Studies in Postcolonial Literature

Edited by

M.Q. Khan
Bijay Kumar Das

ATLANTIC
PUBLISHERS & DISTRIBUTORS (P) LTD

Published by
ATLANTIC
PUBLISHERS & DISTRIBUTORS (P) LTD
B-2, Vishal Enclave, Opp. Rajouri Garden,
New Delhi-110027
Phones : 25413460, 25429987, 25466842

Sales Office
7/22, Ansari Road, Darya Ganj,
New Delhi-110002
Phones : 23273880, 23275880, 23280451
Fax : 91-11-23285873
web : www.atlanticbooks.com
e-mail : info@atlanticbooks.com

ISBN 81-269-0763-0

Printed and bound in India at Syndicate Binders, Noida

Preface

Indian English writers occupy a significant place in Postcolonial literature. Their contributions have significantly added to the rich world body of literature in English. The present anthology is a grateful acknowledgement of their contributions.

The present book focuses on how Postcolonial literature assumes an identity of its own in spite of the writers drawn from different countries with distinct national identities.

In this anthology of as many as twenty-three essays and two interviews, a wide spectrum of writers have been covered and an attempt has been made to offer new insights into their works. The eminent Indian writers and writers of Indian origin included in the book are Sri Aurobindo, Nissim Ezekiel, Shiv K. Kumar, Rohinton Mistry, Bharati Mukherjee, Mulk Raj Anand, Amit Chaudhuri, Vikram Chandra, Vikram Seth, Manoj Das, Ruskin Bond, V.S. Naipaul and Girish Karnad. In addition, the post-Independence Indian English women novelists have also been studied and critically assessed.

Apart from the authors of Indian origin, this anthology attempts to provide a perceptive exposition of works of foreign writers like those of Patrick White, an Australian,

Nadine Gordimer, a South African and Witi Ihimaera of New Zealand.

It is hoped that students, scholars and general readers of Postcolonial literature will find this anthology immensely informative and interesting.

We thank all the contributors for their well-researched papers. We also thank Dr. K.R. Gupta, Chairman, Atlantic Publishers and Distributors (P) Ltd., New Delhi, for bringing out the book in record time.

M.Q. KHAN
BIJAY KUMAR DAS

Acknowledgements

Acknowledgements are due to all the contributors whose papers have been reprinted here from the *Critical Endeavour* (a journal devoted to World Literature in English and published annually by the Researchers' Association, Orissa). Grateful acknowledgements are due to two eminent writers, Manoj Das and Shiv K. Kumar, whose interviews are reprinted here from the *Critical Endeavour*, Vol. IX, 2003 and Vol. X, 2004, respectively.

Contents

1

Glocal Literatures in English Outside Anglo-American Tradition

Bijay Kumar Das

Apart from Anglo-American literatures, literatures are now written in English the world over even outside the erstwhile British colonies. The question of the nomenclature of literatures in English has become increasingly difficult—thanks to the globalisation in the last quarter of the twentieth century and now in the beginning of the twenty-first century. Besides English literature and American literature, we have a substantial body of literatures written in English in Africa, Australia, Canada, India, New Zealand and West Indies in the post-colonial era. These literatures came to be known as 'Commonwealth Literature,' 'Third World Literature,' 'Post-colonial Literature,' 'New Literatures' and 'World Literatures in English.' Each term or nomenclature seemed to be inadequate. Initially, 'Commonwealth Literature' meant literature written in English in the former British colonies which formed an association of their own called Commonwealth countries. Since it is a political term, the countries have the option to opt out of 'Commonwealth' or can be expelled from it leaving the question of the identity of literatures written in English in the these countries open-ended. Moreover, Great Britain being a part of the Commonwealth, English literature is not considered a part of 'Commonwealth Literature.' That makes the nomenclature more problematic. Similarly, all the terms mentioned above with reference to the writings in English are questioned on one count or the other.

The term 'Post-colonial' which politically means post-independence becomes problematic when applied to literature. Helen Tiffin makes a point when she says:

> The term post-colonial is not synonymous with the term "Post-independence." For all the difficulties raised by 'post-colonial' (as a category applied to literary studies), it has proved more resilient than such possible alternatives as 'new literatures' or 'world literatures (in English)' or 'Commonwealth literatures' because it implies the persistence of colonial legacies in post-independence cultures, not their disappearance or erasure... The 'post' in the 'post-colonial,' then, to borrow Terry Eagleton's term in relation to Romanticism, is not 'confidently posterior' to an epoch, but rather 'a product of it,' (158), (Eagleton, 18).

With the development of communication facilities many writers from the erstwhile British colonies now leave for either U.K. or U.S.A. in search of global market and international recognition. The number of expatriate writers, immigrant writers and diasporic writers is increasing now by leaps and bounds. Literatures written in English (i.e. English language—literatures) by writers belonging to different countries of the world are flooding the world market—thanks to international prizes like Booker Prize, Pulitzer Prize, etc. Internet is now a major source of finding out current (should we say nascent?) literatures in English. This phenomenon prompted Bruce King to speak of the emergence of 'International English Literature' in the global context:

> 'English literature' now meant such writers as Wole Soyinka, Chinua Achebe, Nadine Gordimer, J.M. Coetzee, Derek Walcott, V.S. Naipaul, Margaret Atwood, Michael Ondaatje, Les Murray, Salman Rushdie, Vikram Seth, Anita Desai and Janet Frame, none of whom was British, American, or even Irish. As English was the main international language of business, science, politics, travel, education and social change, even nations that were not former English colonies produced English language writers. The new national literatures, national multi-cultural

> literatures and International English Literature were parts of a developing urban global culture, produced by international politics, communication and a world-wide economy which included a heightened awareness of difference partly to assert identity (3).

The point is how to describe English language—literatures in the present context and what are the major themes of such literatures.

International English literature is a myth. It is true that literature is written in a language but what gives identity to literature is not language but nationality and culture. W.B. Yeats makes it clear in his poem, "Under Ben Bulben":

> Many times man lives and dies
> Between his two eternities,
> That of race and of soul
> And ancient Ireland knew it all.

In India we have several regional literatures (now we call them Bhasa literatures, thanks to G.N. Devy who coined this term) which are rich in texture and sensibility but they are grouped under the cover term Indian literature. This is because of Indian culture and nationality which is shared by the writers of our country irrespective of the language they write in. In order to assert his/her identity a writer has to be rooted in a soil. Nissim Ezekiel reiterates it in his poems, 'Island' and "Background, Casually" in the following lines:

> I cannot leave the island
> I was born here and belong.
> ('Island').

> The Indian landscape sears my eyes,
> I have become a part of it
> To be observed by foreigners.
> (Background Casually).

What I want to say is that a writer is always conscious of his identity—past as well as present. It is rightly said that one may take a person out of his/her country but one cannot take the country out of his/her mind. And again, for expatriate, immigrant and diasporic writers there is not one country to think about but two countries and sometimes three as in the case of Salman Rushdie and Derek Walcott to locate or re-locate their identities vis-a-vis their homeland, real or imaginary. If the origin of a writer is of no consequence, how come that the writers from the erstwhile British colonies from Africa, West Indies and India who now live in either U.K. or U.S.A. are not regarded as English or American writers?

There are two distinct categories of writers in English in the former British colonies. One group of writers who stay in their own country and write in English. In this category we can include poets, novelists, fiction writers and playwrights like Jayanta Mahapatra, Kamala Das, Manju Kapur, Shashi Deshpande, Manoj Das, Rushkin Bond, Mahesh Dattani and host of other writers. In the second category, we have expatriate, immigrant, diasporic and what is more important, a group of writers who divide their time between their homeland and U.K. or U.S.A. Here, we can include the names of writers like V.S. Naipaul, Derek Walcott, Bharati Mukherjee, Jhumpa Lahir, Raja Rao, R. Parthasarathy, Vikram Seth, Salman Rushdie, Shashi Tharoor and a host of others. These writers can be better explained by a portmanteau word 'Glocal' (global plus local) and we can call them 'Glocal Writers in English.' That is because they write with a sense of history and contemporaneity. What Eliot says in his epoch making essay, "Tradition and the Individual Talent" (1917), about a writer's sense of history, seems to me very pertinent with reference to these writers in the global context. As Eliot puts it:

> .... the historical sense involves a perception, not only of the pastness of the past, but its presence, the historical sense compels a man to write not merely with his own generation in his bones but with a feeling that the whole of the literature of Europe from Homer and within it the whole of the literature of his own country has a simultaneous existence and composes a simultaneous order (14).

What Eliot says obliquely refers to multi-cultural commitment on the part of a writer. Derek Walcott affirms it in his poem, "A Far Cry from Africa," when he writes:

I who am poisoned with the blood of both,
where shall I turn, divided to the vein?
I who have cursed
The drunken officer of British rule, how choose
Between this Africa and the English tongue I love?
Betray them both, or give back what they give?
How can I face such slaughter and be cool?
How can I turn from Africa and live?

Walcott is conscious of his three identities, African origin, Caribbean birth and his place of work in U.S.A. and makes a multicultural commitment to all these places and cultures. In "The Muse of History: An Essay" Walcott says:

> I needed to become omnivorous about the art and literature of Europe to understand my own world. I write "my own World" because I had no doubt that it was mine, that it was given to me, by god, not by history with my gift (26).

It becomes clear that a writer can write or does write about his own country while living in another country either as an expatriate or an immigrant. That is what A.K. Ramanujan did when he wrote his poetry about family and places in India while living abroad. R. Parthasarathy during his stay in England spoke about the roots in his *Rough Passage*:

There is something to be said for exile
You learn roots are deep.

With the advent of Information and Technology revolution, the world has become 'a global village.' Now no culture is pure and no writer of a country can write in isolation. Everything has become hybrid. English-language writers of the erstwhile British colonies who now move on to either U.K. or U.S.A. to live there permanently or work there keeping their option open to return home write keeping in mind the English language readers the world over. That is why history and time are the two important factors in their writings.

What then, are the trends in literatures written in English by writers of former British colonies living in their native countries or abroad? In the post-1960 era English language poetry in the former British colonies followed American Poetry of the post-war period. As Vinay Dharwadker has pointed out, "American writing had been the original post-colonial and anti-colonial literary tradition in the English language, and hence offered forms of rebellion, innovation and freedom that could work simultaneously in the domains of literature, history, and society" (72-73). Practitioners of American 'open form' poetry such as Ezra Pound and William Carlos Williams, Beat poets like Allen Ginsberg and Lawrence Frelinghetti and Confessional Poets like Robert Lowell and Sylvia Plath influenced the post-colonial poets all over the world. For instance, Indian English poets like Nissim Ezekiel, Kamala Das and Shiv K. Kumar were deeply influenced by Confessional Poets of U.S.A.

W.B. Yeats, T.S. Eliot, and W.H. Auden influenced post-colonial poets particularly in evoking the image of the 'native land' and 'city' in their poetry. Eliot has taught the poets world over how to bring every day conversational language into the realms of poetry. European and Latin American poets too influenced the post-colonial poets. Names of poets like Cesare Pavese (Italian) and Pablo Neruda (Latin American) can be cited in this context. Vinay Dharwadker has rightly stated that, "If the post-war American models enabled poets from the former colonies to break away from older British influences, then the European-language models showed the Commonwealth poets especially from the former settlement colonies, how to re-establish imaginative connections with continental cultures and traditions" (74).

The post-colonial poets apart from being influenced by the American, Latin American and European poets, they also tried to acclimatize indigenous culture and tradition in English language. These poets are also influenced by the regional language poets in their own countries. For instance, A.K. Ramanujan, Kamala Das, Jayanta Mahapatra and R. Parthasarathy in India, and Dennis Brutus, Wole Soyinka and Christopher Okigbo in Africa brought alive their indigenous cultures in English language. These post-colonial poets seek to re-create the image of their 'native land' in their poetry.

A.D. Hope, the well known Australian poet constructs his homeland in a poem called 'Australia' as Nissim Ezekiel does in his well-known poem, "In India."

The fiction writers in the post-colonial period are obsessed with new kinds of realism which determines the subjects of their fiction. The new realisms are 'social realism,' 'psychological realism,' 'historical realism' (Vinay Dharwadker's coinage) 'mythic realism' (Fawzia Afzal Khan's term) and 'magic realism' (Franz Roh's phrase). If 'social realism' deals with the reality that one encounters in the contemporary society as in Mulk Raj Anand's *Untouchable* 'Psychological realism' takes into account the hidden thoughts of individuals which are expressed in their interior monologues as we find in Anita Desai's *Fire on the Mountain*. On the other hand, 'historical realism' imaginatively reconstructs history which is not official while 'mythic realism' seeks to reconstruct the past using myth, archetype, legend, and folklore as we find in Kiran Nagarkar's *Cuckold* (1997). In the post-1950s Chinua'Achebe's *Things Fall Apart* (1958), V.S. Naipaul's *A House for the Biswas* (1961), R.K. Narayan's The *Financial Expert* (1952) and *Waiting for the Mahatma* (1955), Anita Desai's *In Custody* (1984) and *Boumgartner's Bombay* (1989), Kamala Markandaya's *A Handful of Rice (1966)* and Ngugi Wa Thiong'O's *A Grain* of Wheat (1967) can be cited as examples of post-colonial novels which deal with different kinds of realism.

Salman Rushdie's *Midnight's Children* (1980), which won Booker Prize for the year, 1981 and Booker's Booker in 1993 is an epoch making novel. Rushdie introduced the technique of 'magic realism' which became very popular in the world. Writers like Amitav Ghosh, Githa Hariharan and a host of others followed Rushdie in experimenting with magic realism. There is a shift from realism to magic realism which marks a thematic transition in literatures written in English in the last quarter of the twentieth century.

Magic realism heralds an international movement in literatures written in English. The shift from realism to magic realism becomes evident if we in the words of Vinay

Dharwadker "Juxtapose, say, Achebe's *Things Fall Apart* (1958) and *Anthills of the Savannah* (1986), both broadly in the realistic style, with Rushdie's *Midnight's Children* (1980) and *The Satanic Verses* (1988), both works of magic realism" (71).

Feminist writers have given a new direction to fiction in English by asserting feminine identity and demanding sexual freedom in the patriarchal society. R.P. Jhabala, Margaret Atwood, Jhumpa Lahir, Arundhati Roy, Shashi Despande, Manju Kapur and a host of other women novelists have written boldly on man-woman relationship from woman's point of view. In Heat *and Dust,* Jhabala's nameless narrator asserts her right to give birth her child without getting married. Margaret Atwood does the samething in *Surfacing* when her nameless protagonist declares that she will give birth her 'love child' without getting married to the lover. Jhumpa Lahir in *Interpreter of Maladies* (to be specific in the title story) makes her protagonist confess her guilt when she tells the driver that her second son's father is not her husband but his friend. Arundhati Roy boldly asserts a woman's right to choose her lover in her Booker Prize Award winning novel, *The God of Small Things* (1997).

Apart from the new themes, new techniques in the form of code mixing is central to fiction written in English. For example, one encounters a number of Indian words (taken from regional languages) in Indian English fiction. The attempt at creating new idioms based on usages is common to English language poetry and fiction writers in different parts of the world.

Literary criticism such as Culture theory, Feminist criticism, Gender Studies and Queer theory—has become popular in the world. Being influenced by these theories, poets, novelists, fiction writers and dramatists have boldly experimented with the themes of love, lust and gay and lesbian relationships in their works. Playwrights like Wole Soyinka and Mahesh Dattani, have experimented with new themes in their plays. Dattani's two volumes of plays, *Collected Plays* (2000) and *Collected Plays* Vol II. (2005), together contain 16 radio, screen and stage plays on the themes of same sex marriage, sexual exploitation, religious fundamentalism, family relationship and above all, the social problems faced by the 'hijras' in the contemporary society.

Literatures written in English in former British colonies face two-fold challenges—one at home and another abroad. In countries like India where indigenous literature is very rich, Indian English writers face challenges from Bhasa literatures. The national literature in English dealing with the identity of the nation and contemporary problems such as the transition in the society due to international influence becomes closer to international literatures written in English the world over than indigenous literatures at home. This phenomenon brings one important question to our mind. That is, whether English language writers at home and English language writers living abroad either in England or U.S.A. now as immigrants are writing alike or differently. Bruce King makes a pertinent point when he says,

> Just as there is no clear dividing line between the new national literatures in English and their overseas branches in the United States or England so there is no clear division between the new national literatures in English and in local languages (14).

Cross-cultural literary influences work both ways: for example, postcolonial writes living in their own country are influenced by literatures written in English abroad and expatriate, immigrant writers living abroad are influenced by literatures written in English in their homeland. The hybridity of culture and global phenomenon affect all writers. If English language writers living abroad write about their origin, and homeland, the writers who divide their time between their own country and abroad, also write about foreign countries, as Vikram Seth has done in *The Golden Gate* and in *An Equal Music*.

English language writers of the world outside Anglo-American tradition, particularly the fiction writers face a stiff competition among themselves for prizes like the Booker Prize. The Booker Prize is one of the most prestigious literary awards given every year to the best novel written in English. The nominees are selected from the English language novelists in the Commonwealth countries and the Republic of Ireland.

The winners of the Booker Prize include the names of the well known writers such as V.S. Naipaul for *In a Free State* in 1971, Nadine Gordimer for *The Conversationist in* 1974, Ruth Prawer Jhabala for *Heat and Dust* in 1975, William Golding for *Rites of Passage* in 1980, Salman Rushdie for *Midnight's Children* in 1981, J.M. Coetzee for *Life and Times of Michael K.* in 1983 and again for *Disgrace* in 1999, Michael Ondaatje for *The English Patient in* 1992, Arundhati Roy for *The God of Small Things* in 1997, Margaret Atwood for *The Blind Assassin* in 2000 and Kiran Desai for *The Inheritance of Loss* in 2006.

These writers from different countries write about their own country or country of origin and birth and reconstruct the homeland. International themes like women's movement, assertion of feminine identity, cross-cultural encounter, East-West interaction through migration are dealt with by the English language writers.

The narrative techniques employed by the fiction writers is also influenced by the Oral tradition of their nativeland. Salman Rushdie tells this is course of an interview published in *Kunapipi* 7, No. 1, 1985:

> Listening to this man (famous story teller in Baroda) reminded me of the shape of the oral narrative. It's not linear. An oral narrative does not go from the beginning to the middle to the end of the story. It goes in great swoops, it goes in spirals or in loops, it every so often reiterates something that happened earlier to remind you, and then takes you off again, sometimes summarises itself, it frequently digresses off into something that the story-teller appears just to have thought of, then it comes back to the main thrust of the narrative....

So that's what *Midnight's Children* was I think, and I think everything about Laurence Sterne, Gracia Marquez, and all that comes a long way behind that, and that was the thing that I felt when writing it that I was trying to do, (Ashcroft, *et al.*, 181).

English language writers in Africa and India have moulded English to embody their experience. In the context of multilingual situation in African States and in India, English language literature is bound to be national literature there. Ania Loomba reiterates this aspect by referring to Chinua Achebe's observations on the subject. "Achebe suggests that given the multilingual nature of most African states as well as the colonially generated presence of the English language there, 'the national literature of Nigera and of many other countries of Africa is, or will be, written in English.' Achebe invokes the creative hybridity of African writers who moulded English to their experience rather than the other way around, and concludes that:

> for me there is no other choice, I have been given this language and I intend to use it.... I feel that the English language will be able to carry the weight of my African experience. But it will have to be a new English, still in full communication with its ancestral home but altered to suit new African surroundings (Achebe, 103) (91).

Now it has become crystal clear that literatures in English are written by writers of the former British colonies who live either in their native land or in U.S.A. or U.K. or shuttle between two worlds—their homeland and U.S.A. or U.K. If this is the case, where does the writer locate himself? Where does he belong? Elleke Boehmer seems to have provided an answer to this in the following lines:

> For different reasons, ranging from professional choice to political exile, writers from a medley of once—colonized nations have participated in the late twentieth-century condition of migrancy. We might mention the St. Lucian Derek Wallcott, now a commuter between Boston and Trinidad; the Bombay-born Salman Rushdie; the Antiguan resident in New York, Jamaica Kincaid, the black British writer of Caribbean descent, Caryl Philips; the Nigerian Londoner, Ben Okri, the now

> Canadian, once—Trinbagonial poet Nourbese Philip, Amitav Ghosh, Indian but based in the United States; the South African exile in London, Lauretta Ngcobo, Vikram Seth, who writes about Delhi and San Francisco with equal facility, and translates medieval Chinese poetry in his spare time. And so on. In the 1990s the generic post-colonial writers is more likely to be a cultural traveller, or an 'extra territorial,' than a national. Ex-colonial by birth, 'Third World' in cultural interest, cosmopolitan in almost every other way, he or she works within the precincts of the western metropolis while at the same time retaining thematic and/or political connections with a national background, (233).

And again the questions of nomenclature stares in our face. Should we call literatures written in English 'New Literatures in English'? As an alternative to 'Commonwealth Literature' or 'Post-colonial Literature' in the global context? Ania Loomba suggests that, "these literatures cannot be adequately discussed outside of the difficult interplay between their local and global contexts, an awareness that is all too often erased as we celebrate the hybridity or polyphony or magic realism of these texts!" (257). That is why, I call these literatures, 'Glocal literatures in English' and to avoid confusion and secure clarity we should accept the nomenclature "Glocal Literatures in English outside Anglo-American Tradition."

To conclude, let me address the vital question. That is, what should be our approach to Glocal literatures in English? Since, colonialism is linked with modernism and structuralism, post-colonialism is linked with post-modernism and poststructuralism. Hence we can interpret these literatures in English by applying post-colonial theory, post-modernism and post-structuralism in the global context.

WORKS CITED

Achebe, Chinua. *Morning Yet on Creation Day*. New York: Anchorpress/ Doubleday, 1975.

Ashcroft, Bill, Gareth Griffiths and Helen Tiffin. *The Empire Writes Back*. London: Routledge, 1989, rpt. 2003.

Boehmer, Elleke. *Colonial and Post-colonial Literature*. Oxford: OUP, 1995.

Dharwadker, Vinay. "The Internationalization of Literatures." *New National and Postcolonial Literatures*. Ed. Bruce King. New York: OUP, 1996, rpt. 2002.

Eagleton, Terry. *Literary Theory: An Introduction*. Oxford: Blackwell, 1983.

Eliot, T. S. "Tradition and the Individual Talent." *Selected Essays*. London: Faber and Faber Ltd., 1951.

King, Bruce. "New Centres of Consciousness: New, Post-colonial and International English Literature." *New National and Post-colonial Literatures*. Ed. Bruce King. New York: OUP, 1996 rpt. 2002.

Loomba, Ania. *Cotonialism/Post-colonialism*. London: Routledge, 1999.

Tiffin. Helen. "Plato's Cave: Educational and Critical Practices." *New National and Post-colonial Literatures*. Ed. Bruce King. New York: OUP, 1996, rpt. 2002.

Walcott, Derek. "The Muse of History: An Essay." *Is Massa Dey Dead? Black Moods in the Caribbean*. Ed. Orde Combs. New York: Anchor, 1974.

2

Epic of Sri Aurobindo's Feminism: Reading *Savitri*

Haladhar Panda

Savitri: A Legend and Symbol is not only Sri Aurabindo's masterpiece but it is also the longest poem in English and the only completed epic in the language after Milton's *Paradise Lost*. This unique poem retells the story of Savitri's life and her encounter with the god of Death from whom she wrests back the life of her husband, Satyavan. Sri Aurabindo follows closely the story as given in the *Vanaparba* of the *Mahabharata*, changing, however, a few of the details in order to incorporate his evolutionary philosophy of 'the life divine' with descriptions of such mystical and spiritual experiences as are associated with that philosophy. The poem presents an elaborate treatment of subjects like man's aspiration after immortality and divine knowledge; his endeavour to liberate himself from the bondage of time, death and nescience; the course of human evolution from matter and lower mind to the Supermind; and the intervention of divine grace in realizing "the life divine" on earth. The legend of Savitri is said to be thus extended into a symbol of man's spiritual guest blessed by Divine grace.

The looming presence of such philosophical and mystical materials in the poem has led its critics like Gokak, lyengar, Nandakumar, Purani, Singh and Mishra to read the poem as a psychological and spiritual epic like *The Divine Comedy* of Dante. Here is a characteristic comment: "But the greatest value of the epic lies in its symbolic significance, its cosmological and philosophical background and its mystical, psychological delineation of the evaluation and consummation of life."

(Gokak, 20) such reading does grave injustice to the magnificently sketched character of Savitri in the poem, reducing it to just a symbolic prop in an allegory like the character of Christian in Bunyan's *The Pilgrim's Progress*. The dramatic centre of the poem is undeniably the character of Savitri, her personality and action, and this is what strikes the reader most. He remains engaged not so much by the philosophical and mystical ideas of the poem as by the grand figure of its protagonist before whom all other characters of the poem and even all other heroines of Sri Aurabindo's narrative and dramatic works pale into insignificance.

The stress in the *Mahabharata* story is on the splendour of the character of Savitri and Sri Aurabindo's departures from the original serve not to diminish but intensify the same. Thus, Aswapathy's Yoga and mystical journey in Books I, II and III which replaces the simple description of the childless king's austerities and propitiation of the Divine Mother, Savitri, in the original story, highlights the exceptional character of Savitri as the embodiment of divine grace, the *Yagnaphala* as given in the *Mahabharata*. Similarly, other changes in the details of the source story the Yoga of Savitri in Book VII, the temptation of personal salvation offered to her in Book XI, and even the revelation of her as being one with the Divine Mother in Book X—serve to emphasize particular aspects of the character of Savitri. In fact, *Savitri* is designed to be primarily an 'epic of character' like *The Ramayana* to which it was rightly likened by Sri Aurabindo: "It (*Savitri*) has been planned not in the scale of *Lycidas* or *Comus* or some brief narrative poem, but of the larger epical narrative, almost a minor, though a very minor *Ramayana*" (Purani, 35).

The legend of Savitri in the *Mahabharata* had already been turned into a symbol before Sri Aurobindo superimposed his personal symbolism of the spiritual quest on it. The primary symbolism has become a living reality through the ritual worship of the goddess Savitri by generations of Indian women, both wives and maids, on the New Moon Day of the lunar month of Jyestha every year, when they pray to the goddess fervently to bestow on them the great power of true wife's love and devotion whereby they would never be widowed. Thus, the personality of Savitri has been inspiring men and women as the most patent symbol of womanhood, of wife's intense love and unflinching devotion that can overcome all evils including the greatest of those, death. The reader's familiarity with this symbolism as an integral part of the legend, naturally guides his understanding of the meaning of the poem. Sri Aurobindo's secondary symbolism, lacking often concrete embodiment and being merely asserted, fails to suppress or erase the working of the original symbolism in the reading experience.

Sri Aurobindo has not been able to inject sufficient life into all his major characters in order to make them carry the load of his symbolism with success. The one and the only developed or rounded character is Savitri, while the two of the major figures, Satyavan and Aswapathy, are more or less flat ones and the symbolism associated with them either does not work or is confusing. Satyavan, the most sketchily portrayed of the three main characters, has confusing symbolic significance and evokes varied interpretations from the critics. For Iyengar, Satyavan is Truth, presumably because of his name and not for any thing in the poem. "And Satyavan is Truth. Beauty, love and power (the power of devotion and chastity) allied to truth can dare anything, achieve anything." Therefore, Sri Aurobindo has chosen as the fit symbol hero and heroine of his epic of the evolving soul the immaculate Satyavan and Savitri" (Iyengar, 192).

In the poem, however, Satyavan is asserted to be "the soul of the world called Satyavan" (Book X, 1977: 4), "He is my soul that climbs from nescient Night"; and "He is my soul that gropes out of the beast" (Book XI: 1). On the other hand, Aswapathy who is said to be "the Lord of Life" (Book III: 4) is also interpreted as a symbol of "the aspiring human soul down the millenniums of evolution in his search for the truth of himself, of the world and of God" (Purani, 5). Thus, the symbolism of the human soul is both inconsistent and haphazard. Further, the character of Aswapathy remains shadowy and undefined although almost half of the whole poem is devoted to the description of his Yoga.

One encounters a similar problem of inadequate and perfunctory symbolism in the delineation of Savitri as the incarnation of Divine Mother. In the *Mahabharata* story, she is fully human, albeit an exceptional woman; but Sri Aurobindo's symbolism fails to be realised in poetic terms and her being an incarnation is simply asserted. Aswapathy's prayer to Mother Savitri is:

> Incarnate the white passion of thy force,
> Mission to earth some living form of thee.

and he hears the reply:

> One shall descend and break the iron law,
> Change Nature's doom by the lone spirit's power.
> (Book III: 4)

This is Aswapathy's vision of Savitri before she leaves the palace in search of her future husband:

> The strange significant icon of a power
> Renewing its inscrutable descent
> Into a human figure of its works. (Book IV: 3)

What these passages underline is that Savitri is not so much an incarnation of the Divine Mother as an extraordinarily developed soul born to achieve its divine mission—an idea consistent with the traditional belief that one is sent to the earth to fulfil a particular divine purpose. The explicit assertion of the epic voice at a late stage, therefore, fails to carry conviction in its context.

> In a flaming moment of apocalypse
> The Incarnation thrust its veil. (Book X: 4)

Despite the capitalization, the term is haunted by ambiguity of meaning: after all, every human soul is an incarnation of the Divine covered by the Veil of Maya. Savitri impresses the reader as being intensely human, whatever might have been her author's intention.

Once the critical cobwebs surrounding the interpretation of *Savitri* are cleared, one cannot fail to see that Savitri represents Sri Aurobindo's vision of womanhood—a vision which has been developing all through his literary career in poems, plays and prose works. It is the woman's identity and her role in life that constitute the central concern of Sri Aurobindo in all his narrative poems and plays; *Urvasie, Love and Death, Chitrangada, Ilion, The Viziers of Bassora, Vasavadutta, Eric, Perseus the Deliverer* and the like. In all these works, as in *Savitri,* the central figure is a woman and it is her name which often gives the title to the work. Although these works are designed as love romances, the stress in them is not on romantic longing or love, courtship or wooing. They are poetic-dramatic representations of an exalted conception of woman's love and its power of transforming the life of man. Aslaug, the heroine of *Eric,* sings of the nature of such love for all Aurobindonian women:

> Love is the hoop of gods
> Hearts to combine.
> Iron is broken, the sword
> Sleeps in the grave of its lord:
> Love is divine. (*Collected Plays and Short Stories*, 1971: 477)

Love is the divine force that conquers hatred and violence. It is not just a physical passion, but the strong bond that ties one with his fellow human beings as well as with nature and God. It is a union of two hearts, giving one soul to two different bodies, as Vuthsa elaborates:

> We will not be as man and woman are
> Who are with partial oneness satisfied,
> Divided in our works, but one large soul
> Parted in two dear bodies for more bliss. (Ibidem, 288)

and it is capacious enough to include the felicity of different relationships. This is how Vasavadutta speaks to Vuthsa:

> All things at once,
> Wife, mother, sister, lover, playmate, friend,
> Queen, comrade, counsellor I will be to thee. (Ibidem, 292)

Obstacles may threaten the course of love but such is its grand power that it can surmount all of those to effect the happy union of the lovers. The dire plights of Rodogune,

Aslaug, Comol Cummary, Vasavadutta, Andromeda and others do not defer them from their chosen course and ultimately, they reach the goal of their heart's desire. Each of these women's steadfast love and unflinching devotion bestows on her the requisite strength of mind and determination to stand against all impediments. Her egolessness and self-sacrifice make her a heroic figure meeting every challenge to her love with fearlessness and courage. Thus, her great love for Nureddene fortifies Anice Aljalice to stand against the mighty Caliph Haroun Al Rasheed, and Aslaugh's love proves to be "mightier and swifter than the warrior's sword" against fierce Eric's revengefulness.

The grandeur of the power of such love lies in bringing an end to discord and disharmony, violence and brutality, hatred and jealousy, vanity and insolence and making peace, harmony, amity and bliss prevail. The source of this transforming power is the woman's boundless love, her overflowing pity and compassion, her utter selflessness and spontaneous urge to give joy to others, Nureddene, the rake; proud and haughty Vuthsa; carnal and harsh Antioch; Eric, the denier of love and all other heroes of these romances are changed completely by the sublime power of their woman's love. The transformed Eric voices the heroes sentiment:

> As long, the world's sole woman! Thou cam'st here
> To save for us our hidden hopes of joy
> Parted by old confusion. Someday surely
> The world too shall be saved from death by Love.
>
> (Ibidem, 534)

In *Urvasi, Love and Death* and *Savitri,* indomitable love of the woman conquers death. The poetic and dramatic romances, thus etch the distinctive Aurobindonian picture of woman as the devoted and self-sacrificing lover; strong willed and determined to save her love through heroic and victorious fight against all adds; and in her being, the very embodiment of divine grace transforming the life of man. It is this image that gets splendidly magnified and is given the noblest and the most impressive expression in *Savitri* which Sri Aurobindo has lovingly fashioned through repeated drafts over almost fifty years of his career as a writer.

We first meet Savitri on the morning of the fateful day when Satyavan is to die. In appearance, her supernatural beauty and charm is all the more captivating for the magnanimity of her heart: "A wide self-giving was her native act" and "The Universal Mother's love was hers":

> Love in her was wider than the universe,
> The whole world could take refuge in her heart.
> (Book I: 2)

She is acutely conscious of her innate divinity that is imprisoned in the human mould and knows that it is only the power of her spirit that can "lift the yoke imposed by birth in time." Her growth from childhood to youth has already familiarised her with the greatest human problem-transience and mortality; and it evokes in her a constant experience of pain and suffering for mankind. Her own calamity, therefore, gets universalised through her habitual sympathy and compassion and in putting up her lone fight against death, she also takes up "the load of an unwitting race." Conscious of her conjugal felicity with Satyavan in the course of last twelve months, calm and courageous, she prepares her for the great question of her life:

> Whether to bear with ignorance and death
> Or hew the ways of immortality,
> To win or lose the godlike game for man,
> Was her soul's issue with the destiny's dice. (Book I: 2)

Now, deeply aware of the presence of divine light in her, the immutable and immortal soul, she grows into "a flaming warrior" and

> Her soul arose confronting time and fate,
> Immobile in herself she gathered force. (Ibidem)

The beginning of the epic narration *in medians res* is followed by a flashback from Book I, Canto 3 on Aswapathy's yoga, Savitri's birth, childhood and youth and, in due course, we are led to the climactic occasion of Savitri's meeting with Satyavan in the forest in Book V. Theirs is glamorous, mutual love at first sight, neither romantic fancy nor infatuation, but the soul's longing for another—"The soul can recognize the answering soul" because of past affinity and intimacy. The meeting "summed the drift of numberless births." At the sudden sight of Satyavan in the sylvan surroundings of the forest, Savitri felt "A mystic tumult from her depths arose" and "Her soul flung wide its doors to this new sun." On the other hand, "Satyavan looked out from his soul's doors" and "He turned to the vision like a sea to the moon" and felt that "his life was taken to another's life." After an exchange of information about each other, Satyavan invited her to "Enter my life, thy chamber and thy shrine" and Savitri responded "I know and only thou art he." The she bowed and touched his feet and Satyavan "gathered all Savitri into his clasp" consummating the ritual of marriage. In the purity and ecstasy of human love, it is one of the rarest of scenes in literature.

On returning to the palace, Savitri reported her choice to her parents then in the company of sage, Narad. The latter, being pressed by her parents, revealed Savitri's adverse fate: "This day returning Satyavan will die." The Queen became deeply aggrieved and asked Savitri to go forth and choose again. But Savitri remained firm and calmly replied, "Once my heart chose and chooses not again" and "I will have joy only in union with Satyavan." The independent, strong—willed Savitri is not to be cowed by the prophecy of doom and speaks defiantly:

> My heart has sealed its troth to Satyavan.
> Its seal nor Fate nor Death nor Time dissolve.
> Fate's law may change, but not my spirit's will (Book VI: 1)

Narad consoles the Queen saying that Savitri is not weak—kneed and is conscious of her soul's Force and will, therefore be left alone to face her Fate.

Savitri's life at the hermitage with Satyavan and his blind parents reveals another aspect of her character, the devoted and loving housewife willingly undertaking "the labour of broom and jar and will" even being the Princes, and giving joy to all while suffering alone the anxiety and fear of her impending fate. Her yoga undertaken in response to the voice inside her roused her latent soul-force and liberated her from the bondage of body in order to establish her identity with the universal consciousness—Force, the Divine *Sakti*. While the yoga is meant to prepare her in spiritual strength to face the challenge of Death, it also serves to throw a flood of light on her character, particularly through the episode of 'The Triple Soul—Forces.' The three women whom Savitri meets in course of her search for the soul symbolize the three essential aspects of her human personality—love and compassion; might and majesty; knowledge and wisdom.

These parts of herself now get united with "the secret Deity" and become one Being through her soul—realization. Thus completely liberated from time and the world, Savitri becomes the Divine in her will and action although she continues to live in her human body. Savitri's achievement of the highest spiritual attainment coupled with her distinctive humanness makes her the grandest among all the women portrayed in world literature. Her subsequent encounter with Death is designed as a trial of her soul-strength and it highlights her intense love and devotion, overflowing compassion and concern for others, adamantine determination and courage, and her rock—like endurance and fortitude. She patiently undergoes the trials and temptations, cajolings and sophistry of Death, but finally imposes her will on the latter through the revelation of her achieved divinity. Once Death is Vanquished and Satyavan's life is set free, Savitri is offered the choice of Nirvanic peace and felicity as the fruit of her soul-realization. But her womanhood rejects such lonely personal bliss and prefers to be the agent of divine grace on earth and work.

> To take all things and creatures in their grief
> And gather them into a mother's arms—
> and "lift man's soul to God." (Book XI: 1)

Savitri: A Legend and a Symbol is the apotheosis of woman and-her essential power. The *Mahabharata* story stressing the power of woman's chastity and the purity of conjugal love was composed from the perspective of the Vedic and Puranic ideology of woman as the *Sahadharmini* and *Ardhangini* of man. This ideology, while recognising the equality of the sexes, labours under the masculinist bias against woman as being weak and dependent on man. From what has been observed about Sri Aurobindo's portrayal of women in the narrative and dramatic romances and in *Savitri,* the culmination of those works, it is clear that Sri Aurobindo's ideology is a repudiation of the Vedic—Puranic one. For him, the woman has a distinctive and separate identity, self-sufficient and independent of man. Her glory is the tremendous power of her love and compassion that can withstand all challenges against the same and transform all dross into gold. She is, in sum, the mirror—image of the Divine Mother, *The Mahasakti,* on earth. This exalted view of the woman is derived from the Tantric feminism as developed in *Sakta* philosophy and mystical practice. It is a feminism that is characteristically a product of the Indian mind and with its hoary ancestry in Pre-Vedic times. It is distinguish led from the feminism of the present day in as much as it does not plead for the empowerment of woman since it adores her as the Power itself. In Sri Aurobindo's words:

> In the Tantric Sakta religion which puts the female principle highest, there is an attempt which could not get itself translated into social practice....to elevate woman and make her and object of profound respect and even of worship (*On Women*, 1984: 17)

In celebrating this grand and majestic power in his unique epic, *Savitri,* Sri Aurobindo proved himself to be a path-breaker in the field of poetic thought as in many of his other activities in life.

WORKS CITED

Aurobindo, Sri. *Collected Poems*. Pondicherry: Sri Aurobindo Ashram, 1972.

——. *Collected Plays and Short Stories*. Pondicherry: Sri Aurobindo Ashram, 1971.

——. *Savitri*. Pondicherry: Sri Aurobindo Ashram, 1977.

——. *On Women,* Nivadbaran, ed. Pondicherry: Sri Aurobindo Ashram, 1984.

Gokak, V.K. *Sri Aurobindo—Seer and Poet.* New Delhi: Abhinav Publications, 1973.

Iyengar, K.R.S. *Indian Writing in English.* New Delhi: Sterling Publishers Private Limited, 1994.

Purani, A.B. *Savitri. An Approach and a Study,* Pondicherry: Sri Aurobindo Society, 1970.

3 Apart and Yet a Part: Hybridity in the Poetry of Nissim Ezekiel

Mina Surjit Singh

> Do not in your vanity, the tenuous thread of
> difference flaunt but be Asserted in a common
> dance. Participate Entirely, make an end of
> separation. A change of heart requires this
> transmutation (Ezekiel, *Collected Poems*, 56)

The homozygous and ancestral origin is a myth and that everything is always and already hybrid has been well argued out at length by Derrida and the deconstructionists. Yet cultural hybridity in the sense of interpenetration of cultures through historical confluence, interaction, mutual accommodation, transformation and cultural discovery in cross-cultural transactions, becomes a telling index of the extent and depth of the complex impact of such encounters and interactions. It is in this context that this paper proposes to explore how the space that the Bene Israel Jews occupy in the Indian literary world, has been considerably enhanced by the writings of Nissim Ezekiel through his representation of his tribe. However, it is important to remember that his secular, cosmopolitan poetry acknowledges and even celebrates the force that the idea of hybridity has come to acquire in recent times. Also, the poet recognizes the fact that the idea of cultural insularity and homogeneity has given way to the view that all societies are constantly caught up in a process of contact, change and transformation.

In the process of forming such syncretistic configurations, although Ezekiel is identified with another culture, his verse is firmly rooted in the subsoil of India and its' ecosystem, even while it penetrates much deeper into the layers of his Jewish consciousness. Originating from the core of his personal experiences and dilemmas, his poetry has strong biographical underpinnings, but it also reflects alongside, the poet's concern with a socio-cultural perspective that mirrors the paradoxes of his twin identity as an Indian—Jew, an 'alien' native in India, which he considers his home-hell environment:

I've never been a refugee
except of the spirit
a loved troubled country
which is my home and enemy. (*CP*, 209)

Behind the legendary persona of this literary patriarch whose name is "synonymous with Indian poetry in English, particularly abroad" (De Souza: 1), lies the self-consciously alienated urban Indian—Jew struggling to redeem his commitment to both, his Jewish roots and the country of his adoption. Adopting the characteristic double vision and discourse of a natural outsider but a naturalized citizen, the poet attempts to affect a cultural confluence that would provide the basic framework of "difference on equal terms" (Ashcroft *et al.*, 37), within which multi-cultural societies may be fruitfully explored. Veering between his Jewish and Indian inheritance, Ezekiel's poetry thus articulates his constant endeavour to bridge the hiatus between the two cultures:

With, among but never of
nor aloof
not critic, not dissenter, (*CP*, 210).

By birth Ezekiel belongs to the race of Bene Israel Jews regarded as one of the lost Judaic tribes of Israel, shipwrecked some two thousand years ago near the coastal village of Navgaon in Maharashtra, while fleeing from Muslim persecution on Persia. As Ezekiel's biographer R. Raj Rao informs us, these tribes settled down in the coastal villages of the state, adapted to the local culture, got naturalized in the process and have ever since, inherited the wisdom of both these ancient cultures. Quite understandably then Ezekiel's relationship with India assumes critical significance his anxiety to belong, to become a part of the land of his adoption, reflects a sincere effort at cultural adjustment that is propelled by his deep sense of urgency to establish an authentic identity. As William Walsh writes about the poet:

> One is aware of a double impulse in the poet, which on the one hand keeps him at a distance from his environment as he clutches his private history and aspirations and which on the other, by painful act of will, reconciles him to his environment. (*Indian Literature in English*, 130)

These apprehensions come across sharply in poems like 'Background, Casually,' where, in attempting to identify with contemporary India he writes:

> I have made my commitments now.
> This is one: stay where I am,
> As others choose to give themselves
> In some remote and backward place.
> My backward place is where I am (*CP*, 181)

Born and raised in Bombay, the poet grew up as Rushdie puts it of himself in *Imaginary Homelands,* with "an intimate knowledge of and even a sense of friendship with a certain kind of [India]' (18). Ezekiel himself puts his position in clear perspective when he says:

> I am not a Hindu and my background makes me a natural outsider: circumstances and decisions relate me to India. In other countries I am a foreigner. In India I am an Indian, ("Naipaul's India and Mine", 203).

Nevertheless, even while claiming to be an Indian national, the gap that exists between his twin identities can neither be denied, or underplayed, nor ignored, if his poetry is to be viewed as a dramatized representation of the ordeals and conflicts of his hyphenated status. The anguish of his cultural plurality surfaces as a leitmotif through the entire corpus of his work and is reflected in the poet's constant search for an enduring identity.

It is in this context that the nature of the poet's affiliations with his adopted country gains greater significance, in that it's cross cultural and collate methodology questions the very myth of group purity. Alongside, it also implies that hybridization and syncretism can be the "the potential terminating point of an endless human history of conquest and annihilation" (Ashcroft *et al.* 36) that such myths justify:

> One must be out of doors also
> Within, break the barricades
> Of pettiness and pride, overcome
> The schizophrenic agonies
> And dive into the present tense,
> Making for the friendly land
> Of unambiguous speech
> Or corn and wine. (*CP*, 15)

Ezekiel's poetry thus gains maturity and detachment from the fusion of his exiled state with his concern for his surroundings, which is not an India that appeals to the West, but an India that is the only home he has ever known and can truly relate to. The attitude of a foreigner or a complete outsider looking at India through alien eyes would range from amazement to distaste. However, despite the deep sense of estrangement, which is a "recurring motif in his poetry" (Naik, 143), Ezekiel's perspective of India "is all too analytical, thoughtful, compassionate" in Geive Patel's estimation. His world, he rightly avers, is permeated" by an amiability that "alleviates the grotesqueries of poverty, squalor, brutishness" ('Introduction' *CP* xxvi). These larger sympathies render greater credence to his poetic endeavours in a socio-historical trajectory that is marked by a series of repetitive, separatist replications.

Critics like C.D. Narasimhaiah are of the considered opinion that Ezekiel has failed to make any difference to the Indian poetic tradition. This is perhaps because of his "refusal to tap the sources of his own Jewish history" and his "total alienation from the mainstream of the rich Indian life and literature" (10). While this may be arguably true, it is also legitimate to believe that Ezekiel is careful to avoid a casual and blinkered over-absorption in the traditions and texts of a society. Instead, he asserts the importance of his engagement with the immediate socio-cultural reality of Bombay, "the mundane language of the senses" which, even while it "sings/ Its own interpretations" (*CP*, 129), imparts him a sense of identity and makes up for the missing link with his past. External and internal worlds in his poetry appear to mirror each other as if interior language and material reality are one indivisible entity. Nonetheless, re-visioning becomes an important motif, as his poetry interrogates the obligatory relationship of history to fictional discourses:

> A poem is an episode, completed
> In an hour or two, but poetry
> Is something more. It is the why
> The how, the what the flow
> From which a poem comes,
> In which the savage and the singular,
> The gentle, familiar,
> Are all dissolved; the residue
> Is what you read, as a poem, the rest
> Flows and is poetry. This should be so,
> Precisely so. (*CP*, 13)

Not only does the historical and literary inter-textuality of Ezekiel's Indo-Jewish world focus on the predetermined textuality of its characters, but it also suggests a way pf reading literature as a more subtle form of history through its rich and layered subtext:

> I went to Roman Catholic school,
> A mugging Jew among wolves.
> They told me I had killed the Christ,
> That year I won the scripture prize.
> A Muslim sportsman boxed my ears. (*CP*, 179)

Ezekiel often looks back at his Jewish history through allusions to the Jewish Diaspora, the Holocaust, Nazi Germany, his ancestors and most significantly, the wrong Judeo—Christian strain of his early poetry. In doing so then, he is not only living in a fantasy world in which he longs for a motherland he has been cut off from, but more importantly, also underscoring the recurring nature of colonial impulses. Through the use of intertextual and comparative modes, the poet is skillfully reconstructing imaginatively, a history of "imperial self-replication," to use Judie Newman's term (196), in order to emphasize that history is only marked by a meaningless series of repetitive transactions. Ezekiel refers to his ancestors in 'Background, Casually' (*CP*, 179—181), as "aliens crushing seed for bread" One of them who "fought and taught/A major bearing British arms" was even deployed in the Boer War. Hence, by compressing the two-thousand-year-old history of his ancestors skillfully enough for it to seem the immediate past of a race he is integral to, he is exploiting a material reality that is overwhelmingly significant in its bearing witness to the worst horrors of recent history. Although the "poet-rascal-clown," is neither free from the guilt of survival nor a "terror of the strong," he recognizes the conjunctive potential of belonging to a landscape that he has now accepted as his own.

The poet realizes that it is through a process of homogenization alone, that he can create his authentic, hybridized identity as an Indian—Jew. By continuously reexamining and redefining his own ethnicity, the poet attempts to set forth his proposal of a cultural metamorphosis that would signify a complex process of co-operation, and provide the necessary framework for accepting difference on equal terms. Thus, it is hope in the possibility of a mutually progressive crossover and assimilation that he expresses, through his ironic Friday-night musings:

> At home on Friday nights the prayers
> Were said. My morals had declined.
> I hear of Yoga and Zen.
> Could I, perhaps, be rabbi-saint?
> The more I searched, the less I found.

Ezekiel's poetry functions as a form of critical thought then, which allows for the exploration of areas of experience unavailable to the historian, without engaging in any obsessive theorizing:

I did not know that words betray
But let the words come, and lost
That grip on things the worldly prize.

In like manner, although the poem 'Island' (*CP*, 182), is inaugurated by a deep sense of gloom that dispels all suggestions of oriental romance in the metropolitan, slum-scraper city of Bombay, which seems "unsuitable for song as well as sense," the poet is "here to find my way in it." The unreadable quality of the city has some positive consequences:

Bright and tempting breezes
flow across the island,
separating past from future,

There is a spirit of inventiveness and renewal in the city that makes his twin identity relevant in its potential for a heterogeneous inclusiveness and dispassionate relations:

I cannot leave the island,
I was born here and belong
Even now a host of miracles
hurries me to daily business,
minding the ways of the island
as a good native should,
taking calm and clamour in my stride.

Bombay, which for him is India, is the context which enables him to experience openness to cosmopolitan influences, even while it affords him the opportunity to explore new forms of textual and relational interpolations. In his efforts to break out of the self-regarding loneliness of his mixed background, Bombay is the place he throws himself into.

Ezekiel's 'Very Indian Poems in English,' too, are reflective of a cultural infiltration that subtly rejects mimetic linguistic control on the one hand, and allows for a cultural re-mapping through multiple and syncretistic configurations that offer a way out of a confining past, on the other. While these poems lead one into an exploration of the many patterns of power which are associated with British colonial rule, they also contest English cultural hegemony by adopting linguistic patterns that mirror the speaker's mind and social context:

I am standing for peace and non-violence
Why world is fighting fighting
Why all people of world
Are not following Mahatma Gandhi,
I am simply not understanding.
Ancient Indian wisdom is 100% correct.
....
What you think of prospects of world peace?
Pakistan behaving like this,
China behaving like that,
It is making me very sad, I am telling you...
All men are brothers, no?...
Though some are having funny habits (*CP*, 237)

This intricately interwoven admixture of "Indian vernacular and half-baked English" (Kumar, 4), also serves as Ezekiel's critique of the powerful undercurrents imperialistic and separatist tendencies that underlie cultural conflicts and are the wellsprings of social disjunction and dysfunction. The poet's linguistic abrogation serves yet another significant purpose, in that it subverts colonial intentions through structures that reinforce native modes of thought. Digression from normative standards of English infuses a sense of geographical realism into his poetry, which brings about not only a healthy linguistic crossover of two distinct cultures, but also helps the poet realize his distinct national identity through language that is significantly different from that used by the English. In the words of Anisur Rehman, Ezekiel,

> Who has suffered both the loss of Hebrew, the language of his forefathers, Marathi, the natural mother-tongue of Jews living in Bombay, English is the language of his intellectual make-up, thinking, feeling aspiration and basic communication (265)

Being intellectual adequately exposed to Western influences Ezekiel finds a language barrier between the poet and his compatriots who find the English language alien. Hence, the poet develops the typical Indian English idiom to establish his sense of identification with the land and its people. Contrary to M. Prabha's classification of Ezekiel's 'Very Indian Poems in English' as "deliberate mischief "and "disservice to Indian Writing in English" for the "indiscriminate use of... ungrammatical constructions," in order to establish an "easy superiority" (*The waffle of the Toffs*, 180—182), these poems neither lash nor scoff at the "acquisitional inadequacies" of their subjects. The poet himself reiterates that he did hot use the idiom for comic or mock effect or to create humour, but based the language of these poems on the social reality that there are "Indians who speak that kind of English all their lives.... I just connected what was being said in Indian English with some of the attitudes and values of the normal Indian English speaker" (Barucha, 26-27). Since he is a modernist poet concerned about the here and how, that is the *hoi polloi* of Bombay, Ezekiel states that he started jotting down the variegated usage of the language he encountered while commuting on local trains and then composed these poems. These poems help the poet to establish a linguistic proximity with his audience and are therefore sufficiently redeemed by a characteristic amiability that prevents them from becoming "unkind caricatures of people who do not know the language they use" as Patel legitimately states (xxvi).

Ezekiel's *Collected Poems* form a kind of Ezekielean Wisdom Bank that mirrors the valid uncertainties of his twin identity, nonetheless, also expresses his faith in the sanity of mankind to look beyond narrow sectarian divisions. If 'Hymns in Darkness,' have been composed under the influence of Vedic Hymns, in 'Latter-Day Psalms' the poet looks at the Biblical Psalms through the eyes of a modern skeptic (*Naik*, 142). Naik informs us of the very interesting genesis of these psalms, tracing it to an exigency at the Rotterdam Poetry Festival in 1978. As the poet found no other reading material in his hotel room except the "ubiquitous Gideon's Bible" his re-reading of it led to a "modern satirical version of an ancient religious text" (143). The metaphysical theme of both groups of poems however, is reflective of the poet's lack of faith in organized religion. Investing his belief in his own liberal, rational and secular propensities, he articulates, instead, an existential vision that seeks 'God's' blessing "upon/all the people of the earth" (*CP*, 253). As Naik puts it: "repudiating ancient faith, admitting the presence of evil in life, and yet finally asserting that Man will somehow endure" (143), Ezekiel envisions a secular future in which, justice and peace will finally prevail:

> Cast off, scattered for a
> thousand years, where shall
> we live in peace with our neighbours? (*CP*, 256)

In his ceaseless attempts to define himself, the poet thus sits on the hyphen of his dual kinship, identifying with and belonging to the reality on both sides, so as to arrive at the much sought after synthesis of cultural polarities. Putting the whole issue of dual kinship in correct perspective, Balachandra Ranjan foregrounds the opinion that "the presence of two cultures in one's mind forms a wider and therefore saner basis on which to originate the quest for identity." This quest is to be seen as a process of "creative self-realization," he believes, out of which grows a "sense of nationality" (1-2). Likewise then blessed with a fine sense of balance that is borne out of his twin affiliations, Ezekiel is optimistic about being able to make a difference, to look forward to a more meaningful and rewarding future.

WORKS CITED

Ashcroft, Bill Gareth, Grriffiths, Helen Tiffin. 1989. *The Empire Writes Back: Theory and Practice in Post-Colonial Literatures*. New York: Routledge, 1989.

Barucha, Nilufer E. and Vrinda Nabar, eds. *Mapping Cultural Spaces: Post-colonial Indian Literatures in English: Essays in Honour of Nissim Ezekiel*. New Delhi: Vision Books, 1998.

Ezekiel, Nissim. *Collected Poems: 1952—1988*. Delhi: O.U.P., (1989).

——. "Naipaul's India and Mine" *Journal of South Asian Literature*. 11.3-4 (Spring—Summer 1976).

de Souza, Eunice. *Talking Poems: Conversations with Poets*. New Delhi: O.U.P., 1999.

Kumar, Shiv. K. *Contemporary Indian Literature in English*. New Delhi: Manohar Publications, 1992.

Naik, M.K. and S.A. Narayan. *Indian Literature in English, 1980—2000: A Critical Survey*. New Delhi: Pencraft International, 2001.

Narasimhaiah, C.D., ed. *An Anthology of Commonwealth Poetry*. Madras: Macmillan India Ltd., 1990.

Newman, Judie "History and Letters: Anita Desai's *Baumgartner's Bombay.*" *Post-colonial Literatures: Contemporary Critical Essays*. Ed. Michael Parker and Roger Starkey.

Patel, Geive. "Introduction." *Collected Poems 1952—1988*. Delhi: O.U.P. 1989. Prabha. M. *The Waffle of the Toffs: A Socio-cultural Critique of Indian Writing in English*. New Delhi: Oxford and IBH Publishing House, 2000.

Rajan, Balachandran. "Identity and Nationality." *Considerations*. Ed. Meenakshi Mukerjee. New Delhi: Allied Publishers Pvt. Ltd., 1977.

Rao, Raj. *Nissim Ezekiel: The Authorized Biography,* New Delhi: Viking, 2000.

Rehman, Anisur "Nissim Ezekiel's Language and *Diction*." *Essays on Nissim Ezekiel*. Ed. T.R. Sharma. Meerut: Shalabh Prakashan, 1994.

Rushdie, Salman. *Imaginary Homelands*. Harmondsworth: Penguin, 1992.

Walsh, William. *Indian Literature in English*. London: Longman, 1990.

4

The Use of Indian English Idiom in the Poetry of Nissim Ezekiel and Shiv K. Kumar

Sabita Nayak

Poetry written in English today in a different countries of the world is not regarded as English Poetry, for the identity of a literature is based not on language but on nationality and culture. Poets all over the world who write their poetry in English do not write in the same way. The language is English but the expression and mode of collocations are different. That is why literatures written in English in Canada, Australia, and America are known as Canadian literature, Australian literature and American literature respectively but not as English literature or part of English literature. Hence, the Indian English writer should be judged by the intensity of his Indianness. This identification will be possible only when 'Indian English' is treated as a distinct idiom. In this paper an attempt has been made to show that Indian English idiom has established itself as a distinct 'idiom' as a result of which, Indian English Poetry has assumed an identity of its own. Modern Indian English Poetry is now easily distinguished from World Poetry written in English because of its 'idiom' and 'Indianness.' If the use of language, idioms and nuances is instrumental in giving an identity to literatures, then Indian English Poetry has little to fear.

The Indian English poetic movement in the 1960s and after shows its distinctiveness and reveals its authenticity. It no longer follows blindly either the genteel British or confessing Americans. Indian English Poets tried to talk of Indian reality in a frank and original way and attempted to evolve an idiom and imagery and poetic technique suitable for their purpose. Poets like Nissim Ezekiel, R. Parthasarathy, Kamala Das, P. Lal, Shiv K. Kumar, Keki N. Daruwalla, Ramanujan, Arun Kolatkar, Jayanta Mahapatra, Gieve Patel, O.P. Bhatnagar, Margaret Chatterjee—and more recently Imtiaz Dhankar, Bibhu Padhi, Makarand Paranjape, Bijay Kumar Das, Niranjan Mohanty, Shanta Acharya and a few others, are creating a new Indian English idiom in their poetry that is at once recognizable from British, American, Canadian and Australian English.

The aim of this paper (as stated in the beginning) is to make a study of the use of Indian English idiom in the poetry of Nissim Ezekiel and Shiv K. Kumar who have shown not only signs of promise and potentiality, but significant achievement in this field. In course of my analysis and explanation I would like in particular to show how effectively they have made use of a second language for creative purposes, and how authentic and original is the tone of their voice with regard to their Indian sensibility.

Let me begin with Ezekiel. Modern Indian English Poetry could not have been what it is today without Nissim Ezekiel. Ezekiel is to Indian English Poetry, what T.S. Eliot is to Modern English Poetry. Not only did he write poetry in a new style but he also taught other poets including Dom Moraes how to write poetry in English. Unlike other amateurs and aristocrats of Indian English verse, he has shown remarkable ability to give his poems a certain finality of form. In this, he has believed in Yeats' dictum that poets like women "must labour to be beautiful." Adil Jussawalla makes a point when he says that, "Ezekiel is perhaps the first Indian poet consistently to show Indian readers that craftsmanship is as important to a poem as its subject matter" (qtd. in Walsh, 80). Whereas previously Indian English verse was a hobby, something done in spare moments, Ezekiel made it central to his life. As Bruce King rightly observes, "Others wrote poems, he wrote poetry. The difference is reflected in his craftsmanship and purposefulness—, this is as much a matter of will as a talent"*(Modern Indian Poetry in English, 91)*.

Ezekiel published his first book of poems, *A Time to Change* (1952), in London. Back home he published a number of collections: *Sixty* Poems (1953), *The Third* (1959), *The Unfinished Man* (1960). *The Exact Name* (1965), *Hymns in Darkness* (1976), *Latter Day Psalms* (1982) and *Collected Poems 1952—88*, (1989). He won Sahitya Akademi Award in 1983 for his book of verse, *Latter Day Psalms*.

'Self' inevitably brings a concord between one's inner life and the outer life. In the course of an interview given to *Gentleman* Ezekiel states:

> "To start with, my own inspiration is and always was 'my inner life.' And writing is, for me, a way of coping with tension between my inner life and the outer life. Looking back, this from the earliest days seems to be the main source of my writing. Every other source is somehow related to it—even the experiences of other people. My poems are often introspective and therefore, express self-criticism and self-doubt. I also write about my relationship with other people: love, sex, the individual in society etc" (94)

Ezekiel has been consciously Indian in his sensibility to elicit the reader's participation in our country. He has tried to be authentically Indian without having the faults of his fellow practitioners of verse. Though essentially a serious poet, "Yet, his experiments in the levity and frivolity of Indian English have retained their own flavour" (169), says Chetan Karnani, with confidence. He has not only tried to describe Indian culture but he has made good use of 'Babu Angrezi' in Indian English. He has an open mind and therefore, he changes the subject matter of his poetry from time to time. He makes this clear in his poem "Theological":

> I am tired
> of Irony and Paradox
> of the bird in the hand
> and the two in the bush
> of poetry direct and oblique
> of statement direct and oblique

of statement plain or symbolic
of doctrine of dogma....

Ezekiel's contribution to 'Indian English idiom' lies in his attempt to re-create Indian characters in their situation. He has performed half a dozen experiments in this genre. The tone may appear to be mocking but Ezekiel faithfully reproduces these characters as they appear in their real life. The language in these poems is based on colloquial speech rhythm and the tone is conversational. Poems like, "Very Indian Poems in Indian English," "Good-bye Party for Miss Pushapa T.S.," "The Railway Clerk," "The Truth about the Floods," "Hangover," "Healers" etc. belong to this category. In these poems Ezekiel uses English the way most semi-literate Indians write, speak and perhaps understand it. The poem "Very Indian Poem in Indian English," tries to depict characteristic Indian attitudes in Indian English idiom. It is a common Indian practice to use the present continuous tense in place of the simple present:

For instance—
"I am standing for peace and non-violence....
I am simply not understanding....
Everyday I am reading Times of India....
Friends, Romans, Countrymen, I am saying...
Not that I am ever tasting the wine.....
I am not believing in ceremony......
Always I am enjoying your Company... ('The Patriot')

"I am living just on opposite house 'back- side...."
("The Professor")

The further I move
away from madness
towards stability
and a measure of sense,
the closer I seem
to the verge of madness. ("Dilemma")

1. He knows how to speak of hunility without humility.
2. He has lost faith in himself and found faith at last.
3. Darkness has its secrets which light does not know.

(Hymns in Darkness)

The closer you come, the further you move. ("Distance")

Where you are
Is where you have to be.
("Counsel for Shri Hariji," who said it)

In these poems Ezekiel reminds us of T.S. Eliot who used paradoxical language in his later poetry, particularly after his conversion to Anglo-Catholicism in 1927.

In "Passion Poems," the Poet uses erotic vocabulary freely. In some of his earlier poems like "Two Nights of Love," "The Recluse," "Delighted by Love," and in a later poem like "Jewish Wedding in Bombay," the consummation of love has been freely used. In a poem titled "Motives" the persona honestly states his motive to consummate his love with the desired woman and emphasizes his sexual passion in unequivocal language:

My motives are sexual....
Your things are full and round,
thin and flat I'd love them too
There go my aesthetics.

Ezekiel is bold enough in describing and using words from the biological point of view. He uses unconventional words like "unrully thighs," "plopping breasts," "midrif moist" and describes female anatomy as well as garments in his poetry. There is as it were an attempt to create an Indian English idiom to describe love and sex in poetry. Take, for instance, a poem like *Nudes* (2) where the woman takes a lead in the sex act and this is how the poem moves:

I love undressing, she has to say,
as she undresses...
Is this a part of your? she asks
as she holds it, stares at it.
Then, she laughs. 'Put your finger
there; she pleads, as if
I need instructions, It's only
impatience, though becoming frenzy
as I penetrate—'Now' she claims,

Ezekiel uses phrases like, "threshing thighs," "swinging breasts," "buttocks," "stripped bodies," "orgasm," "breasts naked to the waist," quite freely in his poems of love and sex. He has declared that the use of 'nakedness is good' and has acknowledged Sanskrit poets as his ancestors.

Shiv K. Kumar began his poetic career as an imagist poet extending Eliot—Pound tradition to Indian English Poetry. For him the image is the idea. His volumes of poems are *Articulate Silences* (1970), *Cobwebs in the Sun* (1974), *Subterfuges* (1976), *Woodpeckers* (1979), *Trapfalls in the Sky* (1986), *Woolgathering* (1998) and *Thus Spake the Buddha* (2002).

I am inclined to agree with B.K. Das when he says, "Kumar's originality lies in the employment of his imagery. In his image making power, Kumar has a few peers but not many equals among Indo English poets, Kumar starts a poem with an abstract idea like birth or death, identity or flux, choice or commitment, which he tries to naturalize in his imaginative world by reclaiming it through image" (*Modern Indian English Poetry,* 83). Take for instance, the poem, "And Death Shall Speak with Many Voices" which dramatizes a mood of calm acceptance of the fact of death. As G.S. Amur has rightly pointed out that, "The Poem works through a strong visual image, that of a body reduced to ashes by the flames of pyre, reinforced by a series of auditory images" (qtd. in Naik, 129).

> Soft mallet strokes
> on the navel,
> thrumming past the heart
> by its soprano chords
> and outshout its brazen denials
> till the membrane pops to silence.

The Indianness of such poems is evident not only in their unmistakably Indian images like the sandalwood pyre, but in their attitude to death which is one of detached acceptance.

In sexual imagery, Kumar shows a greater imagistic skill. The horse, which symbolizes passion and sexuality is a positive symbol in Kumar's poetry. Whereas the rat which is associated with garbage cans and symbolizes the failure of love and marriages, is a negative one. In "My-correspondent," riderless horses whinny under the red moon' symbolizes uncontrolled passion. In the poem "co-sharer," the rival in love is termed 'co-sharer' and the tone of the poem is potentially mocking.

In Kumar's poetry one encounters erotic images which bear a parallel to the sexual images of Kamala Das. For instance, images like 'vaginal creeks,' 'semen of primeval gods,' 'Blue-Veinedbreasts,' 'Silken Thighs,' and 'nipples smeared with gold dusty-powder/swing hysterically/round swaying waist lines," are very daring and un-conventional. The figures of speech that are associated with these images heighten the meaning and musicality of the poem. In Kumar's "Before the Beginning" the pun on 'eyecatching,' used to suggest attracting and flirting, is an Indian coinage (like 'coleging' and 'gifting') not common elsewhere:

> It is now time to roll up the picnic basket,
> put away the crumbs of bread,
> for she is already eye-catching a stranger
> on the other side of the beach.

I am inclined to agree with B.K. Das when he makes a perceptive comment on Kumar's use of idiom of the following words:

> Apart from employing new themes in his poetry, Kumar has contributed substantially to the creation of a new idiom (i.e., Indian English idiom) and a new kind of 'other englishes' which is a precondition for post-colonial poetry. Kumar's vocabulary is learned like the vocabulary of English Metaphysical poets. His fondness for similes and metaphors, irony and paradox is remarkable. He has a knack for neolism and therefore, one encounters a number of interesting coinages in his poetry. Here are a few examples:
>
> 'Colonial moustache,' 'sabre eyes,' 'fugitive cloud,' 'self-righteous coconuts,' 'scimitar-tongue,' 'virgin transparency,' 'ancestral memories,' 'clipped syllabus,' 'splintered tongues,' 'womb of time,' 'exotic chant,'

> 'choleric air,' 'hybrid moon,' 'champagned ripples,' 'forespent thighs,' 'monolithic rocks,' 'mango ripples,' 'sophomore breasts,' etc. Kumar's innovative images are startling and they make an assertion of the novelty of expression by a post-colonial poet (*Shiv K. Kumar as a Post-colonial Poet*: 112-113).

The Post-Independence English Poet is concerned with the "Indianness" of his experience. That's why the modern Indian English poetry has now taken for its theme various Indian subjects from legend, folklore, to contemporary Indian situation. The new poetry demanded a new use of language and called for the use of everyday speech—rhythm in poetry. Thus there is a demand, as it were, for the creation of an English idiom, to give an identity to modern Indian English poetry. Therefore, the modern Indian poets do not write poetry in the conventional English poetic diction and instead, they write in a live Indian English idiom. They speak to us in our own situation and in a language that is spoken, heard and understood by the English educated Indians of our country.

WORKS CITED

Amur, G.S. "Poetry as Subterfuge: An Introduction to Shiv K. Kumar's Poetry." *Aspects of Indian Writing in English*. Ed. M.K. Naik. Madras: MacMillan, 1979.

Das, B.K. *Modern Indian English Poetry*. Bareilly: PBD, 1992.

——. *Shiv K. Kumar as a Post-colonial Poet*. New Delhi: Atlantic Publishers, 2002.

Ezekiel, Nissim. (Interview) *Gentleman* (July 1984).

Jussawalla, Adil. "The New Poetry." *Reading in Commonwealth Literature*. Ed. William Walsh. London: OUP, 1973.

Karnani, Chetan. *Nissim Ezekiel*. Liverpool: Lucas Publications, 1974. New Delhi: Arnold Associates, 1995.

King, Bruce. *Modern Indian Poetry in English*. New Delhi: OUP, 1995.

5

Imagery in the Poetry of Shiv K. Kumar

Krushna Chandra Maharana

Shiv K. Kumar's arrival on the Indian English poetic scenario was like a powerful current of fresh air which carried in it exceptional fragrance. He made his mark in the seventies and published his volumes of poems in quick succession. His first volume was Articulate Silences (1970). This was followed by Cobwebs in the Sun (1974), Subterfuges (1976), Wood Peckers (1979), Trafalls in the Sky (1986), Woolgathering (1998), and *Thus Spake the Buddha* (2002). A multifaceted personality, Shiv K. Kumar is a class by himself. His poetry is rich in vocabulary and one can find two strains in his poetry. First, he writes in a 'Confessional' mode as he articulates on themes of love and sex but he tries hard to dispel such a labelling. Second, he also writes poems taking national landscape and national identity as themes, employing new images that make an interesting reading. He grapples with ideas and abstractions, images of men and women on several planes, the complex of emotions centering round human activities such as love, sex, companionship and problems relating to his own art. In his image-making power Kumar has few peers but not many equals among the post-colonial poets. To the common Indian reader, Kumar is too much Westernised and his problem is to live upto the expectations of both the Indian and the foreign readers. For this reason one finds a wider range of themes and diverse images in his poetry. Irony, humour and satire are Kumar's forte. There is something of Donne, Eliot and Yeats in his poetry.

He is the fifth Indian English poet to have been honoured by the Central Sahitya Akademi for his book of verse *Trafalls in the Sky* which reveals his Indian sensibility in a brilliant manner. He is a very delightful, charismatic and colourful personality who is full of great promises even today. Readers await with eagerness to find out what this great Indian English poet has in store for us in the new millennium.

The 'Imagist Movement' so assiduously built up by T.S. Eliot and Ezra Pound has no greater impact on the Indian English poets, though the concept of 'image is the idea' is not completely lost upon them. Indian English poets in the sixties and after began thinking of using indigenous imagery in their poetry as a kind of post-colonial resistance. They have deliberately avoided the borrowed images of their predecessors from the Anglo-American tradition and set their minds on Indian imagery. Before examining the use of images in the poetry of Shiv K. Kumar, we would do well to examine the use of imagery in poetry in general.

A poet's sense of belonging to a place or a nation is linked up with the question of his nationality and his identity is dependent on his commitment to the place of his birth or domicile. In other words, a poet's response to the topography of his country, his awareness of the tradition and culture of the land of his birth or domicile and inwardness with the psyche of the people, help him to carve out a place for himself or in post-colonial terminology, to locate himself in his own place. It is said that the Englishness of William Shakespeare, Wordsworth, John Keats and Tennyson lies in their intimacy with the English landscape. Similarly an Indian English poet has to develop an inwardness with Indian landscape, tradition and culture in order to acquire a sense of 'Indianness' in his poetry. As Judith Wright has remarked very aptly:

> Before one's country can become an accepted background against which the poet's and novelist's imagination can move unhindered, it must first be observed, understood, described as it were, absorbed. The writer must be at

> peace with his landscape before he can confidently turn to his human figures (Kohli 1979: 54)
>
> The ever increasing number of Indian English poets has led to a definite growth of English in our country. The increased use of Indian landscape and the dissociation from Christmas trees, lilies, daffodils, dales and nightingale has changed the texture of English in its usage for creative purposes. As Bhatnagar has rightly observed: "consequently, there is a shift in the import and suggestiveness of the language, facilitating ease in taking liberties with the British bound norms and forms of making inflexions, compounds, phrases and pattern of making images and sentences to suit the Indian ethos and imagination" (1991:19).

Shiv K. Kumar makes an interesting point about the use of images and symbols in poetry in general and in his poetry in particular. He opines:

> When you say something through poetry the mode is different from that of prose. You have to say it through images. You have to speak through symbols. You have to say 'like a patient etherized upon a table.' One's experience of agony is externalised through an image, a symbol. But the pain is there. You will never say, 'I am in pain.' You will instead say, 'I am bound' upon a wheel of fire. Coming to a pure image and symbol, I'd say the prostitute in my poem is a symbol. I'm not describing her face or lineaments. She is a symbol of human being 'more sinned against than sinning.' Chirantan in "To a Friend who Died of Cancer" is a symbol. The priest is a symbol. My images expand themselves into symbolic significance. This goes on all the time. It is my visual imagination which always gets excited. This, I believe, is my strength (*JSAL*, 1990:233-234)

Telescoping of images is characteristic of Kumar's poetry. Indian landscapes and images of 'India' have inspired him like other Indian English poets, to create newer and more fascinating images that have not been created ever before. Traditional people in India believe "in a holy communion with nature and therefore, they worship the Himalayas and the Ganges. Many of India's religious rites are performed on the banks of holy rivers after ceremonial bathing. Aldous Huxley wrote a sarcastic essay on Varanasi in which he ridiculed Indians who took a dip in river Ganges. Like Huxley, a rationalist, Kumar could not share the blind belief of the masses and instead, wrote some sarcastic poems on these rituals. His poems "Crematorium in Adikmet, Hyderabad," "At the Ghats of Banaras," "Pilgrimage," "Kali" and "An Encounter with Death" are cases in point. Beggars, priests and carnivorous animals together with vultures surround Cremation places and Ghats of Banaras. Kumar refuses to be swayed away by mere rituals and instead, sees the horror and reality within. He records these incidents with a subtle touch of irony and skilful art of sarcasm in the following manner" (Das, 1993: 55):

> Incessant din of beggars
> and Chants.....
> Perched on the wall a vulture cogitates
> upon human avidity—flesh offered
> to flames, bones and ashes
> to the Ganges. No leaving
> for the living....
> The Priest Chants louder for a generous tip.
>
> ("Crematorium in Adikmet, Hyderabad")

> Between its carrion feeth
> the Ganges can hold three live fishes—
> fins, bones, and eyes.
> A child's lissom body
> in a jute bag,
> the warm ashes of a young courtesan,
> and once I saw a man ferry across
> on a sleazy raft to drop
> his pet dog and bless
> the sharks that carried the Prize away.
>
> ("At the Ghats of Banaras")

Images of India are handled with a consummate skill and keenness of intellect in Kumar's specifically Indian poems like "Indian Women," "An Indian Mango Vendor," "Transcendental meditation," A Hindu to his Cow," "Rickshawallah," "My correspondent," "Karma," "Aftermath" and "Days in New York." "Indian Women" is written on the theme of East-West encounter and Kumar here describes the patience of the Indian Women who sit like "empty pitchers on the mouth of the village well," "waiting for their men's return.' The picture and image of rural and tribal India come alive in this poem. As Kumar puts it:

> With Zodiac doodlings on the sands
> they guard their tattooed thighs
> awaiting their men's return
> till even the shadows
> roll up their contours
> and are gone beyond the hills. ("Indian women")

In "Days in New York" an expatriate Indian speaks to a native Indian. The speaker takes us from inside of his apartment to outwards where there is an imminent snow storm. Outside his door we encounter a black cat, a black maid and the "quart gallon of milk.' Then the scene shifts to India as a mode of contrast. Thus, Kumar writes:

> They wouldn't believe it here
> That Ganges water can work miracles
> Inspite of the cart loads
> of deadman's ashes and bones
> Daily offerings to the river.

Here the protagonist looks at India through the eyes of a foreigner. Kumar's treatment of the theme of love (i.e., man-woman relationship) in terms of the elements of the Indian landscape has the weight of a poetic reconciliation of the Spirit and the country. "The Sun Temple at Konark" catches the spirit of Vyastayan's Kamasutra in Verse, such that the sex images have a transcendental effect and there is a hint of the mystical Union with the Ultimate through sex. His love poetry is intimately connected with the topographical landscape of the country. For instance, the failure of consummation in love is anticipated by the image of the receding sea in Kumar's "Kovalam Beach."

> The Vaginal Creeks
> lie open-thighed
> in insatiable expectancy
> While the sea's thrusts
> break into surf
> then recede
> Consummation thwarted
> each time they
> miss an ovary.

The idea embodied in the above images taking the sea as the masculine principle and the beach as the feminine principle which is fertilised by the waves of the sea, may not be convincing because the saline water of the sea is sterile. One image leads to another and in the final stanza we get the vision of the poet successfully realised through the following images:

> The sea-shells
> conches
> lobsters
> One closed fist
> Clasping abortive dreams.

In Kumar's poetry one encounters failed marriages and receptions in married life quite frequently and such a theme is couched in appropriate Indian imagery. In this context Surjit S. Dulai makes a pertinent observation:

> Conjugal unhappiness continues to be a frequent theme of Kumar's in this collection. He seems to see disharmony in marriage as a rampant phenomenon in the modern world. All the guests in "Twenty-fifth Wedding Anniversary" are wearing a mask of happiness in marriage and wishing the hosts "many returns of the day," while they know full well the truth is otherwise. If possibilities of "extra-marital romance arise, they are smothered by the hovering ghosts of Wedded partners ("Thou Shalt Not Commit" and "Ghosts") "I am a vegetarian" is a light-hearted picture of a husband thinking about the consequences of weakness "a lambs liver, a chicken's breasts"—in his relationship with his "shrewish wife." Most poems about marriage are about a man's

> unhappiness caused by a woman's heartlessness. But the most moving poem on the subject, "First Night—After a Doweried Wedding" describes the feelings of a bride, victim of the common Indian custom of arranged marriage, a custom that pays scant regard to the bride's feelings, making marriage synonymous with death (*JASL*, 1990: 37)

The imagery in his love poems is highly innovative, learned and original. Love and sex are depicted with consummate skill and the ideas are successfully conveyed through the imagery. Infact, in Kumar's love poetry the image is the idea and therefore, the hints and guesses 'Whisper Results.' Thus, he writes:

> Each icon of love speaks
> its own language
> husky cooing in a thistle
> down bed, eyes that seek the meaning
> of pollen wafting from one blue-bell
> to another—and fingers that Weave
> Occult patterns around brown nipples,
> till even Stone melts into benediction. ('Rape')

Likening, the final assault in sex act to legs pinioned like a fowl's/before it is traded off and arousal of sex, to 'moon tide,' or the post-sex act to 'the moon hiding/behind a fugitive cloud/and the stars sniggering,' is to create innovative images to judge human love and sex in terms of the movement of Stellar bodies. In another poem called 'The Ring' the comparison between talisman (i.e. the Ring) and lie, desire and 'an abandoned mackerel' speaks volume of Kumar's insight into image making.

In his sixth book of verse *Woolgathering*, Kumar creates new images as he strikes new notes about the inexorability of reality against which human dreams and fantasies are in noble, albeit futile flight. He searches for meanings and seeks answers to the disasters of earthly existence in the ancient 'Shimla Hills':

Knowing all the answers, they just grin,
only the wind hisses through the sere
leaves of the Oaks.

Though the suggestive omens in 'Sunrise' disturb him, he still keeps alive his faith of facing renewal through rebirth. Kumar writes:

But it's such beginning that befuddle my mind
first a promise of grace and beauty
then descent into the grave.
But how can you confront the Sun
if you don't seek rebirth after each death?

Kumar has used religious "imagery frequently and the titles of quite few of his poems—"Karma," "Relations," "Renunciation," "Genesis," "The unbeliever," "A Hindu to his cow" and "Buddha at a Night Club" suggest his pre-occupation with religious themes. There he carefully avoids pronouncing value judgements from great spiritual heights or putting on philosophical postures. His attitude is one of detached ironic commentator. That is why the priest in the Shiva temple admonishes the truant in Freudian terms, his "Jasmin bracelated hand" caresses the boy's nape. The poet can be seen mocking the culture which vicariously savours sensuous joy through erotic fantasies involving gods and goddesses. Similarly, in "Buddha at a Night Club" where the "tobacco joss sticks" are suggestive of perverted religious rituals, and in 'Wife at Prayer' we have the spirit that is sensual enough "to caress the velvet inebriate." Easing one's nerves is compared to Buddha's peace in a 'Letter from New York." The stones in the 'Temple Konark' are 'Washed by the semen of primeval gods and "since the first adultery/they have pleaded for compassion" "Kali" is perhaps the solitary poem in the entire corpus of Kumar's poetry in which the poet employs a profound religious symbol with sincerity, though the awe and reverence in which the Hindus hold this deity is conspicuously absent in the poem.

Through irony and contrast Kumar expresses his experiences of 'felt life' in Oriental or Occidental terms. His images transcend the narrow barriers of regionalism or nationalism. Whether he talks of "Walking down the Avenue of America" or strolling at "Kovalam Beach," he is always in search of the core of "felt experience." The imagery is Kumar's poetry is both learned and often far-fetched like the imagery in English metaphysical poetry. But he has created images out of his own perception of Indian situations and landscape. The sufferings and pain in his personal life also contributed substantially to the making of new images in his poetry. It will not be an exaggeration to say that Kumar has succeeded in creating an indigenous imagery in his poetry that at once explains the resistance theory of post-colonial literature.

WORKS CITED

Bhatnagar, O.P., ed. *Studies in Indian Poetry in English.* Jaipur: Rachana Prakashan, 1981.

Das, Bijay Kumar. *Critical Essays on Poetry.* Delhi: Kalyani Publishers, 1993.

Dulai, Surjit S. "Shiv K. Kumar's Writing" *Journal of South Asian Literature* 25:2 (Summer, Fall, 1990): 9—48.

Kohli, Devindra, Quoted "Landscape and Poetry." *The Journal of Commonwealth Literature* 13:3 April 1979.

Kumar Shiv K. "Shiv K. Kumar: An Interview." *Journal of South Asian Literature* 25:2, Summer, Fall, 1990, 233-234.

6 Nineteenth-Century Australian Poetry as a Mirror of Australian History: A Reappraisal

Subhas Chandra Saha

Australian poetry is a tantalizing literary phenomenon. The landmass of Australia had been existing since the precambrian age but it had remained physically inaccessible to the Western world till Captain Cook (1728—79) discovered the route to it as late as in 1770. There have been several expeditions to this landmass from various countries but the waves of the ocean, inclement weather and the secretes of time guarded the coasts of Australia from foreigners till Captain Cook discovered Botany Bay, walked over the land, unfurled the Union Jack, and communicated with the Aborigines who had been inhabiting parts of the land in an exclusively nomadic and primitive manner. In 1788, Captain Arthur Phillip (1738—1814), with the First Fleet, full of hundreds of convicts, some gaolers and officers, landed on the coast of Sydney Cove, and began the colonial history of the as-yet-unknown South Land—the Down Under, in the colloquial parlance. In 1901, Australia was granted freedom from the colonial rule, and it became a federated Commonwealth State. During the hundred and twelve years since 1788, Australia went through rapid changes—from a dry intractable landscape into a green country with several cities on the coastlines of the vast continent. The colonial history of the hundred and twelve years also shaped the history of the coming into being of the Poetry of Australia. It was all in English as the Aborigines had not developed a viable script till then. In this paper, I will dwell upon the impact of the colonial history of Australia on the colonial poetry of the country.

Australia came into contact with the white civilization after the landing of the British explorers followed by the British officers along with a host of British convicts. The beginning of white civilization in Australia is mirrored in the English poetry written in Australia during that period of time. Who was the first poet of Australia? He was none other than a convict whose name was Michael Massey Robinson (1747—1826) He arrived in New South Wales as a convict in 1798. Here it may be mentioned that during the first twelve years of British settlement in Australia, the white people were chiefly engaged in transforming the bare land, and adjusting themselves to the strange climate of the Southern hemisphere, and the stark prospect of beginning a new lifestyle on an utterly hostile and stark reality. Hence no Australian verse during the eighteenth century is traceabie as yet. During the first quarter of the nineteenth century, Robinson's odes celebrating the birthday of George III and Queen Charlotte, and praising the activities of Governor Macquarie appeared in the *Sydney Gazette.* In 1818 and 1819, Robinson was rewarded "for his service as Poet Laureate' by a grant of two cows from the Government herd, probably the first royalty to a poet in Australia. Though a minor poet, Robinson is not able for having written about exile in his first published ode in *Sydney Gazette* in June 1810. In his last pieces published in February 1826, he made an attempt to rhyme 'Australia' with 'gala,' in recognition of his new homeland.

Another convict balladist, Francis MacNamara (1811-?) reflects more of the convict's life and Australian social situation in his verses and ballads. He wrote a ballad about the convict Jack Donohoe. The history of Australia of that time is reflected in the minor poetry of these two convict poets.

After these two convict poets, the first officer poet of Australia is W.C. Wentworth (1793—1872) whose long poem *Australasia* (1823), vindicated in a positive manner the lifestyle that was developing in the new country. *The Oxford Companion to Australian* Literature designates this poem as 'one of the first outbursts in Australian literature of nationalistic pride' (Wilde, 1935: 44). A.D. Hope rightly points out:

> The oft-quoted description of Sydney (in *Australasia)* is first-rate depiction and the language shows that ability to combine elevated thoughts and down-to-earth description in the same poem, to mingle classical allusions, new terms like Kangaroo and emu and new names like Parramatta and the Warragemba without incongruity (1974:107)

History is embedded in the poem; for illustration I quote the following lines:

> Illustrious Cook! Columbus of our shore,
> To whom was left this unknown world t' explore;
> Its untraced bounds of faithful chart to mark,
> And leave a light where all before was dark.
>
> (Wilkes, 1974: 3)

Barron Field (1786—1846) is the second officer poet of Australia (he was a judge of the Supreme Court of New South Wales), who published the first book of poems in Australia, entitled *The First Fruits of Australian Poetry* (1819). Field took interest in the flora and fauna of Australia but viewed them wryly, and presented them with a note of satire, as they were very different from those of England. His poem 'The Kangaroo' is an illustration of his point of view:

> Kangaroo, Kangaroo!
> Thou Spirit of Australia,
> That redeems from utter failure,
> From perfect desolation,
> And warrants the creation
> Of this fifth part of the Earth,
> Which should seem an after birth,
> Not conceived in the Beginning
> (For God bless'd His work at first,
> And saw that it was good),
> But emerg'd at the first sinning,
> When the ground was therefore curst;
> And hence this barren wood! (Ibidem: 7)

Charles Thompson (1807—1883), born in Sydney, 'one of the most attractive of the early versifiers' (1981: 276) according to Vivian Smith, published *Wild Notes from the Lyre of a Native Minstrel* in 1826. *Wild Notes* is the first book or Australian poetry published in Australia by a poet born in Australia. His poem, 'Black Town,' records the facts and history of developing Australia. He pays tribute to Lord Macquarie (Governor of New South Wales, 1910—1922) in the following lines:

> To thee, MACQUARIE, was the dictate giv'n.
> Thou wert the chosen Delegate of Heav'n
> Thousands adore thee forth' angelic deed.
> And for thy parted soul invoke the Christian's meed!
> (Wilkes, 1974: 11).

The versifiers, mentioned above, rendered a great service to Australian literature by taking steps to create Australian poetry, and by embedding the history of colonial Australia in Australian poetry. Colonial history and colonial poetry of Australia went hand in hand.

Charles Harpur (1813—1868), initiates the true tradition of Australian poetry in more than one sense. He is not only born in Australia but spent his whole life in Australia, His life spanned forty-five years during which Australia grew from a nascent colony to a well-developed country where not only western culture prevailed but also a new political orientation developed. Harpur reflected the process of the country's development from a barren landscape to a new political entity in poetry that literally grew on the soil of Australia. History and poetry came together in the poetry of Harpur.

Born of convict parents, Harpur grew up beside the Hawkesbury river in New South Wales; hence he was often called 'A Hawkesbury Lad' (Pierce, 1887: 47). He is the first Australian poet who has given vivid descriptions of Australian landscape in Australian poetry. He describes the surroundings of Hawkesbury river with its background of the Blue Mountains in his poem, 'A Storm in the Mountains.' Harpur not only presented the Australian landscape in his poetry but also wrote several poems about Australian people. For example, he wrote a poem entitled 'The Beautiful Squatter,' in which, his tone is ironic and satiric. He wrote several poems on the social themes: for example, 'Bush Justice,' 'Squatter Songs,' 'Tom Brown or Human in the Bush.' He also wrote many poems on the Bushrangers: for example, 'Lost in the Bush' and 'The Bush Fire.'

Thus Harpur made the places, people and social problems of Australia of that period an integral part of Australian poetry, developing in it a new discourse and a new configuration of Australian images and myths, giving it a new turn and direction, making it more capable of embedding Australian nuances and stances. A new genre, called Australian poetry, was born as a result of Harpur's poetic efforts. Thus Australian history got itself imprinted in Australian poetry.

Henry Kendall (1839—1880), represents further development in the process of the integration of poetry and history in colonial Australia. The death of Harpur elicited from Kendall a genuine tribute to him in poetic form. What is striking in Kendall's poem entitled 'Charles Harpur' is his effort to modulate the British poetic discourse in order to incorporate in it the Australian landscape with its flora and fauna. The fact that certain marks of British poetic style still linger in Kendall's poetic technique registers the historical fact that Australian poetry that was gradually evolving originated from the historical situation of the colonial expansion of the British empire. Hence the colonial poetry of Australia, as exemplified by the verses and the poems of the versifiers and poets discussed so far, is to be regarded as a literary outcome of a historical contest. Thus, this poetry is valuable and illuminating for understanding the growth of a new culture in a country which only recently opened to the attention of the white civilization.

Kendall paid a tribute to Adam Lindsay Gordon, the poet who came from Britain to Australia in 1853 and earned wide reputation on account of the ballads and poems that he wrote against the backdrop of Australia. Kendall's response to the landscape, events and personalities of Australia found memorable expression in his poetry, thus evolving an Australian discourse and register in English language.

Kendall wrote several papers on the Australian pioneering characters who contributed to the gradual growth and development of Australia. His poems like 'The Barcoo (the Squatter's Song),' 'Song of the Cattle-Huntes,' 'Camped by the Creek,' 'Song of the Single-splitters,' 'Bill the Bullock Driver' and 'Jim the Splitter' testify to Kendall's approximation to the archetypal Australian characters whom he represents in his poems through an Australian stylistic register. Hence, by the third quarter of the nineteenth century, we watch the evolution of the process of the integration of Australian and English poetry in the Australian colonial context.

Kendall's poems on landscape betray an accent on the peculiarities of the Australian landscape. For example, his poem like 'Mountain Moss,' 'Bell-Birds,' 'September in Australia,' and To a Mountain,' all paint the Australian landscape. The antepodean flora, fauna, waterscape and seasonal variations, all enrich the motifs of Australian landscape poetry written by Kendall.

Kendall's poems on his near and dear ones as well as the haunting natural spats in Australia emphasize the Australian content of his poetry. Poems like 'Rose Lorraine,' 'Araluen,' 'Crara,' 'Mooni' and 'Narrara Creek,' all point to the fact that the colonial context of Australia brought forth a new genre, namely, Australian poetry. The emergence of this new kind of poetry is an outcome of a historical phenomenon, that is, the British colonisation of the Down Under.

Adam Lindsay Gordon (1833—1870), was born in Great Britain but in 1853, he came to Australia. He composed and published his poems in Australia. He contributed a new vibrancy to Australian poetry. He gifted Australian colloquy to Australian poetry, thus heightening the appeal of the local Australian flavour in it. His best poems are about Australian horses and Australian riders. He projected the motif of the horse in his poetry. Geoffrey Serle aptly points out:

> He (Gordon) was the post of the horse—and the horse was all-important in the nineteenth-century Australia. (1987: 34)

Through Gordon's poetry, the Australian reality secured a permanent place in Australian poetry. The charge of imitativeness and nostalgia for Great Britain in the colonial poetry of Australia has to be offset by the recognition of the boldness of the colonial poets of Australia in adapting the language of Great Britain to a new reality. The colonial poets like Harpur, Kendall and Gordon have to be reassessed; and their contribution has to be re-evaluated on the basis of their inventiveness and pioneering' efforts to evolve a new discourse and a new register for a new genre of poetry—Australian poetry which never existed before. The pioneers in Australian poetry have to be given their due recognition and credit.

Gordon is to be treated more as Australian than as an expatriate, for it is he who has recorded in moving memorable lines the emerging Australian identity—the disappearance of the white people's homesickness and the emergence of a clear sense of identification with the land of Australia. His famous poem 'The Sick Stockrider' ends with lines that capture the essence of people's sense of identification with Australian land:

> Let me slumber in the hollow where the wattle blossoms wave,
> With never stone or rail to fence my bed;
> Should the sturdy station children pull the bush flowers on my grave,
> I may chance to bear them romping overhead.

The history of developing Australia and Australian psyche is thus recorded in the colonial poetry of Australia. Both the content and form of colonial poetry of Australia underwent a gradual transformation as the colony gradually moved towards nationhood.

Towards the end of the nineteenth century, the colony of Australia was ready to be free from the shackles of the coloniser. This moment of nationalism is reflected in the poetry of A.B. Paterson (1864—1941), whose volume of poems, *The*

Man from Snowy Riper and Other Verses (1895), has sold over one million copies. Clemment Semmler points out:

> Indeed, the Man from Snowy River and Clancy of the Overflow were to become national symbols of the bushman horse-rider now firmly established in our cultural mythology (1992: XVII).

Paterson's racy vigorous poetic style reflects the strength of the intrepid Australian man who dared face the rough environment of nature. In an article analysing, 'The Man from Snowy River,' Semmler points out:

> In a sense, Paterson is merely restating the theme of the constant struggle our colonist forefathers were involved in, in coming to terms with their environment (1978: 8)

Where as Paterson gave Australian literature the image of the Australian man, it was Ada Cambridge (1844—1926) who projected the humiliation suffered by Australian women, and asserted the women's efforts to liberate themselves from the masculine domination. Her second book of poems *Unspoken Thoughts* (1887), exhibits Cambridge's intrepid handling of feminist issues. Even seventy years before feminism and women's liberation movement appeared in Europe and America in 1960s, women's causes were championed by Cambridge in her poems. The final poem entitled, 'An Answer' in *Unspoken Thoughts* articulates women's liberation from bondage under male domination:

> Thy love lam, Thy wife I cannot be,
> To wear the yoke of servitude—to take
> Strange, unknown fetters that I cannot break
> On soul and flesh chat should be mine, and free.
>
> (Auckland, 1993: 209)

By developing a discourse and style of resistance and opposition in Australian poetry towards the end of the nineteenth century, Cambridge bring Australian poetry to a level of originality and maturity that transcends the narrowness of colonial pre-occupations. That Australia transforms itself from a colony to a nation by the end of the nineteenth century is evidenced by Cambridge's language of freedom.

Thus the nineteenth-century Australian poetry is not a mere document of imitation, pastiche and colonial romance, as is often alleged, but a vital historical document that enshrines the chronicle of the poetic efforts of pioneers in a new land. Whom will we give more credit—to the forefathers who broke new grounds in an alien land or those who followed their footsteps later on? I believe that credit should be given to both the groups of poets. Let us not forget history and historical situations when we level allegations of imitation. Australian poet like Harpur, Kendall, Gordon, Paterson and Cambridge occupy a place of eminence in the chronicle of Australian poetry, since their poetry mirror the nineteenth century Australian history as well as laid the foundation of Australian poetry.

WORKS CITED

Auckland, Michael, ed. *The Penguin Book of Nineteenth Century Australian Literature*. Ringwood: Penguin Books, 1993.

Hope, A.D. *Native Companions*. Sydney: Angus and Robertson, 1974.

Pierce, Peter, ed. *The Oxford Literary Guide to Australia*. Melbourne: Oxford University Press, 1987.

Semmler, Detriment. 'A.B. ("Banjo") Paterson. The Man from Snowy River.' *Australian Poems in Perspective*. Ed. P.K. Elkin. St. Lucia: University of Queensland Press, 1978.

——, ed. 'Introduction.' A.B. "Banjo" Paterson. St. Lucia: University of Queensland Press, 1992.

Serle, Geoffrey. *The Creative Spirit of Australia,* Richmond. William Heinemann Australia, 1987.

Smith, Vivian. 'Poetry.' *The Oxford History of Australian Literature*. Ed. Lesnie Kramer. Melbourne: Oxford University Press, 1981.

Wilde, William H. et al., eds. *The Oxford Companion to Australian Literature*. Melbourne: OUP, 1985.

Wilkes, G.A., ed. *The Colonial Poets*. Sydney: Angus and Robertson, 1974.

7

Three Writers of Indian Diaspora: A Note

M.Q. Khan

International literatures in English is now enriched by the writers of diaspora, exile and immigration. Indian writers of diaspora has immensely contributed to the growth of fiction in English. Of these, three writers stand out—Salman Rushdie, V.S. Naipaul, and Bharati Mukherjee.

Born and brought up in Calcutta, Bharati Mukherjee married a French born writer named Clark Blaise and finally settled in America. Right from the beginning she declared that her main focus would be on the Indian subjects, themes and characters. Apart from her various novels and short stories that mainly deal with Indian themes and characters, *Days and Nights in Calcutta* is the most accomplished non-fiction work written by both the husband and the wife. It is essentially a record of their experiences in India after a long gap of time. But here she does not write like her French husband, on the contrary she strikes altogether a different approach and attitude. She is closer to the understanding of the Indian way of life, Indian scenes and situations and is a sympathetic observer of the changing scenario in India. When she visits the temples at Calcutta, she observes:

> Not only Vishnu the Chief God, but the serpent supporting Vishnu was also the god Vishnu given a magical illusory transformation. My years abroad had made me conscious of ineradicable now, the preparation for the visit to India setting off an explosion of unrelated

> images. Reptiles, lotus, flying bull gods and heroes. All functioned simultaneously as emblem and as real (171).

What is important to note here is the fact that in spite of her being away from India for a long time and having settled in a foreign land for good, there is no significant change in her attitude towards India and her treatment of the Indian characters, scenes and situations is marked by a sense of empathy. Hence in all her works, particularly in her nonfiction, she appears quite discreet and careful in making her statement on India as she herself declares:

> Having been born in pre-Independent India, and having watched my home land change shape and colour on school maps, then having discarded that homeland for another, I know excess of passion lands only to trouble. I am, I insist, well mannered, discrete, secretive and above all, pliable (175)

Herein we have the real attitude of an Indian diasporic writer towards her homeland India and it is this attempt of understanding with a sense of feeling and involvement that brings Bharati Mukherjee in sharp contrast with *V.S. Naipaul,* the well known non-fiction writer.

Similarly when we analyse the works of another prominent writer of Indian diaspora, namely *Salman Rushdie,* vis-a-vis his attitude towards and treatment of Indian situations, themes and characters, we find that he too depicts the Indian characters with insight.

Rushdie has created a significant stir in the field of fiction chiefly owing to his innovative style, narrative structure, pungent irony, and above all his use of paradox. To a casual reader, he may appear to be chiefly interested in history, philosophy and evolution of political processes in India, but a close reading reveals his deeper interest in the fantastic and phenomenal development of Indian mind. He has shown the changing Indian life from independence to the closing decades of the twentieth century. Similarly his analysis of Pakistan reveals a kind of sceptical and ironical discourse that projects the country drifting towards various directions of lawlessness and confusion leaving little room for a proper and meaningful growth of this nation after independence.

The most important factor that emerges in his novels is again the attitude and understanding of the Indian people in the post-colonial period. This is chiefly revealed in his epoch making novel *Midnight's Children* in which he makes a brilliant exposition of the Indian scenes, situations and characters particularly during the transition. He is, at the outset, full of doubts about the new generation, the children born after Indian independence, quite critical of the turning situation and most ironic of the leaders of India vis-a-vis their attitudes to the country. And yet, despite all the shortcomings and darkness, the novelist never loses faith in his country nor does he condemn her completely. On the contrary, there is an underlying hidden current that runs underneath the surface to show his faith, sympathy and understanding of the various multiple, basic Indian situations. Hence the vignettes of the past, especially the personality of Tai and boatman and the episode of love arising through the medium of perforated bedsheet articulate the author's nostalgia for the past which embodied startling qualities like simplicity, sincerity, love, attachment to the soil and a cosmopolitan code of values which are timeless. Similarly the protagonist of the novel, Salem Sinai represents the intellectual, imaginative Indian, who can think, feel and communicate with others, whose mind is a parliament of various viewpoints. As *O.P. Mathur* puts it:

> The superficial objectivity of the narrative perspective and the sharp radiant ironies are woven of the threads of sincerity and love which encompasses the whole of mankind. The protagonist emerges as an Indian at the cross-roads of history, gifted with a fertile imagination, having no illusions and mental cobwebs and cherishing truth, sincerity, love and tolerance even amidst barren and hostile world (177)

Hence we may conclude that the narrator helps us in a better understanding of contemporary society and historical events, figures and trends by interpreting these from a supremely comic angle based on a stance which is profoundly moral, human and cosmopolitan.

It is this approach of human understanding, love, sympathy, tolerance and appreciation that distinguishes Rushdie from *V.S. Naipaul* and his attitude to India. While considering the literary works of *V.S. Naipaul,* we should remember his spectacular success in the art and the new technique of the non-fiction novel. He is one of the pioneering artists who has explored this new form very successfully and thereby paved the way for other writers to follow. Almost all his works, which are in the traditional journalistic form or in the form of travelogues or memoirs, are actually to be considered as the best examples of the non-fiction novels. Among these are *The Middle Passage (1962), The Overcrowded Paracone (1972),* and *India, A Million Mutinies Now (1990),* in which he actually experimented this new literary genre with success.

His total literary creation may he divided into two categories: (i) those written on the general or non-Eastern themes, and (ii) those written chiefly on the Middle East, India, Pakistan and other Eastern countries.

While making a comparative study of the writers of Indian diaspora particularly with regard to the attitude towards India, we find a striking difference in tone, attitude and treatment of Indian themes and characters in the works of *V.S. Naipaul.* In fact right from the beginning he tends to disapprove of Indian civilization, which, according to him, is not only crumbling but is engulfed with thick clouds of darkness. Similarly Indian character and society appear to him to have fallen into a substandard state.

Obviously there have been a good deal of controversial reactions against the award of Nobel Prize for literature to him. The editor of the *Times of India* commented:

> The fact that the Nobel Prize has been conferred on him (Naipaul) at a time when the Muslim World is in a state of turmoil following the terrorist attacks on the United States and the retaliatory action taken against Afganistan will only lend currency to the suspicion that the Swedish

> Academy's choice is blatantly political in nature (Oct. 12, 2001)

It may be noted here that Naipaul has appeared controversial chiefly for his views on India, on the Third World countries and above all, on the Muslim nations and civilization. The basic difficulties lie in the facts that he claims to have knowledge like an insider of a country, or a nation or a civilization, but in reality he remains an outsider. For example, without knowing the deep meaning and implication of Islam and its faith, he expresses his views on Islamic faith, as such his entire assessment of the Muslim world as well as the teachings of Islam contradicts an insider's view.

Apart from his arbitrary venture to comment and express views on people and their countries, of which he has no inside knowledge, *Naipaul* has also disowned the place of his birth and the place of his origin (in India). Edward Said, while making a discerning observation on *V.S. Naipaul,* regards him as:

> A master novelist and an important witness to the disintegration and hypocricy of the Third World, but in the postcolonial world, he is a marked man as a purveyor of sterotypes and disgust for the world that produced him (qtd. in Ahmed, Oct. 12, 2001)

It is significant to note here that *Naipaul* having, completely identified himself with the West, in his works on India in particular and the East in general, presents the European idea of the Orient with a kind of intellectual authority over the Orient and the knowledge of Western culture. In the words of Edward Said, "What he says and writes, by virtue of the fact that it is said or written is meant to indicate that the Orientalist is outside the Orient, both as an existential and as a moral act" (21).

This is what Edward Said has been emphasizing again and again in his book, *Orientalism.* But what is worst is the fact that even after the colonial period when the imperialism was overthrown, there were still writers in the West who continued to regard the Orients from the same angle, the same point of view, the same tone of authority, and control of the subject race. It is a great irony of history and culture that Naipaul is one such author who, in almost all his works dealing with the Orient, speaks in a tone of authority that the various rulers and western leaders have been speaking right from middle of seventeenth country—an attitude that persisted even in the post-colonial period. Hence *Edward* Said clearly points out:

> My argument takes it that the Oriental reality is both anti-human and persistent. Its scope, as much as its institution and all-pervasive influence last up to the present (144).
>
> Said further explains "the meaning of Orientalism, then, is knowledge of the Orient that places things oriental in class, court, prison, or manual for scrutiny, study, judgement, disciplines or governing (41).

Now like the traditional Orientalists of the last two centuries, Naipaul too in his treatment of the Indians or the Orient, betrays his highbrow attitude. His main concern here is to deliver judgement and express his disgust against the people who he considers to be inferior.

It is necessary here to quote some of the famous imperialists and their views on Eastern countries like Egypt, India and others in order to justify their colonization of these lands by virtue of their knowledge of the Orient. One of the most outstanding imperialists is Balfour whose knowledge of Egypt makes him to say:

> We are in Egypt not merely for the sake of the Egyptians, though we are there for their sake; we are there also for the sake of Europe at large (31)

Similarly regarding the poor capacity of Orientals for administration and self-Government, he assertively declares:

> Conqueror has succeeded conqueror; one domination has followed another; but never in all the revolutions of fate and fortune have you seen one of those nations of its own notion establish what we from a western point of view call self-government. That is the fact. It is not a question of superiority and inferiority (31).

Obviously Naipaul, in his analysis of the Eastern countries, has been following these imperialists, whose views and attitude are coloured completely by the Western knowledge of Orientalism. This is amply supported when we find that in his book, *India: A Million Mutinies Now*, Naipaul quotes an eighteenth century British scholar, Sir William Jones who was the judge of the Bengal Supreme Court in 1786, and whose opinion is completely in line with the chief imperialists of the time:

> But your observation on the Hindu is too just: they are incapable of civil liberty; few of them have an idea of it; and those, who have, do not wish it. They must (I deplore the evil, but now the necessity of it) be ruled by an absolute power; and I feel my pain much alleviated by knowing the natives themselves... are happier under us than they were or could have been under the Sultans of Delhi or the petty Rajas (244).

Another important pillar of Orientalism was Cromer who in his *Edingburough* Review in January 1908, termed the Orientals as subject and made vociferous comments on the superiority and authority of the West on the Eastern subjects. He supportingly records the statements of Sir Alfred Lyall on the Orient:

> Accuracy is abhorrent to the Oriental mind. Every Anglo-Indian should always remember that maxim. Want of accuracy, which easily degrades into untruthfulness, is in fact the main characteristic of Oriental mind. The European is a close reasoner; his statements of fact are devoid of any ambiguity; he is a natural logician, albeit he may not have studied logic; he is by nature skeptical and requires proof before he can accept the truth of any proposition; his trained intelligence works like a piece of mechanism. The mind of the Oriental, on the other hand, like his picturesque streets, is eminently wanting in symmetry. His reasoning is of the most slipshod description (38)

Endorsing the remarks of Sir Lyall, Cromer further adds:

> Orientals are invertebrate liars, are "lethargic and suspicious," and in everything oppose the clarity, directness, and nobility of Anglo-Saxon race (39).

He finally condemns:

> I contend myself with the fact that somehow or other the Oriental generally acts, speaks, and thinks in a manner exactly opposite to the European (39).

Such views, opinions and attitude closely echo the remarks and views that Naipaul makes in his record of Indian scenes and situations:

> A million mutinies, supported by twenty kinds of group excesses, regional excesses: the beginning of self-awareness, it would seem, the beginning of an intellectual life, already negated by older anarchy and disorder (15).

Even Naipaul echoes the imperialist Cromer when he talks of the darkness and dark thinking of Indian mind:

> Even now, though time has widened, though space has contracted and I have travelled lucidly over area which was to me the area of darkness, something of darkness remains, in those attitudes, those ways of thinking and seeing, which are no longer mine (16).

Unlike Cromer who seeks support from other imperialists for his views on Orients, Kissingar, another builder of the West, speaks boldly and vehemently regarding the inability of thinking power among the Orientals and as such the absence of any scientific discoveries in the East:

> We had our Newtonian revolution; they didn't. As thinkers we are better off than they are (17).

Surprisingly Naipaul echoes the same remark with the similar belief regarding the poor thinking power of the Indians in the following remarks:

> (i) Social inquiry is outside the Indian tradition. Formal politics became an affair of head counting.
>
> (ii) India is without an ideology and that was the failure of Gandhi and India together.

(iii) The scientist returning from abroad regains the security of his caste identity and the world is once more simplified (18).

What is most important to note here is the tone of authority, superiority and judgement in which the colonists or the imperialists had been speaking in the House of Commons or publishing in various papers in the entire span of the colonial period. Here they appear, as commented by Said, to hold the Orients in the court or prison and thus declare the abnormal features of the civilization of the subject race. Naipaul, in the following remarks made on the Indians in his various books, comes close to the statements of the European imperialists:

(i) It is well that Indians are unable to look at their country directly, for the distress they would see, would drive them mad.

(ii) Indians defecate everywhere. They defecate, mostly, beside the railway tracks. But they also defecate on the beaches, they defecate on the hills; they defecate on the riverbanks; they defecate on the streets; they never look for cover (19).

(iii) I bolted the door, pulled down on all the blinds, trying to shut out the howls of dogs, shutting out intruders, all those staring faces and skeletal bodies. I put on no lights. I required darkness (20).

(iv) This underdeveloped ego, according to Kakar, is created by the detailed social organization of Indian life, and fits into that life (21).

(v) The crisis of India is not political, it is not economic, it is part of a larger crisis, that of a decaying civilization. Indian press... matched the triviality of the politics; it became a part of the Indian anarchy (22)

In the above quoted remarks we find an authoritative tone, a kind of rejective and naive attitude that amounts to a clear stand of the western superiority which holds the Orientals as uncivilized, uncouth and devoid of any trace of culture.

An eminent European psychologist, H.W. Gillden in his article in the issue of *American Journal of Psychology,* February

1972, on his investigations on the various races of the East, records that what is 'aberrant' for the Western is 'normal' for the Arabs and further observes:

> Arabs can function only in conflict situations; that prestige is based solely on the ability to dominate others that ashame culture and therefore Islam itself makes a virtue of revenge (23)

Similarly Naipaul, too, pronounces his judgement on Islam, which is related to and obviously derived from the remarks of *Prof. Gillden,* on the Arabs:

> This late twentieth-century Islam appeared to raise political issues. But it had the flaw of it's origins—the flaw that ran right through Islamic history: to the political issues it raised, it offered no political or practical solution. It offered only the faith. It offered only the prophet, who would settle everything—but who had ceased to exist. This political Islam was rage, anarchy (24)

Nothing can be farther from facts and truth than the above remark. Naipaul's views and comments have no relevance nor do they give the basic elementary idea of the Islamic faith. It is entirely based on Naipaul's personal assumption of his own subjective reading without any understanding and appreciation of the basic tenets of Islam.

Actually an objective analysis of the entire subject discloses that all the views and opinions on India, the East and the Islamic countries are derived from the same source of knowledge that was built by the imperialists of the West to derive power and strength to rule and govern the Orientals which has been very well summed up by Edward Said:

> In a sense Orientalism was library or archive of information commonly and, in some of its aspect, unanimously held. What bound the archive together was a family of ideas and a unifying set of values proven in various ways to be effective. These ideas explained the behaviour of Orientals; they supplied Orientals with a mentality, a genealogy, an atmosphere; most important, they allowed Europeans to deal with and even to see

> Orientals as a phenomenon possessing regular characteristics (25)

It is pertinent to note here that even in his understanding of the outstanding personalities of the East like Khomeine of Iran, Maulana Maudoodi of Pakistan and Mahatma Gandhi of India. Naipaui has been chiefly guided by the Western knowledge of the Orientals for nowhere does he make an attempt to understand their points of view and their insight from the Eastern and Indian angle and herein Naipaul makes the greatest mistake in his basic approach to the history, culture and philosophy of these lands.

After having left the country for years and having identified herself with a different culture Bharati Mukherjee, a writer of Indian diaspora, is filled and overwhelmed with deep feelings and emotions when she visits a temple in Calcutta. Similarly Salman Rushdie, after having settled in the West and having made the most comic and ironical treatment of Indian subjects in his well known novels, still displays sympathy and deep involvement when he comes to consider the common Indian themes and characters. But in case of V.S. Naipaul it boils down to an abject sense of rejection, negation and condemnation, simply because like the great imperialists of the last three centuries he too makes Western assumptions and starts with the basic theory of the post-colonialism as analysed by Edward Said. It is this knowledge that supplies the power, the tone and the language that ultimately prompts Naipaul to make such shocking, disappointing, scathing and the most biased views on the Eastern civilization in general, and on India in particular. His views and visions of the Eastern countries and precisely of India are obviously viewed through the *green coloured lenses* of the Western civilization. He is perhaps the only post-colonial writer of Indian diaspora, who, in spite of being an excellent artist of immense literary achievements, expresses his views and comments which are characteristic of the colonial writings of the imperialist leaders and statesmen who built up their knowledge of the Orientals in order to rule, dictate and subjugate the East.

WORKS CITED

Ahmed, Rashmee Z. *The Times of India.* October 12, 2001.

Mathur. O.P. *Symbolism in Indian Fiction in English.* Ed. R.K. Srivastava. Jalandhar: ABS Publication, 1997.

Mukherjee, Bharati and Clark Bleise. *Days and Night in Calcutta, Part—II.* New York: Garden City.

Naipaul, V.S. *An Area of Darkness.* London: Andre Deutsch, 1964. rpt. New York: Vintage, 1981.

——. *A Wounded Civilization.* New York: Alfared A. Knopt, 1977. rpt. New York: Vintage, 1987.

——. *India, A Million Mutinies Now.* London: Minerva Paperbacks, 1990.

Said, Edward. *Orientalism.* London: Routledge and Kegal Paul, 1978.

8

The Concept of Identity in Indian Immigrant Women in America: A Literary Perspective

Rama Nair

This paper attempts to critically evaluate the concept of Identity in Indian immigrant women in America from a literary perspective. Creative writers from post-colonial societies use various genres and forms of English to explore alternative worlds of experience that were formerly repressed or unimagined to engender a pluridimensionality of experience. Language is also 'both source and womb of creativity, a means of giving birth to new stories, new myths, of telling the stories of women that have been previously silenced' (*Motherlands*, xiii). Women from post-colonial countries are now transforming English to enable new kinds of representation through which they can articulate their intellectual, emotional and psychic dilemmas. I have chosen Meena Alexander's memoir *Fault Lines* and Bharati Mukherjee's novel *Jasmine* for my analysis of the predicament of the Indian immigrant women in America. Meena Alexander and Bharati Mukherjee are women writers of the Indian diaspora. The protagonist in both these literary works are female, and the product of multiple cultures and multiple anchorages. Meena Alexander and Bharati Mukherjee had unwittingly broken out of the traditional patriarchal mould of an Indian society, and had forged ahead with their lives in America. But questions of identity, displacement and rootlessness persist. The truth of art lies in its power to inscribe new dimensions of reality. It is this deeper reality that the spatio-temporal framework of Meena Alexander's *Fault Lines* and Bharati Mukherjee's *Jasmine* lead to. After all, what do multiple migrations and multiple anchorages do to a person's self-identity? Does it intensify feelings of displacement, or do they, instead, add a richer dimension to one's creative self?

Mary Elizabeth Alexander was born in Allahabad, India, on February 17, 1951. She officially changed her name from Mary Elizabeth to Meena (the name she had been called since birth) in her fifteenth year. Regarding this act of defiance, Alexander writes, "I felt I had changed my name to what I already was, some truer self, stripped free of the colonial burden" (*Fault Lines,* 74). Her name itself suggests her own multi-lingual nature. 'Meena' means 'fish' in Sanskrit, 'jewelling' in Urdu, and 'port' in Arabic. Meena Alexander is also the product of multiple cultures. When Sudan gained independence in 1956, Alexander's father applied for a job with the Sudanese government, and the family moved to Khartoum. Between the age of five to eighteen, Alexander moved between Sudan and India, between Khartoum and Kerala, and between her immediate family and her grand parents. When she was eighteen, and had received her degree from Khartoum University, Alexander left for Nottingham University in Britain. She obtained her Ph.D. in English literature there. But she returned to India, and eventually married an American, David Leyveld in Hyderabad, India. Later the two moved to New York City, where they still live with their two children.

These biographical details become crucial in the analysis of the protagonist of *Fault Lines. Fault Lines* begins with lucid moments of self-introspection. When asked by a friend to write her memoir, Alexander's first reaction is justifiably that of confused doubt and self-apprehension. She writes, "The more I thought about it, the less sense any of its seemed to make"(2) for there were any number of multiple selves that clamoured to be let loose from the confines of her body. Then again, she wonders whether she would be able to do justice to all the cities and small towns and village that she had lived in since birth such as Allahabad, Tiruvella, Kozencheri, Pune, Delhi and Hyderabad, all within the boundaries of India; besides Khartoum in the Sudan; Nottingham in Britain; and now this island of Manhattan. She states, "How should I spell out these fragments of a broken geography? And what of all the language compacted in my brain: Malayalam, my mother tongue, the language of first speech; Hindi which I learnt as a child; Arabic from my years in the Sudan—.... French; English? How could I map out all this in a book of days?"(2). Her life did not fall into any of the narrative she had been taught to honour-birth, an appropriate education, followed by an arranged marriage to a man of suitable birth and background, somewhere within the boundaries of India. But now she is in America. And certain questions still persisted. Some of them were "Where did I come from? How did I become what I am? How shall I start to write myself, configure my 'I' as other; image this life I lead, here, now, in America? What could I ever be but a mass of faults, a fault mass?" (2). It is from this candid assessment that we get the title *Fault Lines*. One of the definitions of the word 'fault' is derived from geology or mining. It refers to "Fragments of the adjoining rocks mashed and jumbled together, in some cases bound into a solid, mass called fault-stuff or fault-rock"(3). Alexander states, "That's it, I thought. That's all I am, a woman cracked by multiple migrations. Uprooted so many times she can connect nothing with nothing"(3). Memories of her past in India rescue her initially from being a nonentity in a world that survives only through its ability to define, identify and label people. Memories from the foundational basis of a conscious existence. To establish one's cultural identity, memory is sometimes necessary as Homi Bhabha points out. "Remembering," he writes, "is never a quiet act of introspection or retrospection. It is a painful remembering, a putting together of the dismembered past to make sense of the present" (*The Location of Culture*, 63). But memory itself is unreliable, and there is little sanctity even in remembrance, Alexander admits.

The question "Why did I leave India?" often torments Alexander. She writes, "All I knew was that something had broken loose from inside, me, was all molten." (*Fault Lines*, 146). And what was 'molten' and '*broken loose*' had to do with India, and to write, Alexander finds she had 'to flee into a colder climate.' 'Else I would burn up and all my words with me.'

Marrying David and moving to America might have resolved this trauma. But America proves to be more tormenting. Marrying a man of her choice, coming with him to another country, giving birth and finding a University job within a short span of time do not resolve the inner conflicts of rootlessness and displacement. "Was this what a woman's life had to be?," she wonders. Alexander finds that racism is something that one had to live with in America. Being with David at his workplace in Minneapolis made her realize her 'otherness.' David with his Scandinavian friends and blonde beard was often mistaken for one of them. But she 'stuck out like a sore black thumb,' a grotesque thing. Her alienation intensifies when on one occasion a white man in a black leather jacket and slicked back hair calls her a 'black bitch.' Her plight was akin to those of other Indian women—women who were forced to give up their saris and wear western clothes lest they lose their jobs, or the Asian children in the city schools, or to those Indians who lived through racist stonings and murder in Jersey City, and who lived in fear of the Dot Buster skin heads. Did one know what it meant to be unwhite in America? This piercing question reveals the extent of psychological oppression imposed on the marginalized communities in a country which takes pride in its secular and liberal values. Marrying a white man intensifies the competing anxieties of colour which extends itself to the identity of her children, Adam and Svati. Svati states, "You are brown mama, papa is blond papa, Adam is brown Adam, and I am peach Svati" (170). When a little Indian American child is transplanted into another soil and another earth—what kind of a future could they conceive? When a black man asked Adam, "What are you? American or Indian?" Adam replies boldly 'No..... I'm a Jedi knight,' suggesting a possible escape into a fantasy land where such distinctions were neither necessary nor important. To Alexander's consternation, the children at Svati's School regarded her as a Red Indian. Alexander had to explain the different geographical locations of not only India and America, but also the difference between native Indians, and native American Indians to both her daughter and her teacher and other students at school. The question that raises itself is the question of identity. Alexander asks, "Who are we? What selves can we construct to live by? How shall we mark out space? ...How shall we live another day?"(174). Ultimately, what one needs in Frank O'Hara's words is "Grace/to be born and live as variously as possible"(193). In America, as Alexander states, one had to explain oneself constantly. Her reply that she was a poet writing in America was not enough. Instead, she writes, "Everything that comes to me is hyphenated. A woman poet, a woman poet of colour, a South Indian woman poet who makes up her lines in English, a post-colonial language, making up poems about the disorder and violence in American society" (193). In fact America did not know what to do with the Asian women, who to them were 'exotic, border-line black,' and who never complained.

Though the 'usable past' was a recurrent theme of her poetry once, "an ethnicity evoked, a past that took the form of an ancestor, a grand mother figure"...it had effectively choked her attempts to understand the present. Living in the past, yearning for a life that could never be, was to live in a creative vacuum. What mattered was the American present. But the anguish of displacement continues. "...Is America this terrible multiplicity of the heart?" she wonders, "Am I American now that I have lost my shining picture (of home)? Now that I have no home in the old way?" (200).

But with multiple anchorages and a fractured past, ethnicity enters. Ethnicity lies in being an Indian American, or an Asian American, and the gateway to a life of letters depends on a "splintering of older ways of being...that might have made the mind think itself intact, innocent, without presumption" (202). The multiple anchorages that ethnicity provides means learning from Japanese Americans, Chinese Americans, Fillipino Americans, Mexican Americans, and also Indian Americans. In the opportunity given to become what one wishes to lies the compulsive energy of American. But here again, being dark and being female, prevents one from totally alienating oneself from one's roots. Ethnicity, Alexander states, "for such as I am comes into being as a pressure, a violence from within resists such fracturing" (202). This is an ethnicity that cannot be defined, it is an ethnicity that constantly evolves in the present. In the case of a poet, ethnicity would mean to transcend individualism, and to express in words what comes with rage—the overt acknowledgments of the nature of injustice. The struggle for social justice at a universal level is shaped by forces that 'well up out of us' and dislocate the brittle boundary lines we create to turn us towards the light of truth (193). Meena Alexander's struggle to develop her sense of self-identity lies in being true to her creative self-thus going beyond the boundary lines set by nation, race, gender and colour.

We now come to Bharati Mukherjee who says, "I'm writing about the here and now of America." She writes not just as an expatriate novelist but as a mainstream American writer. Her immigration to the US is to her "a movement away from the aloofness of expatriation to the exuberance of immigration" (*Darkness*, 3). It is this exuberant and energetic spirit of America that she celebrates in her novel, *Jasmine*, *Jasmine* explores this quest for the autonomy of the individual. Bharati Mukherjee, herself is the wife of Clark Blaise, an American, and her insight into American life is based upon her own observations and experiences. In *Jasmine*, the protagonist's name was initially Jyoti. Jyoti's father had migrated to the remote village of Hasnapur in the Punjab from Lahore during the Partition riots. A rich man, he had to live in poverty in Hasnapur. Jyoti's earliest memories deal with the agony of people uprooted from their homesteads. Her agony is compounded by the fact that she is born a girl, and therefore, a burden to her impoverished family. She is constantly remained of her misfortune of being a dowryless daughter. However, luck favours her, and she marries Prakash Vijh, 'a modern man, a city man.' Prakash was Jyoti's Prof. Higgins who wanted 'to break down the Jyoti' she had been in Hasanapur, and make her into 'a new kind of city woman.' To break off the past he gave her a new name: Jasmine. He said to her, "You are small and sweet and heady, my Jasmine. You'll quicken the whole world with your perfume" (*Jasmine,* 77). Jyoti, Jasmine—thus began the shuttling between identities. To

Prakash, love was letting go. Independence and self-reliance was the 'mantra' he instilled in her. This was to stand her in good stead in the years to come. Prakash's sudden death due to a terrorist's bullet, and Jasmine's widowhood at the age of seventeen, change the course of her life. Prakash's dream had been to go to America to study at Florida, to make something more of his life than fate intended. After his death, it became Jasmine's obsession to go America—not to study but to burn the new suit Prakash had bought for his trip and immolate herself on that 'pyre' as a pious Indian wife would have done in the olden days.

Thus begins Jasmine's transition from 'a modern city girl' in Jullundur to an illegal immigrant in the US. With forged papers, she prepares herself for an unknown destination, undaunted, to fulfil her ideal. The illegal immigrants were the 'outcastes and deportees, strange pilgrims visiting outlandish shrines, landing at the end of tarmacs in planes that are not listed in any directory, ferried in old army trucks to roped-off corners of waiting rooms where barely awakened customs guards awaited their bribes (101). Her first sight of America was not very prepossessing. The beach where she landed was strewn with 'Eden's waste; plastic bottles, floating organs, boards, sodden boxes, white and green plastic tied shut but picked open by birds and pulled apart by crabs (107). Her initiation into the brutality of life as an Asian immigrant woman begins with her rape by Half-Face, the scarred white captain of the ship in which she was smuggled into America. Taking on the form of the dreaded Goddess Kali, with her tongue sliced to let the blood drip on her victim, she stabs him repeatedly until he dies. Outside the motel she enacts a purificatory ritual by burning Prakash's suit and her white cotton sari which had been defiled by Half-Face's touch. She had not given even a day's survival in America a single thought. She had come to America to die at Tampa within the premises of the college where Prakash had got admission. As she states, "The vision of lying serenely on a bed of fire under plan trees in my white sari had motivated all the weeks of sleepless, half-starved passage, the numbered surrender to various men for the reward of an orange, a blanket, a slice of cheese" (120-21). But Half-Face's sneers and taunts had denied her even the comfort of death. So begins her journey along the length and breadth of the U.S. Professorji, Lillian Gordon, Wylie and Taylor and then Bud and Du were her family at different stages. She says, "I have had a husband for each of the women I've been, Prakash for Jasmine, Taylor for Jase, Bud for Jane, Half-Face for Kali" (197).

She begins her life in America as a caregiver to Taylor and Wylie's adopted daughter, Duff. America might be "fluid and built on flimsy, invisible lines of weak gravity" (179), but she had begun the process of 'getting rooted.' The Indian Language Department at Columbia used Jasmine as a Punjabi reader. She started tutoring students in Punjabi, and later she became the resource person for all those academics and executives interested in Indian studies. Her money grew. But in America nothing lasts. This was the hardest lesson for her to learn. "We arrive so eager to learn, to adjust, to participate, only to find the monuments are plastic, agreements are annulled. Nothing is forever, nothing is so terrible, or so wonderful, that it won't disintegrate" (181). Taylor and Wylie separate, and Jasmine leaves for Iowa. The next phase of her life center around Bud and Du. Du is Bud's adopted Vietnamese son, and in him Jasmine finds a reflection of her own rootlessness. "In the America Du knows, mothers are younger than sisters, mothers are illegal aliens, murderers, rape victims, parents are unmarried, fathers are invalids, shot in the back on Christmas Eve" (224). Jasmine is pregnant with Bud's child when she finally decides to leave him for Taylor. She loved Taylor, and he loved her. That was enough. "Greedy with wants and reckless from hope" is how Jasmine describe herself as she goes with Taylor. "Time will tell," she concludes, "if I am a tornado, a rubble-maker, arising from nowhere and disappearing into a cloud" (241). Though Jasmine was 'different' with her 'black hair' and 'wheatish' complexion, she learns to 'walk and talk' American, and takes on every opportunity to become American. She absorbs the alien culture, and becomes a personality with a definite identity. Jasmine from a diffident alien with forged documents transforms herself into the adventurous Jase living only for the present. While the other immigrant domestics were suspended between two worlds, Jasmine succeeds in rooting herself in the new culture. She uses her strength to forge new alliances. Her Indian past does not become a cause for nostalgia or sentiment. As an Indian girl she would never have deserted Bud, denying him even his child. But America had taught her that nothing lasts forever. Each phase in her life takes her one step closer towards the affirmation of selfhood. Jasmine stands for a new class of women who have the courage to discard a predictable life of orthodoxy and tradition in a conservative society. She welcomes the challenge of a competitive society—and evolves into a complete individual, notwithstanding her illegal immigrant status.

Both Meena Alexander and Bharati Mukherjee approach the immigrant problem in different ways. But there is a point of commonality. Acculturation or adoption of changes in external behaviour begin early, but assimilation or the ability to react instinctively and emotionally to a culture is a far slower process. Breaking away from one's ethnicity and absorbing a new culture is the only way of survival. Alexander finds a creative outlet for her personal anguish in writing, while Jasmine finds comfort in adaptability. Both are resilient and self-reliant, traits which American society apparently approves of. Both Alexander and Jasmine attempt to position themselves within the context of a self-defined space at a certain moment in history. New models of identity consider the displaced position of the migrant to be an entirely valuable one. As with Alexander's memoir, Bharati Mukherjee's Jasmine is also written in the first person. To live as a migrant is also to live in a world of immense possibility and creativity. In such a situation, one has to create new narratives which will accommodate one's position more positively than dominant narratives of belonging and identity. Alexander's privileged situation as a well educated woman made her feel empowered enough to expose the racial prejudice and social violence in American society. Bharati Mukherjee through Jasmine establishes that most women in divergent contexts are first and foremost victims of different kinds of oppression such as male violence, familial prejudices, economic constraints, and finally, their own sexuality. Jasmine's survival depends on her ability to utilise her inner resources in a way that does not conflict or clash with the culture that she is in. But in both Fault Lines and Jasmine an attempt has also been made to consider the different types of social relations that could be possible between men and women. This comparative analysis reveals that through assimilation or acculturation, an Indian immigrant woman in America can create an identity for herself. But this is an identity that is constantly evolving, being open to change and perpetual motion. This in turn challenges the earlier holistic concept of history, identity and community.

WORKS CITED

Alexander, Meena. *Fault Lines*. Penguin Books, 1993.

Bhabha, Homi K. *The Location of Culture*. London: Routlede, 1994.

Mukherjee, Bharati. "Introduction." *Darkness*. Penguin Books, 1990.

——. *Jasmine*. Penguin Books, 1989.

Nasta, Susheila., ed. *Motherlands: Black Women's Writing from Africa, the Caribbean and South Asia*: Women's Press, 1991.

9

"A Pain in the Posterior": Scanning Minority—Mainstream Relationship in Rohinton Mistry's *Tales from Ferozsha Baag*

A.G. Khan

Rohinton Mistry, a Canada based Indian writer—earned fame with his short stories that brought him two successive Hart House Prizes in 1983 and 1984. Recipient of Governor General's Prize in 1991 for his novel *Such a Long Journey* it stood runner up for the prestigious Booker Prize for Commonwealth fiction in the same year. That Mistry has a gift of telling stories is amply demonstrated by the eleven short stories collected in *Tales from Ferozsha Baag* (1987). Like one of the characters of his stories, Nariman Hansotia, Mistry has a knack of blending his stories with two salient features.

> Unpredictability was the brush he used to paint his tales with and ambiguity the palette he mixed his colours in (147).

The implication of the above is that he told:

> *a funny* incident in a very serious way or expressed a significant matter in a light and playful manner.....[with] lots of subtle gradation of tone and texture (147).

This collection is an exciting as well as absorbing picture gallery comprising interesting, eccentric and even grotesque characters. The blurb rightly describes, "the crowd, throbbing life of India is brilliantly captured." The reviewer in the *Sunday Times* aptly considers it to be "an acknowledgment of human variety." This paper seeks to scan the minority (Parsi) mainstream relationship described in the stories vis-à-vis both the countries—India and Canada.

The Parsis, who are a microscopic community of 120 thousand scattered all over the globe, find themselves in an unusual predicament. They became invisible' minority everywhere—Bombay, Karachi, London or Toranto. They demonstrate a wonderful capacity to adapt to and socialize with the mainstream cultures; they also exhibit extra-ordinary stamina to retain their identity.

Alarmed by the threat of extinction because of decreasing birth rate they are vigilant to adhere fast to their faith. A constitutional malady endanger their welfare.

> .... That is what Osteoporosis does hollows out the bones and turns effects into cause. It has an unusually high incidence in the Parsi Community (*Tales from Ferozsha Baag*, 230).

The internal threat is further increased by inter religion marriages. Dina Mehta and Bapsi Sidhwa have raised the issue in "*And Some Take a Lover,* and *An American Brat:*

> .... there were too many cousin marriages among the Parsees.... what lack of crossbreeding had done to a Small community like theirs. (*And Some Take a Lover*, 37) ... That we should allow our girls to marry outside the community, mate with Parjat?"(37).
>
> .... Once a Parsee—Zoroastrian Marries a non-zoroastrian he or she is deemed to have renounced the fait! and ceases to be a Parsee-Zoroastrian (*An American Brat*, 305).

The other problem that brings the community hostility from the mainstream people is their practice of funeral the dead body being consumed by birds of prey such as the vultures. Mistry describes the controversy in details in *Such A Long Journey:*

> "You; vultures!" the tenants complained, "control your vultures! Throwing rubbish on our balconies!" They claimed that the sated birds, flying out from the tower after gorging themselves, invariably snatched a final bite to savour later. And if the tidbits were lost in mid-flight, they landed on the exclusive balconies (316-17).

In addition to these, social and political developments made their position quite vulnerable. Should the mainstream population turn fanatic or hostile where shall they find a refuge? The Jews have found a homeland but the Parsees cannot cherish such dream. Dina Mehta hits:

> "Whether or not Parsees should return enmasse to Iran, the land of their forebears thirteen hundred years ago" (29) Slogans of Maharashtra for the Maharashtrians and Khalistan for the Khalsas, Pakistan for the Muslims has become an eyesore for them. Mistry pours his venom;
>
> "No future for minorities with all these fascist Shiv-Sena politics and Marathi language nonsense" (*Such A Long Journey*, 55)
>
> "Wait till the Marathas take over, then we shall have real Gandoo Raj." He suddenly worked himself into a real rage; there was genuine grief in his soul (73).

The anxiety is not born merely of the communal hatred, but has its monitorial implications. The Parsees enjoyed privileged and economic extravaganza under the British Patronage. But the circumstances in the post-independence era have turned tables on them:

> Parsis were the kings of banking in those days, Such respect we used to get..... And today we have that bloody Shiv-Sena wanting to make the rest of us into second class citizens.... Parsee crow eaters we shall show you who is the boss (39).

See how Dina Mehta has described this communal hostility in terms of market management:

> ....but the Hindu wore Dhoti; he turned his world into a spittoon by ejecting streams of betel-juice..... his bathrooms stank of urine and kitchens of heeng; he was dishonest in his business practices and mean with his money (*And Some Take a Lover*, 38).

Probably the Parsees had an inkling of the bank scam with strict British procedures absent, a Harshad Mehta was an inevitability:

> Once the British leave scoundrels of the first water will line their pockets from unclean sources, judges will be bribed, juries fixed and your Uttamchands and Mulchandanis will become multi-multi (37).

It is for this reason that the "nostalgia" for the British Raj has a psychic spring:

> Johniwalker scotch freely available under the British could now be obtained only on the black market and was responsible for Rustamji's continuing grief over the British departure (*Tales from Ferozsha Baag*, 15).
>
> They thought they were like British only ruling India side by side (46).
>
> Anglophilia, the Parsee disease (*Trying to Grow*, 161).

II

The five stories of this collection deserve special attention as they give us a peep into the Parsi psyche both home and abroad. They are *Auspicious occasion, The Chost of Ferozsha Baag, condolence visit* and *squatter, Swimming lessons.* An analysis of these stories scan the minority—mainstream relationship.

Rustamji, the protogonist of the first story *Auspicious occasion,* loses his temper when offended by a squirt of tobacco juice from a double decker bus. He explodes into an angry outburst but soon realises his monstrous folly. The crowd comprising mostly the mainstream people had a fun on the *bawaji's* plight. But soon turns militant and is about to pounce on him. Rustamji has to resort to a bit of buffoonery to save his skin. Removing his denture from his mouth he pleads:

> "Look such an old man no teeth even." The collapsed mouth and flopping lips appeased everyone. A general tiltering spread through the assembly, Rustamji the clown was triumphant. Tears of shame and rage welled in his eyes (*Tales from Ferozsha Baag*, 18).

This broken man, his arrogance subdued, on his return have becomes an object of piety:

> This rare glimpse of the softness underneath his tough exterior touched her (20).

Hence while getting inside the car he has to stoop low "to keep the *phyto* from being knocked off his head" (18). The leak in Rustomji's toilet is a symbolic leak in which filth is an unavoidable destiny—"was a steady leak—drip drip drip drip," Shorn of their past glory the Parsees have to keep a low profile. "Plaster from the ceiling had dropped" (5). It is not the condition of the walls at Ferozsha Baag that is described but the fate of the entire community.

It is for this reason that Ferozsha Baag is a *ghetto* that admits no no-parsee except as *ayab* or servant. There is just one Muslim tenent. Hindus are conspicuous by their absence. The communal pride is often reflected in several incidents. The contempt for the non-parsis is expressed without any ambiguity. Whatever is decent and dignified is undoubtedly Parsi; whatever is filthy or disgraceful must be non-Parsi. Boys are often admonished to behave like good Parsis and not like *ghatis*—a term of contempt for the illiterate, low bred, Marathas.

Hence when Rustomji finds the toilet dirty at a place (Tower of silence or *Agyari)* where not a single non-parsi is admitted.

—it was not Parsis who used the WC, he felt, but uneducated filthy, ignorant, barbarians" (15). Naturally, this superiority complex finds expression in such make-believe e.g. when a Hindu priest fails to drive away the *bhoot,* Parsi priest is called to perform a *Jashan* because "Parsi priest has the most powerful prayers of all" (54). But things acquire ridiculous proportion when we are asked to believe:

> Parsi prayers are so powerful, only a Parsi can listen to them. Every one else can be badly damaged inside their soul if they listen (54).

but sometimes the necessity becomes so urgent that a non-parsi is permitted as a concession:

> It needs two Parsis, but I'll do with you (55)

Similarly, when the accomplishments are to be enumerated only those will be enumerated who belong to the community, e.g. while praising Indian Cricketeers not a single non-parsi is mentioned:

> You boys know the great cricketeers Contractor, Polly Umrigar and recently, the young chap, Farookh Engineer (146)

The Maharashtrians have their Gavaskar, Manjrekar, Tendulkar, the Sikhs their Bedi and Sidhu, the Muslims their Azhar and Pataudi, why shouldn't the Parsis praise their Surti and Engineer! Inspite of their modernization/Westernization and enlightenment of Oxford and Cambridge; the Parsis are most conservative. A non-parsi would pollute their powerful prayer. So none is allowed in an Agyari or at the Tower of silence:

> Sam's colleagues from the bank had to stand outside, They weren't Parsee. Their presence would have defiled the fire temple (*Trying to Grow*, 167).

> ......the wall ran the length of the compound sheltering them from non-parsi eyes while they prayed (*Such A Long Journey*, 82).

Feeling miserable in India, the only alternative any minority community works out is migration to America, Australia or Canada.

> And one day, you must go, too, to America. No future here (112).

II

The process of assimilation and adaptation are not so easy as it is commonly believed and advertised. No country, neither Canada nor India has been able to find a solution inspite of sincere efforts, Mistry does not mince words when he describes the travails of an immigrant unable to rise to the standards and expectations of the host country. Mistry first begins with India. Francis and Jacqueline are Goan Christians who have spent almost four decades each in this parsi locality. Francis who came as an errand boy is still marginalised, "the awning of the store still provided the only roof he had ever known" (27). He is not inducted as a full time servant. So is Jacqueline sleeping in the verandah or below the stair well. The house where she worked as Ayah for 48 years does not provide her a roof. Her name has been twisted from Jacqueline to Jackaylee. She complains, "Forgetting my name, my language, my songs" (45). And no wonder her fellow outcast Francis slips in her bed she is unable to recognise him as a person in flesh and blood confusing him to be a *bhoot.*

Mistry tries to exploit the immigration issue by creating a humorous situation. No one is able to resolve the mystery about Sarosh (Sid's) unceremonial return from Canada while people in thousands were rushing to the land of opportunities. Mistry narrated Sarosh's plight in a lighter vein by confiding to us that his bowels refused to obey the dictates of the toilet seat being accustomed to the squatting postures of Indian latrines. Inspite of his best efforts he remains constipated and had to spend hours together. He cannot disclose the cause of his anxiety to anyone belonging to the mainstream. Marked late eleven times in a month he is served warnings by his supervisor. Counselling serves no purpose. The Multi-cultural department is his last refuge. However, his encounter with *Dr. No Illaz* (No remedy) and *Mrs. Maha-Lapate* (Madame Exaggeration) make him more nervous. Mistry ridicules the futility of such hi-fi notions like Multi-culturalism:

> The Multi-cultural Department is a Canadian invention. It is supposed to ensure that ethnic cultures are able to flourish, so that the Canadian society will consist of mosaic cultures, that's their favourite word, Mosaic—instead of one uniform mix, like the American melting pot. If you ask me mosaic and melting pot are both non-sense and ethnic is a polite way of saying bloody foreigner (160).

The inefficacy of counselling is described by explaining how does *Dr. No Illaz* extend his expertise: For the normal natural body function he suggests a mechanical device and then scares the poor man by possibility of complications:

> A small device, Crappus non-interruptus or CNI as we'll call it, it is implanted in the bowel. The device is

> controlled by an external transmitter similar to the one used for an automatic garage door opener (160).

An awe-stricken Sarosh is further warned that once fitted he would become a permanent slave of the device. Moreover:

> There are other dangers too. CNI can also be operated by someone with similar apparatus... very embarrassing if it happened at the wrong place and time..... (161).

Hence when all quack prescription fail he decides to say good bye to the country. The situation becomes bizarre when Sarosh finds that his tummy develops the right kind of pressure and his bowles are ready to discharge when the plane was ready to take off for India. But alas, the air hostess does not permit him to alight but forces him to fasten the seat belt.

Mistry employs the post-modern Jargon to heighten the ridicule. Sarosh questions:

> But wait, something else was happening now. A tiny rumble inside him. Or was it his imagination? Was it really thunder outside which in his present disoriented state, he was internalizing? (164) (emphasis mine).

The "adaptation" was a total fiasco. Mistry parodies the Othello scene:

> When you shall these unlucky deeds relate, speak of me as I am nothing extenuate, nor set down ought in malice; tell them in Toranto once there lived a Parsi boy as best as he could, set you down this; and say, besides, that for some it was good and for some it was bad but me life in the land of milk and honey was just a pain in the posterior (168).

WORKS CITED

Kanga, Firdous. *Trying to Grow*. Delhi: Ravi Dayal, 1991.

Mehta, Dina. *And Some Take a Lover*. Calcutta: Rupa & Co., 1992.

Mistry, Rohinton. *Such A Long Journey*. Calcutta: Rupa & Co., 1991.

——. *Tales form Ferozsha Baag*. New Delhi: Rupa & Co., 1993.

Sidhwa, Bapsi. *An American Brat*. Penguin Books India,1994.

10 The Marriage of the Mind and the Cosmos in Patrick White's *Voss*: An Indian Perspective

K. Chellappan

It was Bradbrook who referred to the epic dimension and the open-minded myth in the novels of Patrick White which the mind of Australia merges with the Australia of mind (141-2). In *Voss* (1957), the central character is an explorer, a metaphor of the mind of man in search of its infinity in the emptiness of the Australian desert symbolizing the human soul before the descent of the divine. Even though critics such as Patricia Morley (1972), and Joan Newman (1995), have referred to the allegoric dimensions of the journey of Voss in Christian terms, an attempt here is made to show that this journey is more universal than simply Christian as it has also affinity with the Indian concept of the identity of Atman and Brahman. This, however does not deny the Christian pattern in the novel, but suggests that it has resonance beyond the Christian framework and becomes a universal parable of the soul's quest for the absolute.

The journey of Voss across Australia from Bonner's world is very much like that of the Ancient Mariner who is shipwrecked in the Pacific as he commits a crime against God, nature and man but at the end learns that, "He prayeth best who loveth best. All things both great and small." Voss thus has affinity with the romantic creed in its region of nature and also in linking God with creativity and love. But Voss in seeking a kind of identity between the creator and the created seems to be closer to the Upanishadic 'Tatvamasi' (Thou art that). Though in the beginning Voss seems to symbolize only sublime egotism, finally there is a progress to a kind of self which is characterized by love for all life. The story seems to enact a cosmic drama as it were, in the Australian landscape in which we see a kind of the eternal triangle of love: here Voss seems to be pursuing the infinite in the Australian landscape though it is only a reflection of the infinite in him. Laura who is pursuing him through his journey has been associated with Christ and Beatrice in his absence. We would consider her as his epipsyche where as Australia is the greater soul, and, Voss dislikes Christian virtue of humility as well as conceives a God like himself. But Laura seems to be concerned with humility and makes amends for others when she says, "I am not in the habit of setting myself limits" (*Voss*, 1957: 90). Voss seems to be seeking an Identity between himself and God, the infinite and the finite, and this identification is like the Upanishadic "Aham Brahamste." But he being an inverted seeker is also like Hiranya who does not want his son to accept any God but himself. Australian landscape, more particularly its emptiness suggests the greater soul, but it is also a correlative to his own soul.

The horizontal movement is paralleled by the vertical journey deep down his soul. Only his mind seems to be real. "All that was external to himself he mistrusted, and was happiest in silence, which is immeasurable, like distance, and the potentialities of self" (Ibidem, 21-22) to him. As William Walsh puts it, "Voss is one whose powers are concentrated with ferocious intensity upon an inner life. The outer world is either a nuisance or a menace" (1977: 44). The landscape seems to be an extension of his consciousness whereas his consciousness becomes an interior landscape. In the early phase of the journey he observed all things as if for the first time. It was a gentle, healing landscape in those parts. So he was looking about him with contented eye, drinking deep drought of a most simple medicine. He preferred shortcuts instead along the bush tracks walking on leaves and silence. White adds: "It was not the volcanic silence of solitary travel through infinity. The German had experienced and had been exhausted by it, winding deeper into himself, into bleaker tickets of thorns" (*Voss*, 124). Significantly he describes, "The world of Gods was becoming the world of men.' In another context, White says that the world of semblance communicated with the world of dream.

Whereas Mc Auley sees Voss as a story organized around the contrast between the urban society of Sydney and the unexplored Bush, to William Walsh, Voss does not rely on this too simple contrast. 'The world of Sydney for example is the Bush, the country of the mind.' He adds that the Bush itself pictures an inner world (48) and the conquest of a continent was an outer aspect of Voss's inward expedition. Australia is the objective correlative to the unconquerable mind as well as the greater self and also enables him to discover the Divine in himself by discovering his humanity through descent into the demonic depths. The relationship between the antihero and Australia is one of love-hate and Voss finally achieves knowledge of the self as inseparable from the landscape. If, in one sense Laura is Voss's epipsyche, Laura also seems to be seeking Voss who affects her like poetry, whereas Voss seeks the interior regions of Australia. They respond to each other by reflecting and recognizing each other. There is something of the sublime both in Voss and the landscape. Caroline Bliss has referred to Laura being the mirror of Voss and a mediator between Voss and us (1986: 62). In their Plantonic love we see the longing of the divided parts for each other. Australia does to Voss, what Voss does to Laura and vice versa. Laura helps Voss to recognize his limits and humanizes him just as Voss humanizes her though in different ways. There is something of the marriage of the finite and the infinite all the time. Again, Voss understands Australia through Laura who has a better understanding of Australia after having suffered with Voss.

The main focus in this expedition is on Voss's determination to wrestle with the rock, to bleed if necessary, to ascend and he tells Laura that he does not intend to stop short of the throne for the pleasure of groveling on lacerated knee in company with Judd and Palfreyman who have the orthodox faith. In this he is not only a heretic and a Gnostic who pits himself against the God of conventional Christianity and Gnostic versions of the God head as suggested by Mark Williams (1993: 68), but is close to some of the Asuras in the Hindu mythology like Ravana, Hiranya or Surpadman who questions the divine only to attain divinity by being destroyed in the hands of God. The imagery of light penetrating earth and water is very significant in this earth dominated novel. Laura is associated with air whereas Voss is linked with earth and fire. Voss recalls "how they had never spoken together using the truly humble words that convey the inner most reality, bread, for instance or water." But when he now looks at the landscape now "we shall understand each other," he said (*Voss*, 190). Then follows the description of the birds. The visionary moment is summed up, "the marriage of light and shadow in the infinite distances of that dun country of which he was taking possession, all, finally would be resolved" (Ibidem).

More important than this is the linking of Voss's creation of the light with creation out of chaos, while commenting on the long passage on the morning when the world seemed to be created again out of shapelessness. The reference to the punishment and the grey creeping over the rocks, slithering in native coils upon the surface of waters is very much suggestive of *The Rime of the Ancient Mariner* with which the novel has a number of affinities. Voss's killing Gyp is like killing of the Albatross and we may associate the suffering of the crew with Voss's egoism, but here Voss like the ancient Mariner becomes a creator. "The creator sighed, and there arose a contended little breeze, even from the mouth of the cave" (*Ibidem*, 63). White continues to talk of the creative work of the Sun and also the water, with water of another kind and light. Williams comments: "Voss regards his mind as the origin of all ocean in the world. The sunrise his creative act and when he sights, a breeze is sent out into the expectant world. Behind Voss's arrogance lies the post-romantic conviction that the mind is the active partner in the marriage into which it enters with the outside world. In the rising Sun scene Voss tests the limits of this nation" (1993:64). This would link Voss again with the Ancient Mariner which also deals with creativity. But here the creative mind is more important than even in the Ancient Mariner.

There are two other passages, which also are concerned with something like nature mysticism. The first is from the journal of Le Mesuirer who also symbolizes creativity and grace and deals with his descent from arrogance to humility, from divinity to humanity.

'I pray that you will take my spirit out of this my body's remains, and after you have scattered it, grant that it shall be everywhere, and in the rocks, and in the empty water holes, and in true love of all men, and in you, O God, at last' (*Voss*, 297).

He wants to be dissolved in the rocks and waters. We are reminded of Wordsworth's Tintern Abbey which talks of one spirit in the setting Sun etc., and in the mind of man. Here, "there is a linking of nature with true love of all men and in you" (294). Laura also while talking of the impact of Rose's death says:

> As I stood there (I hesitate to write you all this, except that it is the truth), as I stood, the material part of myself became quite superfluous, While my understanding seemed to enter into wind, earth, the ocean beyond, even the soul of our poor, dead maid. I was nowhere and everywhere at once. I was destroyed, yet living more intensely than actual sunlight, so that I no longer feared the face of Death as I had found it on the pillow. If I suffered, it was to understand the devotion and suffering of Rose, to love whom had always been an effort! (*Voss*, 239)

Both emphasize the unity of all life as well as unity with nature. Laura seems to suffer while trying to understand the devotion and suffering of roses and later she also suffers while Voss is killed who also through suffering recognizes his humanity and oneness with humanity through which he attains a kind of divinity.

The emphasis on suffering is Christian but here it is a tool to liberate the imagination as in Romantic poetry. We are made to recall not only *The Ancient Mariner,* but the lines of Wordsworth: "Suffering is dark, permanent and real and shares the very nature of infinity." And this again is as much Gandhian as Christian.

But it is Voss who suffers most and attains divinity by accepting his humanity. And he also understands Australia better again by love for all including those who hate him. The cave where Voss's killed to be reborn could also be linked with the platonic cave as well as the cave in Kubla Khan. But here creativity is linked with a better understanding of Australia. And true knowledge only comes of death by torture in the country of the mind. He becomes one with Australia and the mind of Australia becomes one with the Australia of mind. The novel emphasizes that true knowledge comes not through rational understanding but through identification and suffering and the soul's quest for its true identity which comes through a recognition of identity between the soul and greater soul of which Australia is a symbol. This we have tried to show is like the Upanishadic identification of Atman with Brahman and also the need to embrace all life in one brotherhood in relation to the fatherhood of God. In the novel Voss's descent/ascent is linked with the paradox of man in God and God in man, in Christian terms "of God into man. Man and man returning into God" (Ibidem, 383-384). Vedanta also speaks of the ascent of man necessitating the descent of God, the whisper from above responding to the wink from below. Even though the Christian framework is preserved, Voss seems to be close to the Indian philosophy in its concept of unity of the self and also in portraying the hero's usurping divinity whereas Christianity's focus is on humility.

Carolyn Bliss has suggested that in Voss the periphery of self expands to coincide with infinity (1986). But both she and Patricia Merely see Voss exclusively in Christian terms. She makes a distinction based on Eckhart between unitive mysticism which aims at a complete union of soul with the divine and the oriental mysticism which aims at the marriage of a soul to God and which therefore maintains as essential distinction between creature and creator. She also refers to Otto's distinction between East and West and calls these two forms of mysticism as Eros and Agape. But it is not correct to say that the Eastern mysticism does not accept life in its diversity, through the Advaita speaks of total identity between the soul and the greater soul.

Finally the novel in dealing with the psychic journey in relation to the landscape resembles classical Tamil poetry. Its uniqueness lies in its division of life and literature into two major categories, Akam and Puram, inner and outer life, standing for domestic life or the life of the mind and Puram meaning "outer" stands for the larger social life or the life of the heroic deeds. In both, the cosmos provides the setting or primal theme (muthal porul), the human characters provide the kernal theme (karu porul), and the varied recurrent motifs and situations constitute the intrinsic theme (uriporu) that belongs to the poems proper. Both have seven parallel tinais pertaining to the world of love and heroism respectively. Palai tinal of Akam signifies separation whereas Vanchi, its Puram counterpart signifies war.

If we look at Voss from this perspective, Voss signifies the dynamic male world, that of quest and conquest and Laura signifies the static female world of love and dream, (Akam) like Nedunal Vadai which speaks of a heroine, but the focus is on the hero in the battlefield. This can be seen either as an Akam or a Puram novel or both simultaneously. In this respect it is like 'Neuuelvadai' one of the long Sangam poems in which the heroine's pangs of separation are juxtaposed with the hero's bravery in winter (vatai). There are parallels to Akam poetry in Laura's experience and to Puram poetry in Voss's experience. Though we may have to extend Puram to include heroism of the spirit. Here again the land is central to the human drama and the main event is journey. The heroine recreates the hero in her consciousness and the hero's journey takes place both in the Australian desert and in her consciousness. Whereas the desert brings out the hero's heroic qualities, it brings out the heroine's tenderness. The mind is extended as it were into an objective universe and discovered through it. The desert becomes a correlative to his own isolation. The epic novel shows the convergence of Akam and Puram, the mind of Australia and the Australia of the mind. Finally the hero is made to live as a myth, both in Australia and the mind of the people as a tale which serves as Natukal erected to perpetuate his heroic memory.

The Akam—Puram division is the Tamil counterpart to the self-greater self-concept in the Sanskrit tradition. There is a view that only the mystic aspect of love in Sangam poetry is later developed into Bhakthi poetry in Tamil which shows a merging of the two traditions also. It is interesting to see that Patrick White's *Voss* shows parallel to both the traditions in Indian literature.

WORKS CITED

Bliss, Carolyn. *Patrick White's Fiction: Paradox of Fortunate Failure.* London: Macmillan, 1986.

Bradbrook, M.C. "Literature and Society in Commonwealth: 'The Australian Legend.'" *Literature in Action.*

Morley, A. Patricia. The Mystery of Writing, *Theme and Technique.*

Newman, Joan. "The Significance of Christian Myth Structures in Voss." *Prophet from Desert: Critical Essays on Patrick White.* Ed. John M. Choren. Melbourne: Red Hill Press, 1995.

Walsh, William. *Patrick White's Fiction.* London: George Allen and Unwin, 1977.

Williams, Mark. *Patrick White.* London: Macmillan, 1993.

White, Patrick. *Voss.* New York: Vikin Press, 1957.

11

The Migrant Experience in Bharati Mukherjee's Canadian Short Stories: An Indian Response

Viney Kirpal

Writers are known to make statements that prepare their readers for receiving their works with apprehension of their art and philosophy. They do this particularly, when they have attempted something new. Wordsworth and Coleridge did it, when they brought out The Lyrical Ballads in 1798. J.M. Synge, T.S. Eliot, Nadine Gordimer, Raja Rao, Salman Rushdie, Chinua Achebe and Wilson Harris have from time to time put forth the operational sensibility behind their works. Although, not of the same stature as a writer, Bharati Mukherjee has done it too, beginning with her now famous "Introduction" to Darkness, a collection of short stories written in 1984, in Atlanta, Georgia (U.S.A.), during her stay there as a writer- in-residence. Statements by writers certainly assist critics to explain and assess their works in the light of the proffered guidelines. There is danger, however, in not being able to distance oneself from the writer's intention and reading his works entirely in the light of her stated aesthetic aims and positions. Something like this has happened in the case of both Rushdie and Mukherjee who have led most First World critics into accepting that migrancy is a privileged condition because the migrant writer is exposed to multiple cultures (Rushdie, "A Dangerous Art Form, 4"). Both Rushdie and Mukherjee have created the impression that this is so, possibly, because both are themselves migrant writers. Thus, according to Rushdie, the migrant writer is the superior writer because his homelessness qualifies him to become an international writer (Rushdie, "A Dangerous

Art Form, 4"). According to Mukherjee, the migrant writer is not to be pitied for having lost her national identity as she has now acquired "a set of fluid identities to be celebrated" ("Introduction" *Darkness*, 3). Distinguishing between the immigrant' and the 'expatriate,' she has maintained that the former nurses a nativist identity as against the expatriate who is a product of acculturation ("Introduction").

Since both Darkness and The Middleman were written after her migration to America it will be interesting to find out whether or not Mukherjee's representation of migrant Indian characters bear the stamp of the creator's hybrid migrant personality, I shall confine myself to her American stories to establish a point. This aspect has so far not been examined by critics, most of whom have taken the teller (Mukherjee) at her word in reading her tales.

The first story, I examine is "The World According to Hus" (*Darkness*, 35—56). Thirty-three year old Ratna Clayton (half Indian, a Professor at McGill come to an unnamed African island for a short vacation. On the day of their arrival there, the island is placed under a curfew because of an aborted student led revolution. Confined to their hotel, Hotel Papillon, Clayton Ratna recalls the racist attacks on non-white immigrants in Toronto and fears moving to Toronto with her husband who has been offered a chair there. Graeme, being white, does not share her apprehensions. For him, "Toronto is the safest city on the continent" (47). At dinner in the Papillon, Graeme reads aloud of out a scientific article by Kenneth Hsu, According to Hsu, the world had been one, six million years ago the idea sets Ratna pondering the subsequent geographic divisions among the different countries ever since leading to all other divisions. For a brief while, however, she imagines the Papillon to be that one world with all the residents there, united by their need for refuge from the dangers outside and by their knowledge of the English language which had enabled them to converse that night. Offset against the one world vision, is a collage of pictures of difference, unbridged, uncomprehended between husband (Graeme) and wife (Ratna), between white (Canada) and non-white/migrant, between First World (holiday-makers) and Third World (under-developed, politically disturbed, technologically poor) countries like the African island. Notwithstanding, the proposed ideal of the world as a global village where all people are initiated (reminiscent not a little of Ralph Singh's hotel in The Mimic Men by V.S. Naipaul, Mukherjee's model), the story is overridden by the gloom of divisiveness and the inability, as well as, the lack of effort to understand other worldviews.

A similar "Us" versus "Them" position also haunts Mukherjee's other short stories. In "The Lady from Luckow" (21—34), Nafessa Hafeez has an affair with James Beamish a 68-year-old white. While all along, Nafeesa had thought that it was she who was in control of the situation, it is Kate (white woman/Canadian James's wife) who proves the superior adversary on discovering of the liaison. Kate does not become hysterical or emotional (like a Third World women would) she simply plucks off the quilt to uncover the naked Nafeesa and treats her like a joke. The humiliated Nafeesa does not ever recover from the brutal act of shaming. She recalls, by contrast, the story of Husseina, a Muslim girl (her neighbour in Lucknow) whose father had, on intercepting a love note from her heart just broke and she died. Comparing Kate's humiliation of her Hindu lover beaten her with feather sandals Husseina's with the Muslim father's, Nafeesa now feels that the letter's treatment was less unkind because it was straightforward, Kate, by contrast, had been extremely civilized and cool while she had mocked at Nafeesa's passion and reduced her worth in her very own eyes. Mukherjee subtly conveys Nafeesa's state of shame and guilt (a characteristic response of a colonized person) through easily understood psychosomatic symptoms:

> My arms are numb, my breathing loud... The pain in My chest will not go away, I should be tasting blood in my throat by now (34).

The point of the story is to suggest that though it is the Muslim father who would be seen as a savage through First World eyes, it is Kate Beamish, who with her clinically executed degradation of Nafees is more so. Not once does she criticize her husband for his complicity in the affair. Instead, it is Nafeesa, Third World immigrant whom she mercilessly demeans and shows her place.

The contrast has echoes only of two different cultural styles but also of the historical relationship between colonizer and colonized.

While the locale changes from Canada to Detroit (USA) in "A Father" (57—74), the theme remains much the same Mr. Bhowmick who is a devout Bengali and a devotee of Kali is horrified to discover that his 26-year-old unmarried engineer daughter Babli is pregnant. The same distorted, traditional sense of honour that had caused the father in "The Lady from Lucknow" to beat his daughter Husseina, now prompts Mr. Bhowmick to turn violent with Babli:

> Mr. Bhowmick lifted the rolling pin high above his head and brought it down hard on the done of Babli's stomach. In the end' it was his wife who called the police (73).

Although Babli is shown (albeit, simplistically) as having adopted American ways, it is her "permissive" view of life which controverts Mr. Bhowmick's orthodox one and draws blood and destruction from him. The sheer discovery of an unmarried daughter expectant with a child, is enough to shatter the carefully-built economically secure world of the Hindu immigrant Bhowmick, in Canada. A votary of Kali like whom he responds, he carries his India with him.

Thus all the short stories discussed so far share a dark, despair-ridden, pessimistic perspective to the act of migration. The darkness is echoed in the title of the collection itself. The more positive picture of the expatriate as a hybrid of the best of both cultures does not emerge. Only to some extent does the change in attitude come through her short story, "The Management of Grief" (*The Middleman and Other Stories*, 179—197).

Shaila an Indian woman is among the many immigrant families in Canada who lose their near and dear ones in the Kanishka plane crash caused by what the Canadians called "the sikh bomb." The different families try to come to terms with the tragedy in varying ways; her neighbour Kusum leaves for India where she joins a swami's ashram in search of peace; Dr. Ranganathan, a scientist tries for a while, to treat his house as a temple of the dead not even going to sleep there, until unable to bear it any longer he takes up a job in Texas; the illiterate, aged Sikh couple who lose both their sons just a week after they had come to Canada refuse to accept their death by not signing the papers which would enable them to live in Canada on government pension. Their continued refusal irritates the Canadian social worker. Judith Templeton, who cannot understand their 'odd' behaviour.

> In the car, Judith says, "You see what I'm up against? I'm sure they're lovely people, but their stubbornness and ignorance are driving me crazy. They think signing a paper is signing their son's death warrants, don't they?"

I am looking out the window, I want to say, In our culture it is a parent's duty to hope (195; italics in original).

The inability of the whites to understand the culture of the non-white, the Indian others is emphasized in Shaila's refusal to answer Judith, and in Judith's mounting confusion. As Shaila suddenly decides to get out of Judith's car, she pleads with Shaila to sort out the misunderstanding: ("Is there anything I said? Anything I did? .... Let's talk about it." I hear her slam the [car] door (195). Mukherjeeji contrasts the two opposed ways of managing grief (the Indian way, and the contractual way of the Canadian social worker who too is operating under enormous strained trying to help the bereaved.

One recalls Samuel F. Huntington's thesis in The Clash of Civilizations and the Remaking of the World Order that it is a misconception to hold that just because the post-cold war world is a unipolar world ideologically, the people too are a homogeneous bunch culturally who will get along with one another without clashes ("You Read the Essay...." *The Times of India*, 6 July, 1997).

Shaila, alone, among the affected immigrants shows the ability to go on her husband and son's death. Vikram, her husband, appears to her in a vision during a visit to an abandoned temple in a tiny Himalayan village when she is in India for some months after the tragedy. As he communicates with her, unseen by others, the urges her thus: "You must finish alone what we started together" (190, italics in original). Inspired, she returns to Canada to rebuild her life. Though it is not quite clear as to what they had started together, one of the projects surely had been the putting down of roots in the host country. So, instead of mourning as expected of a traditional widow, she returns to fight her way out of her grief, away from parental family ties in India. She sells off her house and is ready to move, urged for the last time by the voices of her family:

> "Your time has come," they said 'Go, be brave.'
>
> I do not know where this voyage I have begun will end. I do not know which direction I will take. I dropped the package on a park bench and started walking (197).

Discarding the baggage of the past-country, home, traditions, ties, she steps forward into the future. Taking the initial step is important, not the outcome. This is one of the Mukherjee's few short stories with a positive end.

In most others, there is a searing sense of homeliness expressed in endless journeys, typical of other migrant characters in Third World fiction (Kirpal, 71), In 'Orbiting' (*Middleman*, 57—75), the Afghan refugee is doomed to circle the world resting only in airport transit lounges. In her novel, Jasmine, the protagonist is endlessly on the move setting up a home-getting dislocated-setting out again in search of a new one.

Despite her claims, Mukherjee's short stories reiterate the theme of homeliness, not as a positive happening, but as a negative event most of the time. The characters do not become expatriates ever. They live in awarenss of their being different from their hosts. Their anxiety to find acceptance as the new members of an alien society is expressed in their endless journeys to make new beginnings.

Mukherjee's stories are very well-written. They move precisely because they defy her declared attempt to represent characters who have adjusted and adapted well to the new environment. The stories reveal the characters' vulnerability, and uncertain hold over the new world. The stories move because they capture the immigrant's attempt to connect, and her sisyphean discovery that she has not yet been able to do so.

NOTE

This is a modified version of the paper published in *The Critical Inquiry, January 1998.*

WORKS CITED

Huntingdon, Samuel F. Cited in "You Read the Essay." *The Times of India* (6 July, 1997).

Kirpal, Viney. *The Third World Novel of Expatriation.* New Delhi: Sterling Publishers Pvt. Ltd., 1989.

Mukherjee, Bharati, 1985. *Darkness*, New Delhi: Penguin Books (India) Ltd., 1990 rpt.

——. 1988. *The Middleman and Other Stories.* New Delhi: Prentice Hall of India Pvt. Ltd, 1989.

Rushdie, Salman. "A Dangerous Art Form." *Third World Book Review,* 1(1984): 3—5.

12 Witi Ihimaera 'Re-writing' Katherine Mansfield

Rama Kundu

> "I know that I am a Maori writer, and this is my world. And so ...[I] attempt to show the view from the other side of the perspective, from the other side of the doorway, from the inside of the house not from the outside"
>
> —Witi Ihimaera

Witi Ihimaera, considered a pioneer in Maori literature, and "the leading male Maori novelist"[1] of the day, rewrites some of Katherine Mansfield's well-known New Zealand stories, including 'The Garden Party,' in his response collection of short stories on the occasion of the birth centenary of Mansfield, the 'canonized mother' of New Zealand literature. Ihimaera's collection, *Dear Miss Mansfield,* which came out on the centennial of Mansfield's birth and offered some distinctly Maori variations of some of Mansfield's New Zealand stories, is but an ironical tribute to this charming 'precursor,' which brings out the 'ephebe's 'anxiety of influence' *vis-a-vis* the illustrious icon, as Ihimaera rewrites story after story of Mansfield with an overt challenge from the post-colonial 'ground beneath [his] feet.'[2] 'This Life is Weary' is a case in point; it is one of those stories in this collection in which the challenge and re-inscription is at its most explicit; here Ihimaera writes back to 'The Garden Party'—the most anthologized story of Katherine Mansfield and also the author's most popular New Zealand story which is generally considered another evidence of her love for the place. Among similar story-doublets in the volume—re-writings flaunting very close connections with their originals—can be mentioned "His First Ball"/"Her First Ball," "The Boy with the Camera"/"The Woman at the Store," "Summons to Alexamlria"/Bliss, "The Affectionate Kidnappers"/"How Pearl Button Was Kidnapped," "The Washerwoman's Children"/"The Doll's House."

It is interesting to note how Witi Ihimaera, in an aggressive gesture to create a Mansfield-like yet very much un-Mansfieldian text, establishes a special hermeneutic relationship with the source text, and thereafter achieves a synchronic transposition and transformation of the original. The intention is apparent in the teasingly ironical paratext of the *title; Dear Miss, Mansfield.* Apparently there is a target for these stories—indeed not one, but two targets—firstly the author [outsider-colonial-white-female] born a century ago, who is invoked with mixed feelings and a slight tinge of irony; and secondly, the reader/s who must recall the original 'vision' to appreciate the aesthetic as well as cultural thrust of the 're-vision.' Unless Ihimaera's reader notes the points of his departure from the hypotext, the thrust of the story is lost. The effect of the story is calculatedly based on the reader's assumed knowledge of the source text, and his consequent ability in perceiving the subtle nuances of the palimpsest lurking behind the bold lines of the aggressive hypertext. In fact Ihimaera deliberately invites the reader to remember—and takes meticulous care to remind him of—the original story; otherwise how would he bring home the implications of his subtle touches towards erasure and re-inscription!

# # #

Katherine Mansfield in her days showed the colonial settler's typical ambivalence of attitude regarding the 'colony,' New Zealand in her case. On the one hand the teenaged girl found the Maori "deeply attractive," owing to "their distance from colonial bourgeois culture" (Stafford & Williams, 31).[3] While in London in later years she even occasionally dressed in the Maori fashion. At the same time, like the typical settler, she also felt drawn toward England.[4] Still Katherine Mansfield, who left New Zealand for London as early as 1908, is recognized by biographers and literary historians primarily as an important figure in the New Zealand literature's early phase. Jock Phillips represents the general view when he writes:

> From the beginnings of European settlement through the first three decades of this century, New Zealand high culture was largely provincial, imitative and undistinguished. In terms of literary quality there was the lonely miracle of Katherine Mansfield whose genius was able to flower once she left her native land. Of native or distinctive traditions there was little trace (Phillips, 520).

Mansfield was indeed a lonely, lofty literary figure in the native land during her own time; and the land, though fascinating, was also alien in a way. She seems to typically epitomise the "intersection of colonial discourse and literary modernism" by which the "movement into exotic geographical space is understood as an inner exploration of the boundaries of consciousness" (Spurr, 146). This is reflected in the exquisitely aesthetic response of her protagonists,—all colonial beings—to the place.

Stafford and Williams explain Mansfield's obsession with the Maoriland,—a "little land with no history" which she would flee, and yet which would continue to insinuate and percolate into her consciousness—in terms of her modernist aestheticism:

> "Inescapably a part of her father's privileged colonial world, Mansfield felt an exaggerated need to establish her distance from her family and from the colonial society of her childhood. Where Maoriland writers tended to mediate the history of settlement by way of myth as a means of controlling its squalors, displacements and violences. Mansfield constructed an extravagant aestheticism by way of compensation for the frustrations and indignities of colonial life. ... Mansfield's aestheticism is always one of self-conscious gesture." (44)

Mansfield's simultaneous preoccupation with New Zealand and modernist aestheticism leads W.H. New to characterize

Katherine Mansfield as the 'problem' in New Zealand literary history: "her very existence cancels all easy generalizations about cultural and historical 'progress;'" because whereas Mansfield's name is associated with the development of European modernism in fiction "she is also claimed by a regional literature springing from New Zealand, where many, and all her major stories are set" (976). Her work has indeed generated a critical and geographical industry there.

After the death of Katherine's young brother in the First War the memory of her early years in New Zealand surged back as something very precious. Preoccupation with death and a serenity of mood have since been the hallmarks of her writing. The death of Laura's happiness, following the death of the carter in 'The Garden Party,' is one of the many variations of the same theme in Mansfield's fiction. But 'in spite of all' serenity reigns supreme; as the face of the dead man seems to murmur to Laura, 'all is well.'

# # #

Ihimaera, on the other hand, presents a polemical discourse as he engages with the same text. Though he too addresses the same themes of death and loss of happiness, he does this all from a new recontextualised perspective. In order to place Ihinmaera's story one must take into account, even if briefly, the genesis of a distinct New Zealand literature which began to emerge only slowly in the 1930s and '40s in the wake of a cultural nationalism; but this new consciousness too could not completely disengage itself from the colonial factor. "The story of New Zealand writing from late nineteenth century to the present," Stafford and Williams observe, "is that of a continuous dialectic between colonial, indigenous and modernizing forces, which has thrown up successive nationalisms, each enlisting elements of the world elsewhere and of the world to hand" (34). In this context writing by Maori authors in the English language is considered no less authentic than traditional oral tales, songs or chants. As a character in Patricia Grace's *Cousins* puts it: "It's not sticking to the old ways that's important,... but it's us being us, using all the new knowledge our own way"(235; cited by Williams, 2). For Ihimaera too the English language is not detrimental to the Maori character of a work "so long as the work speaks for Maori people and rests on a profound and sympathetic knowledge of the Maori sense of the world" (Williams, 2). And Ihimaera himself uses literature "to present a specifically Maori view of the world and of New Zealand history," thereby challenging "the established narratives of colonizers"(Williams, 3). Roimata, a character in Patricia Grace's *Potiki* comes to voice a belief which seems to operate at the core of the Maori Renaissance—that by writing books people but defined themselves, and thereby asserted their own stories against those of their conquerors. Perhaps this backdrop of cultural nationalism accounts to some extent for the general literary hostility towards Mansfield, an iconised story-teller of the land who, in spite of all her love and sympathy for the land and its people, happened to have come from the conqueror's stock.

Mansfield, who had come to be perceived as a cultural icon in her own time, has, perhaps for the very same reason, apparently not always received a fair deal in recent times in course of the literary dialectic between colonial and indigenous forces. Vincent O'Sullivan points out how "no other New Zealand figure has troubled or challenged so many writers to irreverent, defiant or merely exploitative responses. Perhaps the most curious aspect is the underlying assumption that she ever has been an establishment icon." Sullivan also mentions the resistance in 1988, even to the idea of a Mansfield Centennial as discussed in a commentary in *Landfall,* 171 (1989). In any case this very insistence in denying the iconicity of Mansfield by the New Zealand authors displays a degree of 'anxiety of influence.' O'Sullivan writes: "New Zealand's attitude to its national icons being what it is, most literary energy has gone into challenging, subverting or displacing her status. Examples of canonizing, sanitizing or elevating her into a literary progenitor are hard to find. Her stories and life are often now used as the starting point of updated or 're-inscribed' variations" (7). To cite just a few instances: Janet Frame's ironical allusions to Mansfield as 'Margaret Rose Hurndell our famous writer' in *Living in the Maniototo* (1979), Patricia Grace's hints in *The*

Dream Sleepers (1980), at the cultural distance between a teacher's adulation for 'Kay Em' and a Maori schoolboy's real priorities, Ian Wedde's presentation of Mansfield in *Symmes Hole* (1986), as an anachronistic figure in Pacific culture, O'Sullivan's irreverent exploration of the Mansfield-Ida Baker relationship in *Jones and* Jones (1988), Bill Manhire's jocular title *The Brain of Katherine Mansfield* (1988), or Chris Orsman's projection of Mansfield in the poem 'Another Country' (*Ornamental Gorse,* 1994), as a writer imaginative to the point of untruth.

In all these projections Mansfield seems to be at the butt of irreverence and mockery. Ihimaera's *Dear Miss Mansfield* (1989), could be comfortably placed as just another work in this line but for its intent seriousness. Ihimaera provides a 'Maori response' and a challenging interrogation, albeit without a trace of debunking,[5] while at the same time lapping and absorbing, automatically almost, the spell of Mansfield's aesthetic imagination and corresponding beautiful linguistic nuances.

In an interview with Juniper Ellis, in response to the question—'Do you think that writing can help accomplish a decolonization?'—Ihimaera admits: "Yes, of course I do. It's just that the question itself is a difficult one because, yes, writing does subvert that colonization process. However because it is a colonization process in itself, what one has to do is find the techniques by which to subvert it" (Interview, 174).

In his *Dear Miss Mansfield* Ihimaera invokes the legacy of New Zealand literature while at the same time subverting and thereby reclaiming it for a new perception. A synchronic study of the two stories, *The Garden Party* and *This Life is Weary* would bring home the point; while at the same time this will bear out Julia Kristeva's claim about intertextual 'transposition' which involves the assumption that "the passage from one signifying system to another demands a new articulation of the thetic...—of the enunciative and denotative positioning."[6]

# # #

In her story of a rich English family in New Zealand, throwing a garden party at their hilltop house, on the eve of which the report of an accidental death of a poor carter briefly upsets the youngest girl in the house, and she is sent to visit the bereaved family at the end of the 'successful' party, Mansfield makes a mildly ironical but aesthetically exquisite water colour picture.

Ihimaera, on the other hand, scoops up a scrap from this source text and starts working on it to create a poignant picture of beauty and pathos. In the source story—which is of a single day's duration—the Sheridans get ready in the morning with all the usual fanfare for their garden party to be held the same evening, when a report comes about "a horrible accident... a man killed." The baker's man who carries in cream puffs for the party also brings the news: a young chap living in one of those little cottages below, "name of Scott, a carter," was thrown off his horse and killed instantly, leaving "a wife and five little ones." Laura fails to make her mother see the point of canceling the party on the death of such a 'neighbour.' Mansfield leaves enough ironical hints at the insensitivity of Laura's mother, sisters, and eventually of Laura too (a fine hat is enough to make her forget the death for the time being) to leave the reader in any doubt about her own attitude [To be fair to Mansfield one must acknowledge her awareness and implicit critique of the class divisions embedded in the colonial system which is evident in her stories like 'The Doll's House' or 'The Garden Party,'[7]] Still Ihimaera won't consider it enough. So, in order to give us a glimpse of the untold story he would stand back a little and start with the carter and his family.

Ihimaera starts his story by repeating one particular sentence which occurs around the middle of 'The Garden Party.' As Laura, on learning about the death of a carter, insists that the party be stopped, the other Sheridans feel, "That really was extravagant, for *the little cottages were in a lane to themselves at the very bottom of a steep rise* that led to the house" (*M*, 248). Ihimaera starts by looking from this 'bottom' and upwards towards the top, just as the Sheridans look down from the top towards this 'bottom.' This involves an inversion for the hypertext author, an act of 'writing back' which is to be presaged by an act of reverting the lenses. So the hypertext opens with: "*The little cottages were in a lane to themselves at the very bottom of a steep rise...*" (W, 115). This is followed by a quick, fleeting glimpse of *'The Big House,'* which is obviously, undeniably *'big,' 'lovely'* and *'gilded'* as it stands in glaring contrast to the *'little cottages.'* 'The insinuating effect of the allusion is unmistakable as the hypertext draws upon the source for underscoring the contrast between the two kinds of houses. "They were little mean dwellings painted a *chocolate brown*" (M, 248); "*The very smoke coming out of their chimneys was poverty-stricken...* so unlike *the great silvery plumes that uncurled from the Sheridan's chimneys (M,* 248-49). Of course Mansfield on her part clearly distances herself from this point of view of the Sheridan family by her ironical stance. Ihimaera but re-inforces this irony as he mentions "this land *of chocolate brown* houses" and "*the very smoke coming out of their chimneys was poverty-stricken...* not at all like *the great silvery plumes that uncurled from The Big House*" (W, 115). The dearth, however, seems to have been more than made up in Celia's eyes, a poor girl of Laura's age, by the glamour of the personality of her dad, or 'Dadda.' The camera, while it takes in both the big and small houses, would move on to focus the carter, who gets not only a full name, but also a vibrant personality, a voice which is serene and musical, a humble past, a happy present blessed by a modest income, a loved and loving family and friendly neighbours; he is also seen speaking, singing, pleasantly interacting with his dear ones. Jack Scott, his wife and their children are allowed to become life-size, vivid people, whereas the people in the 'big house' appear shadowy, vague as should be natural when seen from distance. Thus the 'absent' elements in the source story emerge and come to occupy the foreground in the later story. Ihimaera does not offer a new story, but rather grafts onto the source story his imaginative additions regarding the 'absentees' there, and adopts the latter's perspective.

Regarding his own work Ihimaera would be rather against such 'labels' as post-modernism or post-colonialism which he dismisses as "international constructs, ... part of a need to look at a work from the outside." He would instead opt for a view 'from the inside out'; as he puts it, "What matters to me is the view from the inside out. I don't consider myself to be a post-modern writer, but I know that I am a Maori writer, and this is my world. And so ...[I] attempt to show the view from the other side of the perspective, from the other side of the doorway, from the inside of the house not from the outside" (Interview: Juniper Ellis, 176).

This is precisely what Ihimaera appears to have done in his story 'This Life is Weary' which rewrites, 'The Garden Party.' It *is* 'from the inside of the house,' but not the house of the white family on the hill top where the party-is held; it is the from the inside of the house of the cart-driver who dies on the day of the party. So, whereas Mansfield focuses a prosperous English family in a far-flung island, Ihimaera's story captures the family of the dead carter, an absentee/invisible unit in the source tale, a tightly knit poor marginalized family—who hail from those 'bottom-drawer people' (to use Ihimaera's cliché-phrase[8]). [They have their own distinctive mark though; they are sent off to school during the week as Mrs. Scott "did not want them *swarming* in the little crowded lanes like many of the other *children* who were kept at home" (*W*, 117); to compare with *"children swarmed" (M*, 249).] The binarial concepts of 'inside/outside,' lying covert and implicit in the original/source story, get transposed in the different context of the later story. The hill-top house is now seen from the 'outside' by viewers who happen to be indwellers of the shabby shanties down the hills, representing the world of fringe inhabited by disadvantaged people. The point-of-view is theirs.

However, Ihimaera takes care to show poverty does not blunt their capacity for wonder as the reader is made to watch the Scott children enjoying their favourite weekend pastime; "crossing quickly over the *broad road between*" (*W*, 117) [cp. "*a broad road ran between*" (*M*, 248)] the kids would go up to '*The Big House*' "to watch the house and the comings and goings of the lovely people who lived or visited there" (*W*, 117). If this is the stage they have no role to play on it; they are just self-invited watchers, indulging in an act of innocent voyeurism, deriving/squeezing all their pleasure from just *see*-ing. Ihimaera peers into the Sheridans' garden, and inserts something between its *"rose bushes"* (*M*, 240; *W*, 117), *"karaka trees"* and *"tennis court"* (*M*, 242; *W*, 117), in order to accommodate the Scott kids somewhere on the outer fringe of the garden; it is "an old wrought-iron loveseat" which "had obviously been thrown out many years ago," now covered with bird-droppings, but nevertheless a seat "perfect to observe from"(*W*, 117). The kids are passive observers to the "gleaming" (117) stage, i.e., the house and its front gateway through which carriages drive in. On some rare occasion their dad can be glimpsed at the "back gateway" used by the delivery vans and suppliers' men. It is the "back way"(*M*, 247) used by the cook, maid, Godber's man, *et al*, where Laura hears about the accident. Men like Jack Scott can at best have access to this "back gateway," but that is sufficient to fill his children with elation: " 'Dadda, oh Dadda! We saw you at *The Big House* today!'— as if grace and divinity had been suddenly bestowed on him." (*W*, 117). Again, Celia, the eldest of the Scott children, keeps a notebook on the house; she is gently encouraged by her parents and the children would go up to the big house every Saturday morning with their sharpened pencils, notebooks, and simple lunch of bread and water. Mam and Dad welcome their reports of the happenings of the day, fondly "taking them as signs that their children would do better than they had to make good lives for themselves"(*W*, 118). The stage/audience [albeit a hidden one] dichotomy, paralleling the top/bottom pattern serves as indicator to the dichotomized geographical-cultural space of the Ihimaera story. The author deliberately draws attention to this division, and the innocent voyeurism and pathetic mimicry generated among the silent, invisible 'audience' from the 'bottom' by this division; an audience from the bottom to whom access to the top will remain denied. "Although Celia had never been to any theatre, watching *The Big House* was just as she imagined a play would be"(*W*, 118). They have no way to know what goes on inside. They may "wonder what her [Laura's] bedroom is like" (*W*, 119), but have to remain satisfied with guessing; their stage constitutes only the outer realms of the house—"particularly the verandahs, top and bottom, and the French doors on to the verandahs. From out of these doors would come the lovely people of *The Big House,* the main actors of every Saturday afternoon performance" (*W*, 118). And "on most occasions, the appearances by the Sheridans were seen from afar" (*W*, 120). The little spectators can only hang around the fringe and get some fleeting glimpses of the 'theatre,' which seems too unreal compared to their place. The actors on this stage, i.e., members of the Sheridan family, are recognizably like their originals with the same nomenclature, appearance and behavioural nuances. The Scott children, on the other hand, are Ihimaera's innovation, and it is through their eyes that we now see the Big House people; and it is left to them, from their invisible 'seat' of spectators, to have picked up the names and other tit-bits about the Sheridans—their dress-up, eating habits, entertainment—by means of which they try to construct the 'play' on the 'stage' and also decide about their favourite character [like Ihimaera himself constructing his story from the small hints and tit-bits left by Mansfield's story].

Whereas Mansfield's story is about a single day, Ihimaera presents his story into two sections, the first section setting the stage through a period of repetitive weeks and months, and the second concentrating on the day of the party which also means,—for both the authors—the day of the death. Thus the second section of Ihimaera's story opens dramatically, on a note of heightened excitement much like the opening of the Mansfield story. One week-end the children return home with the big news of a garden party in the big house on the following Saturday. So to 'see' the party (not to join) they would go up for the whole day instead of just the afternoon. The adults too join the fond game of 'partying' by proxy. The mother manages to sew up some new dresses for the kids from her treasured pieces of velvet, an old curtain, a lace ribbon and other materials. To her daughter's protestation, "But Mam, we're not invited—," she replies: "Hush, child. We can dream, can't we?" (*W*, 121). Dadda also endorses Mam's wish, both verbally and otherwise. Thus by now the entire family has come to join the game of dream-making. To the children's thrilled surprise Dadda has transformed his cart overnight into a carriage with cushions, and jovially hands up the children one by one with the perfect manners 'befitting' the occasion, while Mam gives them a hamper of sandwich and cake, special food for the special day.

As the children set off for the hill top the reader is brought back again to the opening sentence of the source. "*And after all the weather was ideal*" (*W*, 121). The gardener too is there; only a small information is added that he is a Maori: "The *gardener* had been up *since dawn, mowing the lawns and sweeping them*" (*M*, 240); compare this with: "They saw the Maori *gardener* already at work *mowing the lawns and sweeping them*" (*W*, 121), [One can guess the immediate effect by remembering how the epithet is loaded for Ihimaera and his ethnic readers.] From their "position"(121) under the trees the children can see the party from beginning to end, the description of the party closely following the original even in small details,—from the setting up of the marquee to the arrival of the pots of "*canna lilies... radiant... frighteningly alive on ...bright crimson stems*" (*M*, 244; *W*, 122), even Laura coming out with bread-and-butter in hand, to Jose rehearsing on the piano, "This Life is *Wee*-ary," and Godber's man talking to cook, a sudden silence falling on the house, Laura speaking something in an alarmed voice. But that is soon over. The children are "enchanted" by the lovely people, lovely food, lovely band. While the party is bathed in sunlight, "*there in the shadow*" (*W*, 123) the children, in an innocent and pathetic mimicry, imitate the guests and dance to the band, while "always, *far away in the sunlight* was dear, darling Laura"(*W*, 123). Finally as the party comes to a close Ihimaera finds no better or more appropriate expression than Mansfield's to describe the closure: "*And the perfect afternoon slowly ripened, slowly faded, slowly its petals closed*" (*M*, 252; *W*, 123). These are the turns,—such wonderful sentences as those on the 'frighteningly alive' canna lilies or the 'fading' afternoon, which Ihimaera takes verbatim from the source,[9] that betray his admiration for the charm of the precursor in spite of all his aggressive challenge against the [literary] 'mother.' To put it in Michela Mudure's words, "the model invades and fascinates to the point of obliging the emulator to some submission"(189).

Now that the party is over the children reminisce the 'lovely' day while waiting for Dadda. After waiting long they start homewards *down* the 'sordid lanes' and on the way they pass by a youth asking a girl, *'Was it awful"?* (*M*, 256; *W*, 124); once again the two texts overlap and embrace one another.

On reaching home they find, just as Laura saw in the other story, "a dark knot of people stood outside" (*M*, 254; W, 124); but whereas Laura merely saw "beside the gate an old, old woman... sat on a chair, watching" (*M*, 254), Celia "saw Gran, Mam's mother, sitting in a chair, beside the gate"(W, 124). While looking for Mrs. Scott Laura saw a woman, "her face, puffed up, red, with swollen eyes and swollen lips, looked terrible" (*M*, 254). Celia meets the same person, yet with what a difference of feeling! Celia desperately looks for Mam:

> 'Mam? Dadda?' Celia called. 'Mam?' Then another woman was there. Her face was all puffed up and red, with swollen eyes and swollen lips. 'Mam?' Celia whispered, because it was indeed her mother. But she looked so, —so—*awful* (*W*, 124]

This is the difference between looking from outside and feeling from inside. Ihimara elaborately uses the exact words and phrases, sometime full sentences, patches of the Mansfield text precisely in order to highlight this gulf of difference between the insider and the outsider. The outsiders to the 'big house' stage are insiders in this cottage tragedy, and almost the same expressions are used to connote contrastive positions determining contrastive responses.

Again, in both the stories the child is the focus, but without the mutuality of figural relationship. The narrative focus in both is the innocent eye of a child, a technique which is commonly employed by Mansfield in her New Zealand stories. The narrative perspective in Mansfield's story is usually established through a naive girl child encountering the place and people with innocence and optimism.[10] The girl child in Ihimaera's text also goes through a kind of initiation, but in her case it is an initiation attained through terrible grief; because what Laura sees as an outsider is a personal and terrible sorrow for Celia who happens to be 'on this side of the doorway.'

Finally, the title of the story suggests a paratext with an ore of meaning hidden in its grains. It refers to the song Jose, the unmusical Sheridan girl, practices on the piano, in the morning of the party while her face breaks into "a brilliant, dreadfully unsympathetic smile"(*M*, 245). In Ihimaera's story the Scott children would rather have Jose give up the song, not only because of her lack of musical sense, but also, more importantly, because "nobody could sing This Life is Weary' better than Dadda"(*W*, 119). It also suggests an answer, albeit a grim one, to the tentative question of Laura at the end of 'The Garden Party' which remains unanswered there.

> 'Isn't life,' she stammered, 'isn't life—.' But what life was she couldn't explain (*M*, 256)

Laurie's answer,—"Isn't it, darling"- remains evasive. Ihimaera tries to formulate an answer through the title: yes, life is weary, this life of fragile dreams and rude deprivations, of tears and sighs, of too many responsibilities, of the compulsion to 'know' and 'see' premature death is wearying. Thus the stories seem to complement one another; and while the latter draws on ideas and expressions of the former, the mould remains the same. It is within the same frame that the second story is layered upon the first.

Ihimaera seems to have been engaged in an interesting game here; again and again he would bring his story increasingly close to the original, almost twist round it like a creeper, and then would shoot out a stray branch in an unexpected direction by adding the small but poignant touches, touches pregnant with meaning, yet perfectly in tune with the original. Studying this process of continuous conglomeration and rupture, fusion and fission, coalescence and departure by which the two stories continuously converge with and get layered upon one another is interesting and rewarding. After reading Ihimaera one has a feeling that the original itself contained the seed of the later story which Ihimaera brought out from its hibernation and nurtured to blossoming! It may be interesting to note in this context that "KM noted at the end of the manuscript, 'This is a moderately successful story, and that's all. It's somehow, in the episode in the lane, scamped'" [cited Sullivan & Scott 298, n.1].

In this superb negotiation of texts fine details of the source story have been continuously interwoven into the interstices of the later text and the reader gets the added pleasure of recognition, recognition of linguistic echoes which, while serving to highlight the contextual/perceptual ruptures, also disclose a certain degree of admiration—albeit unselfconscious—felt by the rebellious 'ephebe' for his undeniably fascinating 'precursor.'

To cite just a few examples:

> "The house was surrounded with broad swathes of bright green lawn bordered by daisy plants. Just beyond the borders were roses—hundreds and hundreds of glorious dark red roses of the kind that the children had seen on chocolate boxes" (*W*, 117); just to read this side by side with the other description: "... the grass and the dark flat rosettes where the daisy plants had been seemed to shine. As for the roses...hundreds, yes, literally hundreds, had come out in a single night... as though they had been visited by archangels" (*M*, 240). What Mansfield describes as the particular morning on the day of the party is used by Ihimaera as a constant. The opening sentences of Mansfield are as follows: "And after all the weather was ideal. They could not have a more perfect garden party if they had ordered it. Windless, warm, the sky without a cloud. Only the blue as veiled with a haze

of light gold..." (*M*, 240). Compare this with Ihimaera's description of the Scott children's enraptured viewing of the house as if it were a theatre, and, he adds: "Like all theatrical settings, the weather was always ideal up there and the days perfect and made to order. The backdrop was windless and warm, with a light blue sky flecked with gold" (*W*, 118). Thus by lending permanency to the elements of a single morning Ihimaera highlights the feeling of illusoriness which the poor children get at watching the house, and thus justifies their feeling: "It was so unlike the dark and dirty *eyesore* which cluttered the area the children came from. Indeed, sometimes it was difficult for the children to accept that this world was as *real* as their own"(*W*, 118). This can be considered counterpoint to Laura's brief thought of the dead body being carried into the house of the bereaved which is pushed back by the euphoria of the party, so that "it all seemed blurred, *unreal*, like a picture in the newspaper" (*M*, 251). This again echoes back to the unsympathetic perception of the Sheridans [which has been, to be fair, presented with critical irony by Mansfield]: "...the little cottages... were the greatest possible *eyesore* and they had no right to be in that neighbourhood at all" (*M*, 248). It is a long list of allusions—or better to say reverberations—which are intended to be immediately identifiable; and apparently it is no 'accidental confluence,'[11] but very self-conscious convergences, deliberately planned coherences which any perceptive reader would recognize and respond to. Ihimaera's consistent manner of allusive manipulation of the source text seems to bear out "the intertextualist's preference for the communal construction of meaning"(Hinds, 50). The author, instead of abandoning the old story just gives it a slight twist and it is deconstructed to be recontextualised in the 'other' space of the same story, the peripheral space down the 'bottom,' of which Mansfield herself has left enough clues in her text. The hypertext consistently exhibits an "effort to connect"(Hinds, 21) with the source. In order to appreciate the thrust of the elaborate acts of allusive gesturing we have to read both the 'incorporated' and the 'incorporating' texts systematically side by side and notice the finer points of intersection and variation in this close intertextual relationship, which, to use Mudure's beautiful metaphor, "alternate like variations upon a common theme in a musical texture, or like the waves of the sea forever bathing the shores of the two writers' beloved island..." (188).

* Quotations from Mansfield's story are indicated as (*M*), and from Witi Ihimaera's story as (*W*). Emphases within the excerpts from both the texts have been added by the present author.

NOTES

1. To put it in Brian Boyd's phrase, cited by Meklin
2. Allusion is to the title of Salman Rushdie's novel, *The Ground beneath Her Feet* (1999).
3. In her early story "How Pearl Button was Kidnapped" (1912), the Maori figure as a romantic other—capable of stirring fear and desire—to the restricted lifestyle of the colonial settler/outsider.
4. As Mansfield wrote in 1907:
   "I know the bush is beautiful...
   But I, with all my longing heart,
   I care not what they say
   It's London ever calling me
   The live long day." *[Notebooks* I, 86].
5. In his interview with Paul Sharrad Ihimaera said, "we need more critics, and people who will write in an informed manner on our own writers—much in the same way that Katherine Mansfield was turned into an industry..."
6. Cited by Dentith. p. 96.
7. As W H. New claims, it is precisely "these mixed origins, the cultural diversity of her work, her own sense of more than one location, and the record of her life's voyage from the margin to the centre that characterize Mansfield as a writer central to post-colonial discourses; questions about identity, selfhood, gender, and class are instinctively raised and deconstructed in her fiction, particularly questions relating to the position of women in middle-class families" (976).
8. In his story 'Passing Time' Ihimaera refers to this 'under' world as a

possible question mark on the conscience or percipience of those inhabiting the so-called normal world:

> "Those kids *were* disturbing, but perhaps people who lived prime-steak lives needed to be reminded of a reality outside what they were accustomed to: that there were after-hour people, fringe suburb people, bottom-drawer people who lived on the periphery of existence" [cited by Williams, 10].

9. Borges writes about one Pierre Menard who had not altered a single word of Cervantes, and yet written his own *Don Quixote*!
10. New writes: "Her [Mansfield's] New Zealand stories mostly focus on multilayered families representing several points of view but concentrating on that of a child. The childhood perspective in Mansfield's fiction has been influential on twentieth century New Zealand writing; this perspective is also a widespread characteristic of colonial literatures. In Mansfield's case the focus... establishes an optimism and an innocence associated with New Zealand as a landscape of possibility, of spaciousness, and of growth, even though it is offset by the more difficult and more limited point of view of the adult characters" (976).
11. A term used by Hinds to distinguish between 'reference' and auto-intertextuality (Hinds, 20).

WORKS CITED

Borges, J.L. "Pierre Menard, Author of the *Quixote.*" *Labyrinths (1964)*. London: Penguin Classics, 2000. pp. 62—71.

Dentith, Simon. *Bakhtinian Thought: An Introductory Reader (1995)*. London & N.Y.: Routledge, 2003.

Hinds, Stephen. *Allusion and Intertext: Dynamics of Appropriation in Roman Poetry*. Cambridge: CUP, 1998.

Ihimaera, Witi. "This Life is Weary." *Dear Miss Mansfield: A Tribute to Kathleen Mansfield eauchamp*. Auckland, Vikingf, 1989.

——. "The Singing Word: Witi Ihimaera Interviewed by Juniper Ellis"(26 May, 1998). *Journal of Commonwealth Literature*. 43:1, 1999.

Mansfield, K. "The Garden Party." *Selected Stories (1953)*. London: OUP, 1957.

——. *The Collected Letters*. Eds. V.O'Sullivan and Margaret Scott. Oxford: OUP, 1996.

——. *The Katherine Mansfield Notebooks, Vol.1*. Ed. Margaret Scott. Wellington: Lincon UP, 1997.

Meklin, Margaret. 'The Gay Tribe: The Writings of Witi Ihimaera. *The Gay and Lesbian Review Worldwide,* January-February, 2003.

Mudure, Michaela. "Kaherine Mansfield and the Maori Response Texts." *The Atlantic-Critical Review.* 2:1 (Jan.-March, 2003).

New, W.H. *Dreams of Speech and Violence: The Art of the Short Story in Canada and New Zealand (1987);* cited in *Encyclopedia of Post-colonial Literatures in English.* London & N.Y.: Routledge, 1994.

Phillips, J.O.C. "Musings in *Maoriland...*" *Historical Studies,* 81(1983), 520.

Sharrad, Paul. "Listening to One's Ancestors: An Interview with Witi Ihimaera." *Australian and New Zealand Studies in Canada* 8(1992).

Spurr, David. *The Rhetoric of Empire: Colonial Discourse in Journalism, Travel Writing and Imperial Discourse.* Durham & London: Duke UP, 1993.

Stafford, Jane and Mark Williams. "Fashioned Intimacies: Maoriland and Colonial Modernity". *Journal of Commonwealth Literature.* Vol. 37, No. l, 2002.

BIBLIOGRAPHY

O'Sullivan, Vincent: "Mansfield, Katherine." www.book.council.org.nz/writer/mansfieldk.html

Williams, Mark. "Witi Ihimaera and Patricia Grace: The Maori Renaissance" http://www.ucalgary.ca/UofC/eduweb/engl392/492/williams.html

13 Nadine Gordimer's Treatment of 'Apartheid' in her Novels

Ghorpade Pradny Vijay

Nadine Gordimer, who was awarded the Nobel Prize for Literature in 1991, is acknowledged as one of the finest living English novelists in South Africa. Her short stories and novels capture the stresses and ironies of life in the authoritarian, segregated South African Society. Her basic thematic concern is the exploration of the interdependence of the blacks and the whites, keeping aside deep rooted racial prejudices. Gordimer's growth as a novelist is steady. She is a remarkable short story writer. Kenneth Parker in his book *The South African Novel in English* quotes Nadine Gordimer who while explaining her function as a writer, has stated that she has no alliance to South Africa 'as a writer' but 'as a person.' She says: "I have no religion, no political dogma—only plenty of doubts about everything except my conviction that the colour bar is wrong and utterly indefensible. Thus I have found the basis of a moral code that is valid for me. Reason and emotion meet in it and perhaps this is as near to faith as I shall ever get" (1978:5).

Racial exploitation in South Africa has been described by various names; 'apartheid' is only a new name for an old process. Because of the stigma attached to it, the word 'apartheid' is no longer fashionable. Apartheid has evolved from a doctrine of white supremacy to one of 'separate development' and recently to 'plural democracy.' It is based on absurdities and paralyzes action toward a better world. The apartheid system, with its absolute racial discrimination and exploitation has to be maintained by monstrous repressive laws. It also rests upon rigid security legislation for its implementation. The South African authorities could arrest anyone upon suspicion and hold effectively for an indefinite period. Thus, apartheid as a form of racialism bears the stamp of the Afrikaners and their historic situation in the socio-economic development of South Africa.

Nadine Gordimer is conscious of the political-racial issues that affect the people of South Africa. The problem of apartheid is very typical to South Africa. Racial misunderstanding is loudly pronounced in her different novels. In her first novel *The Lying Days* (1953), Gordimer presents her feelings of being a white and the guilt involved. Gordimer delineates the story of Helen Shaw's gradual development as an independent individual with political consciousness. It is set in the period immediately before and after 1948, when the South African policy of apartheid was being enforced. Helen Shaw, the main protagonist and narrator of the novel grows up in the conventional home of her middle class parents in a mining town. As a child, Helen has been taught that mine boys are dangerous and also that girls cannot be left alone in the houses, if there are 'native boys around.' Helen always finds it hard to understand the distinction made by her mother where black boys are concerned. To her, "Native boys were harmless and familiar because they were servants, or delivery boys bringing the grocery or the fish by bicycle from the town, or Mine boys .... dressed differently in any old thing and so were mysterious" (1953: 3-4). In the town of Atherton in which Helen grows up there is a strict maintenance of class stratification with the English—speaking whites in command as masters and blacks as workers and servants. The lowest of all are the Jews who run the concession stores or as Helen's mother puts it in a moment when the constraints of gold mines are suddenly ruptured, 'live among all the dirt and the Kaffirs' (Ibidem, 192). Helen is unable to befriend Mary Seswayo at university, because she is a black coloured student. When Helen wishes to bring Mary Seswayo home for a ten-day study session, Helen's mother is aghast at the preposterous idea of having a black girl living in her house. The life led by Mary opens Helen's eyes to the frustration of fundamental needs by the ruling society of the day-needs for a place to study, for silence, for public toilet facilities, and for human contact with whites through love and quarrelling discovers to her surprise. Helen finds: "There simply was no public cloakroom for native men or women in the whole shopping centre of Johannesburg" (Ibidem, 169).

Gordimer refers to a number of crucial measures of apartheid including 'the Mixed Marriage Act, apartheid in public transport and buildings, the language ordinance separating Afrikaans and English-speaking children in schools, the removal of coloured voters from the common electoral roll' (Ibidem, 255). In Parliament Cabinet ministers spoke of the natives as 'kaffirs.' On a more intimate level there was the social projection of the most obsessional aspects of Nationalist racism. Under the Population Registration Act (1950), every South African had to be registered as a member of one of the officially designated racial groups. The prohibition of Mixed Marriage Act (1949), made marriage between members of different races illegal. In this novel, Gordimer exposes some of the humiliations involved in this legislation such as couples living together for years being woken up in the middle of the night with police torches shining in their eyes. In Helen's quest for independence she becomes deeply involved with Paul Clark and starts living with him. Initially, her parents favour Paul as a prospective son-in-law as he belongs to the province of Natal which is known for its close ties with England. Helen wonders how her parents will react if she brings over an Afrikaner to meet them. Gordimer discusses the political climate in South Africa and writes of the general elections of 1948, when the Afrikaner National Party comes into power, promising white supremacy. She lists the changes brought about by the government: petty apartheid, ban on mixed marriages and suppression of Communism Bill. Helen realizes that for the whites nothing has changed and they continue to live in their world of comfort and leisure. This consciousness of guilt haunts Helen and she tries to overcome it by mixing with some black friends and visiting the locations. During one of her visits to the black township on May Day, she observes the atrocities of the white police. From the safety of her car she witnesses the shooting and death of a black rioter. This makes her realize that in South Africa she can only be an observer but never a participant in the struggle of the blacks, and a Johannesburg "cut...in two" and blind to "half its life" as the result of apartheid.

Gordimer's second novel *A World of Strangers* (1958) relates primarily to the dominance of multi-racialism as the political philosophy of the movements opposed to apartheid in the 1950s and also as a social way of life. In this novel the dilemma of the whites in South Africa is explored from the point of view of an outsider,—Toby Hood, an Englishman who came to replace a publisher's agent. Toby Hood is a stranger in the divided society of South Africa. The social stratification compels the marginal groups to live separate lives. It is a novel which seeks to understand the intricacies of life behind the barriers set up by the government. The novel opens with a description of Africans working on the quay as Toby's ship is anchored at Mombasa. He looks at them with disgust and observes, "Heavy, mild and brutish faces, on which emotion settles momentarily, from the outside, like a fly on the face of an OX.... I hated them in England, those faces in country lanes, red and smiling at nothing....." (1958: 7). He has never had an opportunity to come in close contact with any African before he set out to sail for Africa. When he left England, Toby decided to maintain complete detachment from issues of racism and the struggle in South Africa. He declares that he just wants 'to live.' "I want to see people who interest me and amuse me, black, white or any colour... I want to live" (Ibidem, 36). Although Toby's wants are straightforward, they become impossible in the 'world of strangers' in South Africa. Also, he begins to experience an enjoyable friendship with Steven Sitole, a black activist whose violent death brings that relationship to an abrupt end.

Gordimer depicts the lavish and exclusive world of the whites by describing the fabulous parties given by the Alexanders in High House. In contrast, the black world of Sophiatown is vividly delineated. At the High House, Toby meets a number of whites who are all affluent business executives and industrialists. The Alexanders' wealth is based on the gold-mining industry. The men and women pass their time by indulging in some sport or the other, while the women appear to Toby as 'Gay, quite witty and decorative' (50). The world of the whites is filled with loneliness and monotony. Their world is a reflection of Europe or America. In order to ward off their loneliness, they participate in races, parties and hunting trips. In contrast to the lavish and artificial world of the white suburbs is the other half of Johannesburg comprising the black townships. Its buildings are crowded and full of people. There is a careless attitude to death as every now and then, someone is murdered or shot by the police in the locality. Toby finds that the trinity of life, "survival, food and reproduction" totally preoccupy the men in the township. Toby is at ease both in the white suburbs and the black townships. Throughout the novel, Gordimer has constantly pitted the blacks against the whites. She deliberately chooses a theme in which she can illustrate the differences between the world of the blacks and the whites. Cecil, Toby's mistress and Steven Sitole never meet because of the racial divisions of apartheid. Indeed, Toby deliberately conceals his friendship from prejudiced Cecil, thinking that otherwise he would lose her. In his own person he, therefore, contributes to the maintenance of separate worlds, unfortunately. Toby loses his friend Steven, while he is making a getaway from a police raid on an Indian club. Steven dies in a car crash. Toby is deeply affected by Steven's death and he realizes that he had loved him as a brother. He ponders on the roles assigned to them due to the colour of their skin: "He was in the bond of his skin, and I was free, the world was open to me and closed to him;..."(252) Toby knows that he cannot share his sorrow with Cecil who will be shocked to know that he mixes with blacks. Cecil, late, breaks her relationship with Toby to marry a rich man and her decision is also influenced by the knowledge about Toby's African friends. As Christopher Heywood observes: "*A World of Strangers* exposes the clash of indifference, opportunism, idealism and cruelty which forms the raw material of South African Society" (1983: 17).

In *Occasion for Loving* (1963), Gordimer is disillusioned with racial misunderstanding. In this novel, an affair between a white woman and a black man breaks down under the weight of the colour bar. Also it deals with the consequences of crossing racial barriers. As Judie Newman observes: "In *Occasion for Loving,* Gordimer conjoins racial and sexual themes successfully" (1988: 26). Here Gordimer portrays two couples, one liberal but upholding society's expectations, the other outside or in advance of social norms. The defeated couple in this instance, Ann David and the artist Gideon Shibalo, are separated by the social and psychological forces which oppose their union. The South African state withdraws Gideon's passport. He was the man whose painting had attracted attention overseas and won him a scholarship to work in Italy; but he had not been able to take it because the South African Government refused him a passport, preventing him from taking up a scholarhip to study art abroad.

In the context of institutional repression, there can be no occasion for loving between white and black. Ann is easily accepted by the blacks and her frank nature attracts many people to her. Initially, Ann has no inhibitions about colour, class or race. She takes pleasure in visiting the townships. But, there is a shocked expression on the faces of white people whenever she is seen with Gideon. Usually, Gideon is treated as her driver by the white attendants at gas stations and addressed as 'madam's boy' (Ibidem, 237). Gideon is frustrated with the political situation in the country. When he is denied passport, his friend Sol reacts: "Most of the whites don't want to talk to you.... They are the ones who decide what's going to happen to us. Where we're going to live where we're going to work... (Ibidem, 133). Finally, they see solution in violence and discuss how they can obtain guns from neighbouring black countries. Here, one observes the change in the attitude of the blacks from peaceful resistance to armed violence.

Ann who has always been colour-blind gradually becomes conscious of Gideon's 'blackness.' Whenever they are together

Ann is conscious of his colour and is fascinated by touching his skin, "the dark positiveness of his skin..." (Ibidem: 189). She becomes aware of Gideon as a black first and as a man afterwards. Ann brings only ego and passion to the love affair, not awareness and commitment. Even in an intimate relationship Ann and Gideon realize that 'blackness counts' (Ibidem, 290). Unable to cope with the situation, Ann decides to leave South Africa with her husband. Gideon is very much hurt by the end of the affair and feels that once again he has been betrayed by the white world. He starts drinking heavily and gives up his job as a teacher. He becomes absolutely disgusted with the white women, when Jessie, the central character, approaches Gideon at party to console him, he shouts at her in the drunken manner: "White bitch, get way! (Ibidem, 307). Those words of Gideon are an expression of his hatred of the white world which has deprived him of love, status and dignity. Jessie's belief in personal relationships is broken and she concludes that friendship with black man in a divided society like South Africa is impossible. Apartheid penetrates into the most intimate of human relationships, and the last word on this in the novel is crucial: "...Even between lovers they had seen blackness count, the personal return inevitably to the social, the private to the political.... So long as the law remained unchanged, nothing could bring integrity to human relationship" (Ibidem, 279).

As B.K. Das has pointed out that, "Gordimer sees all human beings as copies in their situation. This is true of the novels like *The Late Bourgeois World* (1966), *A Guest of Honour* (1972), *The Conservationists* (1974), and *Burger's Daughter* (1979)" (74).

Her well-known novel *July's People* (1981), is a study of the changing power relationship between the whites and the blacks. Bam Smales, a white man, is a successful architect. Maureen, Barn's wife, a white woman, is brought up in the Western Areas Gold Mines. July, a black servant, has worked reliably for fifteen years for Bam and Maureen. The theme of racial conflict is a keynote of the novel. Due to the revolution, the Smales seek refuge in July's village. They remain in July's village for several weeks. Even in their village existence, their identity remains constant. They are seen as white and they are treated as white. Relations with all their new neighbours are affected by their alien whiteness and because of this, Maureen begins to understand more about their earlier whiteness in Johannesburg. The book itself has begun two pages earlier with the typical beginning to a white master's day: "You like to have some cup of tea? July bent at the doorway... No Knock; but July, their servant, their host, bringing two pink glass cups of tea and a small tin of condensed milk...with a spoon in it" (1981: 1). Throughout the novel, the Smales family are subjected to the pressures of their newly adopted culture. They are subjected to scrutiny and curious looks by the blacks when they come out of their hut. Maureen remembers the pride they had taken in their whiteness when they lived in the city. Inspite of the realization that the villagers dislike their white presence, the Smales cannot get over their white sense of superiority. When July returns after his first appropriation of their truck, Maureen observes Bam assuming his former role as master: "And where were you yesterday? What's the story?" (53). Most whites stay prejudiced about the entire black race—they brush them off as barbarous and uncivilized. Through the Smales' approach to blacks as 'individuals' not as products of race, with an open mind and without bias of any sort. Gordimer does not ignore racial differences. She traces their genesis to a fear of the unknown and to a basic sense of rootlessness. Typical racial behaviour is not intended to be conveyed either in July's offer of shelter or in Maureen's jumping at the chance of an escape. The collapse of the white military power which the novel assumes is far less disturbing than the collapse of the white moral power. When July realizes it, he feels proud that the whites are powerless. At the end of the novel, Maureen flees. She is not accepted by the tribe and she is unlikely to accept the subservient role of a black woman in the African community. Rowland Smith remarks: "Failure of communication between white and black within the poisoned apartheid world is one of those fictional themes Nadine Gordimer constantly reworks" (1984: 107).

In *A Sport of Nature* (1987), Gordimer describes the problem of racialism. The South African freedom struggle against white dominion and apartheid has formed the subject of the epic saga of human suffering in this novel, which could well be considered her masterpiece. Gordimer traces Hillela's growth through childhood and adolescence, to the growing awareness of her own powers of seductivity. The emotional tensions in the family in which Hillela grows up and the social and political implications of the events around her, sharpen her perception of life. The changes in her own personal life run parallel to the various steps being taken by the black against the white regime. Her social conscience is awakened again and again by the reports of police, torture, beatings, electric shocks, extended denial of sleep to the black activists. In the newspapers were photographs of blacks burning their passes, raising fists and thumbs, staring with elated defiance. Through the events around her, Hillela arrives at an understanding of self. She leaves the country as a political refugee. In South Africa the laws that governed African lives were based on the body (skin colour, relative thickness of lips) and therefore, had to be fought through the body. Hillela realizes that there can be no family life for whites when blacks are denied it, that Hillela cannot "set up home again in the house where only white people could live" (1987: 159). When Hillela accepts a lift from a black man, Pauline, her aunt, comments: ".... in this house I take full responsibility for bringing you up without any colour-feeling, any colour-consciousness. But you must realize that there are risks one doesn't take" (Ibidem, 55). When No Nomzamo was born, Hillela was delighted to have produced a black child, a delight which indicates a clear political orientation: "Hillela sees her conception of a black child as a gesture of her solidarity with Whaila's cause" (Ibidem, 220). When she is expecting their second child, she does not ask Whaila what colour he thinks the child will be; she wants their many children to form a 'rainbow' (Ibidem, 241). This is Hillela's idea, this rainbow family which will be a literal manifestation of inter-racial harmony. After the killing of Whaila, Hillela's maternal role is dispelled. After the assassination of Whaila, Whaila and the unborn 'rainbow' children are the price she pays for having found herself in the answering self of a black man. It is the price demanded by the political struggle against the apartheid. Gordimer often uses the paradigm of man-woman relationship in forging the reconciliation between blacks and whites.

In *My Son's Story* (1990), the racial discrimination and colour prejudice are loudly pronounced in the behaviour of the characters. This is the story of a father told by his son. In the world of black and white, the protagonist of the novel belongs to the 'coloured' category. Except the whites, all other racial groups in South Africa can be bracketed as one for not being privileged to enjoy similar political rights as the whites do. Whenever Sonny, the protagonist, visits the city with his wife, Aila and his children, Baby and Will, he expriences the hardship due to the apartheid laws forbidding any interaction with the whites. He has to stand in separate queues in the stores and take his children to the 'railway station lavatories,' although the department stores have a cloak room reserved for white customers. The blacks appeared in the community hawking tomatoes and onions, putting up a fence, digging a trench, etc. They went back to their own areas when the work was done, remove from the community as the community was from the white town. "Their laughter, their languages yelled from block to block, sounded unceasingly through the day..." (1990: 22).

Initially, Sonny is not interested in joining the black struggle, because the wanted to "better himself, not by going to meetings or getting arrested on the march" (Ibidem: 23). He is so preoccupied with his pursuit of knowledge that he takes little notice of the oppression of the blacks: "...if he had been really black ?—he might have joined, waved a fist. Admiring the real blacks from this sort of distancing, he left it to them. It seemed more their affair" (Ibidem). Here, Gordimer brings forward the distinction between the coloured and the black. The coloured usually feel that they are better than the blacks. By writing about this aspect of the relationship between coloureds and blacks, Gordimer has touched a sensitive nerve of the multi-racial society of South Africa. However, Sonny's attitude towards the blacks undergoes a change when his coloured students join the black solidarity group. He goes with them in their procession as a mediator to face the police and the principal. As a result of his participation in the rally. Sonny is banned from teaching.

There is a violence embodied in the symmetry of the garden, the domain of the rich white man, a violence which produces the parallel asymmetry in order that the domain may be preserved. A description of the spatial discrimination which has governed the lives of Sonny and his family ends with an account of Sonny's exclusion from the library: "The lover of Shakespeare never had the right to enter the municipal library and so did not so much as think about it while white people came out before him with books under their arms; he did not recognize what the building represented for him, with its municipal coat of arms and motto above the pillared entrance" (Ibidem, 12). Here, Gordimer describes the effects of racial discrimination also on literary production. This novel is written in the apartheid era.

In her novels, Gordimer presents different manifestations of 'apartheid,' through which her disapproval of racial discrimination is emphatically revealed. The male-volence consequent of apartheid causes total disruption of human relationship. Gordimer is conscious of the politico-racial issues that affect the people of South Africa. The problem of apartheid haunts her mind without end. She is a representative African novelist who successfully depicts the contemporary reality in her fiction in artistic terms.

WORKS CITED

Das, Bijaya Kumar. "The Fiction of Nadine Gordimer." *Aspects of Commonwealth Literature*, New Delhi: Creative Books, 1995.

Hey Wood, Christopher. *Nadine Gordimer*. Windsor: Profile Books Ltd., 1983.

Newman, Judie. *Nadine Gordimer*. London and New York: Routledge, 1988.

Parker, Kenneth. *The South African Novel in English*. London: Macmillan, 1987.

Smith, Rowland. "Masters and Servants: Nadine Gordimer's *July's People* and The Themes of Her Fiction." *Salmagundi*, No. 62, Winter, 1984.

14 *Hayavadana:* An Approach to the Text

C.R. Visweswara Rao

Girish Karnad's play *Hayavadana* performed by the Madras Players on Dec. 7, 1972 in the Museum Theatre at Madras is a text that is composed of a stereographic plurality of the signifiers that weave it. Based on a tale from the Sanskrit "Vetala Panchavimsatika" as well as on the German Nobel Laureate Thomas Mann's "The Transposed Heads" *Hayavadana* is an intertext which cuts across several works. This is an idea which Julia Kristeva dwells upon in her book *Revolution in Poetic Language* (New York, 1984). A text reveals itself as a composite knowledge of literary traditions and cultures integrating and combining previously existing codes into the new text thus revealing in the new textual manifestation a plurality and complexity of meaning. The emphasis of the deconstructive nature of contemporary criticism foregrounds the heterogeneity of the text. The text is an amalgam of grafts which absorbs and transforms the meaning of other texts.

If the Sanskrit tale solves the problem of the transposed heads logically on the ground that it is the head which governs the limbs, Thomas Mann's story develops the theme of ironic confrontation between opposites in human life—the body and the spirit. Karnad takes up in *Hayavadana* the elements of these two stories and grafts on to them the tale of Hayavadana which is his own invention. *Hayavadana* blends in its structure tales of transformation, akin to Ovidian *Metamorphoses*, but different from them in the sense of a great flux and impermanence associated with life which they suggest.

Hayavadana is, for example, born to the Princess of Karnataka and a great white stallion which, on the expiation of its curse, regained the original Gandhrva self. But the Princess was in love only with the white stallion and not with the transformed celestial being. As a result, she was cursed to become a horse herself and the child of her marriage to white stallion remained a Hayavadana seeking redemption from what the Bhagavata describes as the unalterable writing on our foreheads. Neither visit to the holy shrines nor immersion in the holy rivers nor for that matter "blameless" inculcation of the patriotic spirit and concern for the here and the now helps Hayavadana to change from being a horse-man, for, as Tennyson's poem "Lucretius" so poetically renders in its depiction of the Lucretian philosophical dream, a two-natured thing is no nature. In fact, Hayavadana's conversation with Bhagavata in page 9 indicates how the entire address of Hayavadana is a parody of a way of life in post-Independence India, where, as in the West in the thirties, a new wave of "new irrationalism" or the equivalent of a neo-Christianism, as Kathaleen Nott describes it (1952: 8) has seized people. Hayavadana's birth and antecedents and his sudden intrusion into the play reveals what Coleridge describes as esemplastic imagination, an imagination which creates, rather than reassembles, by dissolving the fixities and definites (the elementary images). Imagination for Coleridge is an organic faculty which operates not like a sorting machine but like a living and growing plant. It is this sense of an essential continuum—continuum with the audience in the theatre as well—which the play *Hayavadana* stresses at several points:

Bhagavata asks Hayavadana:

> Don't take it to heart so much. What happened? What's your grief? You are not alone here. I am here. The musicians are here. And there is our large-hearted audience. It may be that they fall asleep during a play sometimes... (1975: 7)

This drawing of the audience into the fold of the theatre action—audience involvement in the action of the play—is a technique as old as Greek comedy. Aristophanes' play, *The Frogs,* in one of the choric utterances refers to "ten thousand intelligences" (i.e. men of intelligence capable of discrimination) as the strength of the audience at the Dyonisian festival where the play was staged. *Murder in the Cathedral,* again in one of the speeches of the Tempters, underlines the unreality of things material, including the prize awarded for the English essay (1935: 50). The knights stepping out of their twelfth century skins is also a similar device. This is what Eliot found irresistibly tempting to a poet-playwright of the twentieth century who considered that the great vice of English drama was its limitless realism (1951: 111). The attempt on the part of the dramatist, as Eliot envisaged it, was to turn away from the picture-frame stage to a stage where intense fellowship with the audience was invited especially as in the music-hall performances of Marie Lloyd (Ibidem, 457-58).

The mask of Vighneswara brought on to the stage at the beginning of *Hayavadana* by itself images an essentially existentialist predicament—a sense of incompleteness which is an attribute of Vighneswara with his "Vakratunda Mahakaya." It is this irony associated with a God who is worshipped as a Mangala Murthy but who is "Elephant-headed" and incomplete, which is, in terms of an image-idea correlation analysed in the portraits of the old and new and the old-into-new and the new-into-old portraits of Devadatta and Kapila who manifest a dissolving, reassembling, re-dissolving kind of personality represented by disintegration, reintegration and again disintegration. "Integration" as L.C. Knights used the phrase with reference to *The Winter's Tale* seems impossible to catch a glimpse of. This fragmentation of personality dramatized in *Hayavadana* is a typical post-modern phenomenon and the dramatization of this in terms of a rooted Indian dichotomy reveals a pattern of intertextuality at work in the play. The Bhagavata's first utterance thus "foregrounds" (to foreground is to bring something into the highest prominence, to make it dominant in perception) the Vighneswara myth not in the familiar terms in which it is taken but for effecting defamiliarization by literary means. As suggested by Stanley Fish, the meaning of an utterance is not some final, corrected result, but the reader's experience of it and the special sequence of printed word on a page converts itself into a temporal flow of experience in an informed reader.

The chief motif in the Hayavadana story recalls Eugene lonesco's *Rhinoceros*. The protagonist in this play finds himself pitted against a society turned into rhinoceroses because he resists conformism. So he longs desperately to conform and thus, becomes a rhinoceros himself. And he finds that the state of the rhinoceros is impossible and he tricks himself into believing that he is a hero fighting a lone battle for humanity, lonesco in this play shows the absurdity of the human condition. The dolls episode, in its anthropomorphic transformations, suggests, a subversive use of the beast fable that is not possible to be theatricalized in drama. These various elements of *Hayavadana* show that the play is a palimpsest in design enabling us to unlayer several layers of the text which fuse together traditions of the Western and Eastern theatre to unfold a drama of the fluidities of being.

WORKS CITED

Eliot, T.S. *Murder in the Cathedral.* London: Faber and Faber, 1935.

——. "Four Elizabethan Dramatists." *Selected Essays.* London: Faber and Faber, 1951.

——. "Marie Lloyd." *Selected Essays.* London: Faber and Faber, 1951.

Karnad, Girish. *Hayavadana. Calcutta:* OUP, 1975.

Kristeva, Julia. *Revolution in Poetic Language,* trans. Leon S. Roudiz. New York: Columbia University Press, 1984.

Nott, Kathleen. *The Emperor's Clothes.* London: Heinemann, 1953.

15 The Quest for Values: The Case of Nirad C. Chaudhuri

R.S. Pathak

The President, in his address to the nation on the eve of the fifty third anniversary of Independence, pertinently drew our attention to the "unholy alliance between criminals, politicians and important people in the society" and warned us of what he called "the dare-devil heroes of crime and banditry" and the "dark clouds of prejudice and callous unconcern hanging over our society." He was particularly pained to notice that India's "precious heritage of tolerance of different faiths and ideologies" was showing signs of "breaking down." Speaking from the rampart of the Lal Qila on the Independence Day, the Prime Minister also talked about India being a land of diversity in respect of religion, language, custom and tradition and castigated the forces bent upon spreading discord, inciting violence and creating "imaginary enemies." "We are one in many and many in one," he reiterated forcefully. "The whole world is amazed at how India has successfully sustained this magic not just today but for many millennia. This may be a magic for the rest of the world but for Indians it is life itself." Religious intolerance and hate, he added, have never been part of our liberal culture.

Right from the earliest times, Indian society has been, on the whole, liberal, tolerant and accommodating, characterised by a rare capacity for assimilation and synthesis. The tenfold law as laid down by the much-despised law-giver Manu, gives the following characteristics of righteousness:

Dhrtih ksama damo'steyah saucam indriyanigrahah
Dhirvidya satyam akrodho dasakam dharmalaksanam
(*Manusmrti*, 6.92)

("Endurance, patience, self-control, integrity, purity, restraint of the senses, wisdom, learning, truth, absence of anger are the ten characteristics of virtue.") The *Bhagavad Gita* (16.1-3) has also given an exhaustive list of the essential qualities with which a virtuous person is endowed:

Abhayam sattvasamsuddhir jnanayogavyavasthitih/
Danam damasca yajnasca svadhyayastapa arjavam/
Ahimsa satyamakrodhas tyagah santir apaisunam/
Daya bhutesvaloluptyam mardavam hrir acapalam/
Tejah ksama dhrtih saucam adroho natimanita/
Bhavanti sampadam daivim abhijatasya Bharata/

("Fearlessness, purity of heart, steadfastness in meditation for self-realisation, charity, control of senses, worship and performance of sacrifices, study of the Vedas and other sacred text, chanting of divine names, straightforwardness, non-violence, truthfulness, absence of anger, self-denial, tranquillity of mind, refraining from malicious gossip, absence of attachment, mildness, shame in doing things not sanctioned by the scriptures or usage, abstinence from idle pursuits, and sublimity, forgiveness, fortitude, external purity, absence of malice, freedom from the feeling of self-importance,—these are the marks of one who is endowed with divine virtues.") Hiriyanna (1975), and other scholars have talked about the Indian conception of values at length.

India is not the only country which attached so much importance to values. In the West, Philosophers from the time of Plato discussed under 'value and 'valuation' a variety of questions pertaining to the good, the end, the right, obligation, moral judgement aesthetic judgement, the beautiful, truth and so on. Value has been defined in the *Encyclopaedia of Religion and Ethics* (Hastings, 584) as "an attitude assumed towards fact, a weighing of fact in relation to an agent, and his feelings, desires, interests, purposes, needs and acts; and it expresses his appreciation (approbation) or reprobation (depreciation) of it in this relation." The issue of values involves a number of psychological inquiries, while their validity raises the profound questions of epistemology, metaphysics and religion, which are complex and contentious in nature. Ralph Perry (1954) and Paul Taylor (1961), are of the view that issues pertaining to value have a bearing on morality, arts, science, religion, economics, politics, law and custom or etiquette. OED has given eight meanings of value.' There is no need to emphasise that values are absolutely essential for the survival and health of a society. These values may be "eternal or the ones enshrined in the constitution of a country or may manifest as social graces or codes of day-to-day behaviour.

Indian society at the moment is passing through a very critical phase. It is moving very fast towards valuelessness, and all right-thinking persons are worried about the present state of affairs. If this tendency is not checkmated earnestly and promptly, the day is not far when we will witness what Nietzsche calls the 'transvaluation of values.' Today, values and ideals of our age-old cultural ethos such as truth, compassion, non-violence, service and dignity of labour are blatantly given a go by. Instead of them, growing intolerance, self-centredness, recklessness, arrogance, irreverence and fissiparousness are growing at the very basic fabric of the Indian society. The result is that this has resulted in a growing cynicism ("A cynic is one," says Oscar Wilde, "who knows the price of everything but the value of nothing"), corrosive frustration and widespread aimlessness of a large majority of people. Lack of involvement and sense of being marginalised have changed the very complex of our society, and pervasive politicization of our public institutions and nepotism and corruption of a very high order are making people feel helpless. The certainty and security of the Gandhian-Nehruvian ethos has been replaced more or less by directionlessness and we have occurrences of strange role reversals. "Bulbulon ko hai ye hasarat ki hay! ham ullu na hue."

The changes in approach and ethos are primarily due to onslaught of modernity, which is still an unfinished project here (Gupta, 2000). Contemporary intellectuals like Sumit Sarkar, Ashis Nandy, Sudhir Kakkar and others have provided us with hardhitting critiques of modern Indian culture. More recently, Avijit Pathak (2000), has emphatically concluded that modernity is essentially aggressive, masculine, phallocentric, violent and evil. The multiplying loss of values and violence are symptoms of a deep-seated malaise. Violence, says Khushwant Singh, is "the ultimate form of vulgarity." This vulgarity is a behavioural manifestation of a something rotten in our mind and soul. This would explain, incidentally the magnitude of our problems in respect of infrastructure lapses, low productivity (not in population though), corruption, red tapism, new crime waves, rat race and intensified competition and what not. In a corruption ranking done by an NGO, Transparency International, Berlin, Finland was judged the least corrupt country, Denmark being the second cleanest country and Nigeria the most corrupt. The positions of the countries of the Indian subcontinent, I am sure, must be very high in the list. In fact, India remains among the ten poorest, the ten most illiterate and the ten most corrupt countries of the world. We are the past masters of passing the buck on others when things go wrong and snatching away the credit otherwise. Very few countries can beat us in perpetuating the dichotomy between what we preach and what we practise, which makes the matters still worse.

Nirad C. Chaudhuri, despite all his dogmatism, eccentricity and arrogance, has paid considerable amount of attention to the problems that have beset India and Indians and it will not be out of place to refer to some of his views in this connection for diagnosis is the first step and in no way less important than actual cure. In his autobiography, he bewails what he calls "unadulterated decadence" which set in India even at the time of its Independence. "During those years," he writes, "everything about us was decaying, literally everything ranging from our spiritual and moral ideals to our material culture, and nothing really live or organic arose to take place" (1951: 364). The situation was bound to worsen in due course. The intellectuals, who should have given the proper lead, have miserably failed and, as Chaudhuri complains, prefer to live like a group of "alienated Dantean figures, in death sleeping far away from their ungrateful country" (500). Chaudhuri is even more hard-hitting in *The Continent of Circe*. He declares:

> ... a man who cannot endure dirt, dust, stench, noise, ugliness, disorder, heat and cold has no right to live in India. I would say that no man be regarded as a fit citizen of India until he has conquered squeamishness to the point of being indifferent to the presence of fifty lepers in various stages of decomposition within a hundred yards (1966: 22).

India, once Chaudhuri held, is "a classical land of *Jee huzoors*." In his characteristic vein he further observes:

> Life-long observation has convinced me that there is a streak of insanity in the Hindus and that nobody will arise at a correct appraisement of Hindu private and public behaviour on the supposition that they have a normal personality. This madness lurks within their ordinary work-a-day self like a monomania, and the nature of the alienation can be defined in psychiatrist's terms—it is partly schizophrenia, and partly paranoia. In all Hindu activities, especially in the public sphere, can be detected clear signs of either a feebleness of mental faculties or perversion of them (132-33).

Chaudhuri is not content to condemn the majority community alone and what he writes about the Muslims, the Indian Christians and the Parsees is no more flattering. The brunt of his ire falls on the Westernised, timid upper-middle-class of the Indian society in which the desire to improve is "so sheepish and apologetic" (356). Except perhaps Swift's *Gulliver's Travels*, nowhere do we come across this kind of vitriolic attack on a whole society. Most of the problems of the Indians are, according to Chaudhuri, due to built-in contradictions: "collective megalomania with self-abasement, extreme xenophobia with an abject xenolatry; authoritarianism with anarchic individualism; violence with non-violence; militarism with pacificism; possessiveness with carelessness about property owned; courage with cowardice; (and) cleverness with stupidity" (106-107). The key to the understanding of Chaudhuri's mind can be found in the chapter entitled "On Understanding the Hindus" wherein he talks of national character: "there certainly is such a thing as a national character, and once it has been formed it does control all the subsequent evolution of a people" (91). Chaudhuri also talks about the lot of the common people who might be ousted from political and administrative power by their Westernised compatriots. This Westernised class is, according to him, "sunk in an easy-going and affluent materialism," and behind their Westernisation "lies hidden a dangerous void of faith, ideas, courage, and, of course, energy" (355).

Some other issues pertinent to our analysis have been taken up in Chaudhuri's later works. *To Live or Not to Live* revealingly analyses Indian social life, joint family system, marriage, status of women and so on. It lambasts at the inadequacy of our way of living, our system of values, morals, marriage, family and social life. Chaudhuri hits at everything and spares nothing, for nothing is sacred to him. A large majority of people whom he met, he says, should have committed suicide; no one was living in the real sense:

I can get only two versions of living. Those who have done well in the worldly sense say that they have so much money or property; and those who have not, say that they contrived to remain alive. One group mistakes acquisition for living, and the other surviving for living. Beyond that their conception of life does not reach out. Most people sacrifice living for livelihood, a minority would consider themselves lucky for affluence. None live (1971: 8).

What the Indian society particularly lacks is the faculty of self-criticism, which has resulted in vanity. An unbridled love for money is another aspect of modern Indian way of life. Commenting on this "fervid devotion to money," he writes:

> Making money is their *dharma* and, as all Hindus know or should know, one's own *dharma*, even if it leads to death, is preferable to another's *dharma*, which is to be

> feared. This concept of *dharma*, enjoining overriding loyalty to it, is absolutely central to the Hindu view of life (11).

In a healthy community, there are certain groups of people who are honest, indifferent to money and are prepared to make sacrifices for the sake of ideals, principles or the public good. The youth, the intellectuals and the politicians generally belong to this category. But Chaudhuri is pained to notice that "it is precisely among these in India today that one finds the worst treason against moral principles" (11).

Notwithstanding education in the society, people, says Chaudhuri, suffer from 'sex obsession' because the society does not have a proper atmosphere for social interaction. Such is the pull of the society's value system that:

> All over India our best young brains have set their heart on living in slothful ease either as a superior clerk in the IAS or as a superior *mistri* in some technical job. They are toys pursuing baubles. A wife with a personality is likely to be dangerous for them, because, much as they might profess to admire *A Doll's House or Anna Karenina* as a pose, I do not think they would care to give repeats of either the play or the novel in their own lives (123).

Chaudhuri is also not in favour of modern semi-arranged marriages. Even working girls in this system succumb to the position of "only pawns in a process of helpless and often cowardly surrender to external circumstances on the part of their parents." "All talk," he adds, "that the girls are taking to bread-earning to live a richer life or acquire a higher personality is undiluted bunkum" (123). Chaudhuri does not subscribe to the current ideas regarding economic empowerment of women. In a sane society, he says, this issue does not arise at all. "The woman," he holds, "is never a doll in the husband's doll's house, nor is the husband the galley-slave in the wife's galley. It is the hedonism-cum-egoism of a decadent society which divides the husband from the wife, and the wife from the husband" (129). The very system of marriage in our society, he says, has degenerated and deserves an overhaul. Its degeneration gets reflected in matrimonial advertisements. Marriages today, says Chaudhuri, are "sordid scrambles for money" (146). The general pattern that emerges from marriages today is that:

> The daughters of the salaried fathers become typical wives of salaried husbands, and mothers of plump little boys and girls who look embryonic husbands and wives in the salaried class even from the age of ten. Theirs is a self-sufficient world in which disturbing questions of life and values never arise nor are allowed to arise (147).

Indian society suffers, on the whole, on account of shams and inhibitive injunctions and hypocrisy; in it "so long as appearances are saved, nothing is wrong" (152).

In his penultimate book, *Thy Hand, Great Anarch!* (1987), also Chaudhuri refers to virtues. The universe being purposive in nature, the yearning after perfection would be classed with highest values like beauty, goodness, righteousness or holiness. These values, he adds, are at flux because "at every given moment the purpose is incomplete and infinitely potential" (955). He holds the following seven factors responsible for India's decadence:

(a) Complete ineffectiveness of the state.

(b) Concessions made and accepted for expedience and not as a matter of principle.

(c) The installation of incompetent persons at decision-making positions.

(d) Political life and state services being occupied by careerists promoting private interests.

(e) The negative xenophobia, mercenary motives, sterility, lack of originality, and imitativeness in political ideas of the ruling class.

(f) The people becoming either looters or escapists.

(g) The habit of tolerance of or resignation to, anarchy and corruption (859-60).

In the event of fortuitousness, Chaudhuri says in his last book, *Three Horsemen of the New Apocalypse*, one's "rationality, notion of progress, and perception of virtues would be reduced to self-deception" (1999: 15). To highlight the passive acquiescence of the Indian masses, Chaudhuri approvingly quotes four lines from Baudelaire, which in English translation mean: "If rape, poison, dagger, incendiarism have not as yet embroidered the banal canvas of our piteous destinies with their pleasant designs, that is because our heart, alas! is not bold enough" (103). Once again, Chaudhuri is worried about corruption, for "Corruption of the best is the worst corruption" (88). Ever since the country became independent, it got stuck up in "total falsity": "Nothing was authentic, nothing sincere, nothing disinterested in it" (113). The natural outcome of this scenario has been decadence. This decadence "always provides its anaesthetics" (106), which could lead to something disastrous. Chaudhuri mentions two kinds of decadence, i.e. social and cultural decadence, and which is worse, decadence of mental life.

The fall out of a decadent state of affairs can be easily seen in the political sphere, political regimes having "no organic relationship with the general life of the people." The rulers only superimpose "an exploitative, almost predatory, class of men on the people" which maintains "law and order only to the extent that this was necessary for full scale exploitation," (118). The degradation can also be felt in the people's speech, dressing and eating, says Chaudhuri, the three mores indicative of a society's soundness, vitality, authenticity or otherwise (121). While concluding his views on decadence in India, Chaudhuri observes: "As a cultural satellite of the West, India was bound to share its decadence. But there is a difference between the two manifestations. The Western rouses a civilized man to anger; the Indian benumbs him into despair" (124). Chaudhuri is highly dissatisfied with the present condition of both India and the West in respect of their alters and his apocalyptic vision presents a depressing picture of the future. "To a man," he writes towards the end of his last book, "who has an objective historical outlook the future of human existence has become very uncertain, and unpredictable at this moment of history" (136). He considers decadence the natural order of evolution of human life in all countries, and quotes Horace who maintains: "Our Fathers' age was worse than our grandfathers." We their more worthless sons will procreate in our turn a progeny more corrupt.

Chaudhuri's theses are vulnerable on several counts. A hardcore Anglophile, he dedicated his first book to the memory of the British Empire in India, for "all that was good and living within us was made, shaped, and quickened by the same British Rule." He was not averse to some foreign power overpowering India to take it out of the quagmire. "I expect," he wrote in his autobiography, "either the United States singly or a combination of the United States and the British Commonwealth to reestablish and rejuvenate the foreign domination of India" (507). In the Preface to his last book, he claims to have been impartial in his evaluation:

> So far as it lies in my power, I have never allowed my likes or dislikes, my predilections and prepossessions to influence my presentation of my subjects. I have, so to speak, tried to keep the lens of my mind free from chromatic aberrations.

Chaudhuri, however, is a man of very strong likes and dislikes and cannot but be swayed by them at times. He is aware of the fact, as is evident from the preface from which I have quoted above, that "readers in India have always attributed dogmatism, eccentricity and even arrogance" to him, and their reactions are not baseless. His book on *Hinduism* presents him at his blackest, and the line of his argument can be torn to shreds.

Chaudhuri might seem to be exaggerating things but his delineation of the death of moral consciousness in India contains a significant quantum of truth. All right-thinking people will agree, for example, that ours is a society, as Chaudhuri points out in his autobiography, which is "dishonest, self-seeking, venal, mercenary and insensitive to all considerations ... of probity" and is plagued with "a pettifogging pursuit of money" coupled with "a slight stretching of the conscience" (520-21). Thanks to "an undifferentiated promiscuity of values," a vast majority of Indians seem to be "swimming against the current" and are "retrograde and out of sympathy with reality" (526-27). Chaudhuri's diagnosis of the Indian crisis of values, despite his angular presentation, rings true at all essential points. He denies to be a satirist, and even if he were one he would have had to be one "with an abnormally keen appetite for satire to be capable of relishing so putrid a fare" (523). Besides, he affirms the validity of his point of view: "I go even farther and say that my perception of right and wrong is not a whit less valid than my perception of solidity, fluidity, and gaseousness" (527). His generalisations are based on facts, and nothing but facts. He writes in *The Continent of Circe*: "No good literature can be written, and in any case no literary work can come alive without being anchored in reality and without embodying at least the substance of an actual state. If it were not and did not, it would lose all verisimilitude and appeal, and become ineffectual" (235-36). With his astounding scholarship and meticulous observation, Chaudhuri emerges as a formidable social chronicler of Indian reality whom we may disagree with occasionally but cannot dismiss or ignore. He raises right questions may be in an obtrusive way. His conclusions are, essentially, as valid as those of any conscientious and sensitive writer including the poet of the following lines written as a present-day rejoinder to Tagore's well known verse "Where the Mind is without Fear":

> Where education leads to submissiveness, not self-respect
>
> where knowledge and acceptance depend on certificates
>
> where push-out is called drop-out
>
> where repression breeds fear, powerlessness, alienation and marginalisation.
>
> where dependency, not self-sufficiency, perpetuates with helplessness
>
> where discontent is the way of life and dignity is decried
>
> where the system blames the victims to preserve status quo

and the stream of reason is lost in narrow divisions
into that ever-widening hell of majority and minority
O my God,
— let my country not sink in the new century.

(Singh, 48).

WORKS CITED

Chaudhuri, Nirad C. *The Autobiography of an Unknown Indian*, London: Macmillan, 1951.

——. *The Continent of Circe*, Bombay: Jaico, 1966.

——. *To live or Not to live*, New Delhi: Orient Paperbacks, 1971.

——. *Thy Hand, Great Anarch*! London: OUP, 1982.

——. *Three Horsemen of the New Apocalypse*, Delhi: OUP, 1999.

Gupta, Dipankar, *Mistaken Modernity*, Delhi: Harpar Collins, 2000.

Hastings, James, ed. *Encyclopaedia of Religion and Ethics*, Edinburgh: T & T Clark (2nd impression), 1934.

Hiriyanna, M. *Indian Conception of Values*, Mysore, Kavyalaya Publishers, 1975.

Pathak, Avijit, *Indian Modernity*, New Delhi: Gyan Publishing House, 2000.

Perry, Ralph B. *Realms of Value*, Cambridge, Mass, 1954.

Singh, R.K. *Above the Earth's Green*, Calcutta: Writers Workshop, 1997.

Taylor, Paul W. *Normative Discourse*, Englewood Cliffs, N.J., 1961.

16

Post-Independence Indian English Women Novelists: An Assessment

Sonali Das

If British literature has women novelists like Jane Austen and George Eliot, the Brontes and Mrs. Gaskell, Dorothy Richardson and Virginia Woolf, Indian English literature does not lag far behind. Toru Dutt can considered to be our first Indian English Woman novelist of Pre-Independence era. She wrote both a French and an English novel before her premature death at the age of 21 in 1877. Her novels include—*Bianca, or The Young Spanish Maiden* and *Le Journal de Mademoiselle d'Arvers*. Both her heroines—Bianca, a Spanish maiden and Marguerite a French girl—are in Toru's delineation essentially Indian, ardent, sincere, and capable of love and even of resignation.

Post-Independence Indian English women novelists too form a sizeable and significant school. The earliest among them is Ruth Prawer Jhabvala (1927-). She raised a problem for the historian of Indian English Literature as to whether she can legitimately be called an Indian English writer. Born of Polish parents in Germany and educated in England, Jhabvala married an Indian and lived in India for more than twenty four years. She herself has declared that she should not be considered an 'Indian writer' but 'as one of those European writers who have written about India' (Agarwal, 36). Jhabvala's novels fall into two distinct and evenly matched groups—viz. comedies of urban middle class Indian life, especially in undivided Hindu families and ironic studies of the East-West encounter. The first group comprises novels like *To Whom She*

Will (1955), *The Nature of Passion* (1956), *The Householder* (1960), etc. To the second group belong other novels like *A Backward Place* (1965), *A New Dominion* (1973), her Booker Prize Winning novel, *Heat and Dust* (1975).

Heat and Dust narrates the story of a European couple in India. Mr. Douglas is an Assistant Collector at Satipur. His wife, Olivia, suffers from alienation. She falls in love with the Nawab and gets pregnant. She wants Harry to help her in getting the abortion done. But she leaves Douglas, when everything becomes public and lives with the Nawab throughout her life in India.

If Jhabvala is an outsider—insider, Kamala Markandaya is an insider-outsider. She is an Indian who has married a European and settled in London. Her quintessential themes are the East-West encounter, and woman in different life-roles. The East-West encounter takes two forms—first, a direct relationship between Indian and British characters, and secondly, the impact of the modern urban culture brought in by the British rule on traditional Indian life.

Markandaya's first novel, *Nectar in a Sieve* (1954), illustrates all these preoccupations. This novel recalls K.S.Venkataraman's *Murugan, the Tiller*. She has emphasized the role of love and faith, suffering and sacrifice in dealing with the painful realities of life. The narrator, also the protagonist, is Rukmani, a mystic woman. The story of her hard peasant life illustrates the truth of Coleridge's line, 'work without hope draws nectar in a sieve.' The vagaries of nature and the depredations of modern industrialism (in the shape of a tannery) force Rukmani and her husband Nathan to migrate to a city. Nathan dies and Rukmani goes back to her village. She has lost her husband, but she has brought Puli, their adopted son with her. They and the other children, Selvam and Ira, start to rebuild their fortunes on the ruins of the old. Calm after storm, spring after winter—such is the law of nature. What the novelist suggests is that one must hope, and one must persevere, even if one is engaged only in trying to discover "nectar in a sieve!" (Iyengar, 439).

Markandaya's other important early novels include *A Silence of Desire* (1961), *A Handful of Rice* (1966) and *The Coffer Dams* (1969). *A Silence of Desire* shows the clash between the western-oriented rationalism of Dandekar, who wants his wife Sarojini to get operated for a tumour and the traditional religious faith of Sarojini, which relies absolutely on the faith-healing of the Swami. In the end, the Swamy goes away of his own accord and Sarojini undergoes a successful operation and accepts resignedly her separation from the Swamy. Although Dandekar apparently wins, the real victory is with the Swamy.

The theme of Markandaya's *The Coffer Dams* is similar to that of Jhabvala's *Heat and Dust.* It also centers around a European couple in India. Mr. Clinton like Douglas of *Heat and Dust* is a very busy man. He is in charge of the Coffer Dams. He neglects his wife, Helen for his job. Helen, like Olivia of *Heat and Dust* falls in love with an Indian called Bashiam. Bashiam is the chief of the natives and belongs to low rank, unlike Olivia's lover, the Nawab, who belongs to high brow of society. In the end, Helen goes to see Bashiam leaving Clinton alone. Both the women separate from their husbands due to different outlooks and lack of mutual understanding. Both the novels *(Heat and Dust* and *The Coffer Dams)* clearly portray the picture of a "trapped married couple who either wriggle within the cage for better understanding or break loose to live separate lives" (Iyengar, 455). Her other important novels include *The Nowhere Man* (1972), *Two Virgins* (1973) and *The Golden Honey Comb* (1977).

Nayantara Sahgal is the leading practitioner of the political novel in India. Her important novels include *A Time to Be Happy* (1958), *This Time of Morning* (1968), *Storm in Chandigarh* (1969), *A Situation in New Delhi* (1977), *Plans for Departure* (1985), *Mistaken Identity* (1988), etc. But *Rich Like Us* (1985) is Sahgal's best novel. It presents a picture of India in 1975-76, the time when Indira Gandhi declared a State of National Emergency. Sahgal shows that the Emergency was not something that happened overnight, it was the consequence of the slow erosion of moral values which had set in, among the civil servants and the people at large, after Independence. The narrator is Sonali, an idealistic officer of the IAS, but alternate chapters deal with her father Keshav's friend Ram who married an English woman, Rose. Sahgal introduces a struggling Shopkeeper, Kishori Lal, who is also a symbol of the honest common man harassed during the Emergency by the power-drunk police. Sonali represents many restraints faced by a woman, however rich, beautiful, educated or powerful she is. She denies licence to Mr. Neuman, the representative of an American soft drinks company. Mr. Neuman is not interested in Indian society's problem. He believes that if underdeveloped countries "do like we do, they'd be rich like us." He succeeds in setting up the factory by bribing the minister and Sonali resigns even as the Emergency is declared. Sahgal takes a dispassionate look at India, and finds that democracy and spirituality are only skin deep.

In contrast with Nayantara Sahgal, Anita Desai (1937-) is more interested in the interior landscape of the mind than in political and social realities. Desai's protagonists are persons 'for whom aloneness alone' is 'the sole natural condition, aloneness alone the treasure worth treasuring' (Naik, 241). They are mostly women, who, though they have reached different stages in life (from school girl to grandmother), are largely introverts 'trapped in their own skins' (Naik, 241). Her important novels include *Cry, the Peacock* (1963), *Voices in the City* (1965), *Bye-Bye, Blackbird* (1971), *Where Shall We Go This Summer* (1975), *Fire on the Mountain* (1977), *Clear Light of Day* (1980), *In Custody* (1984), *Baumgartner's Bombay* (1988), *Journey of Ithaca* (1995), *Fasting, Feasting* (1999) and *The Zig-Zag Way* (2005). Her new novel, *The Zig-Zag Way* is set in Mexico and narrated by a young American writer, a man who travels to the Sierra Madre without knowing why. Desai admits that this is more like her own experience.

Clear Light of Day (1980), is perhaps her best novel. It deals with two sisters from a loveless home—Bimla, the elder, stays on in their dusty old house in Delhi and looks after their mentally retarded younger brother after the death of the parents. Tara, the younger sister, marries a man in the Indian Foreign Service and visits the house every three or four years when her husband comes to India. When both the parents die, it is Bim who takes charge of the household. Raja, the elder brother follows their landlord Hyder Ali to Hyderabad, where he marries his daughter and inherits his property. Raja sends Bim a letter in the new capacity of a landlord assuring her that she can stay on in their old house as long she wants to. Bim is a new heroine in Anita Desai's fiction, hard-headed and facing life's challenges bravely. She rejects the need of a woman of a man for her spiritual and material happiness. Through the character of Bim Das, Desai does not present an escape from family responsibilities. It instead involves the sublimation of one's emotions, a laying bare of one's soul, until there is no barrier left between oneself and other. A state of openness, peace and detachment are shown as necessary factors in achieving an enlightened sense of being.

Mention must be made of the novel, *Fire on the Mountain,* which won Desai the Sahitya Akademi Award in 1978. The title is taken from William Golding's novel, "*Lord of the Flies*" Nanda Kaul, the protagonist, is the wife of the ex-Vice-Chancellor of Punjab University. She is an old lady tired of formalities, family and even grandchildren. Her husband has not been faithful to her. After his death, she goes to Kasauli, where she wants to be along with pine trees and cicadas. Her privacy is disturbed when her great grand daughter Raka comes there. But Raka too loves solitude. She wants to be alone and she is not even interested in Nanda Kaul's fabricated stories about her life. Ila Das is a social worker and Nanda Kaul's friend. She is nostalgic about her past. The climax comes when Ila Das is raped and murdered. Nada Kaul dies of shock and Raka in her childish prank sets fire on the mountain. The forest on fires is symbolic of the suppressed fire in Nanda Kaul's heart.

Both Anita Desai and Shashi Deshpande explore human relationships in modern Indian society, particularly the husband-wife relationship. Deshpande's women, like those of Anita

Desai's, are tolerant, obedient and submissive. Deshpande's two novels—*The Dark Holds No Terrors* (1980) and *The Long Silence* (1988), establish her identity as a contemporary Indian English novelist. Both the novels deal with the female protagonists search for their self-identity. *The Dark Holds No Terrors* is a feministic rebellion (the protagonist Sarita's) against parental authority and other social conventions. However, *That Long Silence* which won her the Sahitya Akademi Award in 1990, establishes her identity as a major novelist. In this novel, Jaya, the protagonist resents the image of a wife "yoked" to her husband—"a pair of bullocks yokes together." She feels relieved when her husband, Mohan, a well-placed business executive is charged with embezzlement and they have to live in a sort of hide-out. She now feels redeemed as a woman with an identity of her own, seeing her husband dependent upon her.

Other important Post-Independence Indian English women novelists and their novels include Attia Hosain *(Sunlight on a Broken Column)*, Arundhati Roy *(The God of Small Things* for which she won the Booker Prize in 1997), Namita Gokhale (Paro: *Dreams of Passions)*, Manju Kapur *(Difficult Daughters* and *A Married Woman)*. Kiran Desai (*Hullabaloo in the Guva Orchard* and *The Inheritance of Loss*). Whereas previous generation women writers dealt mostly with man-woman relationship; the desire of a woman to gain her own identity, defying social conventions, the present generation women novelists feel free enough to discuss about sex and incestuous relationship in its most blatant form as is evident in the novels of Arundhati Roy and Manju Kapur.

I would like to deal with the novels of Arunthati Roy and Manju Kapur at some length.

Arundhati Roy's debut novel *The God of Small Things* (1997), earned for her Britain's most prestigious award, the Booker Prize. Arundhati Roy explains the genesis of *The God of Small Things* in one of her interview in the following words:

> Writing *The God of Small Things* was fictional way of making sense of the world I lived in, and the novel was

> the technical key with which I did it, it touches things which I could not wish to address in my everyday life. It deals with the areas I do my best to avoid thinking about. It unleashes terrors which I have always tried to get away from. All I know is that there are things which form you before you form yourself. And these things will never go away, for they constitute the deepest part of me (*Frontline,* 106).

The story element in *The God of Small Things* is rather thin. It centers around fraternal twins, Estha and Rahel, and their mother, Ammu, who has been ostracized by her family and society in the small town of Ayemenem near Kottayam, because she had the audacity to divorce the drunken and abusive man she had married and fall in love with an untouchable. The plot of the novel is complex and it moves both ways—backward and forward—and thereby makes the narration difficult and complicated. Thematically it centers round Ammu, her two children Rahel and Esthappen, her parents, brother, Chacko and his wife Margaret and daughter, Sophie Mol and above all, Amu's low caste lover, Velutha, the paravan.

In the words of Meena Sodhi:

> *The God of Small Things*, "a big look about the small things of life," is "Roy's first book and as such is heavily autobiographical, as all first works tend to be. Roy represents her life as a "sample" in its social setting and its ideological situation. The personalized story makes us assume that the writer have felt her individuality to be unique, singular and specific; but she had to go "beyond the actuality also, in order to uncover what was only potential." It had all to be delineated more sharply than the actual life, and hence the need for an artistic re-arrangement and invention. In his way the novel stands by itself though in the form of a "personal book" (41).

Manju Kapur took eight years to write her first novel, *Difficult Daughters* (1998), and next four years to publish her second novel, *A Married Woman* (2002). She tells us how she became a writer:

> I had had no idea of what I was going to write before I began, my story grew in fits and starts. I knew what I was interested in family, marriage, women and education, but I had no notion of how to weave a story around this. Interviews, research, field trips—the tools of an academic—these are what I used, I searched as a I wrote, often not knowing what incident I was going to base the next chapter on (Span, 35).

The plot of the novel is simple and the story is fascinating. It is the story of a woman, Virmati who was hooked on with her Professor, Harish at the latter's insistence. The eldest daughter of Suraj Prakash and Kasturi (the eldest of their eleven children), Virmati had an ambition to be highly educated. As chance would have it, she came in contact with Professor Harish who came to stay in her aunt's house as a tenant.

This married Professor, Harish was not happy with his illiterate wife. He felt attracted towards Virmati and gradually came closer to her. Virmati though initially resisted his love (illicit love and passion), subsequently gave in. Their affair led to Virmati's refusal to marry Inderjit, an engineer, arranged by her family and then to abortion, while she was still in college. The whole family turned against her and she went through harrowing experiences. Finally, the Professor took her home as his second wife. Virmati, won the love of the Professor but lost both the families. Then came the partition and they moved to Delhi and Ida, a daughter was born. The novel here almost comes to an end except the epilogue.

Manju Kapur's *A Married Woman* (2002), deals with the journey of Astha across her middle class life to a world which has affinity with romantic creed linking her with her children, a loving husband and a secure surrounding. In due course, she encroaches on such a setting that she herself feels vague with the sort of association which Pipeelika a much younger woman demands. Astha has a brief expedition to the regions of politics and realms of religion. Initially her focus and determination was to communicate with the world of art and seek an identity.

About one-third of the novel deals with lesbian relationship. Astha-Hemant relationship is the main story in which Babri-Masjid-Ram Janamabhoomi episode and Astha-Pipeelika episode are embedded with an artistic touch in Kapur's fictional reconstruction. At the surface level the novel traces the life of Astha from her young adulthood. In the process she marries, discovers the joys of intimacy with her husband, grows distant from him, struggles to become a painter, becomes a social activist, falls in love with a woman and be friends herself—sort of, more or less almost. The central focus is the relationship between two women. The greatest strength of the novel is its rich social context which the author uses to show her, who concern for a girl, is unrooted from the familiar environment of her childhood, girlhood, youth to mould herself a new in a completely strange environment, and accept a new set of rules to build her present as well as future.

Both Arundhati Roy and Manju Kapur have made experiments with new themes such as gratification of sex from women's point of view and mixing it with the politics of the day. Feminism and contemporary history are dovetailed to give a new dimension to their fiction. Historicising fiction is a significant contribution of Roy and Kapur to Indian English novel. And above all, the feminist fiction of Roy and Kapur makes an absorbing reading in the changing context of Indian society at the threshold of the twenty first century.

The fiction writers in the post-Independence period are obsessed with new kinds of realism which determines the subjects of their fiction. Psychological realism' takes into account the hidden thoughts of individuals which are expressed in their interior monologues as we find in Anita Desai's *Fire on the Mountain* and Arundhati Roy's *The God of Small Things*. Feminist writers have given a new direction to fiction in English by asserting feminine identity and demanding sexual freedom in the patriarchal society. R.P. Jhabvala, Arundhati Roy, Shashi Deshpande, Manju Kapur and a most of other women novelists have written boldly on man-woman relationship from woman's point of view. Apart from the new themes, new techniques in the form of code mixing is central to fiction written in English. For example, one encounters a number of Indian words (taken from regional languages) in Indian English fiction. The attempt at creating new idioms based on usages is common to English language fiction writers in different parts of the world.

WORKS CITED

Agarwal, Ramla. "Interview with R.P. Jhabvala," *Quest, 91,* Sep.-Oct., 1974.

Iyengar, K.R.Srinivasa. *Indian Writing in English.* New Delhi: Sterling Publishing Pvt. Ltd., 1984.

Naik, M.K. *A History of Indian English Literature.* New Delhi: Sahitya Akademi, 1982.

Sodhi, Meena. "The God of Small Things: Memory and Art." Ed. R.S. Pathak. *The Fictional World of Arundhati Roy,* New Delhi: Creative Books, 2001.

17

Situating Post-1980 Indian English Fiction in the Present Context

Gopa Ranjan Mishra

Indian English fiction has come a long way from Bankim Chandra Chatterji's *Rajmohan's Wife* in 1864, to Shashi Tharoor's *Riot* in 2001. This genre of writing has entered the age of self-confidence. While the early Indian English novelists reached out to the Indian mass, the novelists of the 1980s and after have made a distinguishing impact on the whole world. The metropolitan and the cosmopolitan background of these novelists like Upamanyu Chatterjee, Shashi Tharoor and Vikram Seth has given them the confidence to write novels in a new way. The nation itself has moved from the village-centrism of the freedom movement of the Gandhian era to the city-centrism of the post-Nehruvian and post-Emergency era. The novelists of the 1980s and after have made 'a voyage within' as well as 'a voyage without.' To account for the growth and development of Indian English fiction in the eighties the great St. Stephen's factor cannot be glossed over, particularly when a number of writers like Upamanyu Chatterjee, Shashi Tharoor, Allan Sealy, Rukun Advani had their grooming as creative writers there and it has contributed to their skills in writing. The novelists of the post-Midnight's Children era engaged themselves in a search for human living.

While making an evaluation of these, novelists, two things come to our mind; one, in what way these writers have expanded the horizon of Indian English fiction and made it acceptable to the English speaking world abroad; two, in what way these writers will continue to be a source of inspiration for the next generation of writers and what is their real worth, compared to the first two generations of the Indian English novelists. To answer these questions we have to make a comparative study of the opinions expressed by the critics both denigrating and eulogizing the post-Rushdie generation of Indian English writers. One group of critics, particularly the purists, deny any credit to these new writers by saying that they are inauthentic, unoriginal and lesser Indian compared to the regional writers of our country. These critics hinge upon the use of English language as the medium of creative expressions at the hands of these writers. They bring forth a peculiar argument that Indian English literature is not representative in character. We often hear the questions like "Indianness" in Indian English fiction, "Indianness" in Kamala Markandaya's novels and so on and so forth. But we never hear a question like "Indianness" in Anantha Murty's *Samskara* or in the novels of Tagore or Gopinath Mohanty.

Meenakshi Mukherjee deals with such a question at some length in her essay "The Anxiety of Indianness."

> If I were to write a novel in Marathi, I would not be called an Indian writer in Marathi, but simply a Marathi novelist, the epithet Marathi referring only to the language, not conveying the larger burden of culture, tradition and civilization. No one would write a doctoral dissertation on the Indianness of my Marathi novel. But when it comes to English fiction originating in our country, not only does the issue of Indianness become a favourite essentializing obsession in academic writings and the book-review circuit, the writers themselves do not seem unaffected by it, the complicating factor being that English is not just any language—it was the language of our colonial rulers and continues even now to be the language of power and privilege. It is not a language that permeates all social levels or is used in subaltern contexts. Our discourse on Indian novels in English tends to get congealed into fairly rigid and opposed positions. When an earlier version of this paper was orally presented in Delhi, the audience, both general and

> academic, was much more interested in my position in the cultural war between the global and the regional, between English for the world marker and Hindi/Bengali/ Marathi, etc. for an indigenous and therefore presumably more 'authentic' readership than in looking at them an disparate literary products of a complex plural culture (2000: 168).

The question of choosing a language for creative expression is a matter of wide significance. It is not always true that a writer can always express himself/herself freely in the mother tongue. One can write effectively in an acquired language or second language (as English is for us a second language in our country). A noted write and distinguished poet, Shiv K. Kumar once said that he could not write in his mother tongue Punjabi as he lacked the inwardness with that language. The only option available to him was English. Joseph Conrad, a Polish writer, contributed significantly to English literature by writing in that language. M.C. Bradbrook, a noted British critic, once said, "Easy communication makes communication in depth precarious." It is not always that a writer chooses a language. It is the other way about—that is the language chooses the person. Gandhiji once said, "Say your say in any language you like." All our great patriots like Gandhiji, Nehru, Rajaji and a host of others used English as the medium of creative expression. Certainly they were not less patriotic than the regional writers. English has been with us for the last two hundred fifty years. It is no less ours for it's primarily being an English man's or an American's. Moreover, it is included in the eighth schedule of our constitution and is regarded as an associate official language of India. So, the question of being less patriotic or inauthentic cannot be directed against the Indian English writers. It is not the mother tongue or the other tongue that matters. To choose the medium of expression, the deciding factor for a writer is his literary competence. A writer will write in that language in which he/she has acquired literary competence.

Another fallacious notion is to divide Indian literature into two groups: Indian English literature and Bhasa literature. "Bhasa" is a term coined by G.N. Devi in his book *After*

Amnesia and popularized by Meenakshi Mukherjee in her essay. "The Anxiety of Indianness" which refers to other Indian languages except English. Some critics argue that these Bhasa writers are more authentic and original than Indian English writers. This is an untenable argument. One cannot be a lesser Indian just because he writes in the second language. Examples of native Urdu writers writing in Hindi, Gujrati writers writing in Marathi are plenty in this country. Sometimes there is another charge against Indian English writer. The critics argue that the Indian English literature does not have 'a locale' of its own. They forget that English is a pan-Indian language and it is in this sense Indian English literature is a pan-Indian literature. After Sanskrit the only literature which can claim an all India status is Indian English literature. All other Bhasa literatures are regional literatures. Again the term "Bhasa" can be questioned. Bhasa means language. All literatures are written in languages. To say that Bhasa literature is different from Indian English literature and more authentic than it, is not very convincing. Just because Indian English literature is written in English, which is primarily the language of the British, it cannot be less authentic or original than Bhasa literature. It will not be out of place to mention here that English has already been accepted as an Indian language and every year, award is given to Creative Writing done in English along with Bhasa literature books by the Sahitya Akademi. To divide Indian literature into two groups by saying that one is an indigenous Indian literature and the other is an acquired Indian literature is unwarranted. If the world literature written in English language in different countries are known as African literature, Australian literature, Canadian literature, Caribbean literature, American literature and so on, the nomenclature being taken from the native countries, in the same way we can say that literature written in several languages in one country can be taken as one literature. What gives identity to literature is not language but culture and native sensibility. It is in this sense that Indian English literature is as much an Indian literature as Hindi literature is or ought to be.

Another question arises about the percentage of readership with reference to Indian English literature. They say only two per cent of Indians read and understand English. So it is a literature of the elite class. Let us take the other question. What is the percentage of Oriya or Assamese readers. Oriyas are hardly three to four per cent of the Indian population. One per cent of total Indian population would be more than the literary readers of Oriya literature. If Oriya literature is, in the prevailing circumstances, taken as Indian literature, how can we deny the same status to Indian English literature.

The second group of critics tend to blow the achievement of these novelists in the post-1980 era out of proportion. The media too plays a role in this regard. Now books are commissioned by big firms and publishing company. A fabulous amount is given as advance royalty to the writers (Vikram Seth got two crores of rupees as advance towards royalty for his *A Suitable Boy*). Not only that, all the major writers organise a book-launching ceremony to announce their new titles to get publicity. Before the books are read by the readers or even before they reach the readers, an opinion has already been formed and highlighted by the media about the book. This takes us a step ahead of Roland Barthes's announcement of 'the death of the author' for it heralds a new era in which the reader is supposed to be dead and the opinion is formed by the media. In other words, both the author and reader being dead, the text has now been taken over by the media. Texts have been given canonical status by the publisher, media and the award-deciding committee. This is a serious loss. Traditionally books and authors used to take decades and centuries to get canonical status. Now books and authors achieve that status with the book launching function. To put it lightly, it comes to this, that the food has been cooked, the dish has been served and we (the readers) are asked to say that it is delicious. Our writers who are mostly expatriate writers or who spend half of their time abroad are highlighted by the media and the internet and even they are placed above the canonical writers like Raja Rao, Mulk Raj Anand and R.K. Narayan. The supporters of these writers praise them for their mastery over the language and treatment of subjects which transcend the national boundaries. There is some element of truth in their appreciation of post-1980 Indian English novelist but to place them above all the earlier writers is to miss the wood in the tree. Two important critics named C. D. Narasimhaiah and Alstair Niven, one at home and the other abroad, seriously question such kind of estimation. According to C.D. Narasimhaiah:

> "... we should take the greatest possible care in our praise of writers so as not to be posterity's laughing stock ... We should summon all our faculties to ensure a discriminating response" (1999: 242).

He further goes on to say how popularity of a book is determined:

> The American publisher of his (Vikram Seth's) Californian novel *The Golden Gate* had paved the way for it. *The Golden Gate*, a freak, a tour de force, because a novel in verse, and therefore overawed a country with its morbid penchant for novelty—'make it new' is its national motto. It had, besides, Pushkin for stimulus and precedent to add respectability. I have heard it said with excitement in fashionable circles in Delhi 'this thing of anomalous beauty' is written in tetrameter, as if it is a crowning point in its favour. Did they know Dante also wrote his Divine Comedy in terza rhima hut, let it be noted, Dante thought in that meter and did not look on it, as Seth did, to use his own words, us 'a good vessel for a mad novel in verse' which goes clean contrary to the time honoured concept of Vagartha—the fusion of word and meaning. The stuff of *The Golden Gate*, 'the celebration of career climbers,' says Seth, 'is not a classic theme and so he was attracted to it—surface calls to the surface!' He adds he didn't have to 'look for meaning in life,' as if any sane activity can be value-free; and precisely here the theme had to be subjected to the scrutiny of higher values (1999: 242-243).

Likewise Alstair Niven deplores the modern critics' pouring undue praises on the new crop of writers:

> Everyone cottons on the newer generation of writers starting with Rushdie as though they revolutionize Indian writing. But they have predecessors just as good, in some cases better. I feel rather sad that R.K. Narayan, Mulk Raj Anand, Raja Rao, Nirad C. Choudhury, G.V. Desani and Kamala Markandaya are sidelined today. I think it would he hard to find a more fastidious use of language than in Narayan. Choudhury handled the English language magisterially. Anand made an interesting hybrid with Punjabi phrasing and Raja Rao's Sanskrit influences brought in a metaphysical dimension. Don't underestimate the older writers (200: III).

The true merit of post-1980 Indian English novelists lies somewhere between the two opinions expressed above. These post-1980 novelists can be profitably analyzed from the standpoint of post-colonial criticism. They write back to the West, transcend the limitation of nationalism and, above all, make a new use of English language which goes to the creation of an Indian English idiom. In other words, they subvert the Englishness of the English fiction, highlight hybridity (a term popularized by Homi Bhabha). Most of their themes are urban based and international in nature. They have come a long way from Raja Rao's *Kanthapura* where national myths were highlighted to give a kind of prominence to the village-based themes. Since the world has become a global village, these novelists are writing for the English speaking readers the world over. They face a double challenge: one at home by the regional or bhasa writers and the second by the post-colonial writers in the *Third World Countries.*

Shashi Tharoor very convincingly justifies the use of English in the following lines:

> I write of an India of multiple truths and multiple realities, an India that is greater than the sum of its parts. At the same time I remain conscious of and connected to, my pre-urban and non-Anglophone antecedents: my intellectual heritage embraces the Mahabharata, Ottamthullal and Bollywood as well as Shakespeare, Wodehouse and the Beatles, and as a first

> generation urbanite myself, I keep returning to the Kerala villages of my parents, in my life as my writing. Yet I have grown up in Bombay, Calcutta and Delhi; my wife is half Kashmir, half-Bengali; and my mother now lives in Coimbatore... And English is the language that brings those various threads of my India together, the language in which my wife can speak to her mother-in-law, the language that enables a Calcuttan to function in Coimbatore, the language that serves to express the complexity of that multiform Indian experience better than any other language I know (Tharoor, 2000: 46-47).

Sometimes it is said that the contemporary Indian English novelists use Indian words in their writing to sound more authentic to the Western readers. Thus, their attempt in this direction is more utilitarian than artistic. This may be true to some extent but to say that the use of such words is always deliberate and that it has nothing to do with artistic necessity will be an injustice to these writers. My contention is that these writers use such words to give their writing an Indian flavour and also because of the fact that certain words are not easy to translate or they lose much of their significance through translation. Here is a brief list of such words used by Upamanyu Chatterjee, Shashi Tharoor and Vikram Seth in their novels:

> ashram, adaab, aalam, ayah, beti, bhadralok, barfi, chapatis, dal bhat, darshan, dhabas, dharamshala, dhoti, dharma, dharna, grihasthi, gup-shup, haramzada, huzoor, harijan, hazaar, haveli, jawan, janmabhoomi, khat, kerosene, kurta, kundalini, karma, lathi, lungi, mali, maidan, mofussil, moksha, namaskar, nimbu pani, neta, padayatra, panchayat, patideva, puja, paan, puranas, razai, rishi, sainik, sala, satyagraha, shamiana, shastras, sloka, swayamvara, tamasha, zindabad.

The achievement of Indian English novelists of the 1980s in general and Upamanyu Chatterjee, Shashi Tharoor and Vikram Seth in particular is immense. These writers have replaced the grand narratives of the earlier writers like R.K. Narayan, Mulk Raj Anand and Raja Rao by what has come to be known as 'narratives of disintegration.' They have extended the Indian tradition of storytelling by incorporating the Western mode of fiction writing into their texts. Their contact with the west has broadened the range of their themes and thereby made their works acceptable to the western readers. Indian English fiction has gained world wide attention. There is a vital difference between the Indian English writers who have not lived abroad and those who have lived there because the first category of writers lack contact with the spoken word. But writers like Upamanyu Chartterjee, Shashi Tharoor and Vikram Seth have direct contact with the spoken word as they have lived abroad, as a result of which they know how to fasten the English word into their themes. As Joseph Conrad has extended the range of English language, so our Indian English novelists have done a commendable job by creating a live Indian English idiom and expanding the vocabulary of English language through their works. Gunter Grass once said, 'For God's sake open the universe little more.' Our Indian English novelists have done that by incorporating wide range of themes into the texture of their fiction. These novelists write back to the centre and they have done commendable job by making a reversal of *centre-periphery* paradigm in English literary culture by dissolving *the great tradition* of which F.R. Leavis wrote eloquently in the past, into plurality of traditions coming from many races, many regions and many cultures. To conclude, I should say that in the hands of writers like Chatterjee, Tharoor and Vikram Seth, Indian English novel reached a new height that is visible to the English speaking world cutting across countries and continents. Now the authenticity and identity of Indian English novel are beyond question and perhaps, we can say like Othello, "it's better as it is."

WORKS CITED

Mukherjee, Meenakshi. "The Anxiety of Indianness." *The Perishable Empire*. Delhi: OUP, 2000.

Narasimhaiah, C.D. "Spurious Reputations: Salman Rushdie, Vikram Seth, Shashi Tharoor and Arundhati Roy." *The Swan and the Eagle*, New Delhi: Vision Books, 1999.

Niven, Alstair. "Word for Word." *The Hindu Literary Review,* Sunday, May 7, 2000.

Tharoor, Shashi. "Celebrate College, But doubt the School." *The Fiction of St. Stephen's.* Eds. Aditya Bhattacharjee and Lola Chatterjee. Delhi: Ravi Dayal Publisher, 2000.

18 Shades of Light-Hearted Swearwords and Anand's Sense of Humour in *Untouchable*

Ramesh K. Srivastava

Mulk Raj Anand has been well known as a writer with a purpose. For him literature was a means of bringing about reforms in the society wherever needed. It anguished him that a section of the society continued to suffer for centuries due to the Hindu caste system, the feudal social structure and the economic exploitation by the money-lenders. Anand took upon himself the responsibility of championing the cause of down—trodden sections of society, such as, untouchables, sweepers, coolies, tea-estate workers, and wrote about their problems in his novels and short stories.

Anand's *Untouchable* is the story of a sweeper boy named Bakha whose work is to clean latrines in various houses in the forenoon, and to collect chapattis from them in the afternoon. The condition of the untouchables had been so miserable and their tales of suffering so grim at the time his novel was written that hardly a moment of happiness could be found among them. In such a condition, an element of humour is unthinkable. If at all Anand has succeeded in injecting the sunlight and warmth in a rather dark novel through a subdued sense of humour, the credit goes to, what K.R. Srinivasa Iyengar calls, "Anand's sheer exuberance and zest for life" (355).

The poor people, particularly untouchables, did not have good education in the pre-Independent India, nor were they permitted to lead a normal life with decent and cultured people. Consequently, there manners and their speech patterns in everyday life were based on the conditions prevalent among the untouchables living in the outcastes' colony on the outskirts of the town. They mouthed liberal swearwords and abuses - simple, complex, and even vulgar ones—irrespective of the fact whether the son was addressing his father or vice versa. These swearwords are used by the untouchables not so much by a thoughtful choice as by way of habits and manners which were prevalent in their communities for several generations. However, in certain circumstances, an act of employing abuses against one's own people is considered not so much a sign of uncontrollable anger or discourtesy but of warm intimacy. These swearwords and abuses becomes interesting, even funny, when the reader disregards the harsh tone of the abuse-giver, his blood-shot eyes, the surcharged atmosphere, and on the contrary, in a playful mood begins to look at *the literal meanings of the swearwords and abuses,* according to which the abuse-given many times unwittingly turns out to be the abuse-receiver, evoking a lot of fun and humour.

It is quite possible that Anand had no intention of using swearwords as a device for evoking humour. His aim was to ensure the authenticity of characters and the colloquial quality of their dialogues. In order to do so, as Anand himself says, he literally translated "all the dialogues in my novels from my mother tongue" (*The King-Emperor's English, 23*). Since swearwords and abuses normally evoke anger and retaliatory feelings, it would appear paradoxical that these could be considered a source of humour at all. If swearwords and abuses were to be analyzed by the reader, some of them would appear as jokes, and when the jokes are narrated, the listener is taken to a different, alternative, and even unexpected path. It is the discrepancy between the two paths or the trickery in conveying alternative meanings among abuses which evokes humour. Norman Cousins called this process as "train wrecks of the mind meaning that wit causes us to track over to other thinking patterns and perspectives." Most of the swearwords and abuses which are used by Lakha against his son Bakha are ironically but unknowingly directed against his own self, if one were to scrutinize the literal meanings of these abuses. It is this incongruity, this inconsistency, and the ludicrousness of the whole thing that make things laughable. K.R. Srinivasa Iyengar feels that the swearwords often produce "a crude or ludicrous effect" (357). Here are some of the swearwords and abuses spewed by Lakha against his son Bakha:

1. "Get up, ohe you Bakhya, ohe son of a pig!" *(Untouchable, 15).*
2. "Are you up? Get up, you illegally begotten!" (17).
3. "Pig I Dog! You ran away I.... Illegally begotten!" (131).
4. "Son of pig! You have no care for your old father" (131).
5. "Get away, swine, run away from my presence. Don't touch that broom or I shall kill you ! Get out of my house" (132).

The above swearwords have been in use in India for centuries and one can trace some elements of wit in them. By a sudden twist, they could be presented in new, unexpected forms which evoke laughter. The more intelligent, the more ingenious twists and turns are traced in the abuses, the more surprise is created. Consequently, when the starling ludicrous implications flash upon the mental screen, they evoke humour. If one were to look at the literal meanings of above abuses, Lakha, in abusing Bakha, is actually abusing himself, or his dead wife, or his family itself. By calling Bakha the "son of a pig" or "Illegally begotten" or a pig, a dog, a swine, Lakha is abusing himself in the sense that if Bakha were to be a pig, his father too must belong to the same biological category. If Bakha were "illegally begotten," Lakha's dead wife must have had illicit sex outside marriage. A similar situation prevails when Ram Charan's mother Gulabo employs swearwords against her son, calling him "illegally begotten" and he retaliates by calling her a "bitch." Even though these swearwords are exchanged between father and son, on one hand, and mother and son, on the other, they are not uncommon among untouchables. A woman on whose doorstep Bakha had sat uses the following swearwords for him for defiling her house:

1. "Vay, eater of your masters" (80).
2. "Eater of your masters! Why didn't you shout if you wanted food?" (80).
3. But, eater of your masters! Why did you sit down on my doorstep, if you had to sit down at all? You have defiled my religion!" (81).
4. "Spoiler of my salt! Oh, how terrible! You sweepers have lifted your heads to the sky, nowadays" (81).
5. "This eater of his masters has even burnt the bread I was baking by detaining me here" (81).

Now the swearwords that the woman uses implicitly means that Bakha is a gobbler of his masters, which includes her own self. There is no humour in the swearwords themselves, but their meanings and implication make them interesting, even funny.

Normally swearwords and abuses are employed in verbal exchanges, which are uttered and forgotten. It is unusual to have them in printed form, much less in Indian writing in English, as one finds in Anand's *Untouchable,* and hence one cannot resist the temptation of analyzing them. An element of surprise is necessary for humour, which in swearwords comes from two interpretations simultaneously juxtaposed. The printed form creates two situations: one in which the characters exchange swearwords among themselves, and two in which the reader-cum-interpreter is involved. A woman, whose child was injured with a stone thrown by the defeated hockey players, showers swearwords and curses on Bakha. Rather than being thankful to him for helping the injured child, she curses him, uses the worst insulting language, and vehemently expresses her disapproval of an untouchable's act of touching her son. Bakha's silence, instead of cooling her down, accentuates her anger so much that she overwhelms him by the vials of her vituperation, as in the following swearwords curses against him:

1. "Vay, eater of your masters, Vay dirty sweeper!" she shouted. "What have you done to my son?" (129).
2. "Vay, eater of your masters! What have you done? You have killed my son!" she wailed.... "You have defiled my house, besides wounding my son!" (129).
3. "Get away, get away, eater of your masters!" she shouted at him. "May you die!" (130).

Such swearwords and abuses have been employed in many parts of the country for a long time, and more often than not people have not troubled themselves in finding out what they mean or whether they hurt the receiver or not. Some swearwords are light-hearted and are freely exchanged among the persons of low castes to show intimacy among them, particularly if they happen to be either of the same age group or belong to the same social standing. In his story "A Rumor," Anand writes about this phenomenon through the Pathan of Bariwal Woollen Mill when he was using swearwords against Basheshwar Singh. Dhandu thought "that the Pathan was abusing Basheshwar affectionately, as is the custom among intimate friends in Hindustan" (*Barber's Trade Union and Other Stories,* 59). Thus Ram Charan and Bakha exchange the light-hearted swearwords and abuses, as if they were jokes, as in the following passage:

> "Come, brother-in-law," greeted Ram Charan, blinking his lashless eyes and looking up. "I want to be your brother-in-law if you will let me be," said Bakha turning the washer-boy's light abuse into a mild joke, based on the fact that he was known to everyone to be an admirer of Ram Charan's sister.
>
> "Acha, she is being married today, so you are too late," replied Ram Charan, pleased that Bakha would never be able to make the same joke again (*Untouchable,* 39-40).

The term 'brother-in-law' in English has two Hindi equivalents—*saala* and *jija*—the former meaning a person whose sister is married whereas *jija* refers to the person who marries the other's (*sala's*) sister. Since these light-hearted abuses are being used as jokes, it is worth recalling what Freud opines about them. He distinguishes between "innocent" and '"tendentious" jokes and considers that the latter has "a sexual or aggressive context." Here both persons want to address each other as 'brother-in-law' which in sexual terms means sleeping with the other's—*sala's*—sister. In Anand's *Across the Black Waters,* Sepoy Lal Singh asks another soldier Kirpu whether the sepoys will be given land as a reward after the war, and the latter replies. "The son of land! Thank your luck that you are still alive.... Land, he says, the brother-in-law" (1955: 188). Here the term "brother-in-law" (*sala*) has been used by Sepoy Lal Singh to show his disapproval and scorn for the soldier's unrealistic expectation!

The exchange of light-hearted swearwords as jokes can better be seen in conversation between the washerwoman Gulab and Bakha's sister Sohini. Gulabo had her beauty at one time and was still loved by a Hindu gentleman. Being a washerwoman, she was superior in caste to Sohini who belonged to the sweeper's caste. Hence Gulabo looked down upon Sohini as inferior to her own self in caste but also a rival to her because the sweeper girl was more beautiful than her. Gulabo greeted Sohini with light-hearted swearwords and got some support from Waziro, the weaver's wife, who sat near her. The entire conversation among the three ladies is worth reproducing:

> "Think of it! Think of it! Bitch! Prostitute! Wanton! And your mother hardly dead. Think of laughing in my face, laughing at me who am old enough to be your mother. Bitch!" the washerwomen exploded.
>
> Sohini laughed still more hilariously at the ridiculous abruptness of Gulabo's abuse.
>
> "Ari, bitch! Do you take me for a buffoon? What are you laughing at slut? Aren't you ashamed of showing your teeth to me in the presence of men, prostitute?" shouted Gulabo. And she looked towards the old men and the little boys who were of the company.
>
> Sohini now realized that the woman was angry. "But I haven' done anything to annoy her," she reflected. "She

> herself began it all and is abusing me. I didn't pick the quarrel. I have more cause to be angry than she has."
>
> "Bitch, why don't you speak! Prostitute, why don't you'answer me?" Gulabo insisted.
>
> "Please don't abuse me," the girl said. "I haven't said anything to you."
>
> "You annoy me with your silence. Eater of dung and drinker of urine! Bitch of a sweeper woman! I will show you how to insult one old enough to be your mother." And she rose with upraised arm and rushed at Sohini (*Untouchable*, 29-30).

The entire sequence of conversation which begins with simple abuses, rises to vituperation and ends up with billingsgate. According to the *Webster New Dictionary of Synonyms*, billingsgate stresses more strongly than any other words "the offensiveness, often foul or obscene, of the language of attack" (1968: 9). The simplicity, innocence and silence of Sohini gives an impression to Gulabo that the latter is unassailable, and therefore the intensity of her desire to humiliate the sweeper girl rises in crescendo. It can clearly be observed in the above exchanges that such swearwords often end up in quarrels, though they are as quickly resolved as they are begun. Of course, the excessive use of swearwords and abuses has led many readers to criticize Anand on this point. The justification for their use, as Meenakshi Mukherjee points out in *Twice-Born Fiction,* is on the basis of realism. "The Punjabi peasantry with whom Anand's best works deal does have a large repertoire of swearwords in its ordinary conversations. It would be hypocritical to bowdlerize their speech merely because these might appear strange in the English language" (172). Of course, Mukherjee does not seem to be aware of the fun which such swearwords generate among the bystanders in real-life situations, and among readers of these dialogues, even if such reactions are far from the intended purposes.

Mulk Raj Anand in *Untouchable* gives interesting accounts—occasionally humorous—of borrowed tastes and clumsily imitated manners of the untouchables, particularly when they try to ape the white sahib and the upper class Indians. While describing these manners, Anand's intention was not to ridicule or to satirize the untouchables even if they appear to be comical and funny. With vast reserves of sympathy for them, Anand was simply presenting a realistic picture of the society in which the untouchables formed a kind of species who were biologically human, but who appeared to be socially sub-human. They have feelings and emotions, desires and dreams like other human beings but with total deprivation of means of achieving them, they resort to money—like mimicry. James Thurber points out that for him humour comes when expected "future is replaced with an unexpected future. The more unexpected, the more humorous." In Mulk Raj Anand's *Untouchable,* Bakha wants to replace his expected future of the sweeper's with the unexpected future of the white sahib's world. He must have seen that the fashion among the white sahib and the upper-class Indians was to have a neat and shapely blanket rather a shapeless quilt with shifting lumps of cotton inside, even when the blanket does not give as much warmth as the quilt does. Since Bakha wanted to live the life of the white sahib, he did not mind sacrificing many hours of sleep and comfort for the sake of "an unexpected future of 'fashun' which for Bakha was the art of wearing trousers, breeches, coat, putties and boots, among other things. He told himself: "I will look like a sahib. And I shall walk like them. Just as they do, in twos, with Chota as my companion. *But I have no money to buy things*" (*italics mine, 14*). For the satisfaction of his whim to look like a white sahib, Bakha would be willing to go to any extent, though in the absence of money, his desire can at best be termed whimsical. For whim is a trait that turns a person to be comical or amusing by appealing to the sense of ludicrous, absurdity or incongruous. Bakha buys an old jacket, an overcoat, a blanket and a new packet of 'Red Lamp' cigarettes for his use. In his ill-fitting clothes, he might look like a comical figure, a three-dimensional cartoon or a clumsily-dressed western scarecrow but he certainly makes his father angry, while his friends like Chota and Ram Charan make fun of him by calling him—'Pilpali Sahib!' They ridicule "the weight of his body, the shape of his clothes, his gait, which was bit like an elephant's, an account of his heavy swaying buttocks, and bit like a tiger's, lithe and supple" (39). Ram Charan calls Rakha and makes fun of his elder brother Bakha.

> "Don't you go! Don't go!" called Ram Charan naughtily after him. "This your brother, wants to be a 'Gentreman' and to work on the roads, but he wants you do the dirty work at the latrines."
>
> "Don't buk," said Bakha good-humouredly. "Let him go and work for a bit" (41).

Havildar Charat Singh teasingly laughed over Bakha's new uniform and said, "You are becoming a 'gentleman,' ohe Bakhya!" (19). All these derisive remarks of his friends have virtually no adverse effect on Bakha because the satisfaction he draws from the outfits makes him happy within.

Humour, according to a critic on the website of wit and humour, consists of "wit," "mirth," and "laughter"—wit, which is "a thought-oriented experience," mirth, which is "an emotionally-oriented experience," and laughter which is "a physiologically-oriented experience." What Bakha experiences here is mirth, which is an emotional experience even if other make fun of him. Mark Twain is of the opinion that humour implying mirth "is the great thing, the saving thing, after all. The minute it crops up, all our hardnesses yield, all our irritations and resentments slip away, and a sunny spirit takes their place." Bakha feels the mirth inside even if he becomes an object of fun and ridicule to others. This feeling of mirth must have been so much in Bakha in. imitating the ways of the British that he detests some of the Indian habits and manners. He was particularly ashamed of the Indian way of performing ablution—all that gargling and spitting—because he knew the Tommies disliked it. He felt amused, as an English man too might have been, to see a Hindu loosen his dhoti in order to pour some water first over his naval and then down his back in a flurry of ecstatic hymn-singing. Bakha is also opposed to the clumsy habit of taking tea by a large-section of Indians, including his father and younger brother, by making cat-like slurping sounds instead of taking it in a quiet manner.

Anand seems to have caricatured some of the characters in the novel for two possible reasons: first of all, he was trying to inject an element of humour in the novel, and secondly, he wanted to make fun of some Christian missionaries as well as individuals of upper caste society who had ridiculed Bakha—the hero of the novel. Anand makes fun of Pandit Kalinath, Havildar Charat Singh and Colonel Hutchinson, and makes fun of them by exaggerating some of their weak spots. Pundit Kalinath is a hypocrite who, while belonging to the high-caste and looking condescendingly at the untouchables, is shockingly attracted by the beauty of an untouchable's daughter Sohini! He wanted to win the sweeper girl's heart by filling her pitcher with water after drawing it from the well. But it was not an easy thing to do for him. With his skinny, hollow-cheeked, badly-wrinkled face, Pundit Kalinath required a great deal of energy to draw water from the well because "his whole life revolved round endless recitation of sacred verses and the writing of an occasional charm or horoscope with a reed pen. He exerted all his strength and strained to turn the handle" (*Untouchable,* 32). Since untouchables were not allowed to take out water from the well meant for the high caste people, Pundit Kalinath was surrounded by a large of untouchable women who begged him to pour some water into their pitchers. It at all the thought of helping a few of them, his intentions were not altruistic but selfish because he had a good eye for beautiful women but bad ears for the sounds of their requests. He had seen Sohini earlier "the fresh, young form whose full breasts, with their dark beads of nipples stood out so conspicuously under her muslin shirt, whose innocent look of wonder seemed to stir the only soft chord in his person" (39). When he asked Sohini to come and clean the courtyard of his house, "he looked long at her, rather embarrassed, his rigid respectability fighting against the waves of amorousness that begun to flow in his blood" (34). Whereas Kalinath believed that an untouchable could defile a person from a distance of sixty nine yards, he did not hesitate to molest an untouchable girl by teasing and holding her breasts!

Havildar Charat Singh is a broad-minded gentleman who does not believe in untouchability, and is quite kind towards Bakha. Anad has characterized Havildar Charat Singh as a good hockey player, a man of sound character with a balanced mind, but marked with a streak of comicality. His habit was to learn by the goal post and then to fall over the ball the moment it reached him. Thus "the number of scars he had on his body equalled in number, said the babu's son, the marks of sword and lance on the body of the Rajpoot-warrior, Rana Sanga, the conqueror of Akbar, the greatest Moghul. And the most delightful of the injuries which he had ever sustained was to have had his teeth knocked out, for he had them replaced with a row of false ones, mounted with gold. This had led to many a joke, when someone ingeniously suggested that the proverbs 'A straw in the bread of a thief' should be changed to: "Gold teeth in the mouth of the thief" (117).

The entire sketch shows that Anand is laboriously caricaturing a man of sound character in order to inject an element of humour and fun in a person in whom there is virtually no scope for these traits. However, it should not mean that Anand is deficient in humour. In his literary works, he has amply demonstrated that he is capable of writing both comedies and tragedies. K.R. Srinivasa Iyengar writes: "Anand sees life sometimes the modes fuse distractingly" (356), as can be seen in the character sketch of Charat Singh. Since there is sympathy and appreciation in Anand's sketch of Havildar Charat Singh's character, it can be considered neither ironical nor satirical. Even though Havildar Charat Singh is a Hindu gentleman, he is in sharp contrast to Pundit Kalinath by being considerate to Bakha. Anand writes in "Afterward on the Genesis of Untouchable: A Note "that in the original manuscript of the novel which he had shown to Mahatma Gandhi, the latter had asked him to remove his deliberate attempts at melodramatic contrasts of the comic and tragic motifs" (1935: 180) relating to Bakha, but may be those relating to Havildar Charat Singh and other remained. Anand's intention can at best be to make the novel interesting through comic touches rather than to distort Havildar Charat Singh's character.

Colonel Hutchinson, Chief of the local Salvation Army, is a Christian missionary for whom Anand seems to have no sympathy, nor is Bakha enamored of him. Hence if he has been caricatured, it serves Anand's both ends: to inject some comic elements in the sketch in order to bring a little cheer to the reader, and to satirize the Christian missionaries who fail to understand the psyche of the poor before persuading them for conversion of Christianity. Initially, Anand gives certain facts about Col. Hutchinson, which in Indian conditions appear somewhat peculiar. Mr. Hutchinson lived near the outcastes' colony, and to his irreligious wife he "always made the excuse that he was going out for a walk on the hills where the kingdom of Heaven was waiting to be found" (*Untouchable,* 135), whereas in reality he went to the untouchables to convert them to Christianity. Col. Hutchinson had a turban, which had made him baldish! That during his twenty years' stay in India, Col. Hutchinson could convert only five persons to Christianity and those too were from the among the dirty black untouchables. This fact rather than adding a feather to his cap—rather turban-makes a mockery of his achievements. Mrs. Hutchinson, as a barmaid before marriage, "had developed an aesthetic taste for the gem-like, glistening drops of liquor that adorned the edges of Hutchinson's moustache when he had had a drink. She had married him for that" (136). Even the method adopted by Hutchinson for converting people of Christianity is funny because he does it like a thief who would lay "himself in hiding as of yore in deep pits of fifth or behind heaps of dung, to wait for some troubled outcaste who might be tired and hungry and would listen in his despair to the gospel of Christ" (136). A pitiably thin fellow, Hutchinson had a tongue the edge of which was "like a pair of scissors which cut the pattern of Hindustani into smithereens as a parrot snips his food into bits" (137). When Bakha wishes to know who Yessuh Massih was, Hutchinson fails to explain it well; instead, he leads Bakha away with a song, leaving the latter baffled. Unable still to understand the nature of Jesus

Christ, Bakha asks Hutchinson for the third time "Who is Jesus? The same as Yessuh Messih? Who is he?" (141), but instead of satisfying Bakha's curiosity in terms easy enough for an untouchable to understand, Hutchinson sings rhythmically, which only confuses the boy. He finds Hutchinson's words as confusing as a riddle, and gets bored by the letter's act of singing hymns without understanding anything in them. Bakha had followed the Sahib because the latter had worn trousers, which "had been the dream of his life" (143). Similarly, Col. Hutchinson's explanation of how Jesus died for all, how each person is a born sinner and how Jesus's sacrifice was for the sake of humanity failed to make any sense to Bakha. When Hutchinson asked Bakha to confess, it was the proverbial last straw of confusion. How could Bakha confess when he clearly had committed neither any sin nor crime? He heard the angry outburst of Mrs. Hutchinson against her husband in which certain Hindi words like *"bhangis"* and *"chamars"* made him suspect that Mrs. Hutchinson was frowning on her husband because Bakha was an untouchable—a sweeper's son—and thought it wise to run away "as if the Colonel's wife were a witch, following him with raised arms and crooked feet" (148), while her husband was still reciting a hymn. Anand has created a perfectly comic situation by projecting a terrifying image of Mrs. Hutchinson in Bakha's mind so that he had to run away from the missionary. Conversion to Christianity was one of the three solutions discussed by Anand for eradication of untouchability and Bakha opts out of it. The funny characters of Mrs. and Mr. Hutchinson not only provide Bakha an excuse to run away from Christianity, but also give a momentary comic relief to the reader.

In Mulk Raj Anand's novels and short stories, English has been used for two different purposes—for narration and for dialogues. Whereas the English language used for narration is chaste, impeccable, grammatically correct and moves with grace and dignity, the one used for dialogues is often clumsy, ungrammatical and funny, carrying not only words of native language but also literal translations of idioms, phrases and colloquial expression which make it amusing, even comical. It is the use of English—or rather Indian English—for dialogues for which Mulk Raj Anand has periodically been criticized. It is worth remembering that Anand used Indian English in his dialogues, because he was writing about the down-trodden people who were illiterate. His protagonists are untouchables, coolies, tea plantation workers and sweepers who cannot speak chaste Hindi or Punjabi, let alone English. To make them talk in chaste English in the novel would have been the falsification or realistic situation. By giving literal translation of their native expressions or by making them use some words and expletives from the vernacular, Anand was attempting to give authenticity to his characters even if the translated dialogues appear amusing and funny to the English-knowing reader. The following expressions are worth consideration:

1. "And he was, as he said, in the language characteristic of the Indian lover, 'Dead over her" (35).
2. "I thought you were dead or something, daughter of a pig!" Lakha was shouting, "No tea, no piece of bread, and I am dying of hunger" (36).
3. "Why do you eat my head?" snapped Lakha peevishly (36).
4. And he had felt a burning desire, while he was in the British barracks, to speak the tish-mish, tish-mish which the Tommies spoke (44).
5. "Han" the boy agreed (46).
6. Tan-nan-nan-Tan, rang the bell of a bullock-cart behind him (47).

In the first expression, Anad has literally translated the common Hindi expression *"Wah us par mar gaya"* as "Dead over her" for madly falling in love with a girl. If one were to visualize the scene on one's mental screen, it would appear as if his lifeless body lay over hers, but once its Hindi equivalent strikes the reader's mind, the translation makes one laugh over the confusion. Similarly, the expression No. 3—"Why do you eat my head?" is the literal translation of Hindi expression *"Mera sir kyon khate ho?"* (Why do you bother me?), which is often used to tell somebody not to bother him. To the readers knowing English but without being familiar with the native language, Anand's translated version would appear as if the head were an edible item to be served in a plate! The sense of amusement, which is felt by the Hindi-knowing readers, becomes a matter of confusion for English-knowing reader who are not familiar with this expression in the vernacular, and at best it can be humour out of erroneous impressions.

Another trait of native language which has been used by Mulk Raj Anand in his novels is something which is uncommon in English but which evokes humour in the reader when he recognizes certain patterns of expression of the vernacular in English, that is, repetition of an adjective, a verb or a noun two or three times, rather than adding an adverb or some other part of speech. For example, we say "many many thanks" in which the word many has been used two times which may be quite common in Hindi and Punjabi but not so in English. In *Untouchable,* Bakha reflects: "The cruel crowd! All of them abused, abused, abused" (58). Lakha—Bakha's father—wanted to send a message about Bakha's serious illness to Hakimji and said, "I have been shouting, shouting" (90). In both these examples, Anand tries to show that these characters, ignorant of English, speak virtually in their own native language except for the fact that they use English words. This point has also been emphasized in the dialogues of the untouchables by making them use English words with incorrect spellings, such as "santry inspector," as also in literal translations of phrases from native language. For example, Lakh tells Bakha that Hakimji in his anger "was red and pale in turn" (92) which is a literal translation of "*Lal peela hona.*" It is the oddity of the literal translations in such cases, which evokes humour.

The hypocritical attitude and illogical activities of some of the characters make the reader chuckle by finding them not in conformity with their own characters. The shopkeeper who believes in untouchability, and who throws *jubilees* to Bakha, like a cricket ball, to avoid any physical contact with the untouchable, accepts some coins from the sweeper boy, after pouring water over them. Similarly, a woman, believing in untouchabllity, abuses Bakha for defiling her house and her religion by sitting in her doorstep, has subsequently been shown to be so dirty that when her child wants to relieve himself, she asks him to do so in the drain, and rub himself on the ground when none happened to be there to give him water at the next door.

Anand has also shown how superstitious beliefs can create funny situations. Mahatma Gandhi's parents had forbidden him from touching an untouchable. In case Gandhi happened to do so, his mother had told him "that the shortest cut to purification after the unholy touch was to cancel it by touching a Mussulman passing by" (163). This idea of retouching an untouchable in order to remove the defilement from the first touch is altogether illogical and defies common sense, and makes a sensible person smile over the follies of gullible persons. At the same time, the ignorance of a person can also evoke humour. When Bakha happens to be ignorant of the way of wearing a monocle that Iqbal Nath Sarashar wears, his speculations and reflections provoke humour:

> Bakha came back with a start and stood staring at the dignitary who had called him. The man wore a monocle in his left eye and Bakha, who had never seen anything of that kind, wondered how a single glass could remain fixed on the eye without a frame (168).

Anand's *Untouchable* is a tale of poor sweeper boy, ambitious with a jumbo dream before his eyes but without the means of placing foundations under it. Realizing this limitation, Bakha satisfies himself in imitating the superfluities of the white people, such as using a blanket, trousers and shoes, smoking a 'Red lamp' cigarettes, and talking in English—"tish-mish, tish-mish"—because this, in Bakha's view, is what the Englishmen do and which forms an ideal for him. His untouchability, his poverty, his dream and his clumsy way of imitation, on the one hand, portray his pathetic condition while, on the other, they evoke humour, which is not quite pleasant. Bakha is like a poverty-stricken, conscientious circus-joker who through his clumsy-looking, money-like activities provokes fund and humour even when his heart cries out in misery and deprivation.

WORKS CITED

Anand, Mulk Raj. Across *the Black Waters.* 1940. Kutub-Polar, Bombay, 1955.

——. "Afterward on the Genesis of Untouchable: A Note." *Untouchable* 1935. New Delhi: Arnold Heinemann Publishers, 1981.

——. *The Barber's Trade Union and Other Stories.* 1944. New Delhi: Arnold Heinemann, 1977.

——. *The King-Emperor's English.* Bombay: Hind Kitabs Ltd., 1948.

——. *Untouchable.* 1935. New Delhi: Arnold Heinemann, 1981.

Iyengar, K.R. Srinivasa. *Indian Writing in English.* 1962. New Delhi: Sterling Publishers, 1984.

Mukherjee, Meenakshi. *The Twice—Born Fiction: Themes and Techniques of the Indian Novel in English.* New Delhi: Arnold Heinemann, 1974.

Webster's New Dictionary of Synonyms. G. & C. Merriam Co., Publishers, Springfield, Mass. 1968.

19

Cultural Amnesia in Amit Chaudhuri's *A New World*

Bhagabat Nath

'Amnesia' in experimental psychology implies 'violent unconscious repression of memory,' which Freud calls 'concealment of memory.' The Freudian concept read in the colonial context gives expression to the phenomenon of 'cultural amnesia.' Cultural amnesia is an inevitable consequence of colonialism as culture of a colony is in perpetual fear of being obliterated. When the native culture branded as inferior by the colonizers is accepted as such by the colonized, the native people slowly give in to cultural amnesia. 'Cultural amnesia' is a global phenomenon, a problem faced by many post-colonial societies in the world. Immanuel Velikovsky, an American thinker, has made a probing study of 'cultural amnesia' in his book *Mankind in Amnesia.* Many Latin American writers have also dealt with this problem in their works, the most famous instance being Gabriel Garcia Marquez's *One Hundred Years of Solitude.* In it Marquez depicts the loss of linguistic memory to such an extent that the native people have to write down names of all objects in order to remember them.

Amit Chaudhury, a rising voice in Indian English fiction, presents 'cultural amnesia' in his Sahitya Akademi Award winning novel *A New World* (2000). His four novels *A Strange and Sublime Address* (1991), *Afternoon* Rag (1993), *Freedom* Song (1998) and *A New World* (2000), are slim and sensitive. *A New World,* the most provocative of his novels, depicts the predicament of a post-colonial Indian alienated from his country, his culture, his language, his parents, his wife, his everybody in his pursuit of post-colonial success. The plot of the novel is simple—A third world cosmopolitan, working in America for a living, returns to India with his young son and spends his summer holidays with his parents who live modestly in retirement in Calcutta and again goes back to the U.S.A. The story element in the novel is rather thin. Jayojit Chatterjee, more promising of the two sons of Admiral Anand and Ruby Chatterjee, does his B.A. in Economics from St. Stephens, wins a government scholarship to study abroad, but turns down the offer and goes to California for Graduate work in Economics. After the successful completion of his studies he teaches in a college at Claremont in Iowa. He marries a Bengali girl called Amala whose ancestors have migrated from Sind and settled in Jodhpur Park. Amit and Amala settle down in Arlington and have a son after three years of their marriage. After the baby's birth they lose interest in each other and their marriage breaks. Amala runs off with her gynaecologist and lives with him in San Diego in Southern America. After eight years of protracted legal battle both in American and Indian courts the couple get a divorce and Jayojit wins custody of the child for the summer days only. Deep in the heat of April Jayojit visits his parents living in Sunny Park Apartment at Ballygunge in Calcutta with his eight year old, very American son, Vikram to spend his summer vacation and returns to America in June.

'Cultural amnesia' is implicitly manifest in the depiction of Bengali life, customs and affinities, and in the monotonous repetitive details of the engagements of the Chatterjees. The crux of the novel is neither economics nor emigration nor man-woman conflict nor adultery that the novel apparently touches upon nor the existential dilemmas of 'forlornness, anxiety and despair' that the immigrants grapple with but the trivialities of everyday existence beginning from the arrival of Jayojit at his parents' residence till he boards the plane for America. Chaudhuri has no conflict to resolve, no-novelty to explore, no nostalgia for the unattainable, no anguish of personal loss and what is more, there is even no suspense and surprise to engage the readers. The major bulk of the novel consists of sentimental rendering of three generations of post-colonial Bengali Babus but the delineation lingers mostly on mundane banalities. It begins with the petty everyday life of the old Chatterjees—what they eat, how they dress in different times of the day, how they spend their leisure, how they look after their son and grandson, how they remember their old acquaintances, the life they spent in the army cantonments with privileges of high military rank; how Mrs. Chatterjee prepares delicacies for her son and grandson and how indolently she treats her grandson. There is a vivid account of Jayojit's life with his parents—how he chats laconically with his ailing father, resists his mother's dainty dishes for fear of gaining weight, how he visits his bank, confirms his return ticket, encashes his traveller's cheques, converts them into fixed deposits; finally how young Bonny frightened by the 'foreign' local kids retreats to dinosaur games and walks the Calcutta streets with his father. Occasional references to glamours of American life add pleasant deviations to monotony of life at Ballygunge, to the din and bustle of the market places at the adjoining Gariahat, traffic jams, irresponsible and indifferent behaviour of the people at government offices and banks, and the squalor and poverty around. Subroto Roy's remarks on the content of the novel is revealing:

> The bulk of this book is, however, not about adultery or America's Indian immigrants or economics, as the author and publisher have projected it to be. The bulk has to do with the author speaking as he has done before, sometimes in excruciatingly tedious detail, about his own life as he has lived it in Calcutta's upper middle class Sunny Park Apartments, half way between the traditional Bengali area of Gariahat Market and the Muslim/Anglo Indian area of Park Crius and Park Street (*The Literary Criterion*, 10).

I am inclined to agree with Valerie Miner's observation on the depressing mood of the novel which is very poignant:

> Reading the novel is like living inside someone afflicted with clinical depression. One numbingly, unsatisfactory day opens into the next as the increasing heat and

> humidity predict monsoon. Even the vocabulary descends into a dull vagueness about "someones" and "somewheres" (*Span*, 30).

The dichotomy between the two worlds (the First World and the Third World, according to postcolonial terminology), becomes evident to Jayojit when he lands in Calcutta in mid April. "The heat had just become intolerable it was the middle of April. Outside birds cried continuously, sharp, clear obstinate cries" *(A New World, 8)*. He mumbles his disgust for the hot, humid and shabby, Calcutta. Soon he unpacks his survival kit from America:

> Next, he unzipped the shoulder bag and retrieved his shaving things and his and Vikram's toilet accessories, Aquafresh toothpaste, Head and Shoulders shampoo, Bodyline deodorant, a cylinder of Old Spice shaving foam, a Backwood Insect cutter which he'd bought in case of mosquitoes; these things gleamed the most and looked the most foreign and desirable; even the toothbrushes were different and, curving oddly, seemed to belong to the future and some fragile, opulent culture (17-18).

'Cultural amnesia' is symbolised by indifference of the apartment ambience and monotony and fixedness of life in the flats. Families immured in the apartment have exclusive privacy of their own and the relationship of the residents with one another is limited to a perfunctory, "How are you?" Even inside the family the bond is slender and fragile. Description of Jayojit's relationship with his parents is revealing:

> They—Jayojit and his father—communicated, except for a few words and sentences, in English, establishing a rapport, a bluff friendship, which excluded the tenderness of the mother-son relationship—the latter finding expression in the mother's homely, slightly irritating Bengali, and talk centered round questions such as whether her son was hungry, or whether he had a bath (6-7).

Relationship of the Chatterjees with their younger son Ranajit is equally formal and culturally incongruous:

> The thought of his other son, the younger one, Ranajit, married (happily, he hoped) for four years and living in the arborous suburb Vasant Vihar in Delhi, disturbed him only remotely, as would a story he was reading with interest, but mainly to get to the end. No sign of children as yet; his daughter-in-law, Anita, was twenty seven years old; couples waited and waited these days for the opportune moment to arrive as if it were some kind of secret, as if they were gamblers hedging their bets endlessly (67-68).

'Cultural amnesia' is explicit in the American context too. There is conspicuous ignorance about the dates of the main action. Summer holidays in America begin with the Memorial Day at the end of May and end with Labour Day in late August. But Jayojit and his son are holidaying in Calcutta between April and June. Ignorance of American social life leads to fantasy. Amala, Jayojit's wife, decides upon adultery with her gynaecologist two years after the birth of her son because 'love making' with her husband dried up. She gets involved with the doctor, 'a not unpleasant looking man in his forties,' 'balding slightly, and surely not charismatic.' It is "difficult, almost impossible, to imagine how any woman in her right mind could prefer him to Jayojit" (57). She has a strange explanation for her decision: "He was kind to me" (57). Such a situation borders on fantasy. Expectant mothers are to call on their gynaecologist for a few minutes after waiting for an hour or two. There is invariably a nurse present with them and the experience is never pleasant. It is unimaginable that Amala would get involved with her doctor. Moreover an American doctor who runs off with his patient is accused of professional misconduct and might lose his license. The last thing in the mind of a gynaecologist in America is adultery with his patient at the risk of his own marriage and profession; the first thing often in his mind is sneak in some leisure to go fishing with his family.

Portrayal of American life is rather casual and expressive of 'certain fixed ideas' about life 'over there.' Jayojit's life in

America, which his mother cannot conceive of, delineates Chaudhury's idea of an immigrant Indian in America:

> She could not know of his secret life in that continent, of driving down the motor way, going to the supermarket, filling up a trolley with things, his orphanhood and distance from his country and parents, and that of other people like him, wandering around the aisles of the supermarket in shorts, with wives, or perhaps alone, with the ex-wife somewhere completely else, running into each other and saying 'How are you? Still around? 'His mother could not even imagine it' (24).

References to celebrities like Mahatma Gandhi, Jawaharlal Nehru, Indira Gandhi, Rajiv Gandhi, Henry Kissinger, Dr. Karan Singh, Margaret Trudeau, Jacquiline Onassis and the Nobel laureate Amartya Sen appear to be preposterous. Chaudhuri has tried to depict the life of a 'Non-Resident Indian,' a promising economist Jayojit, which seems to have discreet resemblance with Amartya Sen and denied by the author himself. It is evident Jayojit was asked by the waiters in a club:

> But Mr. Chatterjee, do you know Amartya Sen? He stopped bothering telling people he was 'Dr. Chattaterjee.' Sen supposedly introduced as a conversation-opener was, for him, a conversation-stopper. Really he and Sen had nothing in common (given, the fact that they were both Bengali, and economists), except that, now, they had had the experience of a failed marriage as well. Sen, with chastening resilience, had married again, while Jayojit was still trying to grope for a balance in the second phase of his life, and the idea of marriage seemed to him to involve too much spiritual effort (178).

Gandhi has been mentioned to have been deprived of the Nobel Prize on the ground that, 'It's more politics than anything else.' Dr. Karan Singh interviews the hero for a scholarship to Oxford which he does not avail. He is described to have 'dark feminine eyes' and a 'mellifluous' voice. Depiction of these real life character appears ridiculous.

The sum up, Amit Chaudhury does not make the most of both the worlds—the Third World and the First World—but creates a new sociological reality, a perilous territory of not belonging—a new world where every character is a refugee. This world assumes that the most important events of life are not necessarily grand, spectacular or catastrophic but the apparently small and prosaic ones of everyday life. For Chaudhury 'life insists on small movements' and there can be no final place in terms of 'space' in life. Appropriately his hero Jayojit just before boarding his plane to America remembers moodily the Spirit of the Upanishadas and recites to himself: "He moves, and he moves not... He is near, and yet he is far" (195).

WORKS CITED

Chaudhury, Amit. *A New World.* London: Picador, 2000.

Miner, Valerie. "Indian Writers in English." *Span,* January/February, 2002.

Roy, Subroto. "Analysing Amit Chaudhury's *A New World.*" *The Literary Criterion, 36/1 & 2, 2000.*

20 A Critique of Vikram Chandra's *Red Earth and Pouring Rain*

Rabinarayan Sasmal

Vikram Chandra's debut novel *Red Earth and Pouring Rain* (1995), won for him Commonwealth Writers' Best First Book Prize in 1996 for its innovations in theme and technique. Like Shashi Tharoor, Chandra has tried to re-invent the ancient myth in the contemporary context. He advances towards globalization and keeps himself in touch with Eurocentric American perspectives. The grand narrative of *Red Earth and Pouring Rain* dates back to the classical past of Indian heritage and to the roots of our living.

Critics like Edward Said, Homi K. Bhabha and Gayatri Spivak Chakravarty have inspired the novelists to write more and more about cultural encounters between the East and the West. An ambitious and extraordinary first novel of Chandra is above all about telling the stories. It explores history and adventure—passion and power. The fiction intermingles history, myth, folklore and contemporaneity. The novelist goes beyond the post-Rushdic movement and magic realism.

Red Earth and Pouring Rain is a tale told by a young American returned Indian student Abhay and typing monkey, Sanjay. As Salvador writes:

> *Red Earth and Pouring Rain* is composed of hundreds of interwoven told, retold, copied, translated, interspersed stories. Its several characters and narrators are representatives of a huge range of times, spaces, races,

> nationalities, religions, age and gender. Moreover, they come from the animal, human and divine orders (102).

The novel includes in fragments many stories of independent value. The adventurous historical stories of the Franco-Savoyard Benoit de Boigne (1751—1830), the German Walter Reinhardt (1720—1778) and the Irish George Thomas (1756—1802), Sikander of Moghul Empire in the nineteenth century, Modhoji Sindhia, Lord Welsley and a few others are set against the framework of the novel. Besides historical characters, the divine personages from the Hindu pantheon like Hanuman, Ganesha and Yama make the fiction an admixture of history and myth. Along with them Abhay of the contemporary world marches together to give the fiction the flavour of contemporaneity.

The story of the novel goes like this: Abhay, back in India from America after attending college in California is disturbed and alienated. He shoots and seriously wounds an old white-faced monkey that has been stealing from his parents' gardens for years. As a result of his wound, the monkey recalls his past life and states that he is the reincarnation of a nineteen century Brahmin poet named Sanjay Parasher. Deprived of human voice, the monkey Sanjay actually typewrites in order to communicate. Three important Hindu deities arrive on the scene: Yama, the king of Death, Hanuman, the ape-god and the protector of poets, and Ganesha, the elephant god of wisdom. Because of the divine interference, a vital contract is signed. Yama agrees with a condition that Sanjay will stay alive only if he entertains an audience with his stories. Thus, the humanized monkey begins a tale, the tale that had been narrated to Sandeep by the mysterious woman in the clearing, the tale that Sandeep had narrated to the men at the ashram where he was resting and through Sanjay the novelist Chandra tells the readers a story.

Historical events follow the eventful life of Abhay in America and in India as well. Abhay, an American educated Indian loves Amanda, an American who fails to adjust with Indian way of life. After his examinations, Abhay returns to India. Amanda, too, accompanies him. In Bombay they stay in the Rugby Hotel on the Matheran hill station. She suffers from cultural shock. She says to Abhay, "I should go home" and "I'm sorry." Thus, they are separated from each other willingly. In the airport the parting scene is very pathetic. Their conversation is touching. As Chandra puts it:

> When I said goodbye to Amanda in Bombay she said, I'll see you soon, in a few months, and I said yes. But I really didn't know, I felt lost, all I knew was that I had to go home too... Now as we stood in the airport I was telling her that I would come back to the States, that we would be together again.
>
> "I'll see you soon," I said.
>
> "Are you angry with me?"
>
> "No" (515).

Abhay comes back home by train. While remembering America in his discussion with his mother, the white faced monkey takes away his jeans. Hence out of anger he shoots the monkey and the result is *Red Earth and Pouring Rain.*

Abhay and Amanda belong to a new generation. Their love is unlike the love of Sanjay for Gul Jahaan, of Reinhardt for Zeb-ul-Nissa, and of Janvi for Jahaj Jung (George Thomas). Abhay's separation from Amanda is symbolic. The East and the West are poles apart. Kyrie represents the negation of moral values in American society.

The novel moves from microcosm to macrocosm. It deals with "dharma," "karma," rebirth and eternal life. Soul is imperishable. The title of the book bears the Upanisadic philosophy of the existence of human life. The Universe is constituted of *Panchabhutas: Kshiti, Op, Tez, Maruta, Byoma* (earth, water, air, fire, space). 'Red' stands for fire and emotion; 'earth' for soil and flesh, 'Pouring' for sky and air; and 'rain' for water and blood. The characters like Hanuman, Ganesha and Yama are from the space. The word 'and' in the title of the book symbolically connects earth and heaven, human and divine, body and soul and finite and infinite.

In this epic novel, Chandra conceives everything in a grand style. Divine characters, historical heroes, national problems of

India, trans-cultural relationships and eternal life are set in the tapestry of the book. It is a metafictional narrative that introduces magic realism. Sanjay a white-faced monkey communicates his feelings through a typewriter. Chandra has recreated the past in the present context and harks on pre-life and after-life. His language, both polished and chiseled, is the most outstanding contribution to Indian English fiction. He has used many Hindi words to show how code-mixing fits well into the texture of the novel. Even Yama speaks, "Sab Lal ho Jayega" to Sanjay during Janvi's immolation and performing a 'Sati.' Sanjay's sacrifice of tongue to Yama is another pivotal theme in the fiction. Both the sacrifices are related to social life of India—Sanjay sacrifices his tongue to Yama to gain immortality. It symbolizes the sacrifice of the mother-tongue for the love of the other tongue. As Salvador points out:

> Sanjay sacrifices his mother-tongue in order to speak English, to be able to communicate with the colonizers on an equal basis (106).

The learning of English is a colonial process that involves language as a mechanism of oppression. In this context, Sanjay represents the painful learning of a foreign language, the colonizer's tongue. Abhay represents the contemporary hybrid and migrant experience while shuttling between the United States and India.

The fifth book witnesses the war between the colonizers and the colonized. Sanjay kills Sikander for the sake of his motherland, wages Sepoy Mutiny of 1857, and at last dies to incarnate himself again in the form of an animal, the white-faced monkey of the present tale, the present story-teller Sanjay. The time has changed. The British have left India but the colonizer's language retains the prestige of the colonial days and people still look up to the West for guidance. That is why Abhay went to the U.S.A. In these fictional retellings readers meet with stories of bravery, romance and miracles as well as the story of the colonization of South Asia by the Raj. Key events retold here include the fall of the Moghul Empire and the Mutiny of 1857. In this way the novel bears two primary qualifications: one an exceptional literary work and the other a thoughtful political critique.

In *Red Earth and Pouring Rain* Chandra depicts us heroes and heroines who are vibrant, warm and very real. His prose is lively as his approach is an admixture of levity and seriousness. He employs complex literary tools wonderfully and skillfully. Chandra has gathered up in his narrative of love and lives, war and wonders, a lot of questions—political, spiritual, philosophical and cultural. The book is Indian in sensibility and Indian in style. With surprising dexterity and rhythm, the setting relocates back and forth between India, North America, Ireland and England.

The fictional world of Vikram Chandra has variety of expression. The powerful imagery like 'red earth' and 'pouring rain' enhance the grandeur of the book. Most of the time Sanjay utters, "Sab Lal ho Jayega." Towards the end of the same symbolic words are spoken: "The whole map is red now. Everything is red." Red is a symbol of beauty, bloodshed, war, death and destruction. The funeral pyre is red. The battlefield is red. Human blood is red. Mother's vermilion on her forehead is red. The mouth of goddess Kali is red. 'Red' is not only the sign of destruction but also an auspicious sign of newness and new beginning. The earth and rain are complementary to each other. It is natural that the world is a circle and things go on in a cyclic process. 'Red earth' follows 'pouring rain' naturally. It is a deep gut-response, as much in relief from the heat as in recognition of the life-giving properties of water. An entire aesthetic evolves round the artistic tapestry, be it mythical or historical or contemporary.

WORKS CITED

Chandra, Vikram. *Red Earth and Pouring Rain*. New Delhi: Penguin Books, 1995.

Das, Bijay Kumar. *Post Modern Indian English Literature*. New Delhi: Atlantic Publishers, 2003.

Salvador, Dora Sales. "Vikram Chandra's Constant Journey: Swallowing the World DSS." *Journal of English Studies*, 2000.

Teverson, Andrew. *Literary Encyclopedia:* Chandra Vikram <http://www.Litencye.Com/php/Speople.Php?rec=true&VID=817>.

21

A Critique of Vikram Seth's *An Equal Music*

Bhagabat Nayak

The novels of the 1980s are chiefly metro-centric and the texts of Salman Rushdie, Shashi Tharoor, Amitav Ghosh, Githa Hariharan, Vikram Chandra, Vikram Seth and many others consciously present multiple perspectives on fragmented identities. While global migration, multi-cultural commitment positioning of identities dominate the theme of global literature, Seth's works may be analysed in terms of what Homi Bhabha calls 'hybridity.' As a "roaming intellectual" in his migration, he is associated with "expansiveness and elsewhereness" and has experienced life in different commingled cultures. In his "migrancy of the mind" and mapping the culture in imperialism and worldliness, he has alienated his characters from the inter-community mosaic for their meta-identity. In the "fluidities of the contemporary world," in the multiple affiliations and associations in the disparate plurality he has made his novels common signifiers that arise from an international culture, world citizenship and Post-Perestoika age.

Vikram Seth's *The Golden Gate* (1986), an experimental novel in verse form, ignores the immigrant history of Asian communities in San Francisco. His construction of 'home' in *A Suitable Boy* (1993), in the tradition of Pushkin's *Eugene Onegin* and in the dimension of Tolstoy's *War and Peace* is at variance with the fantasy of the homeland as mediated in the works of Salman Rushdie, M.G. Vassanji, Meera Syal and Hanif Kureishi. Seth presents magic realism *in An Equal Music* (1999), to supersede the restrictive boundaries of nationalism and distinct cultural registers through a philosophy of "universal humanism." He expresses an overriding concern for the "human race" by investing love in the story with the fire of passion for music.

An Equal Music appears to be very much unmusical to the readers ignorant of the technicalities of music but the work is outstanding, absorbing, irresistible, tense and deeply moving as the readers show sympathy for the characters engrossed in a world of music. Seth has set the novel in the West and has chosen all the European Characters and presents their problems in their context. Seth's academic career in India or professional career in London has no links with the novel but his passion for music prompted him to study Khayal under Pandit Amarnath at Sri Ram Bharati Kalakendra during his short visit to India. Prior to this his familiarity with Hindustani classical music is evident in *The Golden Gate* and in *A Suitable Boy*. The ghazal performances by Sweeda Begum in *A Suitable Boy* expresses his intimate interaction with the musician and the audience. He has also admitted in many interviews that his interest in Western music grew "in the migrancy of his mind." Music is the core of the novel and it has shaped his creative mind with considerable ease from medieval Chinese poetry to San Francisco Yuppiedom, and from the Hindi belt in North India to the world of Bach and Beethoven in Britain and Vienna.

An Equal Music, "a masterpiece" (De, 6) was published in the same year as that of Rushdie's *The Ground Beneath Her Feet* but the problematics of affiliation in the text rejects the theme of cultural displacement in a new emergent cosmopolitan transnationalism. 'Music' is the core of *An Equal Music:* "In fact music pervades the whole of the novel and admittedly, a knowledge of Western classical music will help one towards a better understanding of the work" (Mishra, 2001: 84). Seth narrates the story of love of an emotional volatile musician, Michael Holden and his passionate relationship with music and deep attachment to Carlo-Tanoni violin which was given to him by his mentor benefactor Mrs. Fromby. The thirty-seven-year-old Michael is the second violinist in an English quartet called Maggoire who plays music in the quartet and supplements his income by teaching violin to rather uninterested students with a bitter realisation: "Leave music to those who can afford indulgence. In twenty years no butcher's son will be violinist, no, nor daughter, neither" (346). Michael is deliberately dismissive of the music of the masses—the music that cab drivers play.

The story begins with the city of London where Michael, a violinist from Rochdale plays for the quartet and gives music lessons to a group of not so-interested pupils. In spite of his desultory affair with one of his pupils he does not forget his memories of love for Julia, a talented pianist whom he had loved intensely as a student in Vienna. Both of them were students then under their teacher Carl Kail. Carl, a perfectionist spotted the rich potential in Michael and urged Michael to preserve his uncompromising nature. Once Michael had a row with Carl over his style of playing piano. When Julia took her maestro's side they had a bitter quarrel. Julia accused Michael of being unable to stand authority in any form. Michael equally viewed Julia's defence of Carl as "an unbearable betrayal on her part" (82). Anger, frustration and betrayal made him to abandon his studies in Vienna and he returned to England. Now he lives like a fugitive even after ten years but in retrospect realises the truth in Julia's accusation and repents for his double loss—loss of a venerable teacher and a beloved. When he tries to reestablish contact with her much later, she refuses to call back or write. He learns now to compromise with his lot and to live a life in "bearable aloneness" (56) only because of his music. Michael remembers his attachment to music "deep as first love, and wild with all regret." "Seth's story of love and loss can hold its own the vicinity of that marvellous line" (Carey, 1999: 13).

It is on his way home after his successful mission, Michael suddenly spots Julia for a few fleeting moments. But his suffering doubles when he learns that Julia has been married to an American banker, James Hansen for nine years and they have a little son. This accidental meeting with Julia at Wigmot Hall helps them to meet furtively and send fazes. This kind of re-union in their lives brings enough changes because of their love for music. As every lover is elated by his beloved's success Michael is overjoyed when Julia is chosen to join the quartet for a concert in Vienna and Venice to perform Schubert's "The Trout." On their brief tour to Vienna and Venice they become nostalgic for their past love and desire to relive in the intimacy of the past. The magical backdrop of concert halls in Vienna and the canals of Venice are captured by Seth's evocative prose in the part five and six of the novel. When Julia remembers that she has her husband and son in London she comes back to her reality and returns instantly as she is reluctant to jeopardize her family relationship.

A number of issues—rift between parents and child regarding choosing a career, agony resulting from being thrown out of one's native place, guilt-feeling associated with extramarital affairs, sexual jealously and above all bitter sense of loneliness play havoc in Michael's life. He decided to go to music school in London to learn classical music. Michael returns to the small town of Rochdale when it has become the victim of industrial planning and the council places a compulsory purchase order with his father's butcher shop. The references to his childhood are important but Michael's desire to escape his part is largely responsible for his present psychological state of mind. He remembers how he had begged Mrs. Fromby to teach him to play the violin and how he got determined to cut off links, with the "distressed and constrained town" (22).

Michael and Julia have lots of difference. But when Michael comes to know the painful secret of Julia's life from her son, he tries to understand Julia's problem. Now Michael can tolerate Julia's passivity for his love but cannot tolerate her love and longing for her family. The night before Julia leaves for London to join her family she becomes restless and uncertain; she feels guilty and afraid. Her choice of an unmusical businessman-husband and rejection of the volatile and moody Michael as well as her denunciation of passion for family and social order is the thematic preoccupation of Seth. The similar subject on music and social themes dominate the subject matter of Rushdie's *Ground Beneath Her Feet* and Shashi

Deshpande's *Small Remedies.* Seth deals with some of the problems of writing about music "by putting music back into the people who perform it... You come at the music through their hopes, quarrels, ambitions, loves, professional contacts they have to make with agents, critics, instrument makers, players..." (Carey, 1999: 13). A lover of "serious music with social obligations and weaknesses can aspire to the condition of music by comprehending this."

Good music is good music. Michael enjoys this in Julia's playing the Art of Fugue to a packed hall. He comments "music, such music, is a sufficient gift" (381) which cannot be possibly formed in the technicalities of a musician. Michael believes in the "fine tradition of music", "where art and literature and music are absorbed without effort or explanation-from speech and travel, from books and records from the very walls and shelves" (81). Music has its objective existence of beauty and it can produce the sensation of the sublime and the eternal. Unfolding the emotional intricacy of Michael and Julia, Seth projects his rare insight into Julia's emotional distress and Michael's psychotic existence. When Julia wants to move on with her life, Michael exists in the past, having monologues with himself; "I am consumed by past love, its germs long embedded, half contained,... I am eaten by futile pity" (247). He broods over his despair at his loss of Julia and has fits of melancholy and panic attacks. He returns to Rochdale listening to the death news of Mrs. Fromby and plays the "Art of Fugue" in memory of her. Though the violin was bequeathed to him by Mrs. Fromby, despair and depression aggravates his mind for fear of her nephew's claiming. For the twelve years he has his companionship with this instrument but the bond between him and the instrument cannot be severed. He cannot play music on someone else's as his relationship with the instrument is the quintessence of his life. In the backdrop of his love it has inspired and consoled him much for loss and has gained much during the fractured sentiments of his mind. The music he has played with the violin has sanitized, civilised and sensitivised his finer sensibilities as a social being music is not only his career but also it serves the purpose for his character. He is almost ascetic for music and continues his endeavour to invigorate his life. His sensuality is redefined in music as it has diverted his mind towards enjoyment of senses. It has also magnified his emotional appeal to produce a feeling of bliss. For him if woman (Julia) is the finest creation of nature, music is the finest creation of man for a bliss.

The novel ends with Julia playing the "Art of Fugue" to a packed hall. Michael has been watching her from her seat in the balcony, listens to her music. He imagines the beauty of her music as clean, lovely, inexorable, phrase across phrase, phrase echoing phrase, the incomplete, the unending and "It is an equal music" (380). He enjoys a perfect peace and bliss and walks away, grateful for having had the privilege of hearing the excellence of Julia's music. In happiness he says, "It is enough, it is to be blessed enough, to live from day to day, and to hear such music-not too much, or the soul could not sustain it from time to time" (381).

It is difficult to polarise love and music in An Equal Music. The blues of music operates the plethora of love in the romantic oeuvre of their life. Music has electrified their sensuality and served a creative spark to their mind. Michael is deeply involved in music. Music has made them aware of commitment for each other and they move from normality to abnormality when they violate the Christian morality in their extra-marital relationship. Through music they perceive, touch, hear, smell and taste the milieu in which they live. The ten years of separation makes them achy, tense and unhappy but during this time music serves as an antidote for their physical and psychological strains. It is their intellectual property they want to preserve with the patent of love. In their decade long separation they have a metaphysical union. Music serves as the fire and flavour of their life and they are the Mars and Venus, a match made in heaven. Through music they have different orientations of life. Michael's rhapsody for piano or concerto is a combination of symphony and a sonata.

The sociology of music in *An Equal Music* is seemingly an outside ideology devoid of ethics or multi-cultural presence.

Seth has contextualised music in love and life but seemingly it is an outside ideology and Michael listens to this music to escape the ideology. The description of music is so real and easy for a lay reader to be familiar with fugues, adagios and allegros to understand and review the finer nuances, stylistic feature and texture of western classical music. One can hear with rapture, the consummate performance of Schubert's Trout or appreciate the quartet's use of present action of Bach's Art of Fugue. Seth illustrates music in the textural world of the novel as "fragmentary, allusive, and romantic." He remarks "music to me is deeper than speech" and "aspires to the condition of music" by rewriting the variegated textures of music and poetry (Chew, 1999: 22). The world of music in the novel is different in degree than that of Ustad Majeed Khan teaching Malati in *A Suitable Boy.* "It is a question of exposure. Exposure and with bit of guidance" (Seth, 1993: 624) which is quite similar in the performance of Bach's Art of Fugue in *An Equal Music.* The quartet produces "the sensation of the sublime and the eternal" music with aesthetic pleasure. Michael is conscious of his relationship with the instrument and the class and kind of music he plays. He envies Julia for being socially privileged, and therefore being brought up in a world unreachably different from his own, "where art and literature and music are absorbed without effort or explanation from speech and travel, from books and records, from the very walls and shelves" (81). He reminds her that she didn't have to earn her living with her fingers. He thinks "a fine tradition of music" can only be imported through institutional patronising and training to the grammar school students. Seth also believes that this tradition can only be preserved by its lovers' affiliation and association to it. He defines Michael's first love for music with that of his for Julia on equal terms.

While searching the source of the novel it is known that Seth was walking across a London Park on a very wet day with his companion Philipe saw someone staring at his own image in the water of serpentine river in Hyde Park. "As they wonder about the man Phillipe suggests that he might be a musician, and thereby the novel took root" (Vidyasagar, April 1999).

It appears that Seth was increasingly impressed and deeply engrossed with this narcissist and thus the novel took the form on the theme of music and love. The title of the novel is derived from John Donne's 'Valediction' describing life after death: "... where there shall be no noise nor silence, but one equal music, no fears no hope, but one equal possession, no foes no friends, but one equal communion and identity, no ends nor beginnings, but one equal eternity" (epigraph to the text). However, it appears Donne's phase of leave taking "yields apt meanings" as it brings out the balance between the unheard music in Julia's heard matching the sound of her playing. Michael's love for Julia, thus is not characterized by the balance, harmony and tranquillity marked by that "one equal communion and identity" in Donne's Valediction.

An Equal Music is about music and the musicians, Seth describes their love life, trials and tribulations and struggle for existence. Their marriage of true minds has become possible only on the strings of their violins. Music has embedded love in them without which he ground beneath their feet slips. Even though the novel is devoid of Indian ethics it will elicit the English reader's response to an Indian "locating a story in the Hyde Park and peopling it with non-Indian characters" (Sharma, 1990: 10). The novel ends with an appropriate emphasis on music. Seth rightly concludes:

> Music, such music, is a sufficient gift. Why ask for happiness, why hope not to grieve? It's enough, it is to be blessed enough, to live from day to day and to hear such music—not too much, or the soul could not sustain it—from line to line (1999: 381).

WORKS CITED

Carey, John. "Vikram Seth's Music for Mind." *The Sunday Times of India*, April 2, 1999.

Chew, Shirley. "The Art of the Fugue." *Times Literary Supplement,* April 2, 1999.

De, Shobha. "There is something about Vikram." *The Sunday Observer*, April 11—17, 1999.

Mishra, Gopa Ranjan. "The Horizon of Vikram Seth's Fiction." *The Ravenshaw Journal of English Studies* 11:12, (January-December) 2001: 77-89.

Seth, Vikram. *A Suitable Boy*. New Delhi: Penguin Books, 1993.

——. *An Equal Music*. New York: Broadway Books, 1999.

Sharma, L.K. "*A Suitable Boy* unfolds *An Equal Music*." *The Sunday Times*, April, 1999.

Vidyasagar, N. (interview) "In the Business of Books." *The Times of India*. April, 1999.

22 The Contributions of Manoj Das and Ruskin Bond to Indian English Short Story

Bilkesh Parveen

It is said that a great writer writes primarily for his own times and his own community but the greater writer transcends his time and place. A writer begins with the 'locale' of his own province but transforms it into universality. The regional or the native element has a place in literature, but a writer worth his salt must transform it into the universal. In a rather neglected essay published in 1922, under the title "The Three Provincialities," Eliot has said that provinciality is not discarded by a writer but transmuted into universality. A writer like Joyce has raised what is provincial to the level of the international and thus, produced literature for the Irish as well as the European public. In a post-script to the essay written in 1950, Eliot writes:

> True literature has in it something which can be appreciated by intelligent foreigners who have a reading knowledge of the language, and also something which can only be understood by the particular people living in the same place as the author (*Littcrit*, 27: 1-2, 2001: 22-23).

This is precisely what great literature does. And this explains the appeal of great writers to the reader of all times and places.

Manoj Das and Ruskin Bond are well known Indian English writers in the postmodern period (It is a coincidence of history that both of them were born in 1934). Both are primarily known as writers of short fiction though they have made their mark in other genres of India English literature as well. It is interesting to note that both of them have won Sahitya Akademi Award for their collection of stories (Manoj Das in Oriya and Ruskin Bond in English). Ruskin Bond's *Our Trees Still Grow in Dehra* is the only collection of short stories in English to have been honoured by the Sahitya Akademi with its Annual Award for the year, 1992 so far.

Indian English short story owes its origin to Shoshee Chunder Dutt's *Realities of Indian Life: Stories Collected from the Criminal Reports of India* published in London in 1885. The Indian English short story, though appeared on the Indian literary scene after poetry and fiction, has exhibited a wide range of subjects in the years preceding Indian Independence in 1947. The short story writers drew inspiration from the ancient Indian fables and tales, such as the Panchatantra and the Jataka Tales. Kathasaritsagara has fascinated the Indian English short story writer endlessly.

The panorama of Indian English short story spanning over a period of seven decades (i.e. from 1930 to the end of the twentieth century) reveals that thematic range of this body of literature is very wide in keeping pace with the contours of change in Indian society.

The great trio-Mulk Raj Anand, R.K. Narayan and Raja Rao who have popularised Indian English novels in the nineteen thirties, have also contributed substantially to the growth and development of Indian English short story during that period. They were followed by K.A. Abbas, Khushwant Singh, Manjari Isvaran. The two great epics, *The Ramayan* and *The Mahabharat* contributed immensely to the thematic growth and range of Indian English short story. For example, stories like Raja Rao's "Kanakapala," Mulk Raj Anand's "Five Short Fables," Manjari Isvaran's "Illumination" and R.K. Narayan's "At the Portal"—to mention only a few of the Indian English early short stories—are based on the fables.

Manoj Das, a bilingual (I should say, an ambilingual) writer has more than 14 collections of short stories in English to his credit. Though Manoj Das depicts love as a theme in some of his stories, human love is not his primary concern in his short fiction. Even when he depicts love in his various aspects he delves into human psyche and portrays characters with accuracy and authenticity. Unrequited love seems to have attracted Das' attention more than the consummated love. However, he excels in other areas such as the depiction of the contemporary society, politics, superstition and above all in coming to terms with reality. And he has built a large number of stories on these themes.

Love is one of themes in his short stories. He has depicted various aspects of love in artistic terms. "The Crocodile's Lady" is an unusual love story between the crocodile and crocodile's lady. This is not a story of human love in the accepted sense of the term. He depicts an unusual relationship of love and affection between the crocodile and crocodile's lady. The crocodile came to the rescue of the crocodile's lady when the latter was unhappy with her life and wept bitterly. She gave her a mantra to recite to get back her human form. The crocodile suggested her that the mantra should not be recited when the latter was in deep water. The crocodile's lady seems to have forgotten her parents and was completely immersed in love. They began to swim from river to river in joy and ecstasy. The tragic end came when the crocodile's lady escaped from the crocodile's control. The latter being a true lover climbed the embankment and was killed.

"The Love Letter" is ironical. It is about the reaction of some people to a supposedly love letter written by Geeta. Goutam, the researcher, found a letter which was actually a scrap of blank paper. When he pretended that he had discovered a love letter of Geeta many people wanted to establish their claim on it. What is surprising that persons like Choudhury, her father's friend became a claimant to this letter. Prof. Das was another claimant. Another person who wanted to establish his claim was Prof. Dhar. All of them claimed to be close to Geeta and threatened Goutam with dire consequences. In the end came the bathos (anti-climax) when it was revealed that the paper was not the love letter but a blank one. The implicit irony is that all these men and the so called lovers having lost their sense of proportion boasted of the love of a young and beautiful girl. It is really shocking that a person of her father's age should think of the girl in terms of falling in love with her.

"The Red Red Twilight" is a story of unconsummated love of Pundarik who later in life confronts with the ghost of his beloved Kumudini. Raghav Sharma's son Pundarik could not marry Kumudini because of the opposition of his father. Later she was drowned in a pond. Her spirit moved around and created nuisance by entering the body of a young girl. One day the spirit entered the body of Kuni, a young girl. His father called for Raghav Sharma, the exorcist to cure his daughter. As he was not well, his son, Pundarik went to heal the girl. Confronted with the spirit in the little girl Pundarik recognised that it was the spirit of Kumudini. Manoj Das recreates the situation in artistic terms in the following lines:

> The look and the smile were not those of a nine year old. The next moment Pundarik realised how intimately known to him, dear to him, they had been.
>
> She continued to gaze and smile at him. Pundarik breathed heavily and sobbed out, "Kumudini!"
>
> Her gaze grew more intense and her smile grew brighter, more alluring. Pundarik could no longer see Kuni. He saw instead a bouquet of rising flames. He would have gladly jumped into them. Perhaps he could not do otherwise.
>
> But the girl suddenly stood up, opened the door and began to run. Pundarik pursued her [Ibidem, 1993: 74].

Pundarik was so much frightened that he ran straight away to his house and entered his father's (Ragav Sharma's) room. The father being an exorcist could know that his son is possessed by the spirit and he got frightened. In a way the spirit of the girl Kumudini took revenge on Pundarik. The significance of the story lies in the fact that if the woman is wronged by the lover and her love remains unconsummated her spirit would not spare the wrong doer. In a sense the story has a kind of poetic justice.

"The Irrational" is a psychological story which deals with the secrets of two innocent hearts and it was a secret which was treated as a prerogative of the two characters. The minister, Subrat Das after a lot of persuasion by the people of the locality visited the village Kakali. He was there to inaugurate the charitable dispensary built by Choudhurani (land lady) in memory of Choudhury. He rested one night in the Choudhury's bungalow as he rested there. There was a flash back which takes us to the past forty five years. The minister is reminded of his young age when he was working as a school teacher in Choudhury's house. In his subconscious mind he took fancy to Jamindar's daughter who was a fourteen year old girl and was his student. Two incidents in their life changed the course of the minister's life.

Like Manoj Das, Ruskin Bond too writes stories about common people probing deep into the human psyche and unfolding the human mind in relation to nature and environment. The incidents and situations depicted in his stories are not wholly fictional. He projects a part of his personality into his stories to make them authentic and interesting. His Sahitya Akademi Award winning book, *Our Trees Still Grow in Dehra* is 'semi autobiographical in nature' and therefore can be read as a disguised autobiography. In the "Bent-Double Beggar" (included in *Our Trees Still Grow in Dehra)* the narrator describes the life of old Ganpat who once upon a time was a family man with a wife and a daughter. Though he was not rich he was not poor either. How he became the Bent-double beggar is the subject of the story. The didactic notes given in the story by the protagonist are highly interesting. Here are a few homilies of the Bent-double beggar:

(i) "'A woman can become jealous of any one, anything,' maintained Ganpat. Even of a Ghost."

(ii) "You must love everyone," said the Bent-double beggar.

Even my enemies? I asked.

It is difficult to love your enemies, much simpler not to have enemies.

(iii) In this life all our desires are fulfilled, on the conditions that they do not bring the happiness, we expected from them [*OTSGID*, 1991: 22].

Ruskin Bond writes a number of ghost stories, (i.e. stories about ghosts) in a lucid language. On being asked by a young student from a New Delhi school, "Sir do you believe in ghosts?" Ruskin Bond answered, "Well I don't believe in them. But I keep seeing them" (Introduction to *ASG*, 1999: VII).

The language makes the reader spellbound. In a story titled "Something in the Water," Ruskin Bond gives the description of events and situations in a lucid manner. This is how the story begins:

> I discovered the pool near Rajpur on a hot summer's day some fifteen years ago. It was shaded by close-growing sal trees, and looked cool and inviting. I took off my clothes and dived in.
>
> The water was colder than I had expected. It was an icy glacial cold. The sun never touched it for long, I supposed. Striking out vigorously, I swam to the other end of the pool and pulled myself up on the rocks, shivering.
>
> But I wanted to swim some more. So I dived in again and did a gentle breast stroke towards the middle of the pool. Something slid between my legs. Something slimy, pulpy. I could see no one, hear nothing. I swam away, but the slippery floating thing followed me. I did not like it. Something curled around my leg. Not an underwater plant. Something that sucked at my foot. A long tongue licked my calf. I struck out wildly, thrust myself away from whatever it was that sought my company. Something lonely, lurking a frightened porpoise fleeing from some terror of the deep [Ibidem, 51-52].

Which struck him in water looks like a 'giant's nail' towards the end of the story. This nail was responsible for the death of the schoolboys.

The supernatural elements grip the readers when a labourer had slipped into the pool and was 'shocked dry' by this nail. It was decided that the pool be left undisturbed. Thus the author ends the story with a note of caution to the readers:

> "The monsoon rains came and the pool filled up again. I can tell you how to get there you would like to see it. But I would not advise you to go for a swim" [Ibidem, 55].

In "A Face in the Dark" Ruskin Bond gives the description of another ghost in an artistic manner. Mr. Oliver, an Anglo Indian teacher was returning to his school late one night when he saw a boy sitting alone on a rock. Oliver became apprehensive for he never imagined that a boy could be there after the dark. When he approached the boy he found that the latter was crying with his "head hung down, held his face in his hand and his body shook convulsing." When Oliver enquired about the cause of his weeping the boy didn't reply. He didn't lift up his face when Oliver's torch fell from his hand and he trembled. He ran towards the school building when he saw a lantern swinging in the middle of the path. The watchman asked Oliver "where are you running"? Then Oliver told what he had seen. Then came the climax of the story in thrilling language:

> "No face, Sahib?"

Manoj Das and Ruskin Bond cannot be evaluated as short story writers in isolation. They should be read along with Mulk Raj Anand, Raja Rao, Khushwant Singh and few others. If Malgudi is the 'locale' of R.K. Narayan's short story North Orissa is the 'locale' of Manoj Das in most of his stories and Dehradun is the 'locale' of Ruskin Bond's stories. Both Manoj Das and Ruskin Bond have universalised the local incidents and situations of their stories and thereby attracted the attention of the readers all over the country and abroad. Sometimes the two writers are also compared to Hardy, Saki and O' Henry and rightly so.

Manoj Das is unique as a writer of short stories in more than one ways. First, he is a bilingual writer who writes stories both in Oriya and in English with equal ease. It would be better to call him an ambilingual writer instead of a bilingual writer. An ambilingual writer is equally good in both the languages. Like Rabindranath Tagore who transcreated most of his Bengali stories in English, Manoj Das has transcreated many of his Oriya stories in English, the great example is his recent collection of stories titled *Mystery of the Missing Cap and Other Stories* which is recreated in English from Sahitya Akademi Award winning collection of short stories in Oriya titled *Manoj Dasanka Katha O Kahani* which was published in 1971.

In Manoj Das' stories myth plays a vital role. Stories are built around myths prevalent in his home state and also in different parts of India. Myths have a purpose in his stories i.e. they give a didactic touch to the themes. Apart from the myths there are also anecdotes in most of his stories. He doesn't speak directly about philosophy in his stories but through the mouths of his characters who embody his basic attitude to life. In other words, the implied writers in his stories can be discerned through the protagonist.

Ruskin Bond on the other hand, writes in aphoristic style and like Bacon's essays most of Ruskin Bond's stories are replete with proverbial lines. The basic purpose is to make the readers aware of the contemporary situation through the realisation of the individual characters. Ruskin Bond makes the reader see into the basic instincts of human nature. There is an unmistakable note of autobiography in his stories. The agony of his personal life arose because of his sad experience with his parents and the early death of his father. Ruskin Bond began to see the agony of human life and the loveliness of an individual. His stories are full of pathos and sufferings of innocent children, boys and girls alike. This is because he too suffered as a child.

Both Manoj Das and Ruskin Bond have an insight into human nature. Their sympathy with the poor people and especially for children are amply demonstrated in their stories. Irony is the predominant mode of their stories. For example, stories like "Mystery of the Missing Cap," "The Submerged Valley," "Encounters," "The Murderer," "The Owl," "The

Kite," "The Misty Hour," "Farewell to a Ghost" by Manoj Das, and "The Woman on Platform No. 8," "The Story of Madhu," "A Funeral," "The Bent-Double Beggar," "Escape from Java," "Untouchable," "Coming Home to Dehra," "All Creatures Great and Small" and "The Last Tonga Ride" by Ruskin Bond are memorable stories in the whole range of Indian English literature.

Apart from broadening the thematic range of Indian English short story, these two writers have successfully created an Indian English idiom similar to that of what Nissim Ezekiel, Kamala Das, Raja Rao, R.K. Narayan, Arundhati Roy and Vikram Seth have done in poetry and fiction. The command of the English language, the felicity of expression and the range of vocabulary have endeared them to the hearts and the minds of the audience. To read their ghost stories is to transport oneself into imaginary world where the supernatural elements have a great sway over human life.

If one cannot understand a W.B. Yeats without his Irish background, one cannot fully understand and appreciate Manoj Das without his North-Orissa background and Ruskin Bond without his stay at Dehradun and Simla. Manoj Das and Ruskin Bond are rooted firmly in their respective background (i.e., North-Orissa and Dehradun). To say the least, both Manoj Das and Ruskin Bond are Indian writers to the core, their medium of writing (i.e. English) notwithstanding. These two writers are no less 'local" than the Bhasa writers and at the same time they are no less 'Indian' in sensibility than them.

WORKS CITED

Bond, Ruskin. *Our Trees Still Grow in Dehra*. New Delhi: Penguin Books, 1991.

——. *A Season of Ghosts*. New Delhi: Penguin Books, 1999.

Das, Manoj. *Farewall to Ghost and Other Stories*. New Delhi: Penguin Books, 1984.

——. *Miracle and Other Stories*. New Delhi: Sterling Publishers, 1993.

Rajnath. "Literary Criticism in the New Millennium." *Littcrit* 27: 1-2, 2001.

23 The Question of Identity: A Note on V.S. Naipaul's Travel—Writings on India and Trinidad

Bijay Kumar Das

The migratory movements across countries and continents are the order of the day. In the last fifty years, or so, people (particularly writers) are migrating either to U.K. or to U.S.A. from former British colonies like India, Africa and West Indies, in search of larger audience the world over for their writings in English. Some of these writers keep multi-cultural and multi-national commitments uppermost in their mind and don't get uprooted either at home or abroad. For instance, Derek Walcott, 1992 Nobel Prize Winner for Literature keeps his multi-cultural commitment and abides by the treble impulse i.e.; fidelity to his African origin, Caribbean birth and upbringing, and finally, to America, where he presently works. V.S. Naipaul, on the other hand, has nothing to do with his origin, that is, India, and the place of birth, Trinidad (West Indies) and is all for his country of immigration, the United Kingdom. In his travel-writings he has come down heavily on India and Trinidad. The purpose of the paper is to show how Naipaul has depicted the country of his origin, and the country of his birth and upbringing, in his travel-writings and the authenticity of such kind of writings.

Before making an assessment of his travel-writings, let us first begin with the beginning—that is, how he began writing and how he wanted to be introduced to his readers the world over. The biographical note which Naipaul contributed to his works published by Penguin reads as follows:

> "V.S. Naipaul was born in Trinidad in 1932. He came to England in 1950, to do a university course and began to write, in London, in 1954. He has followed no other profession."

That means, he has taken his writing seriously and made it his profession. He tells us how he began writing following his father in course of an interview given to *Sunday Times Magazine* on 26 May, 1963:

> "The writing that has mattered most to me is that of my father, which has been published. It taught me to look at things which had never been written about before, and seemed dull in life, yet when transferred to paper became very surprising. A great deal of my vision of Trinidad has come straight from my father" (Salgado, 1987: 317).

Naipaul's three travelogues on India—*An Area of Darkness* (1964), *India: A Wounded Civilization* (1977) and *India: A Million Mitunies Now* (1991)—and one-travelogue on Trinidad titled *The Middle Passage* (1962), in which the author comes down heavily on the country of his origin, and the country of his birth, deal indirectly with the question of his identity. On being awarded the Nobel Prize for Literature for 2001, Naipaul is reported to have said: 'It (the Nobel) is a great tribute to both England, my home and to India, home of my ancestors' *(The Times of India,* Oct. 2001). Critics are divided on the question of the merits of the four travelogues listed above as well as the merit of the Nobel Committee's decision to honour Naipaul with Nobel Prize for Literature. Some critics are of the opinion that Naipaul is honest in his observations on India and Trinidad, as he is on Africa, Middle East Countries and Pakistan in his later books like *Among the Believers: An Islamic Journey (*1981), and *Beyond Belief* (1995). Dom Moraes expresses his deep sense of appreciation and satisfaction for the Nobel Committee's decision to honour Naipaul this year (i.e., 2001). He writes:

> Fifteen years ago I spent a summer in Sweden. I often met the novelist Per Wastberg, who was also one of the judges of the Nobel Prize for Literature. We used to discuss its past recipients and the possible winners in

> years to come. Wastberg said, "May be, in some years, Naipaul. He has some kind of World View." It is no secret in the literary world that Naipaul, though his shoulders were already heavily burdened with laurel wreaths, badly wanted the Nobel, even 15 years ago. Now he has got it, and nobody in English Literature deserves it more (*The Hindu*, November 4, 2001: 3).

What is in question is not Naipaul's merit, and ability to win Nobel Prize for Literature but the authenticity of his observations on India and Trinidad, above all, the problem of his identity. The writings of Naipaul show that he is not at all sentimental about the past and at the same time he has no love for the country of his birth or origin. He is all for his career as a writer and happy with England, the country to which he migrated and made his own. The Nobel Committee has rightly taken him as 'a British novelist and writer.'

C.D. Narasimhaiah and Nissim Ezekiel some years before and Shobha De now take Naipaul to task for his unsympathetic attitude to Indian society notwithstanding Khushwant Singh's wholesome praise for him. Narasimhaiah cites examples from Naipaul's life and work to show how the latter has distorted facts about India and Trinidad, and placed the 'self' above the country:

> "As though the racial instinct never deserts an individual, Naipaul does grasp the full implication of the concept of *Dharma* in his *A Wounded Civilization* when he cites examples from unsuspected sources like Proust to illumine the concept, but before long mocks at it by a wilful distortion as when he seeks to convince the susceptible Western reader with stories like this:
>
> > A foreign businessman saw that his untouchable servant was intelligent and decided to give the youngman an education. He did so and before he left the country he placed the youngman in a better job. Some years later the businessman returned to India. He found that his untouchable was a latrine cleaner again. He had been boycotted by his clan...... he was barred from the smoking group. There was no other group he could join; no woman he could marry. His

> solitariness was insupportable and he had returned to his duty, his dharma, he had learned to obey.

I don't think this propaganda-story, the like of which missionaries working in Afro-Asian countries fabricated to justify their misdeeds, needs comment to this audience. The hundreds of thousands of untouchables who are today the country's engineers, doctors, teachers, lawyers, judges, administrators, public men, in whatever small numbers for their population, should give the lie to this glaring piece of propaganda" (1995: 217).

Naipaul thought that Trinidad was disintegrating and therefore wanted to escape from that country. The opening sentence of *A Bend in the River* seems to embody the authorial voice and vision: The world is what it is, men who are nothing have no place in it. Again the protagonist of the novel says, "I'll go into business, I'll stay." At this point Narasimhaiah makes a pertinent observation:

> But I suspect Naipaul insecurely adds, authorially, "It was the opposite of what I felt... To stay with my community was to be taken with them to destruction. I could be master of my fate only if I stood alone. My wish was not to be good, in the way of our tradition, but to make good"—"make good," an awful phrase, in an informed adult which, as we know, carries its undertones of unashamed opportunism (Ibidem, 2/6).

This view of Narasimhaiah is corroborated by Phil Langran when the latter quotes from *The Middle Passage* to show Naipaul's 'the need to escape' from Trinidad. This is how Langran puts it:

> *The Middle Passage*, (1962) [1], his first work of non-fiction, in which he returns to give his impressions of the region, is frequently cited as summarizing his early views:
>
> > "How can the history of the West Indian futility be written ?...... The history of the islands can never be satisfactorily told. Brutality is not the only difficulty. History is built around achievement and creation: and nothing was created in the West Indies (29)

> I knew Trinidad to be unimportant, uncreative, cynical ....Power was recognized, but dignity was allowed to no one.... We lived in a society which denied itself heroes (43).
>
> The threat of failure, the need to escape: this was the prompting of the society I knew. (45)

He goes on to comment that the West Indian lives in 'a borrowed culture' (73). In Trinidad the 'purely local form,' the calypso, has been 'debased' by the local population in attempting to live up to 'the ideals of the tourist brochure' (75-6).

These comments begin to establish a persona that will become increasingly familiar in his non-fiction. This is distinguished by the expression of unpalatable 'truths,' the appeals to eurocentric notions of history, the discussion of circumstances in which the narrator (in Trinidad and India) has been implicated, and an overwhelmingly negative tone. The key phrase in this context is 'the need to escape,' to acquire and maintain a sense of detachment in the face of Trinidad's 'threat of failure,' (*LC*, 35: 1-2, 2000: 48-49).

However, Langran is not critical of Naipaul for leaving the country because his later works take the themes from that country. The country has never gone out of his mind. Thus writes Langran:

> However, later works confirm that, in terms of subject matter, Naipaul would by no means escape the island. These include a fictionalized account of Trinidadian politics, (*The Mimic Men*, 1967), a history of the island (*The Loss of EL Dorado*, 1969), autobiographical writing (*Finding the Centre*, 1984), and recent fiction that revisits his place of birth (*The Enigma of Arrival*, 1987, and *A Way in the World*, 1994). Furthermore, Naipaul's distinctive voicing of personal involvement and detached observation characterizes his work as a whole, the tension between the isolated individual and the potentially engulfing, imperfect community is a recurring theme (Ibidem, 49).

Naipaul defends his position by stating the fact that though he was born in Trinidad, he was re-born in England as a writer when he went there in 1950. In course of an interview he tells this to Hamilton in 1971:

> I was eighteen when I came (to London) and in a way I have grown up here. I've had my second childhood, a second becoming aware of the world. I've grown out of one attitude and begun to understand the world from another point of view, in my maturity (Jussawalla, 1997: 14).

Aaron Eastley makes an observation on this statement in the following words:

> "And in a sense, this re-birth was inevitable, based on his perceptions of the circumstances he grew up under. I was born [in Trinidad], yes," he says in 1983:
>
> > I thought it was a great mistake.... I [didn't like] the world outside....., I didn't like my family particularly either... (And] I developed a fantasy, I suppose, of civilization as something existing away from this area of barbarity (Levin, 93).

The idea of Trinidad as a barbaric, backward place certainly had a strong impact on Naipaul. He has often directed barbs back at his homeland, provoking much of his unpopularity among post-colonialists. "If you're from Trinidad," he told James Atlas in 1987, "you want to get away. You can't write if you're from bush" (*JCT 1999, Summer:* 37-8).

Chinua Achebe, Edward Said and Derek Walcott take Naipaul to task for his harsh remarks on Africa, Asia and the West Indies. Achebe criticises Naipaul for depicting the African continent as a 'place of darkness' in his African novels such as—*In a Free State* and *A Bend in the River*. Edward Said has described Naipaul's posture as that 'of a Whiteman's nigger' always 'looking down.' As Ravi Vyas has pointed out that "the poet and Nobel Laureate, Derek Walcott, born in St. Lucia, not far from Naipaul's native Trinidad, has derided his fellow West Indian, for an alleged 'abhorrence of Negroes' and for reverting England once Trinidad's colonial mistress over the Afro-Caribbean heritage that he mythologised in his epic poem *Omeros*. As a matter of fact, *The Guardian* in Britain suggested in 1992, that Naipaul had been passed over for the Nobel because of 'reservations about his suitability to represent the Caribbean" (*The Hindu*, Sunday, October 21, 2001: II).

But Naipaul stood his ground. In an extensive interview with the *Times Literal Supplement*, on September 2, 1994 Naipaul said that *he wanted to deliver the truth, to deliver a form of reality based on what I have observed, seen, experienced. Western Writers come from the imperial period without knowing it, without considering themselves imperial writers. They inhabit a world where they don't see the other half or three quarters. For that reason they think reality's all been chartered. I carry many cultures in my head, and these people are much restricted* (Ibidem).

Having stated the views of some of the critics and Naipaul's commitment to his themes, let us examine his travelogues both for authenticity of observations and as works of art. Naipaul visited India for the first time in his thirties with a preconceived notion and negative mindset as a result of which he could write his first travelogue, *An Area of Darkness,* that depicts the dirt and squalor of India devoid of civilized values. Speaking of this book, Naipaul says:

> "Travel writing was new to me, and I didn't see how I could find a narrative for a book about India... I had kept no journal, made few connected notes. But money had been spent, and a book had to be written.....calling up events day after day found a narrative" *(India: A Million Mutinies Now,* 1990: 493).

Naipaul criticises Nehru, Gandhi, Hinduism, language confusion in India, the poverty of the country, the 'death city' of Calcutta almost everything that comes to his notice. Kashmir has no beauty of her own and does not appeal to his mind. Taj Mahal is ill suited to India. He would ideally have Taj shipped to some shining plaza in America. His anti-Indian stance is widely pronounced in this book. Darshan Singh Maini takes Naipaul to task for his onesided approach to India and her problems:

> Of course, the thing which made the book ultimately famous was Naipaul's discovery of defecation in India. A long, wry ode has justly brought him dividends in the West. We hold no brief for the bared bottom in a row seen along the railway lines in the morning or for the 'companionable defecation' of women in the fields or bush alongside the bridle paths, or for the street urchins easing themselves over running open sewers. Surely, we too are shamed into silence at such a brazen unconcern with the simple decencies of life. But, again one needs a measure of understanding. The compulsions of climate and cramped living in old, crowded cities are not basically questions of aesthetics, but of sheer creature existence. The stink is regrettable, but more regrettable is 'the excremental vision' which Middleton Murry and later Aldous Huxley, located in Swift. The energies of art proceed sometimes from mysterious sources! Naipaul's pathological preoccupation with this problem surely suggests a defecation complex. That the thing should be so much on his brain leaves one wondering if he isn't really constipated! Or may be, the 'repetition' urge, which becomes a major concern in Freud's later writing, is the reason for Naipaul's compulsive return to dung, defecation and death (Desai and Amur, 1984: 100).

Naipaul's observations on India is not wholly false but distorted and one sided. Nissim Ezekiel in course of a perceptive article titled "Naipaul's India and Mine" puts things in the correct perspective.

"My quarrel with Mr. Naipaul, which I hope to conduct in a way that will be understandable to him, is not because of these condemnatory judgements of his, so fiercely, so blazingly expressed. My quarrel is that Mr. Naipaul is so often uninvolved and unconcerned. He writes exclusively from the point of view of his own dilemma, his temperamental alienation from his mixed background, his choice and his escape" (1992: 86).

Ezekiel elaborates his argument in the following way:

> "Let me pause to explain again that I see India in most ways as Naipaul sees her. All that he says against the

> grossness and squalor of Indian life, the routine ritualism, the lip-service to high ideals, the petrified and distorted sense of cleanliness, and a thousand other things, all this is true. My dissatisfaction is with his mode of argument, his falsifying examples" (Ibidem, 95).

Ezekiel sums up his argument in the following ways:

> "In one of the rare positive moments in *An Area of Darkness,* Mr. Naipaul writes, 'Anger, compassion and contempt were aspects of the same emotions; they were without value because they could not endure. Achievement could begin only with acceptance.' As always, Mr. Naipaul overstates the case. I believe in anger, compassion and contempt. They are not without value. I believe in acceptance that incorporates all three, makes use of them. I am incurably critical and sceptical. That is what I am in relation to India also. And to myself. I find it does not prevent the growth of love. In this sense only, I love India" (Ibidem, 99).

In his second travelogue on India titled *India: A Wounded Civilization* Naipaul makes a serious attempt to dive deep into the psyche of India by going into the socio-economic and cultural problems that are peculiar to this country but his attitude of India bashing remains unchanged. Thus he writes:

> "How often in India—at every level—rational conversation about the country's problems trails away into talk of magic, of the successful prophecies of astrologers, of the wisdom of auspicious hours, of telepathic communications and actions taken in response to some inner voice !......when men cannot observe, they don't have ideas, they have obsessions. When people live instinctive lives, something like a collective amnesia steadily blurs the past" (1977: 112).

Again he says, "the crisis of India is not political, it is not economic, it is part of the larger crisis, that of a decaying civilization" (Narasimhaiah, 1995: 221).

Naipaul seems to have little respect for and less understanding of the vast changes that swept India between nineteen sixties and eighties, and hence, his lop sided and biased approach to the problems that our country faces during the course of his writing travelogues after travelogues on India. I concur with Darshan Singh Maini when he says:

> If the governing metaphor of the first book on India is that of 'darkness,' reflected in its unflattering title, the metaphor of 'wound' extends Naipaul's thesis in the sequel, written during the troubled and twilight period of "the Emergency." For, *India: A Wounded Civilization* (1977), is simply an example of the 'neurotic' in Naipaul, a compulsive return to a 'strumpet' that will not let him alone. *In the Foreword*, he is candid enough to admit the hopeless nature of his enterprise. "India," he says, "is for me a difficult country. It isn't my home and cannot be my home; and yet I cannot reject it or be indifferent to it..." Thus, the spiritual 'fix' he finds himself in vis-a-vis India, is, in reality, an example, not of divided loyalties—he loudly forswears any kind of allegiance—but of divided energies. It's not, I repeat, a love-hate relationship, and there is no anguish of ambiguity to be encountered here. The transparency of the two metaphors alone dispels such a notion. The metaphor changes, of course, but the misery remains (Amur and Desai, 1984: 103-4).

But by the time Naipaul wrote his third travelogue on India (i.e. *India: A Million Mutinies Now,* 1990), his attitude towards this country has changed a little and thus, he writes:

> "In 27 years I had succeeded in making a kind of return journey, shedding my Indian nerves, abolishing the darkness that separated me from my ancestral past......Twenty-five years or so late (1883)... my ancestors had left as indentured servants for the sugar estates of Guyana and Trinidad. I had carried in my bones that idea of abjectness feat and shame....

What I hadn't understood in 1962, or had taken too much for granted, was the extent to which the country had been remade; and even to the extent to which India had been restored to itself" (*IMMN*, 1990: 516-7).

Naipaul's prejudice against Hindu religion continues to dominate his feelings in this book. As Susheela N. Rao has rightly observed:

> Naipaul's negative thinking on India is incredibly appalling. He can undercut and negate any Hindu achievement ingeniously. When the famous book of Alberuni, an outsider, on India's great achievements in the past is brought to his attention, he says; "Alberunis book was one of the sources for what was known about ancient Hindu science and learning; but Alberuni had also written some famous words about Hindu arrogance in that learning" (*IMMN*, 159). He has the remarkable gift of quickly throwing cold water on a great Hindu achievement and of equally quickly pointing up the bizarre. Standing before the magnificent palace of the Mysore Maharaja, he says: "Nothing in the former mukthesar's account had prepared me for the extravagance of the maharaja's palace. The palace design, with the garishness and mixture of styles..... expressed a kind of Indian self-abasement before the idea of Europe" (*IMMN*, 202-03), His knack for making fun of the Hindus who help him is pathetic. He notes that the Brahmin whom he interviewed and who helped him had a belly which "was curiously narrow and long" and he "appeared to have the shape of cucumber" (*IMMN*, 194). With an insatiable curiosity to collect the most bizarre and grotesque items of information he says that there was in the palace "the lower, curving half of an elephant's trunk made rigid and converted into an ash tray or ash bin, with an iron grille at the top for stubbing out cigarettes and cigars" (*IMMN*, 204). His penchant for collecting gossip is no less impressive. (*LHY*, 1997: 35).

During his travel in India he went to several places particularly to cities and towns like Bombay, Goa, Bangalore, Mysore, Madras, Calcutta, Lucknow, Delhi, Kashmir and some places in Punjab and met only intellectuals and people from middle and upper class. He never met poor people nor interacted with them. He heard about them from middlemen or informants. He came to know only the misery of the poor people but not their sense of dignity or commitment to life. He writes about defecation but forgets their simplicity and warm heartedness. It is on this count the authenticity of his writings on India can be called into question.

Naipaul's travelogues may be faulted on many counts: factual errors about places described, biased attitude against Hinduism and Indian problems but they have redeeming features. First, Naipaul seems to owe allegiance to no institution, to no doctrine and to no religion. He spares none. His commitment is to his own vision of life whatever it may be. Secondly, his magnificent prose, the lucidity of language and felicity of expression hold one's breath. It is the language that charms the readers even when they differ from Naipaul on his observations on India and Trinidad.

Coming to the question of Naipaul's identity one faces an insurmountable problem. He is, not an Indian, let us make no mistake about it. He is not a West Indian, his birth in Trinidad notwithstanding. As Shobha De has rightly observed that, "Naipaul has always occupied No Man's Land. Is that so hard to accept ? He is not an Indian. Let us get that straight. He is also not an English man. Let's also get that straight. He insists he does not feel Trinidadian. Accept that" *(The Sunday Times,* October, 2001). He has no kind words for Indians. Recently after winning Nobel Prize he is reported to have said: "Indians don't read."

But we can solve the question of his identity if we take a liberal view of his position as a writer. If T.S. Eliot could be regarded as a British poet, inspite of his American birth and upbringing, then why can't we accept Naipaul as a British writer? Of course, Indians can have a sense of satisfaction thinking of him as of Indian origin, as Trinidadians can gloat over his success, because of his birth, in that land. It is better left to the person to choose his own country, rather than the country claiming a person as its own on account of birth or origin. A great writer always transcends the limitations of place and time and achieves universality. That is what, Naipaul has done.

WORKS CITED

Eastley, Aaron. "Joking with the Centre: Naipaul's Ambiguous Treatment of Trinidadian English in *The Mystic Masseur*." *Journal of Contemporary Thought,* 1999. (Summer), 25-46.

Ezekiel, Nissim. "Naipaul's Indian and Mine." *Selected Prose,* Delhi: Oxford University Press, 1992.

Hamilton, Ian. "Without a Place: V.S. Naipaul in Conversation with Ian Hamilton." Interview. *Conversations with V.S. Naipaul.* Ed. Feroza Jussawalla. Jackson: UP of Mississippi, 1997. 14-22.

Langran, Phil. "Earl Lovelace and V.S. Naipaul: Representations of Trinidad." *The Literary Criterion,* 35:1-2, 2000, 46-65.

Levin, Bernard. "V.S. Naipaul: A Perpetual Voyager." Interview. *Conversations with V. S. Naipaul.* Ed. Feroza Jussawalla. Jackson: UP of Mississippi, 1997. 93-98.

Maini, Darshan Singh. "The Complex Fate of V. S. Naipaul." *Colonial Consciousness in Commonwealth Literature.* Eds. G. S. Amur and S.K. Desai. Madras: Somaiya Publications Pvt. Ltd., 1984.

Moraes, Dom. "Half Novel." *The Hindu,* November 4, 2001.

Naipaul, V.S. *The Middle Passage.* London: Andre Deutsch, 1962, rpt. New York: Vintage, 1981.

——. *An Area of Darkness.* London: Andre Deutsch, 1964, rpt. New York: Vintage, 1981.

——. *India: A Wounded Civilization.* New York: Alfared A. Knopt, 1977; rpt. New York: Vintage, 1987.

——. *India: A Million Mutinies Now.* London: Minerva Paperbacks, 1990.

Narasimhaiah, C.D. *Essays in Commonwealth Literature:—Heirloom of Multiple Heritage.* Delhi: Pencraft International, 1995.

Rao, N. Susheela. 'Darkness Visible: The Emerging Portrait of India in Naipaul's Updated Indian Travelogue." *The Literary Half-Yearly,* 38: 1, Jan., 1997. 28-41.

Salgado, Gamini. "V.S. Naipaul and the Politics of Fiction." *The New Pelican Guide to English Literature.* Ed. Boris Ford. London: Penguin Books, 1987.

Vyas, Ravi. "His Third World." *The Hindu,* October 21, 2001.

24

Interview

Manoj Das in Conversation with Bijay Kumar Das

(Recipient of Padma Shri in 2001, and Saraswati Samman, a very prestigious award for literature in the same year, Professor Manoj Das is one of the literary doyens of our country. He has won both Central Sahitya Akademi and Orissa Sahitya Akademi Awards for his collections of short stories. He has also been bestowed upon the highest honour from Orissa, namely Utkal Ratna. He was the editor of the prestigious monthly, The Heritage. As a scholar, thinker and distinguished fiction writer, Manoj Das is well known all over the country and abroad).

BKD: In course of an article titled "The Enigma of Draupadi" published in *The Heritage* (January 1986), you have stated that "the only true safety lies in the Divine's Grace; the human supports are unpredictable." I would like to begin with this statement. Does that statement explain your attitude to life?

MD: Yes, indeed, even though I must have stated that with Draupadi's predicament in view—a realisation that dawned on her when she was being humiliated by the Kauravas in the presence of the brave human guardians but the only force that came to her aid was Krishna's Grace. This is an attitude that is unconsciously cultivated by numerous Indians, even though they may not articulate it.

BKD: You are a bilingual writer and your fiction in both the languages—English and Oriya—seems to me obverse and reverse of the same coin, what I mean to say is that it is a harmonious whole. How did you come to write fiction, in the first place?

MD: I began with poetry—very spontaneously—as a child. A time came, while I was in my teens, when my creative urge informed me that there were subjects that can be effectively handled by fiction and not poetry, just as there were inspirations that could incarnate only through poetry and not through fiction. Thus did I come to use the medium of prose.

BKD: When did you publish your first story in Oriya and the first story in English? And when did you publish your first collection of stories in English?

MD: If my memory serves me right—only those who have done research on my works can be depended on for such factual matters—I wrote my first short story in Oriya, *Samudrara Kshudha,* sometime in 1949; the first short story in English was written in 1959 and published in the *Caravan,* a well-circulated literary monthly of the time. My first collection of short stories, *A Song for Sunday and Other Stories,* was published in 1966 or 1967.

BKD: Between your first collection of stories, *A Song for Sunday and Other Stories,* (1967) and *Selected Fictions,* (2001) 34 years have passed. Do you find a pattern that binds all your short story collections in English together?

MD: I believe a pattern is bound to be there, for the observer (I mean the author) of life continues to be the same. His means of observation or outlook may expand; but there can rarely be a qualitative change. So far as I am concerned, my understanding of the nature of mind and men has certainly expanded over the years, but that is one aspect of the things we call pattern. The way you present the characters and situations, your style, treatment of issues, cannot be a radical departure from your basic mode of expression.

BKD: Do you recognise any influence on your short story?

MD: Not one but numerous. From that of the lullaby which led me into my sleep and dreams in my infancy to the great epic poets lines from whom used to be recited by my mother; from indomitable Vishnu Sharma of the *Panchatantra* to Fakir Mohan, the maker of modern Oriya fiction, so on and so forth.

BKD: Do you believe in revising a story?

MD: It is not a question of a belief as a norm or a principle. It is a question of your satisfaction that the idea you wished to put across had been accomplished. If you feel that words or situations had to be changed and you still had the opportunity to change it, you should do it. I do revise.

BKD: Some of your stories have the same themes in both the languages—English and Oriya. Do you first write in a language and then translate it into another?

MD: Of course, I have to write in any one of the two languages first. When I render the same story into the other language, I do not translate but recreate. You see, there is a big difference between a translator and a creative writer. If I were to translate into English a piece you had written, my duty is to be as faithful as possible to your original. I have no right to alter it or even if I could, improve upon it. But I am not a translator of my writing. I am the writer; I write in two languages instead of one. That gives me the freedom to change a story when I work upon the plot for the second time in another language.

BKD: To put it in a straightforward language should we consider your stories having the same themes in Oriya and English as translations or trancreations?

MD: Naturally, transcreations, if you must use a term. For me, it is just an original story, for I am the author of both its content and its form.

BKD: The themes of your stories encompass ghosts, animals, demons, children and adults. Which of the themes appeals to you most?

MD: Natural and supernatural characters and situations, denizens of forests too, are the means through which my themes find embodiment. Whatever I write I write because its theme appeals to me.

BKD: You have made use of superstitions, myths and legends as themes in your stories. Do you believe in them?

MD: I have not used them as themes; they are used as means of driving home certain ideas of reality. If I bring in a superstition to explain the conduct of a character, whether I believe in that superstition or not is irrelevant. So far as myths are concerned, they are often symbols of a complex or occult truth. Legends are different. There are legends and legends—of several categories. Relevance of myths and legends in my writing can be appreciated only in their perspectives.

BKD: Contemporary reality seems to be a favourable subject of your stories. Do you have a didactic purpose while delineating contemporary reality in your stories?

MD: There may be, in a subtle way. After all one has the urge to convey a truth in which one believes. I have some fantasies which are consciously didactic—for example most of the stories in the collection entitled *The Lady who Died One and Half Times and other Fantasies*, published this month (November 2003), by Rupa.

BKD: Irony seems to be a predominant mode in your stories. Is it because of the declining standard of morality in the contemporary society?

MD: Man was always, in all the ages, less than what he ought to be. Hence the element of irony was always there in literature. But in an era of degraded values, satires and irony play a more pronounced role.

BKD: What kind of audience do you have in mind while writing stories?

MD: Only one kind of audience: a sensible and sensitive reader. This is regarding my original stories. It is different when I occasionally write for children.

BKD: Besides being a creative writer, you are a great scholar and thinker. You are well versed in Indian myths and philosophy. Does your learning come in the way of your creative writing? In other words, does the scholar in you obstruct the creative faculty?

MD: You are very generous in your evaluation of me as a scholar. I am a student of the great lores—including mythology, philosophy and mysticism. My interest in such subjects has never stood in the way of my creative writing. They help my inner understanding of truth and life.

BKD: R.K. Narayan has created Malgudi—partly imaginary and partly real—as the 'locale' of his novels and stories. Do you have a 'locale' of your stories?

MD: If I had, you would not ask me; you would know just as you know Malgudi. I have never thought of creating any. Themes and plots of my stories have a large range. A few of them may fall into a group, for example, some stories with Mount Luvurva for their backdrop—but each story and novel has a milieu of its own. The world recreated for *A Tiger at Twilight* is not the world of *Cyclones*. *The Escapist* has yet another world.

BKD: Some of your stories like "Mystery of the Missing Cap," "Encounters," "The Lover Letter" reveal your deep insight into human nature. Which aspect of human life appeals to you most ? And which aspect of human life do you detest most?

MD: I adore the hidden divinity in man; I feel deep empathy—much more than sympathy, for several parts of myself are present in my characters—for the helplessness of man, his propensity for falling into the traps of the darker forces—call them lower nature of Avidya—and I abhor the elements of cruelty and hypocrisy in man.

BKD: Your stories seem to be more psychological than philosophical. Do you agree?

MD: Probably, it is so.

BKD: Is it your empirical personality or implied personality that goes into the making of your fiction? Is there any autobiographical element in your stories?

MD: All these elements will be there; but should we not accord recognition to the most important element that is creative inspiration? Should we not allow that element a bit of mystery? A part of my own consciousness may be the laboratory or workshop where the fiction is shaped, but elements do arrive, rather alight, from outside me!

BKD: Apart from short stories, you have also written novels in English. Why did you choose to write novels after winning recognition as a short story writer?

MD: Why did I choose to write short stories at all? The same urge found a different medium; that is all. Winning recognition was never my destination.

BKD: Besides being a Creative Writer, you are an editor of repute. You have edited *The Heritage* brilliantly. Would you like to share your experience as an editor?

MD: You will remember that when *The Heritage* was published, practically all magazines of any literary merit had closed down. Hence *The Heritage* became immensely dear to writers. I used to shy away from personal contact with writers. As an editor, a new challenge, you may call it an invitation to adventure, knocked on my door. Often I found a gifted writer in a young person, but struggling midway a story or caught up in a knot, I would apply my creative sense and suggest a way. Because they were more or less familiar with my writing, they had trust in me. They would gladly accept my suggestion. I developed some insight into the creative process of others. Apart from that, I had the privilege to edit writings of celebrities of our time. There developed an excellent mutual understanding.

BKD: You have won numerous awards including the Saraswati Samman, the Sahitya Akademi Awards (both national and provincial) for your creative writing. How do the awards influence or affect you?

MD: The problem with the answer to this question is, rarely anybody would say that an award did inspire him or her in any way, even though the truth could be that he or she dying to get it. I know a few pathetic such instances, though I do not wish to mention them. What I mean is, what credibility can I expect when I say that awards had no effect on my writing? They had no effect on me. My only satisfaction is, there are people, constituting a large area of my readership, who rejoice at my receiving some recognition. Personally I feel grateful to those who choose to confer some such recognition on me, but nothing beyond that. I am not elated. Some who deserve do not get; some who do not deserve, get; some who deserve more get less; some who deserve less; get more. I have no illusions about recognitions.

BKD: Apart from being a writer, an editor, a critic, you are also a great orator. Do you consider public lectures as satisfying as creative writing?

MD: I never intended to be an orator—if at all I am. I try to convey as faithfully as possible my understanding of an issue. That's all.

BKD: What do you enjoy more—addressing the public face to face or speaking to the readers through your stories?

MD: I am a willing writer, but not a willing speaker.

BKD: One personal question, please. Why did you move away from Marxism to the philosophy of Sri Aurobindo?

MD: Because I have been a seeker. Personally I found in Sri Aurobindo the light I sought.

BKD: And the last question. How do you like to be termed—Indian English writer or an Oriya writer?

MD: As an Indian writer writing in his mother-tongue Oriya as well as in English. Thanks.

25

Meet The Author

Shiv K. Kumar in Conversation with Bijay Kumar Das

(Elected Fellow of Royal Society of Literature (London), recipient of Padma Bhushan in 2001, and Sahitya Akademi Award in 1987, for his book of verse, *Trapfalls in the Sky,* Professor Shiv K. Kumar is a distinguished academic turned creative writer, who has nine collections of poems, four novels, one play, two short story collections, one book of translation to his credit. A Ph.D. from Cambridge University in English in 1956, Prof. Kumar is well known as a critic and his book, *Bergson and the Stream of Consciousness Novel* is a contribution to criticism.)

BKD: In your poem "Thus Spake the Buddha" you said that, "The way to satiate a yearning/is to sublimate it" I would like to begin with this statement. When did your yearning for becoming a poet begin?

SKK: The line you have quoted from my poem "Thus Spake the Buddha" articulates one of my central beliefs—that the way to salvation is through sublimation of one's yearnings. My desire to become a poet manifested itself when I was just fifteen.

BKD: What was the state of Indian English Poetry when you published your first book of poems, *Articulate Silences?*

SKK: When I published my first collection of poems *Articulate Silences,* there were just a handful of poets writing in English, and we all looked upon Nissim Ezekiel as our pioneer. Incidentally he published my first poem

"Hallucination" in the *Illustrated Weekly of India* for which he was then editing a page "Poetry of the Month."

BKD: Who were the formative influences on your early poetry if you at all admit of any such influence on your poetry?

SKK: Among the poets who influenced my poetry were such confessional poets as Robert Lowell and Sylvia Plath.

BKD: Love is a major theme in your poetry right from the beginning. Is love 'a way down' like Yeats or 'a way up' like Eliot's in your poetry? Or is it like John Donne's when you reflect on various moods of love-both in a playful and serious manner in your poetry?

SKK: Love is a major (recurring) theme in my poetry. To me it's "the way up as in Blake's poetry." Yes, I look upon love as a biological emotion, both "playful and serious."

BKD: Between your first volume of poems, *Articulate Silences* and ninth volume *Losing My Way,* do you have a pattern that unites them?

SKK: There is indeed a consistent theme that unifies my entire poetry—from *Articulate Silences* to *Loosing My Way*. It is the primacy of intuition over reason.

BKD: You have been described as a confessional poet and also an imagistic poet. Do you accept such kind of opinions?

SKK: I would certainly consider myself a confessional poet, partly (as I have mentioned earlier) because I consider Lowell and Sylvia Plath as my mentors. Of course, my verse may also be taken as imagistic, because it is through images I articulate my thoughts and feelings.

BKD: You write topical poems (i.e., poems on contemporary reality). Why have you not explored national myths or archetypes in your poetry?

SKK: I think that even in my so called "topical" poems there are some archetypal concerns—particularly in my poems that appear in the section, "Genesis" in my collection *Trapfalls in the Sky*.

BKD: Which is your favourite book of verse?

SKK: My favourite collection of poems is *Woolgathering* because, in a sense, it reorchestrates all my major concerns.

BKD: How did you feel when you received the Sahitya Akademi Award for *Trapfalls in the Sky* in 1987?

SKK: I was naturally excited on receiving the Sahitya Akademi Award, 1987 for *Trapfalls in the Sky* which incidentally has been translated into Urdu, Hindi, Malayalam, Tamil and Kannada (all published by the Sahitya Akademi).

BKD: Poetry is normally written in one of the two ways: one, under some inspiration—divine or human and two, poetry taken as an art—that is by reading others' poetry and also out of one's experience with life. How do you write poems?

SKK: I write verse only when I feel intensely moved by some happenings—an emotion or personal experience is usually the force that drives me to write poetry. Isn't that one of the basic elements in all confessional poetry? You may call this a compulsive urge or an "inspiration." But since every poem is an artefact one has to craft it into a creative mood. So a poet is also a kind of "artisan."

BKD: Do you revise your poems as a rule?

SKK: To me revision is another form of creation. I have often revised my poems twenty or thirty times. In this respect I look upon Dylan Thomas as my guru for his poem underwent countless revisions.

BKD: In "Birth of a Poem" you have said that, 'words are straws picked up/by a sparrow, from everywhere.' Does that explain the use of multiple themes in your poetry?

SKK: Yes, a poet picks up his images from everywhere—from remote environment to a garbage can. This may explain the use of multiple images in my poetry.

BKD: Why did you turn to *the Mahabharata* for a theme in your later poetry?

SKK: I guess, it is due to my age. At 83 I feel that the *Mahabbharata* can answer several of my questions—spiritual, social or political. Doesn't Bhishma Pitamaha symbolize the consummation of all human experience?

BKD: In "Lord Krishna to Arjuna" you have stated "like the creator/seeing his image in his creation." You being a creator, how much of your personal life can one find in your poetry?

SKK: My personal ideas and emotions are manifest in every poem I have written. I agree with Dostoevsky that a writer discusses himself only in his work. In a sense every poet is "confessional" at heart.

BKD: Your observation 'attachment generates only anguish' has a proverbial ring about it. Does it come from your personal experience?

SKK: Yes, the genesis of all pain is attachment. This is what my personal experience has taught me. May be, I have grown into this belief under the influence of the *Bhagavat Gita*.

BKD: What is the state of Indian English poetry on the threshold of 21st century?

SKK: I believe that Indian English poetry will achieve still greater heights in the 21st century.

BKD: Apart from being a poet, you are also an accomplished fiction writer. What made you write novels after achieving success as a poet?

SKK: I turned to fiction (novels and short stories) and drama in an attempt to cover the gamut of creative writing. But I must hasten to add that poetry would always remain my first love.

BKD: Where do you get more freedom and scope to express yourself: poetry or novel?

SKK: I have already said that it is in my poetry that I see my true self. A brief poem can say much more than a novel of epical length.

BKD: In your fiction you have described love and sex very freely. There are some descriptions of love and sex in *A River with Three Banks* particularly the love scene of Gautam and Haseena, which remind us of some scenes of Arundhati Roy's *The God of Small Things*. One feels that a hint of love and sex could have been better than the explicit description of the physical union. What do you say?

SKK: I agree with your observation that I have often "lapsed" into an explicit description of love and sex. As you have rightly observed that Arundhati Ray also lets herself go in the last scene (in *The God of Small Things*), may be, because sex is such an overwhelming thing that it tempts even such saints as Vishwamitra. Physical aspect of experience is also fundamental to all human beings. No wonder, we have raised such temples as Konark and Khajurao as our tribute to Kamadeva.

BKD: Are your characters in fiction completely imaginary? If not, have you recreated some people of your acquaintance in your fiction?

SKK: My characters (in fiction) are a mixture of fact and fiction. I believe that it is not possible to create a credible and moving character unless it is based on some real persons howsoever remote. But since life never offers a complete character, one has to improvise to a great extent.

BKD: You are an excellent short story writer. Apart from your short story collections, *Beyond Love and Other Stories* and *To Nun with Love,* you have written stories in *The Hindu and* other magazines. Your short story, *The Tomb* published in *The Hindu* is a unique story. Is it based on an actual experience? Isn't the ending a little ambiguous?

SKK: I do enjoy writing short stories. A short story also works as a poem if it uses such poetic elements, revelations and images. I write a story when I find writing a novel too arduous. A poem on the other hand drains one's entire creative energy leaving one somewhat exhausted. So, a short story acts as a bridge between one literary genre and the other.

No, "The Tomb" is purely imaginary though like the protaganist I too migrated to Delhi as a refugee from Lahore. I believe, the end of a story should be a teaser stimulating or even provoking the reader into imagining what is not there in the narrative.

BKD: Apart from poetry and fiction you have also written a play titled, *The Last Wedding Anniversary*. Do you think writing a play is different from writing a poem or a novel?

SKK: A play is different from a story, a poem or a novel in that it presents action on the stage in its direct visual form and also its primary ingredient is dialogue.

BKD: In the last two decades or so, fiction has gained prominence and it has become more popular than poetry and drama. Is it because of Booker Prize and other prizes?

SKK: I attribute the popularity of fiction in recent times to the laziness of readers most of whom are unable to participate in poetic experience articulated through crystallized imagery and metaphorical language. I agree with you that a novel carries palpable and commercial benefits to the writers and publishers. Who will offer a quarter million dollars as advance royalty for a collection of poems? This is where *A Suitable Boy* or *The God of Small Things* so well scored over poetry or drama.

BKD: What is the state of criticism of Indian English literature in our country? Are you satisfied with the criticism and reviews of your works?

SKK: Most of our literary critics tend to be parochial in their stance. Also contemporary literary criticism tends to sound more academic than creative. There are hardly any critic who would care to evaluate poetry. That is where we need most creative critics like yourself.

On the whole I am quite satisfied with whatever critics have said about my works. But essentially speaking I tend to be indifferent to any casual observation about my works—favourable or unfavourable.

BKD: Apart from being a creative writer, you are a critic, a translator and a distinguished academic. As a Professor of English you have few peers and not many equals in India. How do you like to be described: as a poet, a novelist, a critic, a translator and above all a distinguished Professor of English?

SKK: I feel that all the years I spent as an academician was the time wasted. I enjoyed evaluating, analyzing ... but it is as a creative writer (mostly as a poet) that I have discovered my true self.

BKD: Do you have any suggestions to offer to the young Indian English writers how to write effectively in English?

SKK: My advice to younger writers is—be your authentic self. Don't think of your audience while writing because that would make your writing stilted and contrived. One may indulge in lying in real life but creative process demands truth in its ultimate form. This is because literary creation is a kind of yoga—a poem or a novel is born out of meditation of the highest order. So, be thyself, there all the honour lies.

BKD: A personal question, please. You have received many honours such as Sahitya Akademi Award, and Padma Bhushan apart from your professional positions in India and abroad. When did you feel most happy and satisfied?

SKK: I felt happier when I was elected as a Fellow of Royal Society of Literature—a distinction I share with Vikram Seth and Anita Desai. Padma Bhusan and the Sahitya Akademi Award were also happy surprises. But these awards were somewhat burdensome because one has to live upto these honours and not rest on one's laurels.

Select Bibliography

Ashcroft, Bill. Gareth Griffiths and Helen Tiffin. *The Empire Writes Back,* London: Methen, 1987.

Atwood, Margaret. *Survival: A Thematic Guide to Canadian Literature.* Toronto: Anansi, 1972.

——., ed. *The Oxford Book of Canadian Verse.* Toronto: Oxford University Press, 1982.

Beier, Ulli. ed. *Introduction to African Literature.* London: Longman, 1967.

Benson, Eugene and L.W. Conolly, eds. *The Encyclopaedia of Post-Colonial Literature in English.* London: Routledge, 1994.

Bharucha, Nilufer E. and Vrinda Nabar. *Mapping Cultural Spaces: Post-Colonial Indian Literature in English.* New Delhi: Vision Books, 1998.

Boehmer, Elleke. *Colonial and Post-Colonial Literature.* New Delhi: Oxford University Press, 1995.

Cook, David. *African Literature: A Critical View.* London: Longman, 1977.

Cox, H.M.L., ed. *Ten Modern New Zealand Poets.* Auckland: Longman Paul, 1982.

Curnow, System., ed. *Essay on New Zealand Literature.* Aucktand: Heinemann, Educational Book, 1973.

Das, Bijay Kumar. *Modern Indian English Poetry.* Bareilly: Prakash Book Depot, 1992.

Das, Bijay Kumar. *Perspectives on Indian English Poetry: Criticism*. Bareilly: Prakash Book Depot, 1993.

——. *The Poetry of Jayanta Mohapatra,* Calcutta: Writer's Workshop, 1992.

——. *Critical Essays on Poetry*. New Delhi: Kalyani Publishers, 1993.

——. *Aspects of Commonwealth Literature*. New Delhi: Creative Books, 1995.

——. *The Horizon of Nissim Ezekiel's Poetry*. New Delhi: B.R. Publishing Corporation, 1995.

——. *A Reader's Guide to Ten Twentieth Century Indian Poets*. Bareilly: Prakash Book Depot, 1997.

——. *Shiv K. Kumar as a Post-Colonial Poet*. New Delhi: Atlantic Publishers and Distributors (P) Ltd., 2001.

——. *Post-modern Indian English Literature,* New Delhi: Atlantic Publishers and Distributors (P) Ltd., 2003, rpt. 2006.

——. *Critical Essays on Post-colonial Literature*. New Delhi: Atlantic Publishers and Distributors (P) Ltd., 2001.

Davin, D.M., ed. *New Zealand Short Stories*. New Zealand: Oxford University Press, 1976.

Dhawan, R.K. ed. *Commonwealth Fiction*. New Delhi: Classical, 1988.

Elliott, Brian. *The Landscape of Australian Poetry*. Melbourne: Cheshire, 1967.

Ford, Boris, ed. *The New Pelican Guide to English Literature: Present*. England: Penguin Books, 1983.

Frye, Northrop. *The Bush Garden: Essay on the Canadian Imagination:* Toronto: Anansi, 1971.

Gandhi, Leela. *Post-Colonial Theory: A Critical Introduction*. New Delhi: Oxford University Press, 1999.

Hammer, Robert D. *V.S. Naipaul*. New York: Twayne Publishers, Inc., 1973.

Hankin, Cherry, ed. *Critical Essay on the New Zealand Short Stories*. Auckland: Heinemann, 1982.

Heywood, Christopher, ed. *Perspective on African Literature.* London: Heinemann Educational Books, 1971.

Hope, A.D. *The Cave and the Spring: Essay on Poetry.* Sydney University Press, 1965.

Huges, Peter. F.S. *Naipaul.* Routledge: New York, 1988.

Innes, C.L. Chinua Achebe. Cambridge: Cambridge University Press, 1990.

Iyengar, K.R.S. *Indian Writing to English.* Bombay: Asia Publishing House, 1962.

Jones, Elders. *The Writing of Wole Soyinka.* London: Heinemann, 1973.

Kilam, G.D. *An Introduction to the Writing of Nuggi.* London: Heinemann, 1980.

King, Bruce, ed. *Introduction to Nigerian Literature.* London: Evans, 1972.

——, ed. *Literature of the World in English.* London: Routledge and Kegan Paul, 1974.

——. *The New English Literatures - Cultural Nationalism in a Changing World.* New York: St. Martin's, 1980.

——. *Modern Indian Poetry in English.* Delhi: Oxford University Press, 1987.

——. *Three Indian Poets:* Madras: Oxford University Press, 1991.

——, ed. *New National and Postcolonial Literatures.* Oxford: Clavendon Press, 1996 rpt., 2002.

Londfors, Bernth and Bala Kothandaraman, eds. *South Asian Responses to Chinua Achebe.* New Delhi: Prestige Books, 1993.

Loomba, Ania. *Colonialism/Post-Colonialism.* London: Routledge, 1999.

Mandel, Eli, ed. *Contexts of Canadian Criticism: A Collection of Critical Essays.* Toronto: University Press, 1971.

Meauley, James. *A Map of Australian Verse.* Melbourne: Oxford University Press, 1975.

Mongia, Padmini. *Contemporary Post-Colonial Theory*. New Delhi: Oxford University Press, 1998.

Moore, Gerald. *Whole Soyinka*. New York: Africana Publishing Corporation, 1971.

Mukherjee, Meenakshi, ed. *Considerations*. New Delhi: Allied Publishers, 1977.

——. *The Twice-born Fiction: Themes and Techniques of the Indian Novel in English*, New Delhi: Arlond Hienemann, 1971.

——. *The Perishable Empire*. New Delhi: OUP, 2000.

——. *Realism and Reality*. New Delhi: OUP, 1985.

Naik, M.K. *Aspects of Indian Writing in English*. New Delhi: MacMillan, 1979.

——, ed. *Perspectives on Indian Poetry in English*. New Delhi: Abhinav Publications, 1984.

——. Mulk Raj Anand. *Indian Writer Series*. New Delhi: Arnold Heinemann, 1973.

Naik, M.K. and Shyamala A. Narayan. *Indian English Literature 1980-2000: A Critical Study*. New Delhi: Pencraft International, 2001.

Narasimhaiah, C.D. *Commonwealth Literature: A Handbook of Select Reading List*. Delhi: Oxford University Press, 1976.

——, ed. *The Awakened Conscience*. New Delhi: Sterling Publishers, 1978.

——, ed. *An Anthology of Commonwealth Poetry*. Madras: MacMillan India Ltd., 1990.

——. Raja Rao. *Indian Writer Series*, New Delhi: Arnold Heinemann 1973.

——. *Essays in Commonwealth Literature*. Delhi: Pencraft International, 1995.

——, ed. *Makers or Indian English Literature*. New Delhi: Pencraft International, 2000.

——. *The Swan and the Eagle: Essays on Indian English Literature*. Shimla: Indian Institute of Advanced Study and Delhi: Motilal Banarasi Das, 1987.

O'Donell, Margaret J. *An Anthology of Commonwealth Verse.* Madras: Blackie and Sons Publishers Pvt. Ltd., 1984.

Palmer, Eustance. *The Growth of the African Novel.* London: Heinemann, 1979.

Panikar, Kenneth. *The South African Novel in English.* London: MacMillan, 1978.

Parthasarathy, R., ed. *Ten Twentieth Century Indian Poets.* Delhi: Oxford University Press, 1977.

Paterson, Alistair, ed. *Contemporary New Zealand Poets.* New Zealand Pilgrims South Press, 1980.

Pres, John, ed. *Commonwealth Literature.* London: Hememann, 1965.

Rai, Soudha. *V.S. Naipaul: A Study in Expatriate Sensibility.* Atlantic Highlands, NJ: Humanities Press, 1982.

Rajeshwar, M. *The Novels of Wole Boyinka.* New Delhi: Prestige Books, 1992.

Ramswamy, S. *Exploration: Essay on Commonwealth Literature.* Bangalore: MCC Publications, 1988.

Rao, A. Ramakrisnna and C.R. Visweswara Rao. *Indian Response to African Writing.* New Delhi: Prestige Books, 1993.

Rao, K. Damodar. *The Novels of Ayi Kwei Armah.* New Delhi: Prestige Books, 1993.

Sertima, Ivan Van. *Caribbean Writers: Critical Essays.* London: New Beacon Books, 1968.

Shahane, V.A. Khushwant Singh. *Twayne's World Authors Series.* New York: Twaye, 1972.

Shahane, V.A. and M. Sivaram Krishna, eds. *Indian Poetry in English: A Critical Assessment.* Madras: MacMillan, 1982.

Smith A.J.M., ed. *Masks of Poetry: Canadian Critics on Canadian Verse.* Toronto: McClelland and Stward, 1968.

——, ed. *The Oxford Book of Canadian Verse.* Toronto: Oxford University Press, 1965.

Stead, C.K. *In the Glass Case: Essay on New Zealand Literature.* Aukland: Auckland University Press, 1981.

Sundaram P.S. *R.K. Narayan: Indian writers Series.* New Delhi: Arnold Heinemann, 1974.

Trivedi, Harish and Meenakshi Mukherjee. *Interrogating Post-Colonialism: Theory, Text and Context.* Shimla: Indian Institute of Advanced Study, 1996.

Udoeyop, N.J. *Three Nigerian Poet.* Ibadan University Press, 1973.

Walsh, Williams. A Manifold Voice: Studies in Commonwealth Literature. London: Chatto and Widus, 1970.

——. *Commonwealth Literature.* Oxford Paperback. University Series, London: Oxford University Press, 1973.

——. *R.K. Narayan: Writers and their Work Series.* London: Longman, 1971.

——. *V.S. Naipaul.* Edinburgh: Oliver and Boyd., 1973.

——, ed. *Readings in Commonwealth Literature.* Oxford: Clarendon Press, 1973.

——. *Indian Literature in English.* London: Longman, 1990.

Walder, Dennis. *Post-Colonial Literatures in English.* New Delhi: Atlantic Publishers, (Indian reprint), 2005.

White, Landegg, *V.S. Naipaul: A Critical Introduction.* London: MacMillan Press, 1975.

Williams, Patrick and Laura Chrisman, eds. *Colonial Discourse and Post-Colonial Theory: A Reader.* London: Harvester Wheatsheaf, 1993.

Woodcock, George. Odyseous *Ever Returning: Essay An Canadian Writers and Writings.* Toronto: McClelland and Stewart, 1970.

Wright, Judithi. *Pre-occupations in Australian Poetry.* Melbourne: Oxford University Press, 1966.

Young, Rober J.C. *Colonial Desire: Hybridity in Theory: Culture and Race.* London: Routledge, 1995.

Contributors

Bijay Kumar Das: Professor of English, Burdwan University, Burdwan, West Bengal.

Haladhar Panda: Former Professor of English, Sambalpur University, Sambalpur, Orissa.

Mina Surjit Singh: Professor of English, Punjab University, Chandigarh, Punjab.

Sabita Nayak: Head, Department of English, Biraja Women's College, Jajpur, Orissa.

Krushna Chandra Maharana: Former Reader in English, Bhadrak College, Bhadrak, Orissa.

Subhas Chandra Saha: Professor of English, Assam University, Assam.

M.Q. Khan: Former Professor and Head, P.G. Dept. of English, Ravenshaw College, Cuttack and former Vice Chancellor, Berhampur University, Berhampur, Orissa.

Rama Nair: Professor of English, Postgraduate College, Osmania University, Andhra Pradesh.

A.G. Khan: Former Reader in English, Vikram University, Ujjain, Madhya Pradesh.

K. Chellappan: Former Director, State Institute of English, Chennai, Tamil Nadu.

Viney Kirpal: Former Professor of English, I.I.T. Mumbai, Maharashtra.

Rama Kundu: Professor of English, Burdwan University, Burdwan, West Bengal.

Ghorpade Pradny Vijay: Dept. of English, K.R.P. Kanya Mahavidyalaya, Islampur, Dt. Sangli, Maharashtra.

C.R. Visweswara Rao: Professor of English & Rector, S.K. University, Anantapur, Andhra Pradesh.

R.S. Pathak: Former Professor of English, H.S. Gour University, Sagar, Madhya Pradesh.

Sonali Das: M.A. Topper, Ravenshaw (Autonomous) College, Cuttack, 2005, U.G.C. N.E.T. Qualified Dec 2005, D/221, Sector-7, C.D.A. Cuttack, Orissa.

Gopa Ranjan Mishra: Asst. Controller of Examinations, C.H.S.E. Orissa, Bhubaneswar, Orissa.

Ramesh K. Srivastava: Former Professor of English, G.N.D. University, Amritsar. Currently U.G.C. Professor, Bundelkhand University, Uttar Pradesh.

Bhagabat Nath: Dept. of English, K.K. Women's College, Balasore, Orissa.

Rabinarayan Sasmal: Dept. of English, D.K. College, Jaleswar, Orissa.

Bhagabat Nayak: Dept. of English, Kandarpur College, Cuttack, Orissa.

Bilkesh Parveen: Dept. of English, Tangi Mahavidyalaya, Tangi, Cuttack, Orissa.

Manoj Das: Well known bilingual writer and a great thinker. Winner of Saraswati Samman in 2001. He has won both Central Sahitya Akademi Award and Orissa Sahitya Akademi Award for his collection of Short Stories, Professor of English, Sri Aurobindo International Centre of Education, Pondichery.

Shiv K. Kumar: Winner of Central Sahitya Akademi Award for his book of verse, *Trapfalls in the Sky* in 1987. Well known Indian English Poet, Novelist, Short Story Writer, Playwright and Translator. Distinguished Professor of English and Literary Critics. Former Vice Chancellor, University of Hyderabad, Hyderabad, Andhra Pradesh.